PRAISE FOR *The Starlite Drive-in*

"A captivating novel.... Start with a drive-in movie theater in the 1950s. Add a starstruck and lonely twelve-year-old girl, and a handsome drifter, and you have all the makings for a coming-of-age romance. But Marjorie Reynolds . . . added a twist. And there lies this first novel's strength. . . . Told from Callie's perspective, [*The Starlite Drive-in*] captures that childlike innocence and wisdom perfectly. . . . A fine first novel from an author to be reckoned with."
—*Richmond Times-Dispatch*

"Callie Anne is akin to the impressionable heroine of *To Kill a Mockingbird*. . . . *The Starlite Drive-in* is wise in the ways in which families adjust their views of reality to survive."
—*Boston Sunday Herald*

"Moving. . . . A story of confinement and entrapment, and of events that can free the spirit at long last."
—*Publishers Weekly*

ALSO BY MARJORIE REYNOLDS

The Civil Wars of Jonah Moran

The Starlite Drive-in

A Novel

Marjorie Reynolds

HARPER

NEW YORK · LONDON · TORONTO · SYDNEY

HARPER

Dialogue from *The African Queen* courtesy of Romulus Films Ltd. and Horizon Pictures.

A hardcover edition of this book was published in 1997 by Berkley Books in arrangement with William Morrow and Company, Inc.

First Harper paperback published 2011.

Library of Congress Cataloging-in-Publication Data is available upon request.

ISBN 978-0-06-209264-9

11 12 13 14 15 ov/RRD 10 9 8 7 6 5 4 3 2 1`

For my husband,
Michael Shoemaker,
and in memory or our son,
David

Acknowledgments

I want to thank Angela Rinaldi, my agent, and Claire Wachtel, my editor. I am especially grateful to my writing friends: Jane Sutherland, Nancy Jordan, Kay Morison, Karen MacLeod, Stella Preissler, Jerol Anderson, Julia Bartlett, Sue Talbott, Joan Walz, Jennifer McCord and the Pacific Northwest Writers Conference, and James N. Frey and the Oregon Writers Colony. Thanks to Nancy Adams and Joy Glaze for providing second opinions and to T. L. Cannon, "Doc" Richards-Reiss, Robert Bond, Dave Dunbar and Tom Adams for providing technical information.

I should also mention that, although I have borrowed the first names of some Indiana relatives and friends, the characters within these pages are purely fictional.

The Starlite Drive-in

Chapter One

I wasn't there when they dug up the bones at the old drive-in theater, but I heard about them within the hour. In a small town, word travels like heat lightning across a parched summer sky. Irma Schmidt phoned Aunt Bliss and delivered the news with such volume that her voice carried across the kitchen to where I was sitting.

After hanging up the receiver, Aunt Bliss peered at me through her thick bifocals. "With all those farms around there, they could be the bones of some animal."

I picked up the coffee mug, drained it, then set it on the worn Formica table. "They could be."

Pursing her lips, she stared hard at me. "I know what you're thinking, but more than one person disappeared that summer."

"Yes," I said reflectively, "that's true." But my heart was beating faster.

I walked over to the sink, rinsed my cup and tipped it upside down on the drainboard next to a bowl of peaches. My aunt had lived in this house ever since I could remember. I didn't need to look at the linoleum patch to know a hand pump had once jutted from the floor, or at the white wooden cabinets to remember they concealed pulldown bins of flour and sugar. I could almost smell

1

all the peach pies and cobblers she'd baked here the summer before I turned thirteen. With the memories rushing back, I reached for my handbag and car keys.

Aunt Bliss blinked owlishly. "You don't have to go out there, child. Leave it be."

I was forty-nine years old, and she still called me child.

"You know I do. And I need to tell Mom about the bones before she hears it from Irma Schmidt."

She shook her head in resignation. "You always did have a stubborn streak."

Driving out to the Starlite Theater, I passed subdivision after subdivision in an area that once was rural. It used to be, when the Indiana weather was especially warm, strong odors from the cow pastures hung in the air. Now the farms were gone, and the city was creeping toward the countryside on giant Caterpillar treads.

According to *The Jessup Enterprise,* developers were building houses on the drive-in property, tract mansions on postage stamp lots. The architect's sketch in the newspaper showed a man-made pond, with a spray fountain dramatically lighted at night. Workmen had unearthed the bones while digging a trench for the new sewer.

I parked my station wagon alongside the dozen or so other cars at the Starlite entrance, opened the door and climbed out. When I was a kid, my father, Claude Benton Junior, had managed this drive-in. How long was it since I'd been back? Thirty years, maybe more.

I looked up at the theater sign. It was supposed to say THAT'S ALL, FOLKS! but the F in FOLKS had slipped off. I stood there remembering a day in late February 1956. Dad was changing the letters on that sign from CLOSED FOR THE WINTER to OPENING

The Starlite Drive-in

APRIL 1 when he fell off the ladder and broke his leg. That leg was never steady again. Mom always said the doctor removed the cast too soon. Dad walked as if his knee hinges were dangerously unlatched and at any moment the bottom half of his limb might swing outward. It was because of my father's knee that Charlie Memphis came to the drive-in that summer.

I strode past the box office, which had once been a sturdy wooden cubicle with half doors on each side. It used to have shutters on top that folded back so the cashier could lean out to collect admissions. Now the shutters were gone, the doors were broken off their hinges and the little building teetered on its concrete pad. Faded candy wrappers and dead leaves crouched against the high board fence. Dad would never have allowed the place to look like this. Although I hadn't thought about the drive-in in years, I felt a sense of loss. We expect the places of our childhood to be eternal.

As I rounded the corner of the fence, the parking field came into view. I slowed my pace and stared across the few remaining rows of speaker poles perched on their mounds like old monuments. Some were close to toppling over, and loose wires dangled from nearly all of them. Clumps of weeds grew in the gravel where cars had once driven. The movie screen, that inspiration for my young fantasies, loomed in the distance like a ghostly banner. Sections of it were broken or missing, revealing the structure's weathered skeleton. Tears rose to my eyes as suddenly as a midwestern rainstorm, and I had to stop to brush them away.

I walked toward the flashing lights of three sheriff's cruisers. A dozen or so people—neighbors from the nearby subdivision, I suppose, and a few officials in uniform—clotted around a pit, staring at something that held them in fascination. One woman cradled a small white dog that might otherwise have been yapping at someone's heels. Joining them, I gazed into a hole that lay directly in the shadow of the screen. It held a collection of bones, some still half buried. The visible ones were gray and caked with dirt. Seeing in them the form of a human skeleton, I felt a river of cold run through me.

A hand touched my elbow. "Excuse me. Are you Callie Anne Benton?"

I turned to look at the gray-haired, barrel-shaped man in the sheriff's uniform. "Yes. I mean, that was my maiden name."

"Could you step over here, please?"

He led me away from the crowd, moving slowly as if he were in no rush. Drawing two sticks of chewing gum from his pocket, he offered me one. When I shook my head, he peeled off the wrappers, folded the sticks twice and tucked both of them into his mouth. "You probably don't remember me, but I was a year behind you in school."

"I remember."

In high school Bob Jankowski had been a football star, but at some point muscle had turned to fat. Although he had his father's hefty build, his dark eyes were friendlier and less calculating than his dad's had been.

I stuffed my hands in my jacket pockets and waited for him to speak. When he didn't right away, I said, "Your father came to the theater once when it was robbed. How's he doing these days?"

One corner of his mouth rose in a faint smile. "He'd be better if he didn't think he was still sheriff."

I nodded.

He rubbed his chin with his thumb. "You lived here a number of years, didn't you?"

I glanced at the yellow bungalow, an empty, boarded-up shell

that vandals had spray-painted with black graffiti. "Yes, ten alto-
gether. We moved here when I was three years old."

The two-bedroom house at the edge of the theater grounds
had been part of my father's compensation, a "perk" they'd call it
these days. It was common practice to provide a drive-in theater
manager living quarters on the property, but like a hard rain, it
could be a blessing or a curse. It meant he was tied to his job night
and day. During the years we occupied the house, it was white
with green shutters. Lilac bushes provided some privacy, and a
knee-high picket fence ran along the front.

For five long years, my mother did not step outside its walls.

I turned back to the sheriff.

Bob Jankowski maneuvered the wad of gum from one side of
his mouth to the other. "I was wondering, could you look at some
stuff we dug up from that hole and see if you recognize any of it?"

I hesitated. "The bones are human, aren't they?"

"Oh, yes," he drawled, "and I'd say they're old. The coroner
will be able to date them better when he gets them to the lab."

He led me to a dark green van with side doors that were open.
About twenty-five items ranging from a gray button to a metal
container the size of a cigar box lay in a row on the floor. All were
encased in clear, snap-lock bags. As my gaze traveled from one
plastic-shrouded piece of evidence to another, I felt a small jolt.

The sheriff picked up the metal box and handed it to me.
"Look familiar?"

Although it was pitted and discolored, I recognized it immediately. My father had used it for petty cash, and I'd often seen
it on his beat-up wooden desk in the projection booth. Many a
night I sat up there with him. Through the small window, I
watched people traipse back and forth to the snack bar, balancing

drinks and bags of popcorn, calling out greetings to friends. Children darted between the cars, played tag and laughed. For a moment, I heard their voices just as I had on those warm dusky evenings.

The sheriff tapped the metal case lightly to get my attention, and I looked up.

Phantom sounds, that's all they were. Summer memories.

"Think you might have seen it before?" he asked, as he took the box from me and set it with the other things.

"I'm not sure. What's in it?"

"Don't know. It's locked."

A tall blond woman deputy about half my age walked up. "Okay, sir, if we start removing the bones? The photographer's done now."

As he swung around to speak with her, I picked up one of the smaller bags. These things didn't need plastic to protect them, I thought. They had survived decades in that grave. I turned the bag over and examined its contents, the way anyone with a casual interest might do. Then I did something I'd never done before. Knowing perfectly well the risk I was taking, I slipped it into my purse.

When the sheriff turned back, I told him I was in a rush to pick up my daughter. "She's working at Dick's Video Emporium this summer. If I'm late, she'll think I've forgotten her. You know how kids are." I smiled. I was just another housewife in a hurry. "But I'll be happy to drop by your office tomorrow to go through this stuff."

His gaze flicked over me. I don't know whether he believed me or not, but he didn't stop me.

My mind was so consumed with what I had in my purse that my elderly Ford station wagon seemed to find its own way back to town. It wound through the side streets, pulled into the familiar driveway and threaded itself between the fishing boat and lawn mower in our garage. With trembling hands, I pulled out the plastic bag, opened it and held it upside down so that the dirt-blackened cigarette lighter tumbled onto my palm. As I ran my fingers over the cool, gritty metal, I slid effortlessly back into the summer of 1956.

"Callie Anne. Callie Anne. Come here, honey," my mother called.

Running over the gravel, I dodged speaker posts and hurdled the mounds where the moviegoers parked their cars at night. White-hot sunlight sparked off the mica in the rocks and glazed the drive-in with a hazy sheen.

Mom stood in the open door, tugging the bodice of her dress away from her skin so the air would cool her a bit. "You shouldn't be running like that, honey. You'll have yourself a heatstroke."

"Oh, I'm okay."

Her own cheeks were rosy from working in the hot kitchen. In the winter she wore her auburn hair loose so that it fell down her back like a scarf, but in the summer she swept it into soft rolls and fastened them with moss-green combs that matched the color of her eyes. Tiny tendrils had escaped and lay damp against her face. She had the fine features and milky skin of a movie actress. When I looked at her, I tingled with admiration, the way I did when I saw Audrey Hepburn or Natalie Wood on the screen.

Our kitchen was fragrant with the smells of pot roast and yeast rolls fresh from the oven. Mom hurried around the room, pulling

7

out silverware, stirring the gravy, tossing a pat of butter into the green beans. She paused occasionally to swab the moisture from her neck with a small white handkerchief.

"Wash your hands and set the table before your father gets here, will you, sweetheart? And be sure to use Grandma Willard's china." She glanced at the wall cuckoo clock her brother Joe had sent her from Germany after the war. It was one of those little brown houses with a yellow bird that shot out the door and squawked on the quarter hour. About every three days, Dad threatened to throttle "that damned canary."

Noting the time, Mom frowned with worry. "I shouldn't have been working so long on that jingle. Don't tell him what I was doing."

"Did you write a new one?"

"Uh-huh, for Morton salt." She sprinkled flour into the gravy. "Do you want to hear it?"

I arranged the silverware on the table. "Sure."

She stood motionless with the wooden spoon poised over the pan and recited, "Put Morton's in your cupboard. It's the salt of the earth."

"That sounds good, but doesn't it have to rhyme?"

"It's not done yet. It's going to be four lines, but I have to figure out how to use 'worth' in it."

My mother was always entering jingle contests. Aunt Bliss started her on it when she told her about a neighbor who had won five cases of Fels-Naptha soap. I often wondered how that woman found a word to rhyme with Fels-Naptha.

I thought my mother's jingles were terrific. She hadn't won any prizes yet, but I was sure she would someday. Then she'd be famous and get her picture in the paper, like the Jessup woman who had written a patriotic song and was going to be on *The Ed Sullivan Show.*

"They're sure to like this one, Mom," I said.

"Well, you never know."

I reached for the rose-trimmed china plates Grandma Willard had given Mom. "Where'd you hide Dad's birthday cake?"

She gestured toward the pan cupboard. "Now don't be getting in there when he's around."

She'd baked the cake while he was in Jessup that morning, and I'd wrapped his present the night before while he was running the movie. It was a straw hat with a turquoise-and-yellow-striped band. To buy it, I'd had to hitch a ride into town with Mrs. Eggert, who lived on the farm to the east of us. The saleslady at Miller's Department Store insisted the hat was the latest style, and I could picture it over his short brown hair.

"Do you think he'll like his present?" I asked Mom.

She furrowed her brow. "Oh, well, sure. I mean, probably. That cloth band's a little . . . well, a little loud, but otherwise it's . . ." She brightened and added in a firm voice, "Otherwise, it's a fine hat."

I nodded. "I wish we had some balloons to stick up."

She smiled and turned to the sink to fill a measuring cup with water. "Don't you worry. He'll have a fine birthday."

I eyed the steady flow from the faucet. "There's plenty of water now."

She nodded. "It's mostly in the evening it turns into a trickle. Your father says he can hear the pump straining when people flush the toilets in the rest rooms. That's a sure sign the well's drying up."

She drizzled some water into the gravy and stirred. Under her

9

flowered apron, she was wearing the teal dress Dad and I had given her for Christmas. It draped smoothly over her hips and fell into gentle folds. I didn't pay much attention to figures, but I knew my mom had a nice one.

Her name was Teal. She told me it was a shade of blue and green, of lakes and forests, and I thought it was perfect for her. Mom believed names were important, that they should make a person think of pleasant things. She said it was a shame my father's name, which was Claude Junior, didn't have that connection, but still she liked the way it sounded. Mom always called him Claude Junior, not just Claude, because she said the two words together had cadence. She was sorry she didn't have a middle name. Even though Teal was a color, she thought it sounded too harsh. Dad said she should just give herself a middle name, but she said that wasn't the same.

Mom knew some fancy words like cadence. She once told me that after graduating from high school, she had wanted to go to college and become a teacher. Instead, she married my father, who said she didn't need any education because no wife of his was going to work.

I was placing the pressed cloth napkins next to the forks when Mom let out a long sigh. "Oh, honey, just look at your blouse. Have you been down by the creek again?"

"Only for a while."

I'd been trapping frogs and trying to coax them into mud and twig houses I'd built. I wet my finger on my tongue and rubbed the dirt spot. The stain spread to the size of a half-dollar, making the blouse look worse than before.

Mom shook her head. "Be sure to change it before your father sees it."

As I swung around to walk toward my bedroom, I glimpsed a face pressed against the screen. I don't know what it was about Billy that always startled me that way. I used to think his eyes were too big for his face. Then I realized their size wasn't the problem. It was their emptiness, as if the man inside them had gone somewhere else to live.

"Mom," I said, "Billy's at the back door."

She glanced at the clock, then at Billy. When he caught sight of my mother, his eyes glowed as if someone had struck matches inside them. "Hi, Teal."

He was a tall man, scrawny as a scrub maple, with a weathered face the color of an old copper pail. I found it difficult to believe he was my mother's age. His baggy, dirt-brown pants were held up more by suspenders than by his waist or hips, and he'd cut the sleeves off his flannel shirt. I didn't need to look at his feet to know he was shuffling around in the laceless black shoes he always wore.

Mom laid the wooden spoon in a saucer on the counter and walked to the door. Her fingers were long and slender and she pressed them against her chest as though she were out of breath. "Hello, Billy. How are you doing today?"

Bending over so his stubbled face was close to hers, he peered at her through the screen. "I'm going to take dance lessons, Teal, soon as I get the money. At Miss Peabody's School of Dance in Jessup." He had a soft voice, low and wavery, and he sounded as if he were years younger than he was. The tip of his thin nose pushed against the screen. "We danced once in high school. Do you remember?"

"Did we, Billy?" She blew a wisp of hair back from her face. "I cooked a pot roast. Would you like some? With a roll?"

11

"Your hair was shorter then. And you were wearing a yellow dress."

"You wait here. I'll be right back."

She grabbed a plate and filled it with meat and potatoes drowned in rich brown gravy. As she headed for the door, I glanced out the window. "Mom, Dad's coming."

"I'll be there in a minute, honey." She grabbed two yeast rolls that were as light and plump as puffballs and tossed them onto the plate.

I looked again to make sure of what I was seeing. "Mom, he's got someone with him."

She stopped and turned. "Someone with him?"

"Uh-huh."

She handed the plate out to Billy. "Just set it on the porch step when you're finished, but don't let Claude Junior see you. You know he doesn't like you being around the theater."

"Do you think you could come out later and dance?"

"No, Billy, you know I can't. Now run along," she said, without the least bit of sharpness in her voice.

She joined me at the window, where she turned her attention to my father and the lanky man in the white T-shirt and faded blue jeans. "My goodness, who do you suppose that is?"

I shrugged. "I've never seen him before." Because Dad conducted all his business from the concessions building, it was rare for a man to come into our home.

The pointed toes of the stranger's cowboy boots kicked up little puffs of dust. He moved easily, as though his limbs had been tied on with a loose rope, while my father hobbled along beside him. Dad was a broad-shouldered, compact man who stood several inches shorter than the stranger. The heat from the midday sun bored into them, and their tanned foreheads glistened with sweat.

Through the open kitchen window, I could hear the steady murmur of their voices.

Mom said to me in a low tone, "Quick, put another plate on the table." She started toward the front door. "And don't forget the silverware and a napkin."

Once inside, Dad introduced Charlie Memphis. The stranger stood in a patch of yellow light spilling through our living-room window. With his straight black hair, deeply tanned skin and high cheekbones, he put me in mind of one of those Indians you saw in old sepia photographs.

Dad jerked his thumb toward my mother. "This is my wife," he said, not mentioning her name.

Mom rubbed her hands on her apron. "How do you do, Mr. Memphis," she said, raising her eyes only about as high as his belt buckle. It occurred to me she saw strangers, including our nightly moviegoers, only from a distance. I hadn't even realized she was shy.

"I'd appreciate it if you'd drop the mister, ma'am. Most people just call me Memphis." He had a pleasant drawl that was easier on the ears than my father's flat Indiana tones.

Dad wiped the back of his damp neck with his palm. "Mr. Sooter's hired Memphis here to do some of the heavy work on the property this summer. He's going to paint the concessions building and repair the fence—damned thing's falling down." He turned to him. "I guess you'll have to dig up the opening of that septic tank too. It's gone sour on us, and it won't wait until winter. Just about ready to do some of these things when I broke my leg."

Mom brushed a lock of hair from her face and looked at him from under her lashes. When she spoke, her voice was unusually quiet. "We'd certainly be pleased if you'd eat with us. It's nothing fancy."

13

"I don't want to intrude on your meal, ma'am," Memphis said.

"Sure, you'll have dinner with us," Dad said, oddly cheerful and louder than usual.

Mom glanced toward the kitchen, concern shadowing her face. "It's almost ready. I just need to do a thing or two."

Dad kept his eyes on Memphis but gave a little nod toward Mom. "It's funny," he said, although there wasn't a trace of amusement on his face. "She's always in this house. You'd think she could get dinner on time."

Mom seemed to shrink into herself, the way a snail does when it's touched. I stepped back, ducking my head.

Dad moved toward the kitchen, but Memphis gestured for Mom and me to go first. "Ladies."

I straightened a bit. No one had ever called me a lady before.

Mom usually dished our food from the stove, but that day she served it in bowls and platters. When she removed her apron and sat down at the table, Dad glanced at her with curiosity, probably wondering why she was wearing her special dress. But then, he never could remember a birthday, not even his own.

In spite of his name, Memphis was from Louisville, Kentucky. He drew Louisville deep from his throat so it sounded like "Lull-ville." Mom had set up a big old electric fan near the doorway, but the kitchen was still warm and thick with the aromas of our dinner. Memphis thanked her as she passed him the rolls.

Dad glanced around the table, then frowned at her. "I don't see the butter, Teal."

She jumped up, grabbed the butter dish from the refrigerator, and with a quick flustered movement that made me fear she was going to drop it, set it directly in front of Dad. "I'm sorry. I forgot. It was so hot I couldn't leave it out."

14

Dad passed it to Memphis, then gave me a meaningful look out of the corner of his eye. "Callie Anne, your elbows."

I jerked my arms back. If Memphis hadn't been there, he would have reached over and knocked them off. He'd done that a few times and I'd almost bumped my chin on the table.

Memphis was sitting next to me and across from my mother, and I suppose I was staring at him. The lower half of his face was covered with a black stubble. He may have looked as if he'd just tumbled out of bed, but he was the most handsome man I'd ever seen, except for James Dean, of course. His eyes flashed sometimes brown, sometimes dark gray, depending on how the light hit them, and when he turned them on me, I nearly tumbled off my chair. At that moment, I fell in love with Charlie Memphis.

Once the polite talk was over, he ate faster than any man I'd ever seen, even faster than my father, who wasn't shy when it came to food. Memphis wasn't rude or noisy about it though, so I figured his elbows might have been smacked a time or two when he was a kid. He encircled his plate with his arm and shoveled meat and potatoes into his mouth with steady, scooping motions that didn't end until he had finished every last morsel. After a second helping of meat and potatoes, he seemed to surface as though for air and glanced around the kitchen.

I wondered how a stranger would see our house. The refrigerator was dented where Dad, after losing patience with a leaky faucet, had heaved a wrench at it. The linoleum, which looked a little like cement with blades of grass sprinkled over it, was cracked in places and worn to a black ragged edge near the sink. I hoped Memphis wouldn't notice. The rest of the floor shone from Mom's frequent scrubbing and polishing. Our wooden cabinets were white, except for the ones around the stove. Those had turned a light yellow, which was okay because they went with the yellow gingham curtains above the sink. Mom had sewn all the curtains in the house herself and even braided the rug at our front door. Our chrome-rimmed, gray-flecked turquoise Formica table was my mother's favorite piece of furniture. She'd spotted it in the Sears Roebuck catalog, and Dad had finally ordered it after considerable resistance and grumbling.

"Your father's a good provider, Callie Anne," she'd said. "He just has to see the need for things."

We owned a Sears stove, a Sears refrigerator and a Philco radio. We didn't own a television set because Dad said we had all the entertainment we needed right outside our door.

Eventually Memphis's gaze fell on me. I chewed slowly with my mouth closed and tried to pretend I hadn't noticed. But I wondered if he could hear my heart thumping in my chest.

"How old are you, Sallie Anne?" His voice made me think of long grass swaying in a breeze.

I was so pleased he'd spoken to me that I could only stutter, "T-twelve." Then I added, "Thirteen in October."

Mom smiled. "Her name's Callie Anne. It's really Calla. We named her after the lily."

"Sorry, the old ears are going bad." He winked at me. "You can call me Nashville for the rest of the meal, if you want."

I must have grinned like a chimpanzee.

Now that attention had focused on me, Dad gave me a stern look. "You been playing down by the creek again, haven't you?"

I could feel the heat rise in my face. "I . . . I fell."

He looked at Mom as if to say, "Can't you keep her clean?"

Mom bit her lower lip and stared at her half-empty plate. "She's only a child, Claude Junior."

I laid down my fork, and with the side of my thumb, nudged

a few stray crumbs of bread roll under my plate. I wondered if Memphis would think I was one of those white-trash kids who never took baths and wore dirty clothes to school.

Dad regarded Mom briefly, without expression, then turned to me. "You're getting too old to be a tomboy, Callie Anne."

I ducked my head and squirmed in embarrassment. I didn't like the idea of Mom calling me a child, but I didn't like Dad saying I was a tomboy either. I wasn't sure men liked tomboys, and more than anything I wanted Memphis to like me.

Dad poked his fingernail at a bit of meat stuck between his teeth. "Ever worked at a theater before, Memphis?"

Memphis swabbed his face with the napkin. "Never ran a projector if that's what you mean."

Dad chuckled. "Now there's a skill. That Simplex Magnarc's a touchy piece of equipment. It was built in '39, and I'm always havin' to baby it along. No, you wouldn't be running the projector." He broke two dinner rolls in half and slathered butter and raspberry jam on them. Since his accident, he'd put on a little weight, but he couldn't seem to pass up Mom's rolls.

"There's plenty else to do around here though," he said to Memphis. "Some damned fool's always running over a speaker pole. Or a pipe in one of the rest rooms springs a leak. These addlebrained kids we hire to sell tickets and concessions aren't any help. They don't know their asses from a . . ."

"More pot roast?" Mom offered Memphis the platter.

He shook his head. "Thanks, but I'm full, Mrs. Benton."

The color in Mom's cheeks deepened. "Please, just call me Teal. I still think of Mrs. Benton as Claude Junior's mother."

If she had looked at my father, she would have seen him frown. I guess he thought she should have stuck to her married name.

17

Mom refilled Memphis's glass. His dark eyes tracked her movements as she reached for the pitcher on the counter, poured the iced tea, then sat down at the table.

Dad hauled out his pack of Chesterfields, tapped one of the cigarettes several times on his chrome lighter and lit it. He leaned back in his chair, one hand holding the cigarette, the other absent-mindedly rubbing the thigh of his bad leg. People said I looked like him, and I tried to see it now in the ruggedness of his face. I had his sturdy dimpled chin. My eyes were the color of milk chocolate, just like his, but the stick-straight hair that hung down my back in a pony tail was a honey-colored blond, not brown. Mom said it would probably turn dark later.

She jumped up now, grabbed a clean ashtray from the windowsill and set it on the table.

Memphis shook the last cigarette from his crumpled pack, stuck it between his lips and lit it. I liked the way he cupped his hand around the tip, as though a hard wind might blow out the flame. I'd seen John Wayne do that. In *Red River,* I think it was.

Mom carried the dirty plates and bowls from the table, then brought out the cake, with a dozen or so tiny blue candles stuck crookedly in the white icing. She turned a radiant smile on Dad. "I hope you saved room."

Dad raised his hand, as if pushing her away. "Aw, Jesus Christ, Teal, why'd you do that? That's family business. Memphis here's not interested in watching some fool blow out candles."

The smile slid off my mother's face. "But, Claude Junior, we have to celebrate your birthday."

Dad braced his leg with his hand and rose. "We haven't time now. We've got to get working."

As he headed for the door, Mom stood there still holding the cake, her gaze on the floor.

Memphis rose slowly. He leaned toward her, his hand resting on the table. "That was a fine dinner, Teal. We can eat the cake later."

Mom's voice was barely audible. "It's lemon. My mother's recipe."

At that moment, Dad brushed by the counter and sent a bowl crashing to the floor, green beans spewing everywhere. The china dish broke neatly into five pieces that skittered around the room. "Christ on a stick, Teal! Haven't you got enough sense not to set it so close to the edge?"

As Mom's face went pale, I swallowed hard. She dropped to the floor and started picking up the pieces.

Memphis watched her, his face expressionless. I wondered what he was thinking, if he believed, as my dad did, that she had no sense. I wanted him to think well of her, of all of us.

Dad pushed open the screen door. "Come on, let's go."

Memphis hesitated.

"She can clean it up," Dad said. "She's got time."

Without another glance at my mother, Memphis followed Dad out.

Mom didn't move for a long time. She knelt on the linoleum, sections of the broken bowl in her hands. Almost in slow motion, she rose and laid the china pieces on the counter. She hunched her shoulders and folded her arms tightly across her chest. The way she looked, there might have been two strong hands pushing down on her.

"Mom?"

She didn't answer. I picked up one of the bowl fragments that had shot into a corner. The only sound in the kitchen was the whirring fan. The smells of food still crowded the air, making me feel sick to my stomach.

19

I walked back to her but couldn't think what to say. Her shoulders were shaking slightly. I cleared my throat. "Mom, are you okay?"

She brushed her hand across her eyes, then gave me a weak smile and nodded. She picked up the ashtray from the table and emptied it into the garbage can under the sink. "You run along and change your blouse. I'll clean up this mess."

I didn't expect Memphis to come back. People are always saying things they don't mean just to be polite. But he turned up on our doorstep around three o'clock, wearing a battered gray cowboy hat tipped back on his head. "Thought you might bundle up some of that lemon cake for Claude and me."

He must have taken Mom by surprise because she stood there for a minute just staring at him. "Why, yes," she said, her hand still motionless on the door handle. She eventually remembered her manners and invited him in.

He removed his hat and set it upside down on a kitchen chair. I noticed that next to the Stetson name inside was a label for a Boise, Idaho, men's store. He settled into another chair while Mom went for the cake, and I slid into a place beside him, wondering if he'd noticed my clean blouse.

He nodded at me. "Hello there, pardner."

I scooted in and perched my elbows on the table. "Hi."

"You can have a taste while I'm putting this together," Mom said, handing him a plate with a fork and one of the cotton napkins she pressed daily into neat squares.

He looked at her with a half-smile. "Are you trying to suggest I need fattening up, Teal?"

She turned away, reddening. "Why, no, I just . . ." Her voice trailed off.

He sliced off a chunk of cake with the side of his fork and lifted it to his mouth, still watching her. "I can see that if I stay around here, I'll find a lot of things to appreciate."

With his hand folded over the fork like it was a weapon, he polished off the rest in three bites and wiped his face with the napkin. "I had an Aunt Lovene who used to make a lemon cake but it don't even compare to this one. You ever enter it in the fair?"

Mom shook her head. "Oh, no, I haven't been to the county fair in . . . in a while." She turned back to wrapping the slices in waxed paper.

He poked at a few crumbs with his fingertip and licked them off. "I don't mean any little old local doings. You could win a prize at the state fair with this one."

"No, I don't think so," Mom murmured, her head bent low.

He leaned his chair back, tilting up the front legs. She didn't say a word, although I always got into trouble for doing that. I inched closer to him, sitting so near I could smell him. I breathed in, noticing that although he used cigarettes, he didn't have my father's harsh smokiness. He didn't have the soapy sweetness of the male clerks at Miller's Department Store either. He smelled like wood—oak or maple maybe. I'd spent a lot of time in trees, with my nose pressed against their cool, rough bark. It was an earthy smell I knew as well as any other.

He carried his plate to the sink and glanced around. There was no sign of the earlier disaster.

"I could mend that dish for you," he said to Mom.

She glanced away and lifted one shoulder in a half shrug of embarrassment. "I glued the pieces together."

21

"Let's see it," Memphis said matter-of-factly.

She opened a kitchen cabinet and waved a hand toward it as if it were no longer important. "I don't know if it'll hold."

He stuck his head in and inspected it without touching.

"I tend to like things that have been mended," he said, looking it over carefully. "It makes them more interesting." He picked up the sack and the thermos of iced tea. "Thanks for the cake, Teal."

She smiled, a gratitude in her expression I couldn't remember ever having seen before.

From the window, we watched him cross the parking field, his slouchy gray hat pushed back on his head. The late-afternoon sunlight brushed his side and he cast a lengthy shadow, making it look as if there might have been two of him. Eventually he disappeared into the concessions building.

Chapter Two

*M*emphis set to work painting the concessions building the very next day. The paint was the color of Pepto-Bismol and just looking at it made me sick to my stomach. Dad said Mr. Sooter chose it, so I suppose it was on sale.

Although it was only June 6, it was already shaping up to be one of those hot, humid Indiana summers when the perspiration forms a band around your hairline and your blouse sticks to you like wet tissue paper. I stood in the shade of a poplar tree for a while and watched Memphis. When he took off his white T-shirt, I sighed. When he dropped his paint rag from the ladder, I retrieved it. Perching on a couple of cinder blocks stacked against the building, I handed it up to him.

He didn't say much to me, just glanced over occasionally at our house as though expecting someone to walk out.

The next day, he was on the other side of the concessions building, swabbing broad pink strokes across it. I sat on a cinder block reading Zane Grey's *Riders of the Purple Sage*. Halfway through the morning, Memphis stepped down from the ladder and wiped the sweat from his forehead with the flat of his thumb. "So what does a kid do for fun around here?"

I jumped up, surprised that he was speaking to me. "Well, mostly I read, and watch movies, of course."

"I bet your friends wish they could live here."

"I guess." I didn't want to tell him I didn't have many friends, and now that school was out I hardly ever got to see the ones I did have. We were twelve miles from Jessup, which didn't make it easy to go visiting. But the real problem was, I just couldn't get excited about what the other girls were interested in. They sat around curling each other's hair and giggling about the junior high school boys. They came to the drive-in occasionally—Betty Jo Babcock, Edwina Vandenburgh, and some of the others. I was friendly toward them, but I didn't go out of my way to look for them. I heard my aunt Bliss tell Mom that I was probably just a loner.

Memphis wiped his hands on a rag and looked over his shoulder toward our house. "Guess you don't get away from the drive-in much then."

I shook my head. "Only when Dad goes into Jessup or my aunt drives in . . ."

"What about your mother?"

"Huh?"

"Doesn't she ever drive into town?"

I picked up a paper popcorn bag that had drifted against the wooden bench next to the concessions building. " 'Course not," I said, crumpling it into a ball. "She doesn't know how to drive. It wouldn't make any difference if she did, 'cause she always stays in the house anyway." I tossed the paper ball in the air, trying to steal glances at his bare chest at the same time. The black hair there curled and twisted, then dove in a dark line toward blue jeans that rode low on his hips.

I've always been pretty good at catching things, but that rumpled bag shot off on a trajectory all its own. In dismay, I lunged for it and smacked against him, trapping it between his torso and my neck. My face pressed against his warm, bare skin. I jerked back as if I'd hit scorching metal.

He reached out and steadied me. "She must leave it sometimes."

I touched my fingers to my face. "Wh . . . what?" I couldn't even think what he was talking about, and I certainly couldn't look at him, at least not while his naked flesh still branded my cheek.

"Your mother. She can't stay in the house all the time."

I glanced at him from under my lashes, wondering if he was laughing at me. He wasn't. His dark eyes looked perfectly serious.

"Well, she does," I said.

"What about groceries?"

"Oh, Dad drives into town for groceries, for everything, except the stuff Aunt Bliss buys. Sometimes, I get th . . . things for Mom too." I was remembering the boxes of Kotex my father made me purchase.

Memphis swabbed the sweat from his forehead with the rag. His hard-muscled shoulders glistened with a light sheen. "Why doesn't she go out?"

I nudged the wood ladder with the toe of my shoe, not looking at him. "She doesn't like to. She can't breathe, and her heart pounds hard enough to break. I used to want her to go places with me but not anymore, not if it's going to hurt her."

"Has the doctor come to see her about it?"

"A long time ago. I heard him tell Dad it was nerves and she needed rest." I stopped, wondering if I'd betrayed her. I looked up at him. "You won't say anything, will you? She feels bad about it."

"I won't mention it." He picked up the paint bucket and the pink-coated brush. "Seems a shame though. A person can't appreciate flowers or a sunset from inside a house."

"I cut the flowers for her whenever she wants." I didn't tell him my mother hadn't watched a sunset in years because the high board fence blocked our western view.

He squinted in the direction of the house. "Can't imagine being shut up like that."

I stared at the ground, my eyes swimming. "Nope."

I used to have dreams in which my mother left the house. In one of them, I was back in grade school, playing the lead role in *The Ugly Duckling*. I was wearing a swan costume, and all of us, the actors and actresses, were stretched across the gymnasium stage, taking our bows. The sand-colored wooden floor was glossy with polish, and the curtain that closed behind us was a plush red fabric, maybe even velvet. The lights shone directly into our eyes so that all we could see were gray shapes sitting in the folding metal chairs before us. The other actresses curtsied with exaggerated movements, their costumes swishing and crackling. The teacher had carefully glued each white feather to my chicken-wire frame. To avoid bending my swan body or losing feathers, I made only gentle dips.

Then I stood alone. I bobbed slightly, my heart thumping with excitement. Hundreds of hands came together in thunderous approval. I tilted my head and saw her sitting there as if the spotlight had shone on her instead of me. A fine dust that resembled flakes of silver danced in the air around her. Her auburn hair shimmered like a halo, and her face seemed to glow. She held her hands up slightly (the way she clasped them for praying) and applauded with pride and joy. I couldn't hear the individual sound of her hands clapping, but it didn't matter. She was there.

In reality, it wasn't quite that way. I was in the fourth grade play all right, but Edwina Vandenburgh was the swan. I was a talking lily pad with two lines, both of them gossipy and mean. All the kids thought the script, which the teacher had written, was babyish and stupid. We were embarrassed to be in the performance.

And my mother wasn't there at all.

Chapter Three

$\mathcal{I}$t took Memphis two and a half days to paint the concessions building. When it was finished, it looked like the inside of a watermelon that's been left out in the sun too long. While he washed the windows, I stood at the base of the ladder, telling him about junior high school, the stupid boys there, my favorite movies, the books I'd read, every boring little detail of my life. He didn't say much unless I asked him a direct question, but he was a good listener.

I dug a line in the dirt with my shoe. "We don't even get to see a movie until it's played in the big cities first, like Indianapolis and Terre Haute. When it does come here, we have to watch it seven nights in a row. And if it's making a lot of money, it runs for two weeks. Even longer sometimes."

"You know the story pretty well by then."

"Yup." I recited a scene from *On the Waterfront* by heart.

"That's not bad," he said, polishing the glass with a crumpled newspaper.

I jumped over a cinder block, trying to land in a preplanned spot the way I would hopscotching. "Hey, that's nothing. I can watch a movie from our kitchen window and read the actors' lips. I can tell my mom every word they're . . ."

I swung around, and Dad caught me by surprise, thrusting a bushel basket in my arms. "Callie Anne, make yourself useful."

I groaned. One of my chores was picking up litter. Every once in a while I found a coin half buried in the gravel or a bottle I could turn in to the Jessup Piggly Wiggly for the deposit, but most of the time I just found trash. Before Memphis came, I stayed away as much as possible during the day to avoid the work.

As I toted my bushel basket toward the kids' play area, a 1948 Dodge pickup roared into the drive-in, spewing up a cloud of gray dust. It ground to a halt next to our white picket fence and shuddered a few times before coming to a full stop.

Dad swung around, almost losing control of his leg. "Jeeesus Christ."

"It's Aunt Bliss," I yelled, dropping the basket and running breakneck toward the house.

Aunt Bliss was the oldest of Mom's sisters and the only one still living in Indiana. She was a big-boned woman with a stride like a man's. She and my mom had the same color hair, but otherwise they were about as opposite as they could be. My aunt fastened her straight mane back with a rubber band and didn't seem to care if tufts of it occasionally stuck straight out. She wore wire-rimmed glasses, and when she removed them, the bridge piece left shiny pink indentations on her long nose. She often sounded as if she were pinching one nostril shut, but Mom said it was because she had bad allergies. Aunt Bliss lived in Boagle Corner, about forty miles to the south, where my uncle ran an auto-repair business. Every week or two, she dropped by, not bothering to call ahead because she knew Mom would always be home.

Dad, who was strictly a Ford man, disliked my aunt's Dodge truck even more than he disliked her. He said it was a piece of junk to start with, and she'd turned it into an eyesore. It was black except for one fender, which was primed a khaki brown. A lengthy winding crack snaked across its windshield, and the body was covered with so many dents that it resembled an egg carton. It had lost its muffler long ago. When it roared down the highway, it belched and backfired like a disgusting old man. But its real problem was its unreliability. More than once, Dad and Aunt Bliss had huddled over the engine cavity, like doctors over a patient, poking at its insides and glowering at each other while Mom watched nervously from behind the screen door.

The last time it broke down, Dad had bellowed, "Hell's bells, Bliss, can't Augie keep his own vehicle running?"

She had sniffed. "He's busy with customers."

"Well, then, I suggest you get in line."

I'd heard him say to Mom he didn't know how Uncle Augie put up with my aunt. "I sure as hell wouldn't. She doesn't even look like a woman when she wears those bib overalls. Nothing feminine about her. I'll be damned if I'd allow my wife to cavort all over the countryside like that."

Never mind that Mom couldn't cavort anywhere.

This time Aunt Bliss didn't bother to wave at Dad but just charged into the house. When I got there, she was laying out some printed cotton material on the kitchen table and Mom was exclaiming how pretty it was.

My aunt glanced up. "Afternoon, Callie Anne."

"Hi, Aunt Bliss."

She cocked her head and squinted at me out of one eye. "You been running again?"

"No, ma'am."

She turned back to the cloth, stroking it between her thumb and forefinger. It was a light chintz with tiny white flowers on a blue-green background. "Nice weight for a summer dress, don't you think?" she asked my mother.

Mom agreed.

Aunt Bliss looped her arm around my shoulders and roped me in, giving me an affectionate squeeze. "I'll bet there's enough here to make one for you too."

Mom reached into the cupboard for the Hershey's cocoa tin where she kept her pin money. "It's awfully nice. What do I owe you?"

"Why nothing, doll. It's my treat." She gave me another quick squeeze and released me.

"I've got money, Bliss. Now don't you go thinking I'm not going to pay you."

"Nah, it was on sale. I gave hardly anything for it. Don't say another word." Aunt Bliss walked over to the kitchen window, pulled a red bandanna handkerchief from her overalls and trumpeted vigorously into it. "Who's the fellow out there with Claude Junior?"

Mom moved next to her, and I scooted behind them, looking between their shoulders. Memphis had stopped painting and was shrugging into his T-shirt. He happened to glance at the window just as we were staring at him.

Mom stepped back quickly and almost stumbled over me. "Oh, honey, I didn't know you were there." Her cheeks were crimson. Aunt Bliss studied her with lips set tight together.

Mom returned to the kitchen table and picked up the fabric, fingering it absentmindedly. "His name's Charlie Memphis. Mr. Sooter's employed him to do some of the heavy work around the drive-in this summer."

"That old skinflint Sooter?"

"He's not a skinflint. He didn't have to hire him, did he?" Mom folded the cloth, carefully matching the corners.

"Hmmph. Never did trust Sooter. Any man that fat's got to be tightfisted. Where's this Memphis fellow bunking?"

"Upstairs in the concessions building."

"Has he got a car?"

"I don't believe so."

Aunt Bliss snorted. "A drifter, huh?"

Mom didn't answer but the muscles at the corners of her mouth tightened. My aunt's hawkish eyes watched her.

They didn't say anything for a moment, an odd little silence for the two of them. After patting the material into a neat lump, Mom walked over to the shelf that held our portable radio, took down her notebook and leafed through it. She found the page she wanted. "Now tell me what you think of this, Bliss. It's for a Morton salt contest."

"What's the prize?"

"A television set."

"Whooeee, that's a nice one. I was afraid it'd be a lifetime supply of salt."

Mom held the paper up and to one side, the way I'd seen a radio announcer in the movies once do. She cleared her throat and read in a carefully measured tone, "A good cook knows her worth. She puts Morton's in her cupboard, because it's the salt of the earth."

Aunt Bliss nodded slowly. "Yeah, that's good. That's real good. Just one little thing. I think you should say 'cause instead of because. She puts Morton's in her cupboard 'cause it's the salt of the earth. That sounds better."

Mom frowned slightly. "But that's slang. I don't think it's right to use slang in a contest."

My aunt shrugged. "Maybe so. I never was much good at English." She gestured toward the stove. "Speaking of cooking, what you got in there?"

"Oh, my gosh, I forgot." Mom grabbed the pot holders and yanked open the oven door. She lifted out a single-crust pie and set it on the stove top.

Leaning over, my aunt inspected it through her bottle-thick glasses. "Looks done just right. What is it? Pumpkin?"

"Sweet potato. I had some I had to use up."

Aunt Bliss sniffed at the steam coming off the pie. "You sure it isn't carrot?"

Mom smiled as though she had a secret. "Why, of course not. Would I lie? Here, I'll cut you a piece." She reached for a paring knife and sliced into the smooth brownish-orange surface, filling the kitchen with a rich sugary smell.

Aunt Bliss imitated a man's gruff voice. "It'd better not have carrots in it. You know how I hate carrots."

Mom started giggling and dropped the knife on the counter. Soon they were whooping with laughter, until the tears rolled down their cheeks and my aunt had to remove her spectacles and wipe her eyes with the big red bandanna. I was completely mystified.

Aunt Bliss collapsed into a kitchen chair. "Land sakes, I haven't had a belly laugh like that in a long time."

Mom fell into another chair, clutching her arms around her middle. "Me neither. That does bring back memories though, doesn't it?"

Aunt Bliss started chuckling again. "Oh, Lordy, Ma sure could be ornery sometimes."

After a minute or two, their laughter died away, and Mom's eyes got a sad distant look. "It wasn't funny, you know. She may have tricked him good, but she paid for it when he saw the carrot tops in the garbage."

"Hmmph. Beat her so bad that time she couldn't open her eyes for a week." My aunt jammed her handkerchief into her pocket with more force than usual.

I vaguely remembered Grandma Willard, a bony white-haired woman who lived on a farm and shuffled around in ragged slippers with daisies on them. The last time I'd seen her she smelled bad and called me Coral Mae, which Mom said was the name of Grandma's baby that had died. I didn't know my grandfather at all, but I'd heard about his drinking and bad temper.

Mom glanced at me, as if she'd just realized I was there.

I tried disappearing. I'd seen *The Phantom of Dodie McKenna* that spring, and I was doing my best to turn into a ghost. It didn't take hold, but with my attempts at gliding and hiding, I often managed to escape notice.

Mom caught my aunt's gaze and nodded slightly in my direction.

Aunt Bliss eyed me. "Aw, she needs to know about men like that. Callie Anne?"

"Yes."

"Don't ever marry a man who hits you."

"I won't."

Aunt Bliss, her unruly eyebrows arched, stared directly at my mother. "And don't ever marry a man who treats you like a sorry speck of dirt."

Mom drew her mouth into a thin line. "Bliss."

Aunt Bliss flapped a hand at her. "Well, shoot, I don't care if he did have a rotten stepdad. That isn't any excuse."

"He had a stepdad who worked him to the bone and told him all the time he was never going to amount to anything."

Aunt Bliss stuck her nose in the air, like she wasn't going to let mom get the last word on this one. "A lot of men grew up just as hard and they aren't as mean-spirited as your . . ."

"Bliss," Mom said sharply.

They glared at each other for several seconds, until finally I asked, "Well, how come the sheriff didn't arrest him?"

They both turned to me.

"Arrest who?" Mom asked.

Then Aunt Bliss realized I meant Grandpa. She gave a low, throaty laugh. "Why, honey, the law don't interfere in family matters like that. They've got plenty to do catching criminals. They woulda said Ma shouldn't a baked the carrot pie. 'Course now, if he'd killed her, maybe then . . ."

"Bli-iss." Mom rolled her eyes.

My aunt stood and planted her hands on her ample denim-covered hips. "Well, it's true. She's got to know these things before she gets married."

"She's young."

"How old are you now, child?"

I stretched as straight as I could. "Thirteen in October."

She squinted at Mom. "How old were you when you married Claude Junior? Sixteen?"

"Eighteen."

"Eighteen and foolish."

Mom shot right off the chair. "I was not. I knew what I was doing. Why, Claude Junior was so handsome and charming a lot of women would have been happy to . . ."

Aunt Bliss snorted. "Lord amighty, hon, you'd have done just about anything to get out of that house. I would have too. Grabbed the first man that had a decent job and showed a smidgen of kindness. I was sixteen when I married Augie. Took me years to whip him into shape." She pursed her lips, looking like she'd just swallowed a persimmon.

"So there you go." She picked up her black handbag with an air of finality, as though she'd somehow proved a point. I didn't have the foggiest idea what it was, but I felt privileged to have been involved in women talk.

Aunt Bliss rummaged through her purse, then apparently remembered she'd dropped her keys into her bib overalls. She dredged them out. "Gotta go."

Mom stood too, her hands fidgeting with a pot holder. "Oh, don't leave yet, Bliss. Stay and have some pie and coffee."

"I'd love to, sweetie, but I can't." She gave her a firm hug. "Got to drive into Jessup to pick up some parts that came into the post office for Augie. If I don't leave now, it'll be closed when I get there."

Mom watched from the screen door while Aunt Bliss tromped across the gravel muttering, "That damn fool truck'd better start."

After Aunt Bliss left, Mom picked up the material and started toward the bedroom. She stopped suddenly and looked at me with a little spark in her eyes, as if some bright idea had just clicked in. "Ask your dad and Charlie Memphis if they'd like to come in for some pie. Tell them I can't exactly send it out there."

I trotted out to Memphis and asked him first.

He climbed down from the ladder and bent over to tap the lid on the paint can with the wooden handle of his brush. He stood and stared long and hard at our house across the dusty drive-in field. "I'd never say no to a piece of sweet-potato pie."

He tucked his dingy white T-shirt into his jeans. I wondered how he did his laundry or if drifters cared about such things. I thought about telling him my mom would probably wash his clothes for him, but then decided it might not be polite to suggest they were dirty. I noticed he'd shaved the stubble off his chin, but his hair was still long and ragged at the edges.

I glanced around the drive-in field. "Memphis, do you know where my dad is?"

He cocked his thumb upward, toward the concessions building's second-story window. "He had some problems with the projector last night."

There were two ways to the projection booth—through the snack bar and through the rear exit. I walked halfway around the building and opened the heavy wooden door that led to the steep flight of stairs. The stairwell smelled musty and stale, like old cigarette butts. At the top were a small landing and two more doors, one leading to Memphis's room, the other to the booth. I could hear a movie Dad was running to test the projector. I listened, trying to place the exact scene in my mind. The picture had been playing all week as a second feature, so it took me only a few seconds.

"Mr. Allnut," Katharine Hepburn said, "what are these long, round torpedo-like things?"

"Oh, them?" said Humphrey Bogart. "Them's oxygen and hydrogen cylinders, Miss."

"Mr. Allnut?"

"I'm still right here, Miss. There ain't much other place I might be on a thirty-foot boat."

The dialogue ended abruptly. I pushed open the door and saw Dad had stopped the film, although the projector still droned like a beehive and shone its powerful beam toward the tiny window facing the screen.

I made my grand entrance. " 'You're a machinist, aren't you?' " I said in my slightly whiny Katharine Hepburn voice. " 'I mean, wasn't that your position at the mine?' "

My father, the stub of a cigarette twisted between his fingers, swung his wooden chair around on its roller casters. He gave me his lopsided Bogart grin. " 'Uh, yes, kind of a fix–it, Jack–of–all–trades and master of none, as they say.' "

" 'Could you make a torpedo?' "

" 'How's that, Miss?' "

" 'Could you make a torpedo?' "

"Hell," Dad said, "I can't even fix this damned projector."

We both laughed, and I strutted into the room.

Dad stabbed out the cigarette in an ashtray overflowing with butts. "Where you been the last few nights? You haven't come up here."

I studied some black scrape marks on the nearby wall as if they might have been primitive drawings in a cave. "Saw a couple of kids I knew and was talking to them." I didn't want to tell him I'd been following Memphis around.

The place where my father spent his evenings was dreary, even in the daytime. Ever since he'd injured his leg, he'd had trouble going up and down the stairs. And once here, he spent most of the time in his chair, scooting back and forth between the projection equipment and his desk. The only other items of interest in the room were a folding chair, a metal filing cabinet and a Norman Rockwell painting on the wall. It wasn't a real painting, just a framed cover from *The Saturday Evening Post,* but my dad said he liked it because the people in it looked real. I had spent a lot of evenings in this room with him, debating over the hum of the projector whether Jerry Lewis was funnier than Lou Costello or whether Henry Fonda was a better actor than Jimmy Stewart. Dad always said Henry Fonda, that there was no finer actor than he was, but I said Jimmy Stewart because he could be funny or serious. We went back and forth that way, watching the projector's white fog scatter moving pictures across the screen.

For as long as I could remember, I was fascinated with the way motion pictures danced in the air. When I was a little kid, I used to think the images existed somewhere out there in the night and my dad simply caught them and cast them onto the screen for everyone to see. Then he told me how it worked. No matter. I knew any way you explained it, it was magic.

I couldn't think how to tell Dad I'd found something more interesting now outside this cramped room.

He shrugged. Maybe it was the gloomy light in there, but he suddenly looked tired. "Well, maybe tonight."

He picked up a tiny screwdriver and poked at the projector's innards.

I leaned closer. "What's wrong with it?"

"These carbon rods aren't feeding right." He pointed with the screwdriver at some tiny metal pieces. "Probably some dust in the mechanism."

"Uh-huh."

"It's fouling up the carriage. Guess I'll have to remove the gear housing and clean the whole thing out."

"Uh-huh."

I watched him fiddle with the rods. His fingers were stained black from the carbon.

"Mom made sweet-potato pie. She wants you to come have a piece. She invited Memphis too."

He didn't answer. His gaze was fixed on the projector.

"Dad?"

"What?"

"Mom wants to know . . ."

He frowned but didn't look up. "I heard you."

As I backed toward the door, I tripped over three metal film cans on the floor. They clanged and banged together, and I fought to keep my balance.

Dad's head jerked up. "Jesus Christ, Callie Anne, can't you watch where you're walking? You have feet the size of gunboats."

I stared down at them, convinced they had taken on the proportions of the navy fleet. Thinking Memphis also must have noticed how big they were, I felt my face go hot with shame. I wanted to pull them up into my legs, to hide them away.

Dad returned to the projector, muttering under his breath. "Goddamned piece of . . ."

I started to tiptoe out of the room.

"Callie Anne?"

I jumped a bit, thinking I must have done something I shouldn't have. "What?"

"Tell your mom I'll be there soon."

"Okay."

I shut the door softly behind me.

On the landing, I stared at the door to Memphis's room. It was open, but not wide enough to look inside. I chewed on my bottom lip for a moment, thinking I'd sure like to see what he'd brought with him. Of course, I wouldn't have peeked in if the door had been closed. But the way it was, well, it didn't seem so bad. I rested my hand on the knob and gave a little shove, hoping the hinges wouldn't creak. They did, but the projector buzzed on.

Although it had a picture window that faced the screen, this narrow room was drearier than the other. A single bare bulb hung from an overhead fixture. The celery-colored paint was flaking off the walls, and roof leaks had left orange stains on the ceiling and warped the wooden floor in places. I couldn't remember that anyone had ever cleaned this cubbyhole, but I didn't think it was my dad's fault. He had better things to do.

The room held a sagging, coiled-spring bed frame with a thin mattress, where Memphis had tossed his bedroll. Because there was no toilet or sink, I assumed he used the men's rest room downstairs. I wondered how he managed to wash himself there. Mom made me take a bath every two days, three if I was lucky.

A partially deflated duffel bag rested in the corner, and a few folded shirts, two pairs of jeans and some cotton underwear—not white like my dad's but a dull gray—lay on a battered wooden table. I gazed for a moment at his undershorts and thought about how I'd never seen any that didn't belong to my father. I suddenly felt wicked being there. Releasing my breath, which I hadn't even realized I'd been holding, I backed out and cracked the door the way it'd been before.

I ran all the way to the house, vaulting the dirt mounds and slapping my sturdy brown shoes hard against the sand and gravel. By the time I reached the back door, I was out of breath. Memphis was sitting at the kitchen table talking to Mom, whose cheeks were flushed a deep rose.

It seemed to take an effort for her to pull her gaze away. "Wash your hands, Callie Anne," she said automatically, "up to the elbows." She studied me closer. "Have you been running again in this heat?"

I shook my head and, avoiding Memphis's gaze, darted toward the bathroom. I scrubbed my hands and arms twice, wondering how they could get so dirty when I hadn't been digging in the mud or playing with frogs. As I walked into the kitchen, I heard Mom say, "A penitentiary? Wasn't that dangerous?"

41

Memphis shook his head. "Nah, you'd be surprised. Most of those fellows ain't much different from you and me."

Mom raised her eyebrows. "Most of them?"

"Well, we did have a convict named Benny assigned to our drilling crew. Always wore his prison clothes like a tuxedo. Never said much but he was a damned good worker." Memphis gestured toward the center of the kitchen like the man Benny might have been sitting right there. "One day we were perched on a couple of upturned buckets eating our lunch when I turned to him and said, 'Benny, what are you doing time for?' I thought he'd say he'd embezzled money, some quiet little crime like that. At first he didn't answer, just stared at those big penitentiary walls from behind his little round glasses. Finally, he turned and said real casual-like, 'Killed my wife and my father-in-law.' Then he calmly added, 'Woulda killed my mother-in-law too if she hadn't got away.'"

Mom blinked. "Well, I guess you were careful not to upset him."

I think my jaw must have dropped to my chest. Although it was a strange story about some man killing half his family, it was the most Memphis had said to any of us at one time.

I slid into a chair and gazed at him. Already, I knew the hollows that shaded his face, every ropy muscle in his long arms and the tiny blades of white light deep inside his dark eyes. It was as if an actor from the most exciting movie in the world had wandered into our kitchen, and at night, I took this picture of him to bed with me and replayed it through my head.

Mom looked out the window. "You did tell your father about the pie, didn't you, honey?"

I couldn't take my eyes off Memphis, but I nodded. "Uh-huh. He's working on the projector but he said he'd be here in a minute."

Mom set the sweet-potato pie on the table alongside four of Grandma Willard's china plates. "Why don't I just cut you that piece right now, Charlie Memphis?"

If he noticed that she'd used his entire name, he didn't show it. "That's okay. I'll wait for Claude."

I whispered, "You can have two if you want."

A half-smile crossed his face.

"Why, certainly you may have two," Mom said in a light, almost excited voice. "Have as many as you want. I don't even like sweet-potato pie all that much."

Which wasn't true. I knew she loved it.

His gaze swept over it. "Well, it's just about my favorite, that and berry."

"Now that is my favorite," Mom said with the same odd cheeriness. "I love any kind of berry. Strawberries, raspberries. I think I could live off them in the summer." She turned to get a knife from the drawer, then glanced out the window. "Here he comes."

I stood so I could see my father. He was trotting stiffly across the gravel, like a three-legged dog, the tail ends of his white theater manager's shirt working loose from his brown slacks as he limped along. Once inside, he washed his hands at the kitchen sink and tucked in his shirt. The pipes rattled as though straining to bring up water from our near-dry well. Dad lowered himself into a chair, smelling like an odd combination of stale cigarette smoke and Ivory soap.

Mom slid a plate in front of him. "Charlie Memphis has been telling us about working up in Michigan at the state penitentiary."

Dad spooned three heaping teaspoons of sugar into his glass of iced tea. "Lived in Michigan, did you? I wouldn't mind that. Sure is a pretty place."

Memphis agreed. "But cold as a witch's—cold as a deep freeze in winter."

Dad picked up his fork. "Yeah, but it's got all them trees and lakes."

"Hmm." Memphis nodded, his cheek bulging like a squirrel's.

"I'd go up there," my father said abruptly. "My God, I'd move up there, if I wasn't tied to this goddamned shithole"—he stared at my mother—"by a ball and chain."

Her cheeks flamed.

With an easy casualness, Memphis directed his gaze toward the pitcher on the counter. "I'd like more of that iced tea, Teal, if you can spare it. I'm dry as a creek bed in a drought."

"Of course," she murmured, jumping up and grabbing the pitcher. She looked reed-slender in her green-and-white-print dress with its row of tiny white buttons down the front. It was one she'd sewn herself from some feed-sack material Aunt Bliss had brought her.

Dad's voice was thick. "Stuck here like one of the convicts in your penitentiary. Right, Memphis?"

"Well . . ." Memphis drew the word out. "I don't know, Claude. I did leave there and head down here."

With arms as stiff as tree branches, Mom poured his drink and sat back down.

Dad laughed bitterly. "Yeah, but at least you could travel around. Isn't that right, Teal?"

Mom studied her plate and brought a bite slowly to her mouth.

Memphis stood and brushed his hand quickly against the table so that his fork clattered to the floor. His eyes went black. "Leave her alone, Claude."

There was an uneasy silence, and I wanted to fade, to disappear

44

the way actors do when light hits the movie screen. Dad looked at Memphis with surprise, as if he couldn't understand his meaning.

My mother, whose cheeks were the color of ripe peaches, didn't lift her head. A damp wisp of auburn hair lay like a coiled spring across the nape of her neck.

Memphis's gaze swept over her. "There'd be men who'd trade with you," he said, without looking at Dad. He picked up the fork and laid it on the table. "Thanks for the sweet-potato pie, Teal. That's just about the best I ever ate and that's saying a lot for a southern boy." He walked out the screen door without another word to my father.

Chapter Four

*M*y first home was not the Starlite but the Magic Carpet Drive-in. Up to the time I was three years old, we lived in a one-bedroom apartment that was built into the wooden framework of the Magic Carpet theater screen. Mom said all the apartment's windows and doors faced a pasture. That's probably why I don't remember any of that time. I didn't see the movies, their bigger-than-life images shaping my memories.

However, I have an early, mirror-sharp recollection of myself at the Starlite, standing straight in my crib, my hands clutching the wooden railing I had notched with my baby teeth. According to my pictures from that period, I wore one-piece footed sleepers with a drop flap that buttoned at the back, and my tufted blond hair stuck out like a rabbit's ears. In the darkness of my small bedroom, I watched the headlights streak across the walls and blink off one by one as the cars settled on the gravel mounds. I have no idea what movie played that night, but I stood motionless, mesmerized by the silent shapes that flashed and danced just beyond my window.

Dad worked hard during those years too, managing the Starlite seven nights a week from April 1 through the end of September—

sometimes later if the weather held. Mom said he was so good with numbers that in 1950 Mr. Sooter appointed him the inventory supervisor for all the Empire Theater Organization drive-ins, giving him the duties of collecting information from the other managers and ordering supplies. Dad often began his day at eleven in the morning and ended it after the last cars exited about one at night. During the movie, he had to stay by the projector, changing the film reels every twenty minutes.

In the off-season, he worked as an oiler for the county, maintaining snowplows and other heavy equipment. For whatever reason, he hated those cold winter months. He dragged home each dark evening, smelling of grease and sweaty frustration.

When I was around six years old, I first became aware of what I called, in my own mind, at least, the wish box, I suppose because it made me think of the Sears Roebuck catalog, which around our house we referred to as the wish book and which I'd spent many an hour dreaming over. Every Sunday morning, summer or winter, Dad rose an hour earlier than usual, pulled out his square brown cardboard box from the hall closet and set to work on its contents. It contained brochures he'd requested from the Chambers of Commerce of about two dozen towns stretching from Texas to California. He sat on a straight chair in front of the living-room davenport, unfolded them and spread them all out, some flapping onto the armrests. They included statistics about population, weather and local industry. Color photos highlighted such major landmarks as community swimming pools and old Spanish missions. He said these southwestern towns were the places to build a drive-in theater. With their endless summers, a person could operate year-round.

I played at his feet, dressing paper dolls and watching him pay bills and scribble ciphers into a ledger. He wore through pieces of paper erasing and worrying those numbers. Every once in a while, he'd lean over and grab hold of one of the pamphlets. Pointing his nicotine-stained finger at the cloud-free blue sky and deep green palm trees in the picture, he'd say to my mom, "How'd you like to live there, hon?"

And she'd smile and nod.

Then he'd pick up his savings-account passbook and run through the figures again.

It didn't happen, of course. The direction of our lives changed the summer I was seven.

There must have been earlier signs, but I have only vague memories of them: Dad worrying those figures in his ledger harder than ever and yelling at Mom about every penny she spent; Mom staring for long minutes out the kitchen window, her eyes filled with hurt.

Spring eased into the summer of 1951 with an early ferocious heat wave. I remember Mom and me riding into Jessup with Dad and shopping at Miller's Department Store. She looked cool and fresh in her blue going-to-town dress and wrist-length white gloves, a straw handbag tucked under her arm. Hands sticky with perspiration, I fingered the fine satin nightgowns on the lingerie table at the store. The saleslady frowned.

I slid past the brassiere display to a cash register, where I could watch a clerk fold money and receipts into a canister and dispatch it through a tube to an office on the mezzanine. The tube made a gulping, swooshing sound that put me in mind of a fat green snake inhaling a frog.

I was waiting for the canister to spit back out when I heard a soft moan. On the other side of the white brassieres, my mother stood glassy-eyed and panting.

The Starlite Drive-in

I reached her about the same time the saleslady, Mrs. McGarry, did. "Are you all right, Mrs. Benton? Do you feel faint?"

Mom didn't answer. Her hands were clasped across her chest, directly over her heart. Her eyes were as flat and dark as pond water. The rigid way she stood, her legs might have been bolted to the store's wooden floor. She looked like someone who sees a train thundering down on her but can't save herself. I felt the hair on my arms rise on end.

Mrs. McGarry turned to me, squinty with concern. "Where's your father?"

"Down the street, in Mr. Sooter's office."

I wasn't sure if she knew Mr. Sooter, but she gestured toward the wide department store doors. "Go get him. I'll call the doctor."

When I returned with Dad, my mother, her cheeks a feverish pink, was seated in a straight-backed wooden chair. All the terror had fled, leaving the worst kind of embarrassment. A chisel-faced man who wasn't our usual doctor was standing over her, listening to her heart with a stethoscope.

Some of the shoppers wandered toward the lingerie section, pretending to examine the merchandise but stealing looks at her. The store manager scuttled around, assuring people she was just fine, but every once in a while he gave her a nervous glance. I suppose he thought she was bad for sales.

The doctor returned the stethoscope to his black bag with quick, almost impatient movements. The underarms on his white dress shirt were damp patches, and he smelled like Old Spice.

He cocked his head at Dad. "You her husband?"

Dad nodded, his eyes cutting across Mom. "What happened?"

The doctor shrugged, his attention back to the equipment in his bag. "Nerves. That's all. A touch of hysteria brought on by the

49

heat." He straightened and ran a finger along the inside of his collar. "Keep her out of the sun for a while."

Mom hadn't been in the sun, at least not any more than the rest of us. I didn't know what hysteria was, but I didn't like the sound of it. It made me think of polio, and one of the kids in my school had died from that.

Dad took her by the elbow and guided her out of the store, with me trailing along behind. Mom kept her eyes down, not meeting the stares of people in the aisles.

I sat between them in the truck, the rough bench-seat upholstery prickling the back of my legs. Dad shoved the gearshift into reverse with more force than necessary. "Nerves. What does that mean?"

Mom's gaze was nailed to the purse in her lap. "I don't know," she murmured.

"What do you mean, you don't know? We can't afford a doctor for something you don't know."

She shook her head, not answering. Tears splashed onto her handbag and soaked into the straw. I burrowed my head against her arm, inhaling her rose cologne and patting her hand the way she might have done for me.

Dad turned onto Blue Rock Highway and drove past the turquoise-veined boulder that rested in a park at the edge of town. A brass plaque on the rock listed the Jessup soldiers who gave their lives in World War II. Usually I liked to stare at the blue boulder out the rear truck window until I couldn't see it any longer. That day I didn't even turn around.

I guess Dad thought that dwelling on Mom's attack of nerves would only make it worse. We didn't talk about it, and to make sure it wasn't repeated, Mom stopped going into town.

The Starlite Drive-in

* * *

That fall, Mom and I still occasionally walked down the road to buy eggs from one of the farmers on Logan Highway.

During one of those outings, we came to the gray concrete bridge that spanned the White River. It was September, and the hand-sized leaves on the trees that arched over the water blazed yellow and red. The river wasn't wide at that point, only about thirty feet across, but in places it was deep and fast. All of us kids had been warned never to swim in it. A few weeks earlier, after a torrential rain, it had swallowed Jimmy Cousins, who was thirteen years old. Three days passed before it released his body downstream in Bloomfield.

Two identical-looking tow-headed boys leaned over the railing that morning, their fishing poles dangling in the calmer shallows near the bank. I recognized them from school. They were the Moen twins, a year older than I was, and they shared worm bait from a rusty green coffee can at their feet.

A few yards from the eastern end of the bridge, Mom slowed down. When I realized I was outpacing her, I turned. "What's wrong?"

She didn't answer but got that same blank, terror-struck look in her eyes that she'd had in Miller's Department Store. Her breath came in shallow gasps.

I felt my own breath quickening. "Mom?"

I couldn't think what to do. The Moen twins were staring now, my mother suddenly more fascinating than the fish that lurked in the treacherous river. I stepped between her and them, but I wasn't anywhere near tall enough to shield her.

I glared at the boys. "What are you looking at?"

I could have been a bump in the road as much as they noticed me. Their stony gazes were fixed on her.

I tried to take her hands but they were balled stiff and tight as tree roots. "Mom?"

Her eyes darted around, lighting on nothing in particular. Although it seemed as if an hour passed, we probably stood there no longer than five minutes. One of the twins got a bite on his line, temporarily distracting them.

Finally, Mom came back, not quickly but gradually. She was trembling, and she wouldn't look up. I uncurled her hand and led her away, as Dad had done.

That was the last time she left the house.

Dad didn't give up on the brochures right away. For a year or so after that, he brought out the wish box every Sunday morning as usual—until the autumn I turned ten. We had just finished the drive-in season, and he was closing the place for winter. It was twilight, and I remember him walking across the field toward the concessions building, the cardboard box under his right arm and a brown paper bag in his hand. There was something in the droop of his shoulders that made me think things weren't quite right. I watched him disappear into the building and guessed where he was going.

He sat in the projection booth for more than an hour, the overhead light in the room winking on when the sky darkened. I saw him walking around in there, stopping occasionally near the projector to tip a bottle to his lips.

Clumps of ground fog, thick and white, settled into low areas of the drive-in, and a moon the size of a dinner plate floated above the treetops. I was getting chilly, but I couldn't bring myself to leave. I knew something was wrong with Dad—although I couldn't have said what—so I squatted on the ground, propped my back against a speaker pole and waited. Through my light-weight jacket, I felt the cold metal pressing against my spine.

Dad settled in next to the projector, intent on something I couldn't see. After several minutes, he rose and staggered toward the open window. He thrust out his cupped hand, held it there for a moment, then turned it over. Bits of paper, visible in the square of window light, fluttered to the ground like candy-colored confetti. A few minutes later, he dumped out another handful of paper.

I don't know what time he returned home that night. I had already gone back to the house before him, and I was asleep when he came in. But I woke before anyone else the next morning and tramped out to the drive-in field. The air was crisp and cold and the newly risen sun so bright it hurt my eyes. I knelt on the frosty ground directly under the projection window and picked up every scrap of paper that was larger than the head of a nail. I dropped the blue shreds of western skies and green fragments of palm trees into a shoebox, then carried that box back to my bedroom and hid it in a corner of my closet. Don't ask me why.

Chapter Five

Two days after Memphis had sampled Mom's sweet-potato pie, he turned up on our living-room doorstep. It was early evening and cars were just starting to file into the parking lot. Dad had already stationed himself in the projection booth, and I was taking advantage of his absence by tuning in rock 'n' roll music on the radio. Dad felt the same way about music that he felt about cars. He stuck to his own brand, mostly slow ballads. More than once, he'd called rock 'n' roll a communist conspiracy.

Mom was sitting in an easy chair, darning Dad's white socks, and I was tapping my foot to the beat of the song, when Memphis knocked lightly on the screen door frame and said, "Hello."

We both jumped in surprise. Mom stuffed the sock, needle and all, between the chair arm and cushion and hurried to the screen door.

With a smile that made me catch my breath, he handed her a gallon coffee can filled to the brim with strawberries.

Her eyes lit up. "Why, Charlie Memphis. What is this?"

"I happened to be walking past a farmer's field, and he asked if I wanted to pick some. Right away, I thought of you."

I didn't know any farmer in the area who'd give away fruit,

and I might have searched his face for evidence of a white lie if I hadn't been staring at the berries. A good number of them were green.

Mom didn't seem to notice. "I could make us a shortcake if you'd want to stay awhile."

"I wouldn't hear of you baking on a hot night like this." He took a step back off the porch. "I'll just be running along."

"No, please, come in." She wore that same fearful look she got whenever Aunt Bliss stood up to leave. "Please," she added softly.

I noticed he was wearing a clean blue-denim shirt with a collar that was slightly frayed and his beat-up gray Stetson. He'd shaved recently and he must have put something on his face or hair because he smelled like fresh-cut grass.

"Well, I guess I could stay a minute," he said, stepping into the living room. He caught sight of me. "Hey there, pardner."

"Hi, Memphis."

Mom carried the coffee can into the kitchen, flipping on the light as she went. The yellow canary shot out of our cuckoo clock and squawked the quarter hour. Mom nodded at one of the chairs. "Now, you sit right down, Charlie Memphis."

He lowered himself onto the seat and stretched out his long legs. I flopped down across from him and tucked one foot beneath me.

Memphis fished a Lucky Strike from his shirt pocket, stuck the cigarette in his mouth and touched his lighter's blue flame to the tip. He drew the smoke in deeply and blew out a long gray ribbon. "Sure has been a hot one, hasn't it?"

"Sure has," Mom said, as cheerfully as if he'd just declared there'd be two Christmases this year. She took down a bowl from the cupboard.

I pushed the ashtray over the Formica toward him. "The radio says this might be the hottest summer ever," I announced. "Can we . . . I mean, may we have powdered sugar on the berries, Mom?"

She nodded. Lifting out a handful, she held them in midair and stared at them. I guess she wondered the same thing I did. Why would anybody pick them green?

As though reading her mind, Memphis jerked his thumb toward the bucket. "You're going to have to sort those out," he said, blowing another band of smoke in the process. "I imagine there's some there that ain't ripe."

She looked at him in surprise. "You can't see if they are or not?"

He shook his head. "I'm color-blind. Can't tell the difference between red and green."

She rinsed them in water, gently lowered them into the bowl, then gave him the sweetest, most endearing smile. "They're beautiful, Charlie Memphis, just exactly the right color."

I scooted closer so I could peer into his eyes. I figured they'd look different, like the glass eye Mr. Gibbons, the pharmacist, wore. His left one always seemed to be staring at you even when the right one was checking out the lady at the magazine rack. Except for having that gray-brown effect which made you wonder what color they really were, Memphis's eyes looked all right to me.

I pointed to my mother's cornflower-blue sundress. "What color's that?"

His gaze traveled over her, lingering until she turned away in embarrassment. "Blue, maybe."

I was disappointed. "So what colors can't you see?"

"I can see them all. Sometimes I just can't tell which is which. Red and green look about the same to me."

"How do you know what to do when you come to a stoplight?"

He smiled. "Red's always on top."

I made a face. "Yeah, I didn't think of that. Did you get into trouble at school for not knowing your colors?"

He laughed. "At first."

I peppered him with half a dozen more questions until Mom made me stop. Soon we were sitting at the table eating fresh strawberries dipped in powdered sugar, and he was telling us about the time he painted somebody's kitchen orange when it was supposed to be sunshine yellow. He almost had the whole room finished when the owner of the house, a rich, fussy lady, stopped by and nearly passed out. The store had mixed up the paint cans.

Then he told us a longer story about a fortune-teller that he and his friend Earl had met in a small town in Oregon. Seems the old woman, who looked about ninety, wore rags and had the piercing eyes of a crow. The woman told Earl he was in danger and needed to beware, and she told Memphis that he was going to come into some money, which he should spend wisely. If he didn't, his luck would disappear for many years after.

Memphis popped a sugar-dusted strawberry into his mouth. " 'Course we went away laughing. Earl was one of those fellas who never had a care, and we was both flat broke."

I scooted closer to the table. "Did the fortune come true?"

He shook another cigarette from his pack. "You're getting ahead of the story, but, as a matter of fact, it did. That afternoon, while we were scouting this burg, we tromped along a good-sized river called the Willamette. I happened to look down, and what should I see staring back at me but a fifty-dollar bill."

"Honest?"

"Honest. There it was, just as the old lady had said."

"Gosh, I guess you were surprised."

"You bet. Earl and I got ourselves haircuts and bought the biggest dinners we'd eaten in weeks."

Mom just smiled, not saying a word. Already, my skin was beginning to prickle. Visions of Earl being gunned down in that wild frontier town rose in my head. I was afraid to hear what happened next, but I had to know.

"Did he die?" I asked.

Memphis smiled. "Who, Earl? Nah, nothing quite that bad. That night he drank more than he should have, fell off a steep roof and mashed his arm. I had to spend the rest of the money getting him patched up."

I sighed in relief. Then something occurred to me. "What was he doing on the roof?"

Memphis glanced at my Mom. "Well now, I can't really recall, but he shouldn't a been there."

She lowered her gaze. After a moment, she stood, picked up the bowls and carried them to the sink. Both Memphis and I watched her, suddenly running out of words. It occurred to me Mom was wearing her hair a bit different. She had gathered it up at the back and fastened it with the mother-of-pearl comb I had given her for her birthday. A few wayward strands fell damply across her neck, which was pale as milk.

Memphis rose and stretched until his bones cracked. "Guess I better be moving along."

I jumped up. "It's still early. The first feature isn't even over."

Memphis glanced out the window, then at Mom. She didn't say anything.

He rubbed his jaw with his thumb. "Got to get up at dawn

tomorrow, pardner, and work on that building before I can fry an egg on it."

Mom stepped beside me and put her arm around my shoulders. I could feel her cool hand through my thin blouse. "Thank you for the berries, Charlie Memphis," she said. "There's still some left, and I know Claude Junior will enjoy them in the morning."

"My pleasure, ma'am."

Outside, evening had deepened into night. The cicadas carried on as if they were forming their own buzz-saw band, and beyond the kitchen window, the movie flickered on the distant screen. Wordlessly, we all three watched it for a minute. Then Memphis started for the door, with Mom and me behind him.

I was still thinking about the money and Earl. "How did you know you were spending the money the way you were supposed to?"

"Often wondered that." He turned but looked at my mom, not me. "Didn't have much luck though, until I came here."

I grinned. "We're sure glad you did. It was boring before you showed up."

Mom didn't say anything. She kept her eyes down, her arm still looped around me, her hand absentmindedly stroking my shoulder. Memphis stood there so long I began to wonder if he was really going to leave.

He fingered the brim of his Stetson. "Always good seeing you, Teal."

He turned her name into two syllables that rolled smoothly off his tongue. Dad always pronounced it as one sharp word, and I think she noticed the difference. She looked up and smiled.

Finally he put on his hat and strode out.

Chapter Six

$\mathcal{F}$or some reason I could never understand, my mother insisted on washing my hair every Sunday evening. It was an ordeal I couldn't avoid, but I usually tried to delay it by hanging out in the projection booth. It was the third Sunday in June, and Memphis had been at the drive-in about two weeks. I'd spent hardly any time in the booth with Dad since his arrival and I was feeling pretty guilty about it. By the time I climbed the stairs, the first feature had already started. On the top step, I hesitated. The door was open, and my father sat alone in the cramped room, sipping iced tea from the screw-on cup to his vacuum bottle. Although he'd seen the movie twice before, he was staring at the screen with a kind of glazed look. The only light came from the whirring projector.

As I stood on that top step, I had every intention of walking in, but I just couldn't bring myself to stick one foot in front of the other. I thought about how hot and smoky it was in there and how I'd already seen this movie and didn't like it all that much the first time and how it was silly to put off going back to the house. The whole state of Indiana could be hit by an atomic bomb, and Mom would still wash my hair every Sunday night just to make sure it got clean. Once it was over, I could go looking for Memphis.

The bell that signaled the changing of the film reel dinged its two-minute warning, and Dad stirred. Before he could notice me, I tiptoed down the stairs and out the rear exit.

Mom was laying out the shampoo and the towel when I walked into the house.

"Just in time," she said with a cheery smile.

I sighed and dropped so heavily onto the kitchen chair that the vinyl cushion made a little wheezing sound.

She unfastened my ponytail and parted my hair for inspection. She poked at my scalp and made little noises of disapproval, as if she'd discovered a nest of ants there.

I wriggled from under her touch and muttered, "Washed it in the bath this morning."

"Not well enough," she said, motioning me over to the sink. "Or else you've been crawling through the weeds at the crick again. It looks filthy."

"Isn't my fault. You said yourself blond hair gets dirty quicker."

In every other way, my mother was a kind and gentle woman, but when she applied the Prell, she turned from Dr. Jekyll into Mr. Hyde. She wet my hair and kneaded in the shampoo, which had a fragrance I associated with slow torture. Then she knuckled, pummeled and scoured until I yelled for mercy.

"You don't want cooties, do you?"

"But I don't have them."

"And you never will. Now, why do you suppose that is?"

She routinely rescued spiders, bees, ladybugs and even flies that wandered into our house, but for some reason she felt no remorse over killing innocent cooties once a week.

By the time she reached for the vinegar rinse, I felt as though I'd toppled headfirst into a patch of nettles. She towel-dried my hair and ran a comb through it. "There now, I'll bet that feels better."

Compared to the pain, it did. I slumped limply onto the kitchen chair.

Then the brushing began. She said another ten minutes of sitting there wouldn't kill me, and besides, it would make my hair shine. By the time she'd finished, it must have gleamed like automobile chrome in the sun. With a hand like a vise, she gripped my ponytail to fasten it with a rubber band. I heard a knock on the back door and jerked my head around. Mom held tight, and I bellowed.

Through the screen, I could see Memphis delivering one of his rare smiles.

"Guess I came at a bad time," he said.

Mom let go of me. "Oh, no, it's fine. Please come in."

She opened the door, shooing away the bugs that tried to sneak in with him. Her eyes brightened in the overhead kitchen light.

"I won't stay long," he said. "I was wondering, Teal, if you had a needle and thread I could use." He was carrying a plaid shirt over his arm.

"Of course," she said, motioning him to a chair. "You sit right there while I get them."

Mom was back in a minute, carrying her round wicker sewing basket. She walked in just as Memphis stood and grabbed for a moth that was flapping around the kitchen light.

"Looks like I let a critter in after all," he said.

Luckily he didn't catch it on the first try. When Mom saw him go after it, her eyes widened in horror. "No!"

In one quick motion, I dragged the kitchen chair over and

hopped onto it. Without a word, she handed me a canning jar from the cupboard. I trapped the moth within seconds, having done it many times before, and clamped my hand over the opening.

Mom smiled her approval. "Just release it out the front door, honey, where it's darker, and no more'll get in." She lifted the lid on her sewing basket.

I guess it never occurred to her that anybody else might think our lifesaving routine was strange, but Memphis watched in silence.

While I was opening the screen door, I heard Mom say, "A jar's better than hands, because it doesn't damage their delicate wings."

"Uh-huh."

I caught the amusement in his voice and guessed what he was thinking. Standing there in the dark, I felt the heat crawl up my neck and cheeks. If he was laughing at us, I wasn't sure I could face him. I wrestled with my thoughts. So what if my mom didn't kill bugs. Better she was that way than someone who stomped all over them, like a lot of the stupid boys I knew. And if he thought she was crazy, well, too bad. Maybe he wasn't so great after all.

I set my jaw and marched back in.

Mom selected a needle from the padded pincushion built into the lid of her sewing basket. "Any problem, honey?"

I shook my head, not looking at Memphis.

She chose a spool of blue thread and held it against his shirt. "Well, good. He's probably flying around out there thinking he sure had a close call. Right, Charlie Memphis?" She turned her face up to him, and in the umbrella of light from the overhead fixture, her eyes looked especially large and green.

He stared directly into them. "I'd say you're right, Teal."

I blinked. He wasn't making fun of her after all. The seriousness in his voice told me he understood her perfectly, just as I did. My heart soared, and he towered to ten feet.

"Hey, Memphis, you going into Jessup with Dad tomorrow?"

"Might. How about you, shortstuff?"

I grinned, not even minding the name. "Maybe, if you give me a nickel for a candy bar in town."

Mom's eyes widened in shock. "Callie Anne."

He reached into his blue jeans and flipped me a quarter. "If you promise to bring one back for your ma."

I caught the coin in midair as easily as if it'd been a baseball and pocketed it. I flopped onto a kitchen chair. Already I was thinking about cozying up to him on the truck's bench seat and leaning into him when Dad took the sharp corners.

"You're spoiling her, Charlie Memphis," Mom said, but there wasn't any scolding in her voice. She dug around in her sewing basket, then looked up. "Have you seen my scissors, honey?"

"No, but I bet I know where they are," I said, jumping up and heading toward the living room. I switched on the three-way floor lamp next to the easy chair where she had been darning Dad's socks a few nights earlier. Sure enough, I found the scissors between the chair arm and the cushion.

When I returned, they were standing next to each other and Memphis's shirt lay in a lump on the table. His sun-browned hand was clasped over her slender fingers as though to stop her.

"I wasn't asking you for that," he said.

Mom's head was tilted down a little, but I could see her cheeks burned bright. "Oh, I don't mind. It won't take any time at all to sew it up."

I walked over and dropped the small pair of scissors so they bounced and clattered onto the tabletop. Mom's head flicked up. Memphis released her hand but not with any rush.

"Found them," I muttered.

Without another word, Mom slipped into a chair and cut a length of thread from the spool. She stabbed that blue thread at the needle with such a shaky hand I couldn't help but stare.

Whistling tunelessly, Memphis sat down at the table, dug a nickel out of his pocket and, with a flick of his thumb and middle finger, set that coin spinning on the table. Fascinated, I watched it twist and tilt. When it finally came to a rest, it stood on edge.

I think my chin must have dropped to my chest. "How'd you do that?"

A slow smile worked its way to his mouth, but he didn't answer.

I glanced at Mom. She had managed to thread the needle and was making tiny stitches in the shirt where the seam had come unsewn. Through the window behind her, *The Tender Trap* flickered on the screen.

Memphis pulled a cigarette from his pocket and tapped it gently on the table. The nickel fell over, but he left it lying there. "Had me a dog once named Nickel."

"Really?" I stuck my elbows on the table and propped my chin in my hands.

He lit the cigarette, closed his lighter with a snap and leaned back. "Yup, funniest-looking mutt you ever seen. Short-haired and ugly as a warthog, but, boy, was he smart. We called him Nickel because he could count money."

"Aw, Memphis."

"Sure could. Got him as a pup when I started working in a little one-horse town in Wyoming. Once he grew up, I never

65

could get him to stay to home. But around four o'clock every afternoon when I'd have a beer with the fellas at the local tavern, that mutt would turn up." He glanced at Mom, as though checking to see if she was listening. She looked up and smiled.

"Anyway," he said, picking up the coin and tapping it on the gray-flecked turquoise Formica. "I'd be playing with the nickel, just like this, and before you know it, here comes the dog. Well, he jumps onto a chair and starts to eyeing it. After a bit, I looks at him and says, 'Guess you want a candy bar, huh, Nickel?' Then I flip the coin and he catches it in his mouth, quick as you, shortstuff."

I grinned.

"And off he trots to the grocery store. Pretty soon he's back with a big old Milky Way in his mouth." Memphis inhaled his cigarette, tilted his head back and blew a carefully formed smoke ring, a thin gray circle that danced in the air. "Well, Nickel hops in the chair and drops the candy bar on the table. 'Course all the guys are watching 'cause this dog's sharp as a tack. I ignore him but he keeps picking it up and dropping it. Pretty soon I peel off the paper and he takes it over to the corner and eats it."

In my imagination, I saw this clever dog guarding his candy. A thought nagged at me. "How'd he know he could buy a Milky Way with a nickel?"

"I don't know, but he did," Memphis said, looking up at the ceiling as though in fond memory. "Once, one of the fellas thought he'd play a joke on him and give him a quarter. So Nickel takes the money and trots off as usual. Pretty soon he's back with two candy bars and the change. Well, the guys thought that was funny. Only problem was, Nickel ate both of them and got sicker than—well, sicker than a dog."

I laughed, but Mom looked sympathetic.

Memphis stubbed out his cigarette and shrugged. "That's the problem with a dog. He ought to have more sense than to trust a man."

Leaning back in my chair, I thought about owning a dog like Nickel and how popular he'd make me with the kids at school. He could probably learn any number of tricks and would be almost as good as a horse. "Gosh, Memphis, I sure wish you still had him. Where is he now?"

Memphis grew somber. "Well, you see, Nickel was a fool about some other things too. He had a habit of chasing tires and got clipped by a logging truck when he weren't much more than two years old."

I guess we all looked mournful for a moment.

By the time I fell into bed that night, I was too excited to sleep. I kept thinking about Nickel and wondering how Memphis knew when he named that pup that he was going to be smart enough to count money. I wasn't quite sure, but I thought Memphis might have put one over on us.

Chapter Seven

As it turned out, we didn't go into Jessup the next day the way we usually did on Thursdays. Mr. Sooter's old maid sister passed away, and he had to fly to Atlanta to make arrangements for the funeral. Dad said there was no point driving into town if he couldn't meet with Mr. Sooter, but of course he had no way of knowing that quarter Memphis had given me was setting fire to my shorts pocket.

I don't think Dad had any idea that Memphis was stopping by our house after the movie started, and Mom never said a word about it. Anyone could see my father and Memphis didn't have much use for each other. They rarely spoke, except to discuss what needed fixing next.

As soon as he finished painting the concessions building, Memphis began excavating the area around the septic tank. He had to work in the full sun, but I stayed in the shadow of the movie screen while I kept him company. His sweat-dampened hair clung to his neck and his arms knotted with exertion. The steaming mountain of dirt he was loading into my father's three-quarter-ton pickup smelled worse than the skunk that had crawled under Aunt Bliss's house and died.

"Why's it stink so much?" I asked Memphis.

He jammed the shovel in the earth and squinted at me in the bright afternoon sunlight. "Filled with sewage that oozes out from the septic tank. Worms and bugs usually gobble it up, but sometimes they don't eat fast enough and the ground gets choked with it."

That sure gave me a whole different attitude toward worms and bugs. When he said sewage he really meant shit, but I wasn't allowed to use the word. You couldn't have paid me enough to dig around in that dirt, so I felt sorry for Memphis, who didn't have much choice. I decided to keep him company as long as I could, although it wasn't easy carrying on a conversation while pinching my nose and breathing through my mouth. For some reason, he didn't seem to mind the stink. He said a person gets used to it, but I never did.

After he hauled away the clogged soil, he constructed yellow-painted wooden barriers around the cavity so people wouldn't stumble into it. It was in a place where they weren't supposed to be, but Dad said that didn't matter because you couldn't overestimate the stupidity of adults, much less kids. A truck was supposed to come the next day and pump out the sludge in the septic tank. Then Memphis would cover it with fresh earth. But something happened that night that was a lot more exciting than a kid falling into the hole.

It was Saturday, and people were packing the drive-in to see *Abbott and Costello Meet the Mummy*. I left the playground area, having already tired of watching pajama-clad kids tumble off the monkey bars and run to their parents crying. People said I was lucky to have a jungle gym, seesaw and swings in my front yard, but when you're playing on them alone in the middle of the day, they get pretty boring. Dad wanted to install a miniature train that would carry passengers in a circle around the screen. He'd heard about a Kansas theater that had one, and it attracted families from as far away as the next county. Mr. Sooter said he'd think about it, but I could have told him it was a good idea.

Two boys ran between the cars, yelling and playing tag and snagging fireflies. They held them in their cupped hands while the bugs flashed their bright yellow signals. I didn't mind as long as the kids eventually let them go. Every once in a while somebody threw a lightning bug on the cement and scraped his shoe across it, leaving a long phosphorescent streak. There was a time, a few years back, when I would lose all sense and jump any kid who did that. I might have been short and scrawny, but I could slug and holler my way through a fight if I needed to. And the surprising thing was how many of those bug-murderers turned out to be weenie little snot-noses when pinned to the ground. More than once, Dad broke up the fight, snatching me by the waistband of my shorts while I flailed my arms and jabbed and kicked. Hauling me up to the projection room, he said he wasn't going to have any daughter of his charging around the drive-in and whomping the hell out of money-spending customers. It was either I sat up there with him or I stayed in the house with my mother. I guess that's how I started spending so much time in the projection booth.

Wandering toward the theater entrance, I swerved around a guy carrying a fold-up canvas lawn chair. Inside one of the cars, a dad was attaching the speaker to the window, and the mom was pouring Kool-Aid from a jug. Two little kids stood in the backseat. The boy, who looked like he was about four years old, wore Hopalong Cassidy earmuffs and six-shooters in a leather holster strapped over his pajamas. His sister, who was clutching a yellow-haired dolly in one hand and a paper cup in the other, was crying and accusing him of taking aim at her. Up and down the rows, people settled in with their drinks and popcorn, waiting for the sun to draw its last breath of the day and sink below the horizon.

At least twenty vehicles were still lined up outside the theater entrance, but I was more interested in the high school boy manning the box office.

I flipped back my hair the way I'd seen Lauren Bacall do it. "Hello, Virgil."

"Hi, Callie Anne." He didn't even glance at me. His gaze was on a shiny new two-door, turquoise-and-white hardtop Chevy that had just pulled up. He counted out change from the cash drawer and passed it to the driver.

Finally, he turned his lake-blue eyes on me. "Sure is busy tonight."

"I'll say."

The box office rested on a concrete pad that was about four feet square. I dropped to the ground near Virgil's feet and leaned my back against the door, which had been propped open to let in air. Staring up at him, I could see on his jaw the thin white scar he got falling off his uncle's palomino. As if his interest in horses and his bravery weren't enough, he possessed two more fine qualities. He was smarter than the other boys I knew, and when he had the time, he was willing to talk with me. Cars crept by, one by one, and their drivers handed over the admission price. The next vehicle, its muffler rumbling like someone's overwrought stomach, pulled alongside the box-office window.

Virgil stiffened. "Damn."

I glanced up in surprise. He wasn't the type to cuss. Without looking down, he spread a warning hand for me to stay put and eased the cash drawer shut with his other hand.

I heard a man growl, "Hey, kid. See this."

Virgil nodded.

"If'n you don't put all the money you got into this here sack, I'm gonna blow your head off." His words were thick and slurred, and I felt my insides go all cold.

"You don't have to do that," Virgil said, a snail trail of perspiration forming on his upper lip. "You can have the money."

He took the brown paper bag that had HENBARGER'S BAKERY stenciled in dark green on the side. I poked my head up just enough to see a gleaming short-barreled gun pointed unsteadily in Virgil's direction.

Virgil peered inside the sack, then wet his lips nervously. "It's got a doughnut in it."

"Huh?"

"Well, there's a chocolate doughnut in it. Looks pretty sticky. You want me just to dump the money on top?"

A hand reached out and yanked the bag back. "Leroy, you idiot, what the hell's that doing in there?"

Another boozy voice whined something I couldn't make out. While they were busy with the sack, Virgil made a slicing gesture with his right hand that clearly told me to take off. Soon the sack reappeared through the window, and Virgil tugged on the cash drawer under the counter. As I crept away on legs that had gone soft as bread dough, I heard him say, "Gosh, fellas, it's stuck."

I stayed close to the board fence, glancing once over my shoulder at the two men inside the old maroon Studebaker that shook and shimmied under the bright entrance lights. They wore cowboy hats pulled low and bandanna handkerchiefs over their faces. When I reached the open field, I straightened and ran as fast and hard as I could. I smacked directly into Memphis, who was leaving the concessions building. Behind him, Lou Costello, larger than life, cavorted across the movie screen.

"Robbers," I gasped, pressing a hand against the stitch in my side.

"What?"

My breath came in a gasp. "The box office. They're gonna shoot Virgil and steal the . . ."

He bolted before I even finished the sentence. I took off right behind him, but I couldn't keep up with his long stride. He stopped at the corner of the fence, where I caught up with him.

"That it?" He nodded at the gray Plymouth next to the box office.

I shook my head and wheezed, "Guess they're gone."

He walked cautiously toward the cubicle, with me at his heels.

Virgil was collecting money from people and adding it to neatly stacked coins and dollar bills on the counter. His brown freckles stood out like a stampede of bugs across his chalky face.

Memphis slid in beside him. "They get the cash in the drawer?"

"Not yet," Virgil said. "They're back in line."

Memphis stared at him. "What?"

"Well, I told them the drawer was stuck. They started fighting with each other about what to do. People were yelling out their windows and blowing their horns so I suggested they drive to the end of the line. I said by the time they'd get back up here, I'd have it open."

Memphis laughed. "And they bought it?"

Virgil shrugged. "Just dumb and drunk enough to. They're in that rattletrap Studebaker."

"How many men and how many guns?"

"Two guys, but only one gun I could see."

Memphis took off running toward the Studebaker.

I paused long enough to say, "I'm glad you're not shot, Virgil."

He gave me a weak smile and nodded.

As I reached the car, Memphis was yanking the driver's door open.

The robber lunged at him, yelling, "You sonofabitchin' pissant."

The blood rose in Memphis's face, and he jerked the driver from his seat. The robber threw the first punch with his left hand, although it didn't do much more than graze Memphis's jaw. The bandit's beat-up tan cowboy hat fell to the dirt and his mask flopped down over his chin. He narrowed his yellowed eyes on Memphis and raised his right arm. I saw a glint of reflected light. Memphis's fist shot out and hit the bandit's wrist with a loud *thwack*. The pistol squirted into the air like a wet bar of soap and landed near my feet.

I snagged the gun and backed up. It crossed my mind to run, but I didn't want to miss the action. Besides, Memphis might need my help. After all, I'd shouldered my uncle's single-shot twenty-two and nailed many a tin can on a fence post under his supervision. I positioned my finger on the pistol trigger, aiming downward. The grip felt moist from the robber's sweaty palm.

I don't think the other robber, a slack-jawed fellow, ever saw the gun. After tumbling out of the car, he staggered toward Memphis, his soiled T-shirt straining over his belly. He tried to hammer Memphis on the back of the neck, but his fist couldn't dent those hard, tight muscles. Memphis reached behind and swatted at the balled hand like it might have been a horsefly, then swung around and with a few good blows smashed the man to the ground.

Watching them, I got all excited, almost drunk myself with the thrill of the ruckus. Behind them, people were tumbling out of their cars and hurrying toward us.

The weaselly-eyed man seemed to sober up quick. He bared his crooked brown teeth and charged Memphis with an out-stretched fist, trying to sock him below the belt. I had seen enough movie fights to know that wasn't fair. I could tell Memphis felt the same way because his eyes went all dark and narrowed to slits a dime couldn't have passed through. Somehow he got hold of the guy's shirt and twisted it close to his neck. For a few seconds they spun around together, their boots grinding against the gravel and stirring up a cloud of dust. Then Memphis punched and punched, opening a cut above the robber's left eyebrow. Blood gushed and streamed down his face.

The man was clearly beaten, and I waited for Memphis to re-lease him, to let him fall to the ground. But Memphis just kept on, holding him up and jabbing at him until the robber hung limp in his hands.

An uneasiness passed through me. Nothing showed in Mem-phis's eyes but an eerie blankness.

The bandit's forehead pulsed red. He opened his mouth and gurgled. Red foam rose to his lips and dribbled down his chin. It was unlike anything I'd ever seen in the movies and I felt my insides twist.

"Memphis," I yelled. "Memphis, stop!"

He slugged him once more, square in the face, and I heard a dull sound like glass crunching. I flinched.

A boom like a cherry bomb going off blasted near my feet. Dirt and gravel chips spit into the air. When I felt the throb of the recoil in my arm, I realized I had squeezed the pistol trigger.

I heard a thud as the robber dropped to the ground like a bag of dirty laundry, and I nearly passed out right then. I realized to my great horror I must have shot him. The smell of gun smoke hung in the air. Memphis turned, his eyes still black as snake holes. Behind him were a dozen or so men standing motionless in the shadows.

The sweat was pouring down Memphis's face, trickling through streaks of blood and grime. It took a long time for his eyes to start tracking again, to take on a human glow. And when they did, he was staring at the robber as if he didn't quite know where he'd come from, as if some fellow with bloodier hands than his own might have pounded the living daylights out of him.

Memphis turned his gaze on me, and I saw him wince. "Callie Anne."

"Yeah?"

He measured out each word, in a strangely controlled tone. "Callie Anne, very slowly now, I want you to give me that gun."

I looked down at my hand. I was about three feet from him, aiming the pistol directly at his midsection.

"Oh, shit." I dropped it as if I'd been stung, and Memphis snatched it up.

The robber, who I thought was dead, groaned and tried to sit up. He fell right over again. I hadn't shot him after all, but he looked like someone had taken a hammer to his face. A flap of dark meaty flesh dangled from the end of his left eyebrow, and his lids were almost puffed shut.

About that time, my father showed up, red-faced and full of questions. The men who had streamed out of their cars were all talking at once. Several loudly insisted that if they had known those fellas were holding up the theater, they'd have rushed in to help. Memphis stood there quietly now, the blood seeping from his split lower lip. His white T-shirt was splattered crimson. No one said anything about me shooting the gun, and if anyone cared about the beating, they didn't mention it. It had scared me to see Memphis that way, to watch that deadly veil drop over his eyes, then lift again. But having been in a fight or two where I went a little berserk, I understood how it might happen.

They made a big deal out of locating rope and tying up the robbers, who were in such bad shape they couldn't have escaped anyway. Three county sheriff's cars barreled in, red lights flashing, sirens screaming and tires spewing up so much gravel and dust we could hardly breathe. Soon everybody inside the drive-in discovered there was more action outside than there was on-screen, and they came rushing back through the entrance. Finally, Dad stopped the film for a twenty-minute intermission so people could watch Sheriff Ralph Jankowski and his deputies untangle the ropes, handcuff the robbers and haul them off to jail.

About the time the movie started again, the sheriff asked where Memphis was, and I went off in search of him. I found him sitting on a bench outside the concessions building, his head in his hands.

I hovered a few feet away. "Memphis, whatcha doing here? Everyone's looking for you. The sheriff wants to talk to you."

He lifted his head so the light above the snack-bar door cast an amber glow on him. The streaks of blood and dirt were gone from his face so he must have cleaned up in the men's room. A crusty splotch darkened his lip, and he looked tired and suddenly old.

He rubbed the back of his hand across his forehead. "Tell him to talk to Virgil. He's the one who caught those men." He got up and strode into the darkness, in the opposite direction from the box office and the flashing lights.

I stared after him, wondering what was wrong. Figuring Sheriff Jankowski could track down Memphis himself, I walked back toward the house. As I neared the front door, I saw my mother's anxious face pressed against the kitchen window, her hair fanned

77

out like a tangled halo. A wave of guilt swept over me. I had been so caught up in the commotion that I hadn't even thought how frantic she must be, hearing it from a distance.

Inside, she treated me as if I'd just returned from the war, grabbing me and feeling my bones all over. "What's happened? Are you hurt?"

I squirmed away. "I'm okay but we had a robbery. Memphis caught the bandits and saved the money."

She went white as chalk. "Your father? Where's your father?"

"Back in the projection room, I guess. He's okay."

"And Charlie Memphis? Is he hurt?"

"Not much. The other guys looked a lot worse."

She released me, ran to the door and opened it. For a moment, I thought she was going to run outside, but she stopped dead on the threshold, hitting some invisible barrier. She glanced back at me, terror widening her green eyes.

"Everybody's okay, Mom. Honest. The sheriff took the robbers away." I couldn't stand to see her like this, and I tried to think of something to distract her. "Do we have any cookies? I'm sure hungry."

That drew her attention back to me, and she rushed about setting out homemade apple bars and milk. It took me a half hour to describe the night's events. Of course, I had enough sense to leave out my part with the gun and the awful beating the robber took. As I told the story, it seemed less scary and more like something I might have seen on the screen outside our door. By the time I'd finished, it was clear to me Memphis had saved the drive-in, no two ways about it, just as good as John Wayne or Gary Cooper could have done it.

I sighed. "It was exciting, Mom. You should have been there."

I could have bitten my tongue as soon as the words left my

mouth. A shadow passed across her face. She picked up my empty milk glass and the cookie plate, saying something about Memphis needing iodine, maybe even stitches.

I walked over to where she was standing in front of the sink. "Aw, he's okay. Why, I bet he'll stop by tomorrow night and tell you the whole story himself."

She turned, pulled me to her and laid her cool cheek on my forehead. Her loose hair fell across my face, her mother-of-pearl comb hanging by only a few strands. She smelled fresh and sweet, like the roses in our garden.

My thoughts strayed. I began to think of Memphis rescuing me, just me alone, from the hooded bandits. He galloped in on a barrel-chested white stallion, scooped me up and wrapped his powerful arms around me. I pressed my head against his warm, sturdy chest and held on tight. Behind him, on a smaller, less impressive horse, trailed his faithful sidekick Virgil, who desperately and silently loved me, but who would never betray his friend. It was a magnificent scene as we all three rode into the sunset.

Chapter Eight

𝒯he following day, a big truck arrived and pumped the sludge from the septic tank. It was just as smelly as you'd think it'd be.

It was a full twenty-four hours after the robbery before Memphis turned up on our doorstep again. He was carrying three cold bottles of orange soda pop, which was almost as good as Grape Nehi. From what I could tell, his split lip and bruised knuckles were healing fine, but Mom brought out the iodine anyway. She applied it as gently as if she were tending me, crisscrossing his skin with bright orange slashes. I thought he'd mind her fussing over him like that, but he acted as though he enjoyed it.

His hand landed on hers. "This makes it almost worth it."

Her voice was so light it seemed to float. "Now, sit still, Charlie Memphis, and behave yourself."

I figured that once Mom was sure he wasn't in danger of bleeding to death, we could hear his version of the robbery. Instead, he started talking about the septic tank, of all things. Then Mom said something about the well drying up, and before I knew it Memphis was describing a half-Cherokee water witch he once knew. Using an eagle feather, this medicine man found water every time.

He was famous throughout southern Idaho, and no one would drill a hole in the ground without him.

It was an interesting story, but I didn't think it was anywhere near as exciting as our adventure right here at the drive-in.

After he finished, he took a swig of his orange pop, then gingerly wiped his mouth with the side of his hand.

"Memphis?" I said.

"Hmm?"

"Aren't you going to tell Mom about last night?"

She looked at him expectantly.

He set the bottle down on the table with a clunk and leaned back in his chair. "Well, shortstuff, I figured you'd already done that."

"Not like you could."

"Callie Anne says you're a hero, Charlie Memphis."

With an odd, lopsided smile, he rose slowly from the chair, walked over and picked up the ashtray sitting on the windowsill above the sink. He returned to the table, and I propped my elbows on the Formica and scooted in, ready to listen. I knew we'd hear a real wingding now. He pulled a cigarette from his pocket and lit it, the blue flame curling toward him as he drew in a breath. His scraped knuckles shone dark purple in the kitchen light. I was surprised he didn't blow smoke rings the way he usually did.

He gave my mother a long thoughtful look, then turned to me with a weary smile. "There were no heroes last night."

He didn't say any more. I scrunched down in the chair, feeling he had made a liar out of me. I had heard there was almost three hundred dollars in the cash drawer. Everyone else thought that was important even if he didn't. Maybe he figured Jessup wasn't important. That's why he talked about those towns in Michigan and Idaho and California all the time.

The conversation soon slowed, like a mechanical toy winding down. Even Mom seemed disappointed. When he stood to leave, I started out the door with him.

She gave me a warning glance. "Don't be long now."

"I won't."

No more than thirty feet from the house, I blurted, "I guess you don't think what happens here makes any difference."

"What?" he turned toward me, but in the dark I couldn't read his expression.

I looked down at my feet. "Well, why else wouldn't you tell her?"

"About the robbery?"

What did he think I was talking about? "Yeah. You're always telling stories. Why not that one? It's as good as any other." Although I didn't intend my voice to sound accusing, I knew it did.

He waved a hand. "See up there?"

At first I didn't know what he meant. I stared at the screen. Once again the mummy, dragging tattered gray bandages, was chasing Lou Costello. "The movie?"

He walked up and over the gravel mound between two cars, and I had to hurry to catch up with him.

"You mean the movie?"

"Entertainment, just like the stories. What happened last night was real, shortstuff. People ain't the heroes you think they are. You better learn that while you're young."

"But you saved the drive-in."

"Me and Virgil. Remember Virgil?"

"Okay, so you and Virgil."

He stopped and turned toward me, his eyes glittering in the darkness. A kid passed by, swinging a flashlight, and it made cone-shaped patterns on Memphis's face.

He gripped my shoulder hard. "There weren't nothing good about last night, and I ain't a hero. You got that, kid?" He released me and walked off.

I remained where I was, slightly stunned.

Even if Memphis didn't believe they were heroes, everyone else did. An eager, gum-chomping reporter from *The Jessup Enterprise* came to the drive-in on Monday afternoon and scribbled page after page in his notebook. Memphis didn't want his picture taken, so the fellow photographed my father and Virgil shaking hands outside the box office. Then Sheriff Jankowski happened to drop by, and the reporter took a few shots of him and Dad examining the empty cash drawer, which made no sense at all because the money never was stolen. The sheriff's grin was so wide that I wondered if he'd acquired a new set of teeth. You would have thought he had captured the robbers, but Dad said later he was just running for office.

Memphis leaned against the board fence, away from everyone's notice, and with his arms folded across his chest, silently watched the picture taking. After it was over, he walked toward the concessions building, and Virgil headed toward his truck.

I fell into step with Virgil. "Gosh, won't people be surprised when they see your picture in the paper? 'Course, most people have probably heard about it. I mean, everybody says it's the biggest thing since . . ." When it occurred to me my words were banging together like boxcars in a train wreck, my face grew hot. I said more quietly, "What you did to those robbers was brave, Virgil."

He stopped and stared at me for so long I began to wonder if he thought I was goofy in the head. Finally, he said, "I didn't decide to be brave. I didn't think about how it might turn out."

He stuffed his hands in the pockets of his blue jeans, which were so new and stiff they didn't appear to bend at the knees. Some of the farm kids wore shabby clothes and never scrubbed their fingernails, but not Virgil. Even when he wasn't getting his picture taken, he had what my dad called a clean-cut look.

I gazed up at him. "You were smart to trick those bandits like you did."

"It didn't take much doing."

"Well, they still could have shot you."

He nodded. "Memphis said he got in a fight like that once and a man got killed."

I swung around. "You mean Memphis killed somebody?"

Virgil shrugged. "I don't know. He just said someone got killed."

The idea of a shootout sent a thrill through me. I could see the outlaw strutting down the street, Memphis facing him, cool and fearless, pulling his pistol a split second before the other guy drew his.

Virgil started walking again, and I skipped beside him, trying to match his long stride. "How did it happen?"

"He didn't say. I think he just wanted me to know it doesn't always end so well."

Even so, Memphis began to look more and more like Gary Cooper in my mind.

We reached the flatbed Ford truck that belonged to Virgil's dad. Virgil was only fifteen, but being a farm kid, he was allowed to drive it around the countryside without the sheriff stopping him. The truck door creaked as he opened it. He swung himself into the driver's seat, just as I remembered I had intended to ask him a favor.

I dug deep into my shorts pocket and pulled out a handful of change. "I was hoping you might buy something for me the next time you go into Jessup."

I told him what it was, and he listened thoughtfully.

He took the coins but didn't pocket them right away. "Why don't you buy it yourself?"

I dug the toe of my shoe into the dirt. "I don't know how long it'll be before I get to town." It was a lie. Mr. Sooter had returned from his sister's funeral, and Dad would drive in as usual the following Thursday morning.

Virgil looked at the assortment of dimes, nickels and pennies. "You sure your dad's not going to mind?"

"No, absolutely not. You don't have to worry."

He dropped the money in his shirt pocket. "All right then." He pushed the truck starter button until it caught and shifted the Ford into gear. It lumbered down the road like an old black bear.

On my way back to the house, I caught sight of Billy scuffling past the lilac bushes, looking like a stick figure in a baggy brown suit. I glanced over my shoulder and saw Dad limping toward the concessions building, his gaze on the talkative newspaper reporter beside him. I smiled to myself. The empty plate would be on the back step. Once again, Billy had escaped with a full stomach.

Chapter Nine

$\mathcal{I}$t took a few days for the drive-in to return to normal. Then, on Wednesday, the story came out in *The Jessup Enterprise,* and people got excited all over again. With business better than ever, Dad joked that he wouldn't mind a small robbery once in a while. I cut the article from the newspaper and taped it to my vanity mirror. It was a good picture of Dad. Mom had pressed his theater manager's shirt to a white stiffness, and he'd slicked down the cowlicks in his brown hair. With his square jaw, and the military-straight posture he'd managed to keep in spite of his bad leg, he looked solidly in charge. Virgil put me in mind of Jimmy Stewart, kind of long-boned and embarrassed to be there. If you examined the photograph closely, you could see Memphis standing in the shadows.

That night, I sat on a mound of gravel to the far right of the concessions building so that people trekking back and forth wouldn't trip over me. More than once I'd had popcorn and drinks dumped on my head. We were still playing *Abbott and Costello Meet the Mummy.* If I'd wanted to, I could have turned up the sound on the nearby speaker, but I didn't. It was the eighth night of the movie's run, and I already knew the big scenes by heart.

I stood, stretched and ambled toward the snack bar. The humid June air was so heavy and motionless, the aromas of fresh popcorn and hot butter hung like a cloud over the concessions building. With no customers to wait on, the two teenage girls behind the snack bar talked and giggled. One was a brunette, the other a glossy blonde. They glanced at me but didn't stop chattering. I wasn't surprised. I'd decided long ago that there was no one more stuck up than a high school girl.

The snack bar was an L-shaped stainless-steel counter. Just beyond the point where it bent, Virgil stood up, balancing a stack of paper cups in his hand.

The dark-haired girl, whose mouth was as pink and full as a rosebud, nudged him and squealed, "You're just awful, Virgil, hiding behind there like that. Did you hear what we were saying?"

Virgil blinked and set the cups down. "I wasn't hiding."

She flicked her hair to the side, her hand fluttering across it like a bird's wing. "Oh, Virgil," she breathed.

I eased toward him and tried out the movie-star smile I'd been working on. "Hello, Virgil."

He smiled back. "Hey, Callie Anne."

He moved toward me, his big raw-boned hand skimming the top of the counter. The dark-haired girl glanced at me, then turned to her friend and whispered something. They both laughed.

I lowered my voice. "I don't suppose you had a chance to . . ."

"Yup, got it right here." He opened a cabinet drawer, pulled out a thin package wrapped in brown paper and tied with white string and handed it to me.

"Gee, thanks. Thanks a lot." I gave him a dopey grin, completely forgetting how I might look.

He smiled uneasily in return. "You're positive your dad won't mind."

"Oh, it's no problem. You won't mention it though, will you?"

"No, I guess not, but . . ."

"Thanks, Virgil." I backed away.

People were thronging into the concessions building, signaling the start of intermission. I hurried out the door, bumping into a pudding-faced woman with two little kids. She scowled, and I slid around her, clutching the parcel to my chest.

Its contents had taken all of my savings, except for the quarter Memphis had given me for the candy. I wanted to rush right back to the house and try it out, but when I returned home, Memphis was sitting in our kitchen. The package had to wait until morning.

My father ate his meals at the same time every day. He went to bed and rose at the same time, and on Monday and Thursday mornings he drove into Jessup to the Empire Theater Organization office. I should have waited until he was safely away from the drive-in before I opened the package, but that would have meant missing the trip into town. Reaching into my pocket, I felt for the quarter Memphis had given me. I thought of riding next to him in the truck and trailing along behind him to the hardware store. Then I thought of the package again, and it seemed to me that if I was careful I could have it all.

Dad usually spent a half hour going through the weekend receipts before he left for town. I waited until he tramped stiffly off to the concessions building. Mom was in the kitchen, writing a toothpaste jingle. She'd gotten as far as "Pepsodent gives you teeth that are whiter than snow."

After softly closing my bedroom door and shutting the window, I retrieved the flat parcel from my bureau and unwrapped it. Virgil hadn't let me down. I slipped the 45 RPM from its paper cover and positioned it on the turntable of my portable record player.

The music of Bill Haley and the Comets reached out and grabbed me with the swiftness and ferocity of a wild animal. I quickly turned the volume lower, but even then its foot-thumping power rushed over me.

I'd first heard "Rock Around the Clock" when we'd played *The Blackboard Jungle* at the drive-in. It was a movie Dad hated. He didn't get to choose the pictures we played, so he occasionally had to show ones he disliked or disapproved of. The teenage kids loved *The Blackboard Jungle*. They poured into the drive-in by the carload, the oil from their greased-back hair practically leaving a slick across the parking lot. Dad said it was the kind of trashy picture that gave them evil ideas, and maybe he was right, because he had to break up half a dozen fistfights during those two weeks.

All I remembered from the movie was that music.

I was bouncing around my pink-walled bedroom, dying for someone else to hear it, wishing I could fling open the window and turn the volume as loud as I wanted. It occurred to me that Mom might have seen bits and pieces of *The Blackboard Jungle* from our window and she'd heard Dad rail endlessly against it, but she'd never heard the sound. She wouldn't know where the song came from.

I unplugged the record player and carried it into the kitchen. "Mom, you have to listen to this."

She laid down her pen and smiled indulgently. I plugged in the equipment, cranked up the volume and positioned the needle. Bill Haley and the Comets blared from the tinny speaker, a sound that was both primitive and musical. Immediately caught up in the beat, I hopped around the kitchen, wiggling my butt the way I'd seen the teenagers do.

Mom tapped her fingers in time on the table's speckled Formica. "Catchy, isn't it?"

I grinned and held out my hand. "Come on, Mom."

She shook her head. "Oh, no, I couldn't."

"Sure. It's easy." I gave a slightly less frenzied performance. "Come on. You can do it."

Grabbing her hand, I pulled her into the center of the kitchen. I was stomping and swinging and rocking while she laughed shyly and, almost in spite of herself, swiveled her hips to the beat.

My back was to the door when Dad walked in, and the music was too loud to hear his warning footsteps. I saw Mom's shocked look at the same time the needle screeched across the record.

He spun me around and thrust the record in my face, leaning so close I could smell coffee and cigarettes on his breath. A flat red burn surged up his neck, and the muscles of his jaw worked furiously.

"Where'd you get this?" he growled, little flecks of spit collecting on his lips.

The heat rushed into my cheeks. I stared at his nose the way I always did when I intended to lie to him. As I opened my mouth to speak, my mind suddenly emptied. I searched desperately for some answer, anything he might accept. I swallowed hard. "Found it in the drive-in field, propped against a speaker pole."

There was a heartbeat of silence, and I realized I'd made a serious mistake.

His eyes narrowed, and he fixed me with a look that could have singed my hair. "Like hell you did," he breathed.

He stepped back a few feet, held the record up and pressed his thumbs to it. Thinking only of that extraordinary music and how long it had taken to make it my own, I screamed and lunged. The snap of the record was dreadful, almost deafening. Clasping one broken half in my hand, I crumpled to the floor and sobbed like a five-year-old.

I heard Mom say, "Claude Junior, what have you done?"

Looking up through my tears, I saw Dad shaking the other half of the record at her.

"Do you have any idea what this is, Teal? If you ever got out of this goddamned sorry house, you'd know."

I'm not sure what possessed me or where I found the courage, but I whispered, "I'll buy another one."

There was a moment of absolute stillness.

In one quick motion, he brought his hand down, grabbed the record player from the kitchen table and gave it an upward jerk. The short black cord popped from the electrical socket and swung around so that the flat side of the plug caught me on the cheek. I heard only one sound, my cry of pain, but there must have been a second, the tremendous crash as the record player hit the floor. I fell to my knees alongside it, knocking against the kitchen chair as I went down.

An instant later, Mom was on the linoleum beside me, pulling me to her. "No, Claude Junior. No!"

I touched my numb cheek, expecting to find blood, but the plug hadn't broken the skin. A few seconds later, a dull throb began inside my mouth.

My father, his eyes no more than slits of rage, stared down at us. "You buy any more of this trash, little girl, and I swear to God . . ." His hands were trembling with fury, as if he wanted to throttle us.

He didn't finish the sentence, but he didn't need to.

Mom bowed her head, pressed it against mine and gathered

me in tight. I was too stunned to do anything but sit there on my heels, my chest heaving as if I'd run a great distance.

He hovered over us for some time, his mouth twisted into a grimace of disgust. "Jesus Christ, what's wrong with you, Teal, letting her listen to that junk? And you dancing around like that, shaking all over like a wet dog."

Dad spread his fingers and ran them through his hair as though he didn't quite know what to do with either of us. He leaned against the wall, easing the pressure on his leg. The anger had drained out of him.

The turntable lay a few feet away, its arm broken off at the stem. The fake-lizard case had caught the edge of the kitchen table, denting its metal trim. When I saw the damage, my heart sank two inches, because I knew how my mother loved that table.

Mom and I were still cowering on the floor when Memphis appeared at the screen door. Without an invitation, he stepped inside and surveyed the scene. At that moment, we didn't look much like the kind of family Norman Rockwell would have painted.

Memphis's face turned a slow dark red, a blaze flaring beneath his skin. I felt my stomach twist, a new knot of dread forming there. Judging by his clenched hands and his cold-eyed silence, he was going to do something he shouldn't, something that would only make things worse.

Mom must have realized it too. Clutching the edge of the table, she jumped up and with a deliberately casual gesture smoothed her skirt. She brushed a shaky hand across her pale cheek.

"Gosh, that sure made a racket. I . . . I tripped." Her voice sounded higher than usual. She stared at the record player on the floor as if she were still trying to figure out how it got there. "It dropped, but it'll probably be okay."

Any moron could see it wouldn't.

She finished weakly with "You must have heard the commotion."

Dad looked at Mom as though he wasn't quite sure who she was.

Memphis didn't answer. He was staring at my face, and it was all I could do not to raise a finger to the welt that must have formed there. I could hear a pounding in my ears. I wiped my sweat-slick hands on my shorts.

Shifting his gaze to Dad, Memphis appeared coiled to strike, searching for any excuse, any little reason. The knuckles on his fists turned white as bones. I thought of the robber, the shiny red foam bubbling from his mouth. Dad refused to meet Memphis's steady look. His eyes were still fixed on Mom.

A far-off dog barked crazily, as though it had finally snagged a passing car.

Memphis looked back at my mother. It was clear he wanted only a signal from her. Her eyes were large and round, the pupils wet-black with apprehension. She didn't move or speak, but her wordless plea hung in the air.

After a long moment, he smiled thinly and dropped his hands to his sides. My mother touched her fingertips to the edge of the table, steadying herself.

I hadn't moved the whole time.

Memphis stepped over and helped me up. "You okay?"

I nodded, although I was still trembling.

It was several seconds before Mom or Dad moved. Then, in the way grown-ups have of pretending nothing is out of the ordinary, Mom picked up the record player, set it on the table and pushed the chairs back to their usual order.

"There now," she said with forced brightness. She turned to my father. "When are you going into town, Claude Junior?"

He stared at her for a moment. "Uh, right now." Not wanting me to forget who was in charge here, he gave me a stern glance. "You come along, Callie Anne. You can visit Mr. Sooter with me."

Any other time, I might have groaned out loud. I loved going into Jessup, but spending time in Mr. Sooter's office wasn't my idea of fun. He'd call me young lady and offer me lint-speckled Life Savers he kept in the pocket of his gray suit coat. Then I'd have to sit quietly for an hour and a half while they talked business and Dad worked on the inventory.

I followed Dad and Memphis out to the pickup and scrambled in beside Memphis, whose face still had a hard edge to it. He gazed out the window at the drive-in field as though there were actually something to see there besides dusty gravel and row after row of speaker posts. Neither he nor my dad had yet spoken directly to the other.

On the way into Jessup, Dad did all the talking, his voice loud and overly cheerful, his words directed toward no one specific. Memphis didn't answer, just eyed the passing landscape. The hot air from the window whipped my hair around and stung my eyes. The jolting turns threw me against Memphis, but I felt no joy, only a rawness in my stomach.

In town, Memphis took off for the hardware store, while I followed Dad into Mr. Sooter's stifling office. An hour and a half later, when we stepped out into the midday sun, Memphis had loaded some lumber into the back of the truck and was climbing into the cab with a small paper sack in his hand. I fingered the quarter in my pocket, knowing it would go unspent until the next visit to town.

Conversation on the return trip wasn't much more exciting than it had been on the way in. My father said Mr. Sooter was going to hire a company from Bloomfield to drill the new water well at the Starlite. Dad described sewage and water problems he'd had through the years, and Memphis listened, with no more expression on him than a cigar store Indian.

After we reached the drive-in and climbed out of the truck, Memphis handed me the small brown-paper sack. Dad was lowering the tailgate, but he glanced up. I took the bag with some uneasiness.

Memphis deliberately ignored my father. "Open it."

I hesitated. I flicked my tongue over my dry lips, tasting the road dust there and thinking how it had already been as rough a day as I ever wanted. Dad didn't move. I opened the sack and pulled out two big Hershey chocolate bars.

Memphis turned and stared steadily at my father, challenging him. "One for you and one for your ma."

Dad pushed the lumber in the truck bed aside, as though searching for something. His hand came up empty. "Callie Anne, get in the house and help your mom with dinner." Then, without waiting to see if I obeyed, he swung around and limped away.

I closed the bag. "Thanks, Memphis." Digging the quarter from my pocket, I offered it to him.

"Save it for another trip."

I nodded and managed a smile.

Walking to the rear of the truck, he unloaded the two-by-fours, gripped them under his arm and strode toward the concessions building.

Chapter Ten

I slept poorly that night, not only because the house was hot and close but also because the air was still thick with the day's tension. I'd heard that rain was moving in, but I had no hope of its cooling everyone down. My father's sudden explosions of anger tended to affect me the same way a jack-in-the-box did when I was a little kid. After it popped up the first time, I nearly went crazy waiting for it to spring out again. It always took me a while before I could rest easy.

I didn't want to be around when Dad awoke the next morning. Soon after the sun rose, I tugged on my clothes and fixed myself a breakfast of shredded wheat and milk, mashing in three tablespoons of sugar. The demolished record player, an uncomfortable reminder of my foolishness, lay on a kitchen chair. I crept out of the house and headed toward the creek. Misty sunlight spilled over the treetops, and somewhere in the distance, a rooster crowed. My shoes clicked noisily on the gravel. It seemed to me God could do away with the middle of the day. The best parts came around sunrise and sunset, when everything had a kind of glow. Even the flowers smelled the strongest at those times.

If I'd left our house at any other moment that morning, I

would have missed seeing Memphis. Later, I thought about how amazing it was that two people or two cars or two railroad trains could hit the same spot at the same time without some planning ahead, and how different people's lives might be if their timing were just a minute or so off. Ours certainly would have changed that morning.

As it turned out, I was approaching the concessions building when the rear door swung open. Memphis stepped out and sucked in a deep breath as if he couldn't get enough fresh air.

I was all set to say "Boo!" or something like that to startle him when I noticed he was carrying his duffel bag. He hoisted the bulging canvas tote over his shoulder and without catching sight of me set off toward the theater entrance.

It took me a few moments to grasp what was happening. When I did, I shouted, "Hey, where're you going?"

He stopped and his back stiffened. He was wearing faded Levis, his worn blue-denim shirt rolled up at the sleeves and his gray cowboy hat pushed back from his forehead. Keeping his gaze pinned on the theater entrance, he hitched the bag a little higher and continued walking.

I ran after him, not catching up but staying a few feet behind. "You weren't even going to say good-bye, were you? How could you leave without saying good-bye?" I didn't like my voice, the way it sounded high and strained.

He didn't answer; he just kept going. I moved faster, kicking up dust and almost tripping on his heels. We passed the box office and the theater sign and came to the road. He still hadn't spoken or looked back at me. He stepped onto the pavement, and when we heard the muffled rumble of a concrete truck as it rounded the bend, he stuck out his thumb. It lumbered by, and he started hiking along the shoulder.

After two cars and a truck loaded with crated white chickens rolled past us, he yelled, "Go home, shortstuff. Nobody's going to stop for me if you stick around."

"Why are you mad at me? I didn't do anything to you."

It took another minute or so, but he finally slowed his pace, turned and set the bag at his feet. "I ain't mad at you."

"You ain't . . . I mean, you aren't?"

"No, but that don't mean I can stay."

"Why not?"

He regretfully watched a sleek blue and white Pontiac sedan whiz past. "Because if I hang around here, there's going to be trouble and the last thing I need is more trouble."

My mouth dropped open. He wasn't behaving the way he was supposed to. What had happened to the man who had saved our drive-in from bandits?

I felt my whole face tighten and I shouted, "What kind of hero are you? Did Gary Cooper run away from trouble? No. He stood up to a whole gang of outlaws. Alone." I lowered my voice and stared at him. "What kind of trouble are you talking about? What kind of trouble were you in before?"

He shook his head, as if he couldn't believe he was having to deal with me. "Look, kid, just go on back to the house. This don't have anything to do with you."

He hoisted his bag and took off again, more slowly now but with a determined stride. In front of him, the gray ribbon of highway unfurled. It meandered up a green swell of farmland, thinned to a dark thread and dropped over the other side.

I followed him, keeping about twenty feet between us. I couldn't bear the thought of his walking out of my life. No one else in Jessup, maybe the whole state, was anywhere near as handsome or exciting as he was. And I was certain I'd never love another man as much as I loved him. My lungs were closing up, giving me the same breathlessness I had when a school bully, Spike MacDougal, once sat on my chest.

I heard two loud toots from a horn behind me. Stepping off the pavement, I let an old pickup loaded with empty wooden crates clatter by. It pulled alongside Memphis and shuddered to a stop, the slatted containers banging into each other. The driver, who looked like some farmer all gussied up in his town clothes and a straw hat, leaned out the window and asked Memphis where he was going.

"As far as you're willing to take me," Memphis said.

The man motioned him to get in the passenger side. Memphis stepped onto the running board and swung his duffel bag into the truck bed so that it landed with a thud between two crates. As he moved toward the cab, his gaze caught mine.

I barely raised my voice. "And what about my mother? I'll bet you didn't even tell her you were leaving, did you?"

He didn't move.

I propped my hands on my hips, all wound up now. "She hasn't got many friends, you know, stuck in the house the way she is. She said she really appreciated the way you been nice to her." She hadn't said that, but I was reaching for what I could. "I guess that doesn't matter to you though, does it?"

I heard the driver yell, "Hey, fella, you coming or not?"

"Yeah, I'm coming." Without another glance at me, Memphis hopped in the pickup, and it rattled down the road.

I turned back toward the drive-in. "Go on then if you want to," I muttered under my breath. "See if I care." I kicked an empty bean can into the weeds, then tramped over and booted it again.

I finished with "He was nothing like Gary Cooper. I don't know where I ever got that idea." I could feel the tears pooling in my eyes and sliding onto my cheeks.

I heard the squeal of brakes and the sound of those rickety crates smacking against each other. Figuring the farmer must have hit an animal in the road, I spun around. The truck had jerked to a stop all right, but I couldn't see or hear anything it might have struck.

Memphis climbed out. He barely had time to grab his bag before the farmer ground the gears, accelerated in a cloud of dust and clacked lickety-split down the highway.

The way Memphis strode by me, I might have been a Burma-Shave sign along the road. Without saying a word or even tossing me an offhand smile, he trudged toward the drive-in, his duffel slung over his shoulder. When I saw him next, he was painting a bench in front of the concessions building.

I expected things to return to the way they had been, with Memphis digging holes and painting buildings and looking more scruffy as time went along, but that's not what happened. The next morning, which turned out to be his day off, he hitched a ride into town. Returning with several cardboard clothes boxes from Miller's Department Store, he slipped into the concessions building before I could ask him what he'd bought.

That evening while Dad was in the projection booth cranking up the movie, I was fiddling with the radio dial, trying to tune in a station that played rock 'n' roll. I'd listened to Elvis Presley singing "Heartbreak Hotel" on an Indianapolis station the night before and thought it was the best music I'd ever heard. Mom was cutting out a dress pattern on the kitchen table and not paying much attention to me.

She was the first to catch a glimpse of Memphis at the screen door.

"Why, Charlie Memphis." She walked over and opened the door, then said the same thing all over again.

It was enough. He gave her one of his rare smiles and stepped into the kitchen.

I had to look twice to make sure it was him. He removed an expensive-looking black cowboy hat from his head and plopped it on a chair. His creased black slacks and his stiff white shirt with pearly snap buttons crackled like the pages in a new book. But what I liked best was his belt buckle. Stamped into the metal was the outline of a grizzly, massive head raised, fangs bared. It was just the sort of buckle a real cowboy would wear. He'd polished his boots until they gleamed, and he'd had a trim and a shave. I liked his hair longer, but he looked more respectable now. To top it all off, he smelled like one of those fancy men who come from Indianapolis to Jessup looking for property to buy. I tried hard not to let my jaw flop down in surprise.

He nodded at me. "Hey there, pardner."

"Hi, Memphis." I was glad I was back to being his pardner, instead of just "kid."

We went through a few awkward moments of everybody trying to figure out what to say. Mom hurried around, gathering her sewing materials from the table and setting out chocolate cake.

She said how nice he looked tonight, and then backpedaled and insisted he always looked fine but especially so tonight. At that point Memphis sort of took over and told us a story he'd heard at the barbershop about a local man whose big toe got bit off by a catfish. He said the man was swimming in some lake over in Mar-

101

ion County and the fish attacked him for no reason. I said that didn't make any sense at all because I'd been swimming in Clear Lake where there were truckloads of catfish, but I'd never seen any with teeth big enough to chomp off a man's toe. Memphis said that was the point, wasn't it? This wasn't just any fish. So, things were back to normal, except that something other than clothes was different about Memphis, something I couldn't quite put my finger on.

Mom and I were sitting at the table with our backs to the door and Memphis was on the chrome-framed kitchen chair across from us when he leaned over and said in a low voice, "I don't mean to scare you, but there's someone on your porch step with his face pressed against the screen."

Mom and I twisted around. If I hadn't seen Billy at least once every few weeks for the past several years, he would have given me the heebie-jeebies.

"Oh, it's all right," Mom said, rising from her chair and walking to the door. "Hello, Billy, how are you tonight?"

He pulled back, offering her a shy smile. "Hi, Teal." He snuffled a little and rubbed his nose on the sleeve of his ragged shirt. "I was wondering if you could come out?"

"Not, tonight," Mom said softly. "I'm a little busy right now."

I whispered to Memphis, "We can't let him in. Mom did that once and he wouldn't leave."

Memphis nodded.

Billy edged in and out of the shadows. "I have something for you, Teal." He pulled his left hand from behind his back and thrust out two pink roses that looked suspiciously as if they might have come from our yard.

Mom opened the door and took them. "Why, thank you, Billy, they're lovely. Would you like some chocolate cake?"

"I'm taking lessons at the dance school." His eyes glowed like burning coals in his gaunt face. "My uncle gave me the money. Will you come out and dance with me when I get good enough?"

"Someday, Billy. Now, you wait right here while I get you that piece of cake."

She wrapped a good-sized piece in waxed paper, stuck tooth-picks into it to hold it together and handed it to him. "Now run along, Billy, but don't bother anyone."

I leaned toward Memphis and whispered, "He pokes his head inside people's cars and begs food off them. If you ever hear a scream come from the drive-in field during the movie, you can figure it's just Billy scaring the daylights out of someone. Dad doesn't like him."

Memphis nodded with a half-smile.

Billy drifted toward the deeper shadows and Mom returned to the table.

Memphis sipped his coffee from the earthenware cup Mom had refilled. "I seen him around Jessup once or twice. Who is he?"

Mom sighed. "He didn't use to be this way."

Thinking that didn't tell Memphis much, I chimed in, "His name's Billy Watson. He lives with his uncle who has a farm about halfway between here and town, but a lot of the time he just wanders around."

"What happened to him?" Memphis asked, stirring sugar into his coffee. "He get kicked in the head by a horse?"

"He went off to the war," Mom said. "He no sooner gradua-ted from high school than his dad marched him down to the army recruiting center. When he came back from overseas, he was like this."

"Shell-shocked," I piped up, "That's what Aunt Bliss says And he hasn't gotten any better over the years."

"I suppose that's true," Mom said with a pained look.

"He acts like he's still in high school," I added. "If anybody asks him certain things, especially things that have to do with the war, he gets all upset."

Mom stared at our empty plates, as though remembering another time and place. "He was the sweetest, kindest boy in high school. And so smart. Why, we were all sure he'd go off to college and make something of himself."

"But Betty Jo Babcock's mom said he was quiet and kept to himself a lot." I'd heard the story so many times I knew everybody's version of it.

After a moment, Mom's eyes glistened a little and she looked away. "Oh, I suppose he was, but he didn't bother anybody. I don't know why people have to be so hard on a person for being quiet and shy."

It suddenly occurred to me the whole conversation was dredging up bad memories of Mom's own troubles. Before I could think of what to say, Memphis jumped up and began carrying the cake plates to the sink.

"Goodness, you don't have to do that." She grabbed the dirty coffee cups and leaped up too.

He set the dishes on the drainboard. But I guess he didn't realize she was right behind him, because he turned and crashed into her, knocking a cup from her hands and sending it sailing into the air. He caught it before it hit the floor but it still had coffee in it. A thin brown geyser shot up and streaked the front of his gleaming new white shirt.

I shouldn't have laughed but for some reason I couldn't help it. Watching Memphis juggle that cup made me think of a slapstick scene in a Jerry Lewis movie, and I had such a fit of giggles I couldn't stop.

Memphis just stood there like it was no big problem, but Mom's eyes grew large as silver dollars. "Oh, no, your new shirt, Charlie Memphis. I'm so sorry."

He shrugged. "Don't worry about it, Teal."

"I can clean it," Mom said. "You wait right here." She darted into her bedroom and returned with one of dad's white shirts, yanking it off the wooden hanger as she came. "Now you just put this on while I wash yours. It might be a bit small but . . ."

Maybe he thought she was going to unbutton his shirt right then and there because he grabbed her hand. "Teal, you don't have to."

For a long moment, she didn't do or say anything. Then she pulled free and backed up a few steps, pink circles dotting her cheeks. I thought she looked a lot more solemn than necessary.

She lowered her gaze. "It might be better if you had your own to change into."

"It's not important," he said softly. "You don't have to wash it."

She busied herself returning Dad's shirt to the hanger and fastening every single one of its buttons. "Oh, no, I want to. I'm the one who spilled it."

She hadn't, but he didn't argue with her.

"Guess I'd better be getting back," he said, grabbing up his new Stetson and working the crown with his fingers. His hands still had yellow bruises from his fight with the robbers. He didn't say what he had to get back to, but he thanked her for the cake and left.

Stammering some excuse to Mom about being tired, I ducked into my room. I switched on the light, flopped on my bed and picked up a Nancy Drew mystery. I tried to read but couldn't keep my mind on it. I thought about Memphis reaching for Mom's hand and watching her closely. I suspected that in some ways he liked my mother better than me, and I didn't care for the way that felt.

Chapter Eleven

The more summer wore on, the more my love for Memphis grew. He looked as handsome as any movie star I'd ever seen on our screen, and I dreamed of our future together as it might unfold. He would ask me to run away with him when he left for the next town, declaring his love for me just as William Holden had for Jennifer Jones in *Love Is A Many Splendored Thing*. We would marry and travel to those exciting western cities he talked about— San Francisco, Boise, Seattle. I saw them in my head, like bright picture postcards, like the slick brochures Dad used to collect. We—Memphis and I—would be such a striking couple, people in those big towns would nudge each other as we walked by.

"Look at him, so tall and good-looking," they would whisper, "and her, so pretty and so poised for someone that young." I would lift my head a little higher, a serene smile on my lips while I pretended I hadn't heard.

Someday I'd meet his parents. Were they still alive? I wondered. I'd never heard him speak of them. Well, if they were, he'd take me to visit, returning to see them after many years away. His mother and I would become immediate friends. I saw his mother and me in the living room of her large, impressive home, sitting on a wide, flowered sofa, gazing out over their sprawling lawns and drinking coffee from gold-rimmed china cups so delicate they chimed when we set them on their saucers.

His mother would fold her hand over mine and give it a squeeze. "Bless you, my dear, for bringing him back to us. I can see you've made him so happy."

I wanted to tell Memphis I loved him, but I couldn't get up my courage. I was afraid he might say he didn't love me back. Or worse yet, he'd say I was too young.

It didn't help that we were showing *Picnic* every night that week in early July. As William Holden danced under the paper lanterns with Kim Novak, I dreamed of Memphis holding me in his hard, muscular arms. When I came upon a sweat-stained T-shirt he'd shed while working, I considered pinching it and hiding it inside my pillowcase. I thought of burying my face against it while I slept, but then I left it where it lay, figuring he didn't have any shirts to spare.

I took a long look in the mirror above my dresser. It didn't seem fair that Mom should have naturally wavy hair while mine was straight as a measuring stick. The funny thing was I'd never cared before, so I didn't even own a set of curlers. I located some heavy cardboard cylinders in the snack bar, hacked them into short lengths and wrapped my hair around them, fastening them with shiny metal clips that dug into my scalp. It was like sleeping on chunks of a tree branch, but I figured it was worth it.

The next morning I stood before my mirror and pushed, poked and pinned my hair into a style like Kim Novak's. I wriggled into my favorite shorts and a scoop-necked white blouse, the only one I owned that might loosely be called low-cut. I dug out an unused tube of bright ruby-red lipstick I'd found in the bathroom medicine cabinet, and peering at the mirror so closely my breath fogged it up, I colored my lips—which I'd always believed were too pouty.

When I stood back and checked the reflection, I nearly gasped out loud. The woman staring at me smoldered more like Lana Turner than Kim Novak but that was all right with me. I wanted a pair of those spiky high heels like Lana wore, but Mom didn't own any. I finally decided on bare feet, figuring I could play the role of a country girl.

I carefully plotted my appearance before Memphis. I'd sneak out of the house before breakfast and intercept him as he left the concessions building. Once he'd been charmed by my astonishing beauty, I'd rush back to the house, scrub my face and comb my hair. If Dad spotted me before that, I could forget about ever reaching the age of thirteen.

Memphis came out early, just as I'd hoped.

I tried to make my voice sound like Lana's. "Hello, Memphis, isn't it a lovely day?"

He looked at me with a half-smile. "A lovely day?" He glanced around and I could see he was so stunned he hardly knew what to say. I felt a little glow.

"Well," he ventured, "it's a bit like yesterday. . . ." He kicked the ground with the toe of his cowboy boot, stirring up dust. "A shade on the dry side maybe."

I thought I detected some amusement in his voice, but the line of his mouth had gone perfectly straight. Not a hint of a smile.

I thrust out my hip and planted my hand on it. "I'd sure be happy to bring you some lemonade if you'd like."

With his gaze fixed on the landscape, he took in a long breath and released it. "No, that's all right. Thanks anyway." He edged toward the storeroom on the back side of the concessions building "I'd better get started."

He collected his tools, and I followed him out to the middle of the drive-in field. As he reset a speaker post somebody had knocked over, I sashayed past him. "Sure was busy here last night."

"Yup."

"Want me to hold that pole while you tap it in?" I asked, leaning forward to get a grip on it.

He turned away. "Nah, but if you could just hand me that hammer with the wooden mallet." He rubbed his fingers across his mouth and I was certain now he was trying hard not to smile.

After giving him the mallet, I hunched my shoulders and slunk away. When I reached my bedroom and examined myself in the mirror, I saw the problem. My finely textured hair had come undone and drooped in the humid July air, making it about as attractive as corrugated cardboard. Worse yet, I'd applied the lipstick too heavily. Red chunks clung to my eyeteeth, and when I smiled broadly, I might have been Bela Lugosi dripping blood.

Using about half a roll of toilet paper, I scoured my mouth hard enough to bruise. "Damn, damn, damn. Should have known I could never look pretty."

I stomped on the cardboard cylinders and hurled them into the wastebasket, then flopped stomach-down onto my Hollywood twin bed, furious with myself for the little-girl sobs I couldn't seem to control. By the time Mom came to see why I wasn't at breakfast, my eyes and mouth were so red-streaked and chapped that it was all I could do to convince her I wasn't sick. I moped around for a day or so. When Memphis didn't mention my silliness, I began to hope he thought he'd gone sleepwalking and I had been merely a passing nightmare.

✴   ✴   ✴

110

It was a whole week before I started to think about love again.

A girl in my school, Betty Jo Babcock, once told me that when adults talked about love, they really meant sex. I wondered if she was right. We were in fifth grade at the time, and the only reliable thing I knew about sex was that the word shouldn't be said out loud. It never occurred to me to ask my mother for explanations. She couldn't know much about it. She never left the house. And asking my father seemed as crazy as talking to the trees, something I'd given up when I was seven.

At the time, Betty Jo and I were at the school playground watching a goofy sixth grader swipe Edwina Vandenburgh's hat. Betty Jo told me her seventeen-year-old sister Mary Alice did "it" with boys. It took me some time to figure out exactly what "it" was, and when I did, I was horrified.

"No," I said.

"Uh-huh." Betty Jo nodded with the confident air of being one up on me and loudly smacked her pink bubble gum.

In my mind, I conjured up the body parts and goings-on she'd described. "But why would they do that?"

She rolled her eyes upward, imploring heaven for patience. "So they can have a baby. Why else?"

"Gosh, why does Mary Alice want a baby?"

"Well, she says if she gets pregnant, then Mom will have to let her marry Duane. She hates Mom and would rather live with Duane." Betty Jo dislodged a sizable lump of gum from her molars and rolled it between her thumb and forefinger before tossing it into the bushes.

"But he doesn't have a job, does he?" I said.

"Yeah, he does. He works at the Shell station."

"How many times does she have to do it to get a baby?"

Betty Jo shrugged, her shoulders grazing the ends of her Toni-

111

permed brown hair. "I don't know. As many times as Duane wants to, I guess. Mary Alice says it doesn't hurt."

I wanted to ask her more, but the bell clanged and recess was over. I hurried back to class, wondering if Duane knew what Mary Alice was planning and whether he'd marry her if she did have a baby.

Although I didn't especially trust Betty Jo, much of what she said made sense. It gave me an idea of what was going on in my parents' bedroom every Tuesday night when they closed the door and I heard those muffled noises and creaking bedsprings. I couldn't avoid the horrifying conclusion that, in spite of their age, they were trying to make a baby.

It also explained why Aunt Bliss didn't have kids. There was no way she would let my uncle do something like that to her.

Whenever I wanted to learn about a subject that wasn't in *The Saturday Evening Post* or *Reader's Digest,* I visited the Jessup Public Library on Center Street. So it seemed the natural place to turn when I wanted to find out about love. I knew I wasn't going to find what I was looking for in the children's section, but the adult area upstairs was off limits to kids under thirteen without a parent's permission.

I wangled Mom's approval, and on my next visit to town, I scaled the polished wooden stairs, clutching my passport to the new world. I entered the adult library through the double-wide oak doors and gazed with awe toward the high ceiling, then down to row after row of books. The massive room smelled strongly of floor wax and musty paper.

The Starlite Drive-in

Everyone in there was old. Mr. Perkins, who owned a farm out on State Road 59 and always wore bib overalls, was reading *The Owen County Grange Journal* at one of three rectangular tables that were as big and hefty as barn doors. Blue-haired Miss Watson, who worked in ladies' wear at Miller's Department Store, shuffled toward the section marked "Gardening, Quilting and Homemaking." She was probably on her coffee break. I thought I recognized the bowlegged man who stood near one of the towering windows, but I didn't know his name. He held *Dairy News* in the sunlight and squinted at it.

I was unprepared for the silence in that cavernous vault. Not even the drive-in at two A.M. was that quiet.

I tiptoed, thinking I'd sneak among the rows before anyone noticed me. The rubber sole of my shoe caught on the glossy wood floor and screeched louder than the tires in a three-car pileup. All the adults including the librarian turned toward me, and I felt the fire rush up my neck. Dad was right about my gunboat feet. If ever I wanted to chop them off at the ankles, it was then. The hawk-nosed librarian didn't frown, but her eyes measured me. Just as I was ready to bolt and run back down those wooden steps, Miss Watson inclined her head in recognition. I nodded back. Her kind gesture gave me the confidence I needed to continue my mission. Gripping the form with Mom's signature, I set my shoulders and marched across the floor without a sound.

The engraved gold nameplate on the heavy oak desk said MISS IRIS MONHAUT, LIBRARIAN. In spite of the heat, Miss Monhaut wore a lightweight gray sweater draped over her shoulders and fastened at the neck by a pearl clasp. She studied me over black-framed reading glasses that were perched on her substantial nose and anchored to a silver chain around her neck. When I noticed she kept her pencil secured to the counter by heavy twine and cellophane tape, I began to suspect Miss Monhaut liked to have things tied down.

I set the piece of paper on the high counter in front of her and squeaked, "I have permission."

She examined it as though she thought I might have forged my mother's name.

Miss Monhaut had one very noticeable feature. In the crease that ran between the left side of her nose and her mouth, there was a round dark mole about the size of my smallest fingernail. Two black hairs sprouted from it like a bug's feelers. Try as I might, I couldn't keep my eyes off them.

She looked me over, the mole bouncing and twitching. "You're the girl from the drive-in, aren't you?"

I nodded.

Suddenly, the mole disappeared and the two hairs clawed wildly at the air. She was smiling. "Let me know if you need any help."

"Thanks," I said, already hurrying toward the long stacks.

Cruising the rows, I searched for titles that suggested some promise. I briefly considered *Many Desires,* a thin hardback blighted with mildew, then rejected it and moved on.

Forty-five minutes later, I slid two books in front of Miss Monhaut and waited, my breath suspended. She opened *Women in Love* but didn't mark the due date on it.

"Hold off on this one, honey." She laid it aside and reached for the next. She cheerfully stamped *Passion Among the Pines.*

I was disappointed about *Women in Love.* I wasn't sure I would find what I needed to know in the other one, especially if it got Miss Monhaut's approval. Walking away, I looked wistfully over my shoulder.

Miss Monhaut smiled and patted the forbidden book. "In a few years."

That afternoon I read the first six chapters of *Passion Among the Pines*. What a disappointment. The story was about an artist who lived in the woods and devoted his life to painting pictures of trees. It wasn't about love at all.

On my next trip to the Jessup Public Library, I checked out *The Loved One*, which got Miss Monhaut's cheerful approval. The book was written by some lady named Evelyn Waugh, and with a title like that you'd expect it to be romantic. But it was more about funerals, caskets and tombs than it was about love. The only naked bodies in it were dead, and I had to look up a lot of words I'd never heard of before, like *mausoleum, effigy, embalmer,* and *vestal virgin,* which is not what you'd think it would be. It seemed to me the book's title was deceptive, another word I learned from reading it.

Chapter Twelve

$\mathcal{A}$ few days later, I was strolling across the drive-in field in late afternoon, going no place in particular, when I spotted Billy. He was shuffling toward the theater entrance directly ·on a collision course with Dad and Memphis, who from what I could tell hadn't yet seen him. Dad had caught him on the drive-in property three times within the past week, and with each incident I could see my dad's anger growing blacker, building like a storm. For several seconds, while Dad fixed his attention sometimes on Memphis, sometimes on the ground, my heart raced like a revved-up car engine.

"Run, Billy," I urged under my breath. "Get out of here."

It was a ridiculous suggestion, of course. With those flap-tongued shoes, he couldn't run anywhere. Besides, he probably had retreated to his own strange world where the danger came from warplanes dropping bombs overhead.

I saw my father's head snap up and focus on Billy. The muscles in Dad's shoulders tightened, and he leaped forward the way a dog does when he spots a rabbit. Then he seemed to remember his knee and caught himself. I don't think Memphis realized what was happening. When he glanced up, he seemed startled that my father was no longer beside him. And when Billy saw Dad, he froze as still as the rabbit who fuzzily suspects the worst kind of trouble is bearing down on him but can't seem to move. I took off running toward them.

Dad charged across the field and clamped his fingers onto Billy's scruffy shirt. "You goddamned moron," he bellowed, twisting the cloth and shaking him. "How many times do I have to tell you to stay the hell out of here?"

Why Billy didn't at least raise his hands to push my father away, I don't know. Although Dad may have weighed more, Billy was taller and could easily have whacked him in the face. Instead, he just squirmed like a hooked fish while his eyes turned glassy.

Memphis seized Dad's shoulder. "Leave him alone, Claude. He ain't hurtin' anybody."

Dad dug his elbow back into Memphis's midsection. "Get away. This isn't any of your business." He released Billy's collar and started to turn, but he must have changed his mind because he whirled around and grabbed Billy by the neck.

When he didn't let go, Memphis wrapped his arms around Dad's torso and pulled. I sucked in my breath and danced around all three of them, trying to figure out what to do. I kept watching Memphis's eyes, hoping they wouldn't go all dark and flat the way they had with the robber. The afternoon light sent shadows playing across Memphis's face, but his eyes were clear.

Finally, Memphis managed to drag my father off, or maybe Dad let go of Billy. I wasn't sure which.

"Get out of here," Memphis yelled to Billy.

He pitched sideways, took a few steps to steady himself, then without uttering a word loped toward the drive-in entrance.

Red-faced and sweating, Dad swung around as quickly as his leg would allow, and with both hands shoved Memphis on the chest. "I told you to stay out of it."

Memphis staggered, then regained his balance. "Come on, Claude. We got better things to do than chase that poor soul out of this drive-in."

His soothing tone only seemed to make my father angrier. "That son of a bitch pokes his head in people's cars while they're watching the movie and scares the shit out of their kids. Last night, three people demanded their money back. But even if he didn't do a damn thing, you got no right to tell me how to run this theater. You keep this up and I'll kick you out so fast your head'll spin."

Memphis shrugged. "From what I been told, Sooter does the hiring and firing around here." He turned to leave.

Dad sprang toward him, grabbed his arm from behind and tried to shove him around. "Don't walk away from me while I'm . . ."

Memphis snapped his arms upward with such quickness and force that my father toppled to the ground.

Dad sat down hard with a grunt. He leaned forward and growled, "You son of a bitch."

Memphis's shadow fell across Dad, and he stared at him with an expression so cold it pricked my flesh with goose bumps. But he didn't go after him. Instead, he turned and strode toward the drive-in entrance. My father rose to his feet, his white theater manager's shirt flapping open so that I saw the pale roll of flesh above his belt. He brushed himself off, rebuttoned his shirt and shoved in the tail ends. As he lifted his head, his gaze caught mine. He looked away, but not before I saw the fear in his eyes. He was afraid of Memphis, truly afraid of him, and it went much deeper than whether one was going to be punching the other one around.

I stepped back, feeling the momentary shock that my father wasn't the fearless man I'd always believed he was.

"Son of a bitch should mind his own business," Dad muttered.

I knew he was saying that for my benefit, telling me he had been just doing his job and Memphis was in the wrong. But I didn't like the way any of it made me feel.

The fight had taken place beyond the point where the fence curved. I knew my mother couldn't see it, but the shouting had been loud enough for her to hear. She'd be worried, and I'd have to explain what had happened.

Midway between the concessions building and our house, I heard the squealing crunch of brakes, followed not long after by the sound of excited voices. As I turned and headed back, Memphis came charging toward the building.

"What's wrong?" I yelled.

"Billy got hit," he shouted back. "I'm calling for an ambulance."

I ran as fast as I could toward the highway. Near the corner of the drive-in, just over the fence from our house, a great black hunk of a car with pointy fins—a Cadillac, I think—sat in the middle of the road like a beached whale. Several feet away, Billy's long, gangling body lay stretched on the pavement, his blue-veined eyelids closed, a bright red river pulsing from his forehead. The blood streaked down his temples and pooled on the asphalt.

A fleshy, broad-shouldered man squatted beside him.

I dropped to the pavement on the other side of Billy and grabbed his dry lifeless hand. "You killed him!"

"I. . . I didn't mean to," the big man stuttered in a drawl that was thick as river mud. "Did you see what happened? He stepped right in front of the car."

"Can't you make the blood stop?" I pressed the edge of my blouse to Billy's forehead, where to my great horror I could see the white bone shining through. The pink cotton fabric soaked the blood like a wick. I wanted to yank off my blouse and press it against the wound, but with the man there I couldn't. "Don't you have a towel or something?"

He glanced toward the car, his face twisted in confusion. "No, I don't think so."

I stared at the short-sleeved white shirt he was wearing. It had pearly snap buttons and blue curlicue stitching above the pockets. Finally he looked down at it too.

"Well," he said hesitantly.

"Please. All this blood's gushing out of him."

He nodded and peeled off his shirt, leaving behind a stringy little tie that was cinched by a smooth turquoise rock as big as my fist. Grabbing the shirt, I mashed it against Billy's forehead. He stirred and moaned.

"He's alive. Did you see him move?" I bent closer to his face and pinched his hand. "Can you hear me, Billy? Squeeze hard if you can hear me."

He didn't squeeze, but he groaned again, making me feel a hundred times better.

The big man pushed his cowboy hat back. "I think I just clipped him. He shot sideways like he was tossed by a bull."

A lumber truck came along, and he directed it on by, waving two burly arms that switched in color from brown to pasty white a few inches above his elbows.

He looked down at Billy and one of his eyelids twitched ner-

vously. "I sure hope he don't die. Where's that ambulance coming from?"

"I don't know. Jessup, I guess." I glanced at his license plate.
Oklahoma. I didn't think I'd ever met anyone from Oklahoma
before.

"Jessup. Funny name for a town. Is that the closest one?"

"Uh-huh." I didn't bother telling him Mechanicsburg was
only five miles away because, as Dad often said, it didn't have so
much as a pot to piss in.

I dabbed at Billy's wound, which seemed to be oozing rather
than spurting now. The blood had collected in the crevices around
his eyes and he had a scrape as big as a rose on his arm, but at least
he no longer looked like he was going to bleed to death.

Memphis came running up then with a green army blanket
from his bed and a couple of frayed towels. Dad followed close
behind him. Memphis laid Billy's head on a folded towel and covered him with the blanket.

I tried to give the Oklahoma man's fancy shirt back to him.
He started to take the bloodied wad between his thumb and fore-
finger, then drew his hand away. "I guess I won't be wearing it
again. Throw it in the trash, will you, honey?" He glanced around.
The pointy tips of his black tie rode the summit of his white belly.
"Where do you live anyway?"

"At the drive-in."

"No, I mean where's your house?"

"It's at the drive-in theater on the other side of this fence."

"Oh."

I thought he was going to say, "Funny place to live," but he
didn't.

About ten minutes later, an ambulance led by a sheriff's car, sirens blaring, rolled to a stop in front of us. A deputy and two men wearing white coats got right to work and lifted Billy onto a stretcher. He woke up for a moment and mumbled something none of us could understand. Memphis said it was a good sign anyway. Then the ambulance went blasting down the highway with the man from Oklahoma close behind in his black Cadillac.

"Do you think Billy will be okay?" I asked, as we walked back. Memphis shrugged. "Can't tell."

"Maybe it'll knock some . . ." Dad started to say. Eyeing Memphis, he didn't finish the sentence.

I nodded toward the ancient flatbed Ford pulling into the drive-in. "Virgil's coming to work already."

Dad glanced at his watch. "He's early."

I was tempted to visit with Virgil while he set things up in the snack bar, but I knew Mom would be frantic with worry by now. I headed for the house once again.

Chapter Thirteen

As soon as I stepped inside, I knew something was wrong. I felt her absence as strongly as if all the fresh air had been sucked from the room.

It was nearly seven o'clock, the time she should have been preparing supper for the two of us. But her writing materials were strewn across the kitchen table. Her stubby yellow pencil with the chewed eraser lay on the floor.

"Mom?" My steps echoed as I walked through the empty hall to the two bedrooms.

"Mom," I called again, my voice sounding strained and hollow.

I returned to the front door, stepped onto the porch and surveyed the deserted drive-in field. It was too early for cars to arrive. A crow swooped down and grabbed something, a bug maybe or a kernel of popcorn that had been missed earlier in the day. Seeing its wings beat the air like shiny black fans, I shivered. A bad omen—that's what crows were, Aunt Bliss said.

From the corner of my eye, I saw movement, a tractor kicking up dust in the Eggerts' pasture, but no sign of Mother. In the back of my mind, I wondered where Memphis had gone. As I hurried around the corner of the house, I scanned the leafy lilac bushes, knowing she would look for the calm safety of an enclosed place. I expected to see her crouching in that shrubbery like a terrified mouse.

Once, a few years before, Aunt Bliss had persuaded her to step outside our kitchen door. I stood nearby, offering encouragement. When Mom reached a patch of grass, she anchored there. She couldn't go backward and she couldn't travel forward. She trembled all over, showing the whites of her moss-green eyes like a spooked horse. Her breath came in quick gasps. Aunt Bliss ordered her to move, as if she were no more than a stubborn child. Then we both grabbed her slender wrists and tried to pull her forward. We might as well have been tugging on a marble statue. Finally, Aunt Bliss gently wrapped her sturdy arm around Mom's shoulders, uprooted her and guided her back inside.

I still feel ashamed when I think of that day.

Afterward, I just accepted my mother as she was. Given the choices, I would rather have had her stay in the house. I couldn't bear to see her fear-struck.

In the backyard, my gaze swept over our little vegetable garden, the climbing rose trellis, the maples, the birches and then rested on the green-shingled shed that contained our garden tools. Instantly, I knew where she was. I felt her presence as if she had cried out to me.

The door was cracked open. I touched my hand to it, and it swung inward with a creak. "Mom?"

She was curled against the far wall, wedged in the shadows, her head tucked down, her breath reduced to a wheeze.

"O-oh, Mom."

Lifting her paper-white face, she stared at me with glazed eyes. She was beyond terror.

I ran over, slipped my arms around her and clumsily struggled to raise her. She leaned against me and I felt her heart thumping against my chest. In that eerie stillness, I could have sworn I heard it loud as a drum. Her rapid little puffs of breath grazed my cheek.

I propped her up, and somehow we managed to cross the yard and scale the porch steps. As I opened the back door, Memphis rounded the corner.

I shook my head. "Don't! Stay back. She . . . uh, fell, but she's okay. I can take care of her."

He stopped, taking in the scene. I knew how we must look, my mother clinging to my neck like a child and me staggering under her weight. He wore his belt with the grizzly on the buckle, and for a moment that silvery bear glinted in the fading light. He took a step forward.

"Don't come any closer! She doesn't want you here." My voice sounded shrill and harsh, and I suppose my ferocity surprised both of us.

I couldn't read his expression, but he backed off.

Inside the kitchen, Mom collapsed into a chair. She sat there for several minutes, sucking in air like a woman who has come close to drowning. Her eyes were blank, way beyond tears, and her pupils so big that seashells of light seemed to waver inside them. She was scaring me. It had been a long time since I'd seen her this way.

When she finally spoke, I could barely hear her.

"I'm sorry, so very sorry."

Great hot waves swelled against my eyelids. "You shouldn't have gone out there."

Still seated, she slumped against the wall. "I thought something had happened to you," she whispered, her lids half closing, "I heard sirens. And I saw Memphis and your dad running . . ."

"It was Billy, Mom. Not me."

"Billy?"

I nodded. "He got hit by a car. Memphis called an ambulance."

When I saw the fear flare in her eyes again, I added, "He's going to be all right. I'm sure of it. Even Memphis said so." I rubbed the back of my hand fiercely across my wet cheeks. "Anyway, you shouldn't have gone outside."

"I had to know you were okay."

"I was fine."

"I wanted to be . . ." She tried to say "normal," but she got only half of the word out. She doubled her fingers into a fist and pressed them to her mouth.

I couldn't stand having her like this. I tried to think what would make her feel better, what she used to do when I skinned my knee or when Dad yelled at me.

"You want a cookie?" I asked.

She shook her head. She remained in the same position for a long time, holding her hand against her mouth and staring wordlessly at the green-flecked linoleum, until the light in the kitchen turned the shade of iced tea.

Finally, she looked at me. "You're probably hungry."

"No." I couldn't have considered putting anything into my stomach.

She rose unsteadily from the chair. "Look at me, all silly like this. You'd probably give anything to have a mom like your friends have."

"I don't want anybody else's mom."

She took my hand and squeezed it. "You're my lily, the prettiest, most special thing in my life. You know that, don't you?"

I nodded my head vigorously, the tears streaming down my cheeks.

That night the projector broke about three quarters of the way through the movie. When Dad couldn't fix it, he had to return the admission money to people.

"Come back tomorrow evening," he told them. "It'll be up and running then."

They slowly drove their cars out the exit, their headlights streaking across the high board fence. The teenagers cleaned the snack bar and left, the downstairs lights winking off one by one. I wandered out to the kiddie playground at the base of the screen and looked back toward the small projection window, which was lit by a dim glow. I could see Dad's head bent over the equipment, and I knew he'd stay there until it was repaired, even if it took all night.

After a few halfhearted swings and penny drops on the monkey bars, I returned to the concessions building and flopped on an outdoor wooden bench. With only a white thumbnail of a moon, I could see more stars than I'd seen in a long time. I thought about wishing on one of them, then decided I was too old for that. Besides, they'd never done me much good in the past.

It seemed to me I'd had just about as bad a day as a person could have, what with Dad and Memphis fighting, Billy getting whacked by the car and Mom crawling into the garden shed.

I heard the far-off whistle of a train and shortly after that the soothing hoot of a barn owl. In the distance, an animal crossed the field, a coyote maybe, sleek and ghostly, with pinpoints of light glinting off its black-water eyes. Now that the movie was over and people had left, he prowled his own playland, blending into the shadows at will. More than anything, I wanted to be like him.

Mom thought I was in bed, of course, but it was difficult to stay there when the animals were roaming. I often crept out and watched for them. More than once, I had neglected to return before my father locked up the concessions building and trudged across the gravel to our house. More than once, I'd had to climb on an upended pail, remove the screen from my bedroom window and crawl in.

From the corner of my eye, I glimpsed a ruby-red flicker and realized it was the burning tip of a cigarette. I'd been looking so hard at the shadows that I hadn't seen or heard Memphis walk up. Great Indian scout I was.

He eased himself onto the bench, stretched out his legs and reclined against the concrete-block wall. "Thought you'd be in bed by now."

I stared straight ahead. "Couldn't sleep."

Neither of us said anything for a long time, but I didn't feel particularly uncomfortable. I couldn't see his expression in the dark, only his sharp profile and the glowing ember of his cigarette.

"Ain't nothing better than this," he said.

"Yeah, I guess so. But in the winter it sure gets lonesome out here."

He drew on the cigarette, the tip brightening to orange. "I used to feel that way in Idaho when I worked the range alone for weeks at a time. Then I learned the night sky is the best company a man can have."

I tilted my head back and surveyed the silver ribbon of the Milky Way. "I never thought about it."

"A ranch hand taught me that. An Indian. Can't remember what tribe. His people believed the world began in the stars."

We sat there for another hour or so, while he repeated the legends the ranch hand had told him. It wasn't what Memphis said that night that mattered so much. It was what he didn't say. He didn't mention my mother. He didn't ask me what was wrong with her or why she didn't go out of the house or if my friends made fun of her or if she was sick in the head. He seemed to realize I needed to think about something else, if only for that night.

Chapter Fourteen

The next evening around eight o'clock, I was walking toward the house when I saw Memphis stepping out our back door. He was wearing a new plaid shirt and carrying his black cowboy hat in his hand. At first I thought he might have come to see my father, but that made no sense. Memphis knew as well as I did that Dad was in the projection booth by that time. Then I realized he must have been checking to see that my mother was all right.

He came the next evening too with news of Billy. The sun had dipped below the drive-in fence but some of its glow still bloomed behind Memphis as he stood on the kitchen steps. Mom opened the door, her fingers twisting a stray lock of hair into place as she invited him in.

"Billy got banged on the head real hard," Memphis said. He laid his hat on a chair, announcing his intention to stay. "But the doc says he's going to be fine. They'll keep him in the hospital a few more days just to make sure."

Mom spread both hands across her chest in relief. "Oh, that is good news."

I slid into a chair at the table and tucked one foot under me. "I'll bet that fellow from Oklahoma was glad to hear that."

The Starlite Drive-in

Memphis sat down opposite me. "Sure was. Said he didn't care
a bit that his best shirt was ruined. You should have seen him
strutting down Main Street wearing just his blue jeans, his Stetson
and that scrawny little cord around his neck."

I smiled at the picture that came to mind, but I felt the man's
happiness that Billy would live after all.

We had just finished playing *To Catch a Thief* and were beginning a run of *Bad Day at Black Rock.* Even though the movies at
the drive-in that summer were just about the best I'd seen, I was
reading more than ever before. Miss Monhaut kept recommending
books she called "classics," but I hadn't given up my search for a
good one about love. I discovered *Dreams and Desires,* which had
already turned out to be better than *Passion Among the Pines* or *The
Loved One.* It didn't tell me any more about love than I knew
before, but at least it was romantic. An English girl traveled far
from home to become a governess at a castle in the Swiss Alps.
The owner of the castle, an English lord, was a melancholy man
whose wife had died a terrible death in a fire. He fled with his
daughter to Switzerland to escape his wife's memory. The little
girl managed to bring her father and the governess together after
what I thought were some pretty obvious tricks. Anyway, he finally kissed the governess but swore he wouldn't do it again because he didn't intend to take advantage of her.

I wondered if Memphis, if anyone, would ever take advantage
of me. The book made it sound as though it were every girl's
dream, only the English lord and the governess just didn't realize
it. So they spent a lot of time trying to stay away from each other,
kissing in feverish desperation, then changing their minds and

avoiding each other all over again. Along about Chapter One Hundred and Eighty-two, when they couldn't stand it any longer, and I couldn't either, they crashed into each other's arms with the force of two meteorites colliding. On the last page, when they finally decided to marry, I breathed a grateful sigh.

During one of my library visits, Miss Monhaut suggested *Tom Sawyer* and *Huckleberry Finn,* which I took a chance on. It didn't take long for me to decide they were the best books in the entire world. I walked around unaware of anyone and anything else, my nose pressed to the pages. About that time, Mom decided I needed my eyes checked. She called for an appointment, then told my dad about it after dinner while he was poking at his teeth with a toothpick.

He flung the pick in the ashtray. "And when is this appointment for?"

With her head bent almost to her chin, Mom started gathering the dirty dishes. "Dr. Finn's nurse says she can come in on Friday afternoon."

"I don't drive into town on Fridays, Teal. You know that."

She collected the silverware and laid it on a plate, metal clinking against crockery. "Well, I thought maybe just this once. Otherwise, it'll be a month before . . ."

"Well, you thought wrong. If it can't wait another few weeks, get your sister to drive her in."

"Oh, no, Claude Junior, it wouldn't be right." She was twisting a napkin but I don't think she realized it.

I sat motionless as a rock, prepared to go blind if it would stop this conversation.

"Well, it sounds like something a woman should do anyway. How much is this going to cost?" He turned to me. "Don't be thinking you're going to get some fancy expensive glasses, missy."

I nodded unhappily and rose. I was just outside the screen door when I heard Dad say, "We don't have the money, Teal."

The following Friday, my aunt drove me to the optometrist, who peered at my eyes with a little red flashlight and settled his face so close to mine I could see the cavernous pores on his skin. To Dr. Finn's surprise but not my own, I could barely make out the big E on the chart. I chose blue plastic frames that had tiny silver flecks in them. Aunt Bliss said they were fashionable and looked real pretty on me, but I felt miserable and homely.

I dipped my head as if I were a bird flying into a stiff wind. "Dad'll say they cost too much."

She drew herself up and thrust out her bolster-sized bosom. "Don't you worry about that. I'll deal with your father if I have to."

Memphis and I were standing outside my house waiting for Dad to drive into town. With my index finger, I nudged my glasses up the bridge of my nose for the umpteenth time in the three days that I'd owned them.

Memphis leaned against the truck and puffed deeply on his Lucky Strike. "They're real nice, Callie Anne. They look natural on you."

I sighed and made a face. "I hate them. They make me look more stupid than ever."

"No, don't you go saying that." Suddenly he loomed over me, and I thought for a moment he was going to shake me.

He clamped a hand on my shoulder. "And don't listen to anyone who tells you that, you hear?"

I nodded and tucked my head down, kind of digging into myself and wondering what I'd done wrong.

I was to hear almost those same words a few nights later as I stood in the dark outside our kitchen screen door. I'd been down by the creek reading *Love's Rainbow* when the sun gave out on me. I had told Mom I was going to sit with Dad and watch the movie from the projection booth, but I decided to return to my room and finish my book instead. As I approached the back steps, I heard Mom speaking. I don't know why I didn't just barge in the way I usually did. I guess there was something in her voice that made me stop, a softness and a joyfulness that I didn't recall ever hearing before.

She gave a small laugh. "They're just silly verses, of course."

"Could I see them?"

"Oh, no, I'd be too embarrassed."

I heard the scrape of a chair and the clink of silverware against glass.

"What do you do with them?"

"Oh, I send them in. They're always announcing contests on the radio or in magazines. My sister knows a woman who won . . . well, it was just a case of Fels-Naptha, but . . ." She laughed lightly. "I'd love to win a car or something like that. Wouldn't Claude Junior be surprised? He says I'm stupid to think I'm ever going to . . ."

"Well, Claude Junior's wrong." He had that same angry tone of voice he'd used with me. "You're not stupid. You're smart, and you're pretty."

There was a stunned silence, the kind you hear after a firecracker goes off.

134

"But you don't believe that, do you?" he asked. The chair scraped again.

It was a few seconds before she softly answered. "No, I don't suppose I do."

"Well, you are. And don't let him tell you any different."

She didn't reply, and I began to wonder what was going on. I moved over a few feet and pushed aside the twisted branches of a honeysuckle vine so I could see them through the screened window. They were seated next to the table, their chairs facing each other and close together. They seemed locked in a stare. The way Mom's eyes glittered made me wonder if she was crying.

She turned and bent her head low. "I'm not like other women."

He folded his hand over hers on the tabletop. "I wouldn't want you to be."

"I can't go outside." Her voice was breathy, almost a whisper. "I'm afraid to."

"I know."

"But don't you see? I'm peculiar. I don't know anyone else who's this way."

He seemed to consider her words for a moment, weighing something in his mind. "I do."

She tilted her face up, almost hopeful.

He drew in a deep breath and set his jaw as if he'd made some decision. "Maybe not exactly the same, but he's someone who'd understand what comes over you. You're scared of all that wide open space out there." He jerked his thumb toward the window that faced the drive-in field.

She nodded.

He said, "Well, he don't like being trapped in a small place. Every time he gets shut in somewhere, even in a crowd of people, he can't breathe and his heart thumps against his ribs till he's sure they're going to split."

"Yes. Yes, he does know. And he can't let himself get caught like that, can he?"

"Never."

"How did it happen? When did it start?"

Memphis dredged up another breath. "He was about ten when his brother and him got locked in a closet with old coats and rubber boots, and no air. Maybe there was some, but it didn't seem like it. He tried to get out. Clawed the door and screamed for hours. He probably would have scratched his fingers to bloody stumps if his brother hadn't . . ." He looked at my mother's horrified eyes and stopped.

They were both quiet for a moment. A pale moth flailed against the kitchen light above them, but neither of them seemed to notice.

"Who locked him in there?" she asked, and I could see her thoughts were only for him now.

"His ma."

I heard her swift intake of air and then the question, "Why?"

"She run off. Took the baby and left him and his brother to stay with their pa. She abandoned them." He used "abandoned" as though it were a cuss word.

"Why did she leave?"

"Their father gambled and stepped out on her."

Tears rushed to my mother's eyes. "It hurt her to leave them behind. It must have killed a part of her soul."

He glanced at her sharply. "How do you know?"

"I just do. I'm a mother."

He turned away. "She never said that. She never told them. All she said was 'Your pa'll be home soon.' "

"She couldn't bear to see their tears."

"If she loved them, she should have taken them with her."

"It's hard to be a woman alone with one child. It'd be almost impossible with three children. She loved them enough to leave them with their father who could take better care of them."

His face hardened. "To him, they were just two mouths to feed."

"Did the boy ever see her again?"

"Once, years later, when he was about twenty. She was working in a beat-up diner that stunk of grease and stale cigarette smoke. He wouldn't have even gone in if his brother hadn't talked him into it. He didn't recognize her. She just looked like some washed-up, middle-aged woman with faded brown hair and chapped hands—nothing special."

"Did he speak to her?"

Memphis reached across the table for the ashtray. "Nah, he didn't care about her anymore."

Mom laid her hand gently on his arm. "I think he cared very much."

He shrugged. "She left him behind. It made him wonder if anybody ever did love him or ever would."

"I'd love him," my mother said. "If he were here in this room right now, I'd love him."

He stared at her for a moment. "You would?"

Her eyes shone bright and steady. "Yes, I would."

He touched his fingertips to her cheek, as though unsure how she might react. When she didn't flinch or pull away, he slipped his arm around her back and drew her to him, cupping her head in his hand. Their first kiss was soft and tender, the kind I'd seen a hundred times on the big screen just beyond our house. Then he lifted her to her feet, his blue workshirt straining taut across his shoulder muscles. He clamped his arms around her so tightly I was afraid he'd crack her bones, and I wondered how she could breathe. She didn't struggle against him but instead laced her fingers across the back of his head and made a soft noise deep in her throat.

He moved his mouth all over her face and neck. Strands of her hair escaped their pins and tumbled onto her cheeks.

They seemed to kiss forever, with the warm night air drifting through the open window and the moth fluttering dreamily above their heads. She finally pulled away, her breath quick and shuddery.

That's when my thoughts came crashing in on me. Standing there in the overpoweringly sweet blossoms of our honeysuckle bush, I realized this was my mother he was caressing. No man should be touching her that way, not even my father. Memphis had no right. Besides, he was supposed to fall in love with me, not her. I wanted him to like her. Goodness knows, she needed a friend. But to love her? And my mother, what could she be thinking? She should have pushed him away, slapped his face. She had to be crazy to act like this.

They began kissing again, eagerly and fiercely, while I watched in numb horror. They were still holding each other as I crept away, the ground no longer steady beneath my feet.

Chapter Fifteen

I stumbled into the shadows beyond our kitchen and leaned—no, fell against a knotty maple, my pulse thudding in my ears and my fingers digging into the dry tree bark. I felt sick to my stomach, but I knew I couldn't stay there when just a few feet away, my mother and Memphis were kissing.

I crossed the yard to the far side of the house, feeling as though a great black cloud had suddenly wrapped itself around me. When I reached the comforting white glow of the movie screen, I picked up speed. I ran across the parking field, past the cars and the speaker poles, past the concessions building and the box office, past the flickering yellow neon arrow that pointed incoming customers toward the theater entrance. Virgil must have seen me and called out, because somewhere in my head I heard his voice. But I didn't stop. I ran onto Logan Highway and headed south, away from the drive-in and everything I'd ever thought I cared about. I stayed on the gravel shoulder, but even so, a station wagon that was coming around the bend had to swerve to avoid me. With my head down and my heart pumping, I kept going full out, until I felt the pain cutting into my legs and chest. When I got down to my last rasping breath, I dropped onto a strip of grass along the road and

139

gulped for air. My thin cotton blouse was soaked with sweat. The grass was cool and dry and I laid my cheek directly against it. Finally, I sat up, folded my arms around my knees and hugged myself to keep from shaking.

I stayed there for several minutes, with no energy left to cry and barely enough to figure out what I wanted to do. I heard the wail of a nearby train and the thought came to me that I could hop it and travel on it to the end of the line, until I arrived in one of those cities Memphis was always talking about. I would be going alone, not with him as I had once dreamed. Memphis. I raised a tiny bit of saliva in my mouth and spat onto the ground. How could he? How could *she*? Talking to him in that voice she'd used only with me. Kissing him as though she wanted to crawl into his skin. I'd seen her kiss my father sometimes—quick, routine touches of their lips when he left or returned home, but never the fierce eagerness she'd shown with Memphis. And to think I'd followed him around, trying to look like Kim Novak just for him. He must have been laughing inside. He didn't care about me. It was my mother he'd been after the whole time. The humiliation burned through me.

Well, I'd show them. I'd run away, hitchhike to Hollywood maybe and work in the movies. I wouldn't have to be a big actress right away. I could take my time.

Just as I was about to get up, a car rounded the curve, its twin headlights catching me full in the face. It slowed, then stopped, and the driver leaned out the window. Although I could tell by the beefy shape of his head and his crewcut hair that he was a man, there wasn't enough moonlight to see his features. I hoped it wasn't anyone I knew.

"You all right?" he asked.

I didn't recognize the voice, but I jumped to my feet and croaked, "Uh-huh."

"Don't you know it's dangerous to sit that close to the road, honey?"

It seemed to me I should be able to sit anywhere I wanted, but I knew better than to say that. "Well, I was just taking a rock out of my shoe."

"You're awfully young to be running around at this time of night. Does your mom know where you are?"

"I'm on my way home." I pointed toward a lighted farmhouse across the pasture, hoping it wasn't his. "I live right over there."

His head swiveled in that direction, then back.

I edged toward the fence behind me. The last thing I wanted was an offer to drive me down the dirt road to that house. They probably owned half a dozen dogs that would bark their heads off as soon as his car came within two hundred yards of it. "I guess I'd better get going. Mom'll wonder what's keeping me."

"Okay, but stay off the highway, you hear? Some automobile could come around that bend and swerve right into you."

"I'll be careful. Thanks, mister."

He gave a quick wave and nosed his car back into the night. I hunched my shoulders and slipped between the barbed wire into the pasture.

People like him were sure going to make it difficult to run away. It didn't help that I was a scrawny little runt for my age. They'd always assume I was younger than I was. I trudged along the pasture just inside the fence, occasionally pausing to kick a rock or a lump of dirt.

I had to think about this, about what would happen if Dad found out about Memphis and Mom. Besides, I couldn't run away now, wearing no more than a short-sleeved white blouse and a pair of green shorts. I'd need a bedroll, some clothes, food and money. Even Huck Finn had that when he struck out for the river. I decided I could leave tomorrow, or the day after that. Dragging my feet, I turned homeward.

By the time I reached the drive-in, the second feature was in its last half hour. Avoiding the kids who were cleaning the snack bar, I climbed the rear stairs to the projection booth. The door was open. My father sat in semi-darkness next to the humming projector, drinking coffee from his thermos cup and staring fixedly at the screen. Humphrey Bogart was shaking his fist at Van Johnson in *The Caine Mutiny*. I sighed, wondering if Dad had any idea what was happening in his own home.

I'd tell him. Sure, that's what I'd do. He'd probably beat the tar out of Memphis, who'd have to leave the drive-in, of course. But then, Memphis was a drifter. And Mom? Well, maybe Dad would beat the tar out of . . .

I didn't go in. I just glanced at the closed door to Memphis's room and tiptoed down the stairs.

We didn't shut bedroom doors in our house, except on Tuesday nights when Dad and Mom closed theirs, and their bed made those groaning and creaking noises. But that following morning, anyone coming into my room would have had to get past a barricade consisting of the door, my pink-cushioned vanity chair, a wooden toy box plastered with horse decals, and an enormous stack of books.

There was a hollow-sounding knock. "Honey, don't you want breakfast?"

"No." I pulled the pillow over my head and pushed my face against the cotton sheet. It smelled slightly scorched, like the hot iron Mom had pressed it with.

She was silent for a time, but somehow I knew she hadn't left.

"Sweetheart, are you all right in there?"

"I'm fine. Go away."

I poked my head out. More silence, then finally I heard her light step tap down the hall. I'd expected her to keep pestering me, and when she didn't, I felt worse than ever for some reason. It didn't take long to realize I couldn't stay in my room all day. It was miserably stuffy, and I was thirsty and hungry. I should have stashed some provisions, but I hadn't expected a long self-imprisonment. I thought about removing the screen and crawling out the window, but that struck me as something a little kid would do. After a few hours of reading a book that I couldn't concentrate on and dredging up from the bottom of my closet a one-eyed teddy bear and a frowsy yellow-haired doll I hadn't seen in years, I took apart the barricade and walked into the kitchen.

Mom was standing by the sink, a paring knife in one hand, a puckered brown potato in the other. Dad was nowhere in sight.

She looked at me steadily. "What's wrong?"

I boldly took three oatmeal cookies from the fat ceramic bear, knowing she wouldn't stop me. "Nothing."

"Is it because . . ." She couldn't seem to finish the sentence.

"No," I said quickly. I knew we were talking about the same thing but I didn't want her to say it aloud.

She slowly laid the potato and the knife on the drainboard, then turned to me. "There are so many things I wish were different, and I don't know how to change any of them." She folded her arms across her middle, a hand clutching each wrist as though to hold herself together. "Do you understand what I'm saying?"

"Yeah," I said sullenly. I bit a chunk out of one of the cookies, hunched my shoulders and hurried out the door.

Ignoring Memphis's friendly wave from across the field, I ran toward the creek. I built a castle with rocks from the creek bed. I trapped a few frogs, but they managed to slither from my cupped hands and hop away. Even so, there was something soothing about them, about their spongy flesh on my fingertips and the warm mud on my bare feet. I would have stayed there all day but I knew if I didn't show up for dinner, my absence would set off an explosion and Dad would come looking for me. As it was, I moped at the table, putting him in the worst kind of mood.

He jabbed his fork at the meat. "What the hell's the matter with you?"

"Got a stomachache." I nudged the broccoli around my plate, hoping I could avoid having to eat it.

Mom glanced at me sharply. I stared at her hard, jutting out my lower lip but not saying a word. She jerked back almost as if I'd hit her.

I could feel Dad tense up, annoyed at us for disturbing his dinner. He turned to Mom. "Well, can't you give her something?"

She nodded. "I will." She poked at her own stack of broccoli, not much hungrier than I was.

Dad shifted his gaze from her to me, then back again. "For chrissakes, she has a bellyache. Get her some Bromo-Seltzer."

Mom jumped up and headed for the medicine cabinet.

Dad stood, wadded the napkin that Mom had cross-stitched with tiny blue flowers and threw it on the table. "Both of you picking at your food like a couple of dumb chickens," he said as he stomped out.

I slipped out the other door before Mom came back. The last

thing I needed was Bromo-Seltzer. I'd lost my mother and I didn't think even Doc Graham, our family doctor, had medicine for that.

Memphis no longer waved at me, but he still came to our house every evening, and when I was there, he nodded and said, "Hey, pardner," the way he usually did. What amazed me was that I still wanted to be with him. I wanted to wrap my arms around his hard shoulders and bury my face in the curve of his neck, just as Mom had. But then I'd see the way he looked at my mother and I'd leave.

One evening after supper, Mom was staring out the window. "Maybe it'll rain tonight," she said to me. "I see some clouds in the sky."

"It isn't going to rain. Anybody can see those clouds aren't dark enough for that," I said, in the same scornful tone I'd heard my father use with her.

She didn't move.

I stood and pushed in my chair, scraping it across the linoleum just the way I'd been warned not to do. "I'm going to watch the movies from the projection booth with Dad." I wondered if the mention of him would return her to her senses.

I slouched toward the door, jamming my hands in my shorts pockets. "I'm not coming back until the second feature's over," I added, knowing she couldn't do a thing about it. "So you might as well not wait up for me."

She turned away, but not before I saw the hurt swamp her eyes. I felt a brief, mean satisfaction, then a backwash of guilt. All of a sudden, I couldn't wait to get out of there. I ran from the house, the screen door slap-banging behind me.

But I didn't climb the stairs to the projection booth, and I could hardly have told anyone what was playing on the screen that week. I walked around the drive-in grounds, then returned to the house and stood outside the kitchen in the petunia beds Mom had planted earlier in the spring by dropping seeds out the window. Batting away whining mosquitoes, I watched her and Memphis through the screen. I spied on them intentionally now, telling myself I hadn't witnessed what I knew in my heart I had.

They talked about a lot of things, and occasionally they leaned toward each other and kissed. Hours later, after Memphis had left, I sneaked into my bedroom. Looking in the mirror, I could see the screen's smudged imprint on my nose.

One evening, I was eavesdropping on them again from among the flowers when I heard Mom say she wondered if God would punish them for what they were doing. I shifted so that I could see them better. Memphis was in a chair, and she was at the sink, her back turned to me. I could see on her legs the straight dark seams of her nylon stockings, which as far as I knew she hadn't worn in years. She must have put them on after I'd left the house. I noticed she had drawn the shade over the window that faced the drive-in field. She used to lower it occasionally, but now she pulled it down every evening.

She walked to his side, her fingers smoothing the skirt of her print dress. It was a new one she had sewn from the fabric Aunt Bliss had brought her.

She laid her hand on his shoulder, caressing him. "I know what we're doing is wrong, but somehow it doesn't feel that way. Even if God said it was wrong, I don't think I could stop. Do you believe in God, Charlie Memphis?"

He reached for her hand and brought it to his lips. "I believe in miracles."

Chapter Sixteen

Dad picked up my book and slammed it hard on the kitchen table. "Get this out of here. Didn't I tell you to quit your reading during dinner?"

It didn't seem to make any difference that we had finished eating. I grabbed *Little Women* and clutched it to my chest.

Mom, who was filling the sink with hot water, looked up with the same dreamy smile she'd worn for days and brushed the back of her hand across her flushed forehead. "Oh, she's fine, Claude Junior. Just let her be."

Someone should tell her, I thought miserably. Someone should warn her she shouldn't act that way. He'll notice, if he hasn't already. I could see he was tracking her movements with more interest than usual. I'd seen him staring at her over dinner, as if he were tallying numbers in his head, trying to come up with the right answer.

He glared at me and pointed a calloused finger at the table. "Next time I see a book there, I'll burn it. You hear?"

I nodded. He stubbed out his cigarette with the kind of fury he usually reserved for squashing ants in the snack bar, then limped out of the house. Carrying the dirty glasses to the sink drainboard,

I could see him through the window. He looked as though he were carrying the midday sun on his slumped shoulders.

Mom tunelessly hummed some Frank Sinatra love song and swabbed one of the dinner plates for a full minute before she caught herself and rinsed it under the slow trickle of water from the spigot. I picked up a dish towel that had been a flour sack in its previous life and dried the dishes. Occasionally Mom glanced at me, and I suppose she was wondering how to make things the way they used to be between us.

Although I didn't like the anger and meanness growing inside me, I couldn't seem to do anything about it.

That night, which was Tuesday, I heard Dad come in after he'd closed the drive-in. His leather shoes tapped eleven sharp steps down the hall to their bedroom. I counted them.

The door swung shut and I waited for the creaking bedsprings and my father's eventual deep-throated moan. I didn't hear them. Instead, there were muffled voices. At first, I couldn't make out any of what they were saying.

Then Dad's voice rose. "Why not?"

My mother's reply was murmured, too low for me to catch.

Billy returned to Jessup around the third week of July. The doctors had sent him to a hospital in Terre Haute, and from there to one in Indianapolis—not because his injury was so bad but because he still acted strange. At least that's what people said.

A few days later, he showed up at our back door, a white rectangular bandage that was gummy and soiled around the edges plastered to his forehead. His eyes glowed just the same as before.

I should have been happy to see him, but I didn't even ask how he was. By then I was barely talking to anyone.

He pressed his face against the screen of our back door. With his flattened cheeks and sunken eyes, he looked like Lon Chaney in *The Phantom of the Opera*.

"I came as soon as I could, Teal," he said in his sad, husky voice. "Uncle Toby wouldn't let me out of the house until today."

Mom smiled at him. "I'm glad you're mending so well, Billy."

He straightened and beamed in that gawky, embarrassed way he had. Although it was about eighty degrees outside, he was wearing a letterman's sweater with the entwined initials JHS for Jessup High School on the pocket. His clothes looked almost respectable, except for the unlaced, flap-tongued shoes.

The corners of his mouth suddenly folded down. "I had to miss my dance lessons while I was gone."

Mom glanced over her shoulder at the stove. I knew she had cookies in the oven, but I didn't offer to check on them. She turned back to Billy. "I'm sorry to hear that, but I have something for you. You wait right here."

As usual she fed him, bundling an egg salad sandwich in waxed paper for him and adding a warm oatmeal cookie. He shambled off toward the drive-in entrance, not bothering to check if Dad was in the vicinity. I wondered if the blow to his head had scrambled his brains even worse.

Aunt Bliss arrived the next day like an early morning squall and dropped a bushel basket full of peaches on the kitchen counter.

She pulled a red bandanna out of her overalls, snorted into it a few times, then cast her bespectacled eyes on Mom.

"Driving in," she huffed, "I saw Claude Junior and that Memphis fellow tinkering with that old Ford truck of Claude's. I stopped and told Claude he should save himself the aggravation and get a Dodge." She chuckled, her shoulders quivering like a bird dog.

I looked out the window, expecting to see the remains of a blown powder keg. What I saw instead was Memphis and Dad draped over the truck's front fender, their heads concealed by the open hood. Sometimes I wondered how my aunt got away with what she did.

She set down her purse as if she meant business and narrowed her eyes. "Wanted to take a look at this Memphis man up close."

My mother's cheeks flared. She must have said something about Memphis to Aunt Bliss during one of their occasional long-distance telephone conversations. I didn't like the thought of that. Between my aunt's party line and ours, it was possible to have as many as three other people listening in, their heavy breathing making the connection sound like a wind tunnel.

"I'm your sister, Teal. You don't expect me just to sit back and . . ." Aunt Bliss stopped abruptly and shifted her gaze to me. "Honey, go out and get those canning jars off the front seat of my truck, will you?"

Not wanting to miss the conversation, I pretended I needed to tie my shoe first. When I moved too slowly, she frowned. "Go on now."

I darted off like a jackrabbit, banging the screen behind me. For some reason, my aunt had parked her black and khaki Dodge truck halfway across the drive-in field. I found the glass Mason jars on the front seat under a burlap sack. She had packed them in an open box and stuck wads of newspaper between them. Considering Aunt Bliss's driving habits, I thought that was a smart thing to do.

I raced back into the kitchen in time to see her shake her head solemnly. "Lordy, Teal, what are you doing? Claude Junior is a skunk who needs a lesson, but . . ." She stopped when she saw me. "Put those jars right over here. You didn't run with them, did you?"

I gave her my not-me look, while Mom turned away and dabbed at her eyes with the embroidered handkerchief she kept in her apron pocket.

Aunt Bliss harrumphed. "Now, where do you keep that big canner kettle of yours?" She glanced around the room as though she expected it to come marching across the linoleum. Once again, her piercing gaze landed on me. "Do you know where it is, child?"

I nodded, reluctant to tell because it meant another errand. "Probably out in the garden shed."

"You wouldn't mind getting it, would you, hon?"

I shot out the door. It took me several minutes to locate it on a dark shelf under an overturned galvanized washtub. Brushing off the cobwebs, I scuttled back to the house, the lid tucked under my arm, the speckled black kettle banging against my leg. I slowed just as I reached the porch steps. Through the screen, I could see Mom hovering over the sink sorting through the peaches.

Aunt Bliss stood nearby, her arms folded across her well-harnessed bosom. "I'll say it right out, Teal. You're getting yourself into a mess here, carrying on with that drifter. A man like that can't be trusted. He'll flatter you and tell you how pretty you are, but you and I both know what he's looking for. Does he realize you can't leave the house?"

Mom nodded.

"Well, then," Aunt Bliss said, picking up a paring knife, "he doesn't have to worry that you're going to want to run off with him, does he?" She grabbed a peach. "I sure wish you could leave this damned house though. Because if what you really want is to get away from Claude Junior, I'd stick by you. You know I never have liked how he treats you."

"Please, Bliss," Mom murmured, "you don't understand how it is."

"Aw shoot, Teal, I understand perfectly. You're cooped up here with that mean-spirited husband of yours and this good-look-ing drifter comes along and treats you nice for a change. But it can't end well. Don't you see that? Think of Callie Anne. Think of your responsibility there. I sure don't have any fondness for Claude Junior, but that fellow Memphis will break your heart. Anyone with half the sense God gave women can see that."

I stood outside the door, watching the two of them but not making a peep. Mom had her head bent over the sink. When she turned her face toward Aunt Bliss, I expected her to be crying. I saw to my surprise she wasn't. She looked my aunt right in the eyes, and it wasn't the usual dreamy stare she'd been giving Dad and me lately. "It's my life, Bliss, not yours. And I'll conduct it exactly the way I see fit."

Aunt Bliss took a step backward and blinked.

Mom's voice softened. "Charlie Memphis is a good man. I know that in my heart."

"Well, what kind of fellow goes around stealing another man's wife?" She leaned closer and peered nearsightedly at Mom. "Huh? You tell me that."

Mom opened her mouth to reply when she caught sight of me.

Aunt Bliss followed her gaze. "Well, child, what are you doing standing out there in the sun like some brainless mule?" She walked over and held the screen door for me. "Bring it inside."

They had started to blanch and skin the peaches, and the kitchen was filled with a sweet, ripe fragrance. I set the kettle on the counter, removed my glasses and wiped my face on the lower edge of my blouse. A second later, Mom's cool hand was on my forehead. "You shouldn't be running in this hot weather, sweetheart. You'll have yourself a heatstroke."

I shrugged away. "I'm okay."

Aunt Bliss removed the quart jars from the box and lined them up on the counter, then looked around again. "Now somewhere there's a bag of sugar from the A and P."

I sighed.

She tapped two fingers on her forehead. "It's a sad thing, Callie Anne, when an old lady's memory goes. Be a doll, will you, and . . ."

I nodded, already halfway out the door. After it banged behind me, I heard my aunt say, "I'm just thinking of you, sweetie. I don't want to see you hurt."

This time, I walked. I didn't even bother running.

The next evening, Mom and I ate our supper of leftover meat loaf and cleaned up the dishes without saying more than a few words to each other.

I bunched up the wet dish towel and dropped it on the counter.

"I'm going to sit up in the booth with Dad again tonight," I announced. I frequently lied to Dad, usually to get out of trouble, but I had never made a practice of fibbing to Mom. Now I did it with a grudging anger, as if she'd forced me.

"All right." She wiped up the sink, not meeting my eyes.

I didn't visit Dad, of course, partly because his mood wasn't any better than mine, but also because I intended to spy on Mom and Memphis as usual.

I waited until it got dark though, stopping by the box office to talk with Virgil until the movie started. I returned to the house then. Rounding the corner where I had planned to take up my position in the flower beds, I nearly crashed right into Mom and Memphis. He stood on our back stoop, holding the door open, and my mother teetered on the threshold, clutching his hand. They didn't see me, and I dodged behind the garden shed.

I could tell by the glazed, saucery look in her eyes that he was trying to coax her outside. He wasn't tugging on her, the way Aunt Bliss and I had, but just standing there and speaking to her in a voice so quiet I couldn't catch the words. My heart shot into my mouth, not because I'd almost been caught (after all, I was allowed to walk into my own house), but because I was afraid for my mother. And I was suddenly furious with Memphis. I had told him she couldn't go out, that if she did she might have a heart attack.

A thought formed in my head that I could jump from the shadows and kick him off the porch. Then I saw Mom move one foot onto the top step. He wrapped his arms around her and spoke gently to her for the longest time, while every moth and mosquito within ten miles flew through the open door into our kitchen. After watching them for almost an hour, I backed away.

A few nights later, I found them doing the same thing, but now I was more cautious when I approached the house. He held her on the top step, never making her go farther, while he stroked her back and arms and whispered into her ear. The whole time my heart crawled up my throat as if it were trying to escape.

After a while, I began to realize who Memphis reminded me of in a small way. I'd once watched Uncle Augie break a filly to a halter. He didn't just throw it over the scared little horse's head and wait for her to stop thrashing around. He let her sniff it and grow accustomed to it. Then one morning he strapped it over her neck. He did that for several days without forcing the hard bit in her mouth. When he finally did ease it in, she made a little fuss, but nothing like I'd seen some horses do. I used to think my uncle was the most patient man I'd ever met.

As I slid behind the maple tree, the warm still evening seemed little different from the previous ones. They stood just inside the screen door, a bright crescent moon grinning down at them. He held her against him, his arm resting on her waist with all the assurance of a man who might have been her husband. The nightly chorus of crickets nearly drowned out their voices.

He ran his thumb along her cheek as though she were the most beautiful thing he'd ever seen. I wondered if my father had ever touched her that way. More than once, he had swatted her behind, and he kissed her daily, when she handed him the black metal dinner pail that held his sandwich and thermos and he left the house. But I had never seen him caress her. I had never seen him run his hands over her or look at her with the dark heat I saw in Memphis's eyes.

Memphis lowered his head toward her upturned face, and they kissed for what seemed a long time. Finally they parted, but he held his mouth near her ear, speaking so low I couldn't hear the whisper of it.

He opened the screen door, stepped onto the porch and said clearly, "I believe it's going to cool off a little."

As soon as he said it, a puff of wind lifted the leaves on the trees.

"Can you feel the breeze, Teal?"

"Yes."

"We'll be able to sleep better tonight."

"I won't. I'll be thinking of you—of us."

"I'll be thinking of us too."

He moved down the steps. Alone. My mother held the screen door open a few inches. I saw her stiffen.

He called softly to her, "Teal, the breeze is better out here. It's like a light hand on your skin. Remember how it strokes you, how fresh and soothing it is on a warm night?"

"Yes."

If he heard the reluctance and fear in her voice, he didn't act like it. He squatted, spread his fingers and ran them through the thick grass, then released a long breath. "Yeah, nothing quite like this. How long has it been since you walked barefoot through the grass?"

She didn't answer.

"How long, Teal?"

"I don't know. Years, I guess."

Her voice sounded like a thin echo, full of remembering and yearning. It made me want to cry. He didn't say anything for a minute, so maybe it caught him that way too.

He stood up. "I don't guess I've done it since I was a kid. I shouldn'ta waited so long either. People get old too quick, putting away things that feel good, things that are kind to their souls. We shouldn't do that. I'm going to take these boots off, and I'm going to walk barefoot. Yeah, that's just what I'm going to do."

When he started looking around, I backed farther into the deep shadows. He spotted the tree stump near the rosebushes, strolled over to it, just as casual as you please, and sat down.

He tugged off one of his tan-leather cowboy boots. "I'd sure like to have you with me, the two of us together, walking through these long cool blades, feeling their stillness deep inside. Sorta like God's carpet, wouldn't you say?"

No answer.

"What do you think, Teal? I know you'll enjoy it. It'll bring back good memories."

The screen door opened a little more, then wavered.

"I don't know. Maybe." Her voice sounded small and distant.

Memphis was working on the other boot. "Yeah, it's peaceful out here. Just these crickets and frogs singing. Whenever the night critters are fussing, you know things are safe. I like their sound, don't you?"

There was a murmur from the door.

I could imagine the tremor he was sending through her. I knew her heart was pounding because mine was hammering against the wall of my chest.

I understood what he meant about running barefoot. I'd done it every summer since I could recall, and it represented a freedom I couldn't even begin to explain. I wanted my mother to have that freedom. I wanted her to be happy and unafraid again. But not at the risk of her heart giving out, not at the risk of losing her.

Memphis wriggled his toes in the long grass for a minute or two, then strode in a circle around the yard. "This sure feels good. I'd honestly forgotten."

He glanced over his shoulder. "Teal, did I tell you that I love you? Because I do."

A sound almost like a sob from the doorway.

He started walking toward her. I poised to spring from the shadows, to yell at him to leave her alone, that he had no right to torment her this way.

But I didn't move. I was filled with uncertainty, fear and an assortment of the most confused emotions I had ever felt.

Now he stood about six feet from the base of the steps, his hand extended to her. The door opened again. Slowly, she put one foot onto the porch, then another. She stayed there briefly, making a low frightened sound like the whimper of an animal. After a moment, she retreated.

"I love you, Teal."

It must have taken several more minutes for her to come out again, to get to the second step, then the ground, to that point where the door closed behind her. She was swaying so violently her entire body seemed caught in a storm. The color had drained from her face, leaving it pale as a seashell. She had probably stopped breathing. I know I had.

She stretched her trembling hand out, but it didn't quite reach his. He could have moved forward, but he didn't.

She took one more step.

I'll always remember how they looked, washed with moonlight, only the tips of their fingers touching. She was wearing a simple cream-colored cotton dress, her cinnamon hair sprawled across her shoulders. She turned briefly so that I saw her eyes, the pupils enormous, like two deep wells that drank up the light. As if waiting for her, as if sensing the importance of that moment, the crickets quieted, and I could hear the quick rasping of her breath.

Memphis stood straight and tall, wearing his new clothes and his love in his eyes. They held each other only by the light touch of their fingers for what seemed forever. Finally, she took two more steps, and he wrapped his arms around her. She leaned into him as if she had come home.

I released a quavery breath. They might have heard me then, but I don't believe they could hear or see anything but each other. All I could think about was that she was outside now, out here in the open space, and her heart hadn't given out. She was unsteady, but I hadn't lost the mother I'd protected so long.

He embraced her, rubbing her bare arms until she stopped shivering. All the time, he spoke quietly to her, "I don't believe I've ever held anything so soft," tender words made even more soothing by his gentle drawl. With his arm tightly around her, he led her halfway across the yard.

He squatted down, and while she leaned her hand on his shoulder, he removed her straw-colored shoe. Then he lifted her dress, unfastened one of the nylon stockings from her garter belt and slipped it off her leg. She dipped her toes into the grass, giving a little gasp as if she were a child experiencing the newness of it. He took off her other shoe and stocking and laid them aside. Before she lowered her foot, he cupped it in his palm, almost a gesture of reverence, and ran his lips along the top of it. She touched her fingers briefly to his face.

With her hand practically welded to his, she walked slowly from the tree stump to the Queen's Lace rosebush. They must have strode back and forth across that yard fifty times before she seemed to relax. I was growing so weary I had trouble keeping my eyes open. I had crumpled to the cool ground behind the maple, and I probably would have spent the night there if they hadn't returned to the kitchen.

He took her out four evenings in a row, patiently walking with her, reassuring her when she needed it, releasing her hand only when she felt safe. Each time she appeared a little more confident.

On the fifth night, they played. I don't know how else to describe it. I'd never seen adults act that way, but that's just what it was—play. They rolled on God's carpet, as Memphis called it, splashed each other with water from the birdbath, and buried their faces in the roses. They ate the warm ripe tomatoes Aunt Bliss had planted, straight from the vine, drizzling juice and seeds all over their clothes. I remember thinking they were too old to do that, but still I liked hearing my mother's soft laughter. They kissed too, not even minding the tomato juice that ran down their faces.

I sneaked into my room through the front door that night and crawled into bed, pulling the white, pressed sheets over my head. As I waited for my limbs to grow heavy with sleep, my feelings warred against each other. I was grateful that Memphis had released my mother from her own prison, but it angered and saddened me that he had broken her fear when I couldn't.

The next morning I carried a wicker basket of laundry outside to our backyard. I wasn't tall enough to reach the high clothesline and I realized for the hundredth time that I probably never would be. Mom and Aunt Bliss said I was obviously destined to be short like my Grandma Willard. I stood in the warm sunshine on a squat metal step stool pinning Dad's white theater manager shirts on the line and scooting the stool every few feet with some resentment because it seemed to me this was a chore Mom could do now. I dragged the wicker basket back into the house.

After dinner that day, Mom was at the window, following Dad's progress across the parking field. "He thinks the projector might go on the fritz again," she said, lowering the plates into the dishwater. "He'll be up there the rest of the afternoon working on it." She delivered this information as though it were wonderful news.

"Hmm." Dad's repairs on the projector had nothing to do with me.

Drawing her hands from the soapy water, she gave them a quick shake over the sink, wiped them on her apron and turned to me. "I have something to show you."

I kept my face expressionless. "What?"

"You'll see."

She took my hand. I didn't pull away, but I must have flinched because she gave me a quick, regretful look. Her skin was still warm and damp from the hot dishwater. She led me to the screen door, pausing long enough for me to see the light in her eyes and the secret smile tugging at her mouth.

I knew perfectly well what she was doing, but I pretended not to. "What is it? You want me to cut some roses?"

She opened the screen and stepped unsteadily onto the porch. "Thanks, but I can do it myself."

I could feel her hand trembling in mine, but she let go and moved lightly down the stairs, wearing the kind of heavenly expression you see on people in stained-glass church windows. She took several steps in the grass while I lingered on the threshold.

Turning, she stretched out her hand. It was still shaking, but her eyes glowed with triumph. "Come on. It's beautiful out here."

I hesitated a few seconds.

She walked over to the clothesline and began to unfasten the white shirts, draping them over her arm and slipping the clothespins into her apron pocket. "See, I can do this now." She glanced over at me.

"You won't tell anyone?" she said, her eyes glinting with an excitement she couldn't seem to contain. Her skin was so pale it looked like porcelain in the bright sunlight. "It'll be our secret, at least for a while."

It seemed to me everything was backward, out of sync, with her in the yard, me in the doorway. My heart ached. I knew it wasn't right, but for a moment I wanted things the way they were before Memphis came. There was an orderliness about it then. Her duties had been in the house—cooking, cleaning, taking care of Dad and me. There was nothing else to distract her. She had once relied on me to help her, to protect her. Now she had Memphis, and I wondered if she needed me any longer.

Then I remembered how she used to be—frightened, shy, sad much of the time. Crazy, scared of her shadow, some people said, laughing behind her back. I looked at my mother standing there under the cloudless blue sky, her face absolutely radiant, and I felt the weight of that burden lift off me.

"Come on," she said again.

I walked down the porch stairs and into the yard to join her.

Chapter Seventeen

It was during the last week in July that I found the turtle. I was trudging along Logan Highway, which bordered the front side of the Starlite Drive-in, kicking the heads off dandelions and day-dreaming about Memphis. Even though it was only ten in the morning, my sleeveless blouse clung to my moist skin and the road shimmered with heat. Every once in a while a car zoomed by.

I thought of Memphis holding my mother and tried to picture his arms wrapped around me. I couldn't get the image quite right though. His face wouldn't come into focus.

I reached down, yanked out a reed of grass and popped the clean end into my mouth. Some thirty feet away, a box turtle resembling an upside-down, greenish-brown cereal bowl inched over the scorching pavement. I wondered if he was hot in that shell and if the road was blistering his feet. As I stood watching, a dusty maroon Plymouth bore down on him.

"No!" I screamed, the grass falling from my mouth. I ran toward the turtle, thrashing my arms and screeching at the driver, "Stop!"

Maybe because the driver saw him or maybe because he was

trying to avoid me, the car swerved slightly. Even so, I heard a faint crunch as it breezed by.

I turned and shook my fist. "You idiot. You goddamned, fucking idiot."

I stopped dead still, half expecting my father's strong hand to clamp down on my shoulder for cussing. Except for the turtle and the car, which was now just a maroon speck in the hazy distance, the highway was empty.

"Well, Dad swears like that all the time," I muttered to myself.

The turtle lay where I'd first seen him, his head and feet drawn in, his shell dented and cracked along one edge. The damage extended in about an inch. I sank down on the road, not even minding the asphalt that smelled like hot grease and stung my bare legs.

I gathered the motionless turtle to my breast. "You poor little fellow."

I don't know why I thought he was a boy, but it never crossed my mind to think otherwise. Now that I could see him up close, I realized how truly magnificent he was. A faint yellow pattern swirled across the muddy green background of his shell, as if some artist had painted elaborate and exotic designs on him. I felt a stab in my heart at the possibility this beautiful creature might die.

Holding him up, I peered at his tucked-in head. I wasn't sure if the unwavering dark-red beads that seemed to stare back at me were his eyes or not. I lowered him into my lap, patting him lightly, cooing and reassuring him. Wedging my finger under the crushed edge of his shell, I managed to pop it out a bit.

"There, doesn't that feel better already?" I asked in the same tone I'd heard people use with babies.

No movement. How could I save him if he was already dead?

The Starlite Drive-in

I lifted him again and poked cautiously at his head with my forefinger. "Hey, are you alive in there?"

He was alive all right. He shot out and seized the end of my finger, clamping on to it with the speed and ferocity of a powerfully built alligator.

I screamed and flailed my arms, reacting as much to the viciousness and disloyalty of the attack as to the pain. I must have looked like a crazed warrior as I hopped all over the road from one foot to the other with a turtle locked on to my right hand. He reminded me of the Chinese paper toy my uncle from California had sent me. The more I tried to release him, the tighter he gripped.

After one long excruciating minute, I gave my wrist a quick snap and flung him off. He landed in a thick patch of weeds with a plop, and I heard the rustle of unseen critters scurrying into the underbrush. I thrust my finger in my mouth and sucked, certain I could taste blood. When I pulled it out and examined it, the finger was red and swollen, but the skin wasn't broken.

I stomped over to the turtle, which was lying upside down in some ugly-looking nettles, and hollered at him, "You . . . you goddamned dopey moron. Go find someone else to save your life."

Nursing my injury, I set off down the road, muttering and cursing the turtle with every step. I went about forty yards before I began to consider how I might feel in his circumstances. Okay, I might have been scared at first, too, if a car had run over me and then someone had picked me up and stared at me with big eyes. But the turtle should have eventually figured out I was trying to help. I thought of him upside down in the weeds and wondered if he'd be able to flip over, especially as he was near death.

I was halfway to the theater entrance before I turned back. He was in the same place, waving his stubby feet in the air and trying to right himself. I picked him up, accidentally touching a nettle with my pinkie. Now two fingers throbbed with pain.

Carrying him with my right hand outstretched, I headed toward the drive-in again. "This is your last chance," I said, using the tone I'd heard my father use with me all my life.

In the snack-bar storage room, where it was cool and smelled strongly of popcorn oil and disinfectant, I set him on the concrete floor and hunted for a cardboard box that still had its flaps on top. The turtle remained motionless, hunched tight in his cracked shell. Once I'd found the right-sized container, I placed him inside on a clean rag. In spite of what I'd said, I had no idea how to save him. I'd never had a pet before. I didn't even know how to take care of him. Yet somewhere in the back of my mind I was already thinking of him, smashed and crippled as he was, as my pet and my responsibility. If he died now, it would be my fault. I folded the flaps on the Bang-O popcorn box and tucked them in.

Dad and Memphis were already in the pickup, and Dad was cranking the starter when I came out of the concessions building with the box. Another minute and they would have left for town.

Dad leaned his head out the window. "Where were you?"

"Oh, just around."

"Well, you have to be where I can find you if you want to go to town with us. I can't be running all over the place."

Memphis climbed out of the truck so I could sit between him and Dad. He gave me one of his can't-you-stay-out-of-trouble grins as I scooted across the seat with the popcorn carton in my lap. I made a face at him as he hopped back in. He slammed the door, and we drove away.

Telephone poles clicked by. We passed the sign that said JESSUP

12 MI., TERRE HAUTE 36 MI. On both sides of the highway, baked and colorless pastures wavered under the bright sun. Heat mirages rose in front of the truck. I shifted my bare legs away from the prickly bench-seat upholstery and clutched my cargo.

We were two miles down the road when Dad gestured at it. "What's in it?"

"Nothing."

"Uh-huh," he said. "You just like to carry around empty boxes."

"Uh, I meant nothing but a turtle."

Memphis, who'd been staring out the window, glanced at the box but didn't say a word. His gaze snapped back toward the passing landscape, and I could see he was going to stay out of this.

As we approached a sharp curve, Dad shifted down, the gearshift knob tapping the cardboard. "What are you doing with it, Callie Anne?"

"Well, I . . . I found him in the road. A car ran over a bit of his shell, so I thought maybe Doc Graham could fix him up." I don't know what made me tell the truth, except that I didn't have time to think of a good fib. "I mean, I couldn't just leave him there."

"Doc Graham isn't a veterinarian, Callie Anne," Dad said, "and even if he was, we don't have the money to be fixing turtles."

I gazed down at the box. "Well, I know but . . ." Heck, any ten-year-old knew he was a regular doctor, but Dr. Crofoot, the veterinarian, was a mean old coot. Everyone in town knew that too.

Dad set his mouth in a flat line and ran his stubby finger inside the collar of his white dress shirt. I saw right then I wasn't going to win this one.

"When we get back," he said, "you find a good place to let it go, maybe down by the creek. If it's meant to live, it will. If not, there's nothing you can do about it."

I didn't take the turtle to Doc Graham's the way I wanted to, but I decided on the way home I wasn't going to turn him loose either. Hugging the box tight against me, I made up my mind. I was going to save him.

Chapter Eighteen

$\mathcal{T}$wo days later, I was keeping Memphis company while he repaired a hole in our slat-board fence.

He smacked at a bluebottle horsefly on his neck, its iridescent wings catching the light as it tumbled to the ground. "You didn't let the turtle go yet, did you?" he said, giving me a look that made me think he already knew the answer.

I shook my head. "I'm waiting for him to get better."

He lined up the new board where the broken one had been, took a nail from his shirt pocket and hammered it in. "Where you hiding him?"

"Behind the garden shed. Dad hardly ever goes out there, and it's shady and cool in the bushes. I've been giving him water and food, but I don't think he's eaten anything since I found him."

"You still got him in that cardboard box?"

I nodded. "I put some holes in the side so's he'd get air."

Memphis looked like he was going to say something more, but he didn't speak again until he'd pounded in all the nails. Then he laid the hammer down, selected a Lucky Strike from his full pack and lit it. Drawing deeply on the cigarette, he studied our eastern landscape. I gazed in that direction too although I couldn't see much that would interest him, just the drive-in field, more fence and the dried-up farm pasture beyond.

He exhaled smoke in a long gray streak. "Callie Anne, I reckon I wouldn't feel like eating if I had to stay in a box all day without any light or the earth under my feet."

It bothered me that he didn't call me shortstuff or pardner. I dug the toe of my shoe in the dusty soil. "Well, I visit him a lot and every once in a while I put him down in the grass so he can walk around."

Pinching the cigarette between his thumb and forefinger, Memphis sucked the smoke in again and blew it out, giving me that extra time to think.

"Would you like to live that way?" he asked.

I unearthed a small rock with my shoe and gave it a kick. "Well, no, but I don't know how else to keep him from leaving. I'd put him in my room if I thought I could hide him there. Mom wouldn't mind, but if Dad found him, he'd probably kill him, and me too."

"Why don't you let him go?"

"Because if I did that, I couldn't save him. I got some horse salve from Aunt Bliss and I've been putting it on his wound. So it's for his own good, keeping him in the box, I mean."

I wanted Memphis to know it wasn't because I was selfish. I tried to look noble and dedicated, like the picture of Florence Nightingale in my history book. The Lady of the Lamp, they called her. I thought it would be wonderful to be like her, to have a name that reminded people of a magnificent songbird and a healing light. My mind drifted off, thinking of the possibilities. I'd wear an elaborate headpiece, not that silly little white cap Doc Graham's nurse wore.

I heard Memphis's voice from a distance, ". . . call him."

"What?"

"What do you call this turtle?"

"John Wayne." I had no idea where the name came from. It just popped into my head and traveled out my mouth before I had time to think about it. But as soon as I'd said it, I knew it was the right one.

"John Wayne, huh?" He was smiling through a haze of Lucky Strike smoke. "Well, he's going to have to be strong and brave to survive his treatment." He reached over and tugged on the new fence board to make sure it was secure. "Seems to me though, you're going to need something better'n a box for him until he gets well."

I tried to think what else I could hide him in, but nothing came to mind. "I don't have a cage or anything like that."

He gathered up his tools. "Well, I suppose we'll just have to build him one."

I perked up. "You mean that? You'll build a cage for John Wayne?"

He laughed. "No, I said we would. That's you and me, pardner. You know how to hammer a nail, don't you?"

I nodded, although I didn't, of course.

"When?" I asked, hoping he'd say the next time Dad went to town.

He picked up the broken board. "Right now, seeing as how I'm done with this fence."

"Now? But what about Dad? He'll see us."

"You can't be hiding that turtle forever, shortstuff. John Wayne's going to have to defend himself."

I was sure I saw a gleam of amusement in his dark eyes, although, when I thought about it later, I realized it could have been something else—devilment maybe, as Aunt Bliss would say. He headed toward the concessions building, with me trotting beside him like one of Uncle Augie's bird dogs.

"Dad's not going to like it," I said.

"Well now, don't be so sure. What're you feeding this critter?"

"I put some of Mom's beef stew in a jar lid. I thought he'd eat that, but he didn't."

"Try worms and grasshoppers. A turtle wouldn't know good food if he tripped over it."

We reached the cement block building, and I followed him around back. "Regular old worms?"

"Nightcrawlers if you can find them. Ain't gonna be easy with this drought."

"I know where I can get some. And I can catch grasshoppers too." I clapped my palms together, forming a cup. "Snag them in midair."

He stopped and eyed me. "I'll bet you can. Grab them quicker'n any frog, right?"

I grinned.

He opened the door to a storage area where Dad kept the toolbox, broken speakers, paint buckets, lumber and an assortment of just plain junk. Rummaging through the collection, he dragged out a scrap of plywood and a length of screen that had been taken off a door. The screen had a rip and several small holes in one end of it.

"These'll do," he said.

I glanced around. "Dad's going to see us. He might come down from the projection booth any minute." I was starting to get a little prickling feeling in the pit of my stomach.

"Now, don't you go worrying about your pa," Memphis said as he set the plywood across two sawhorses. "How big do you figure we ought to make this cage?"

I surveyed the piece of wood. "About this size, I guess." I stretched out my arms full length.

He shook his head. "Not enough screen. We're going to have to measure it." He dug out an oversized yellow pencil and a carpenter's tape measure from the tool box. "Here, hold the end of this."

We marked the base on the board, and Memphis started cutting it.

"You ever think about the word *cage*, shortstuff?" he said. "Ain't even got a pleasant sound to it. Kind of grates on you, don't it? Like running your finger across a chalkboard."

I shivered at the thought.

The cut piece of board dropped to the ground with a sinister-sounding clunk, like a period at the end of his words. "It's no good to cage things that are wild by nature. They'll go crazy."

I remembered that he had worked at the penitentiary. "Did the men in that prison go crazy, Memphis?"

He stared at me for a long moment, as though his mind were in some other place. Then he slowly nodded his head. "Once in a while." He handed me the end of the tape measure. "Hold it right there." He pulled it taut. "You're going to let that turtle go when it's healed, right?"

"Oh, yes, that's what I'm going to do." I saw myself in my Florence Nightingale uniform, tears of joy in my eyes as he padded off. Only a slight dent in his shell would show where his near-mortal wound had been. He lifted his clubby front foot, and it seemed for a brief moment he was waving good-bye. It was a bittersweet scene, one I might have watched in a movie, *The Yearling* or *So Dear to My Heart* perhaps.

"Is that a promise?" Memphis asked.

I nodded eagerly. "Oh, yes, I promise."

I was still pondering my nursing career when Dad rounded the corner of the concessions building and came to a dead halt. He took in the plywood and the screen and Memphis and me, and his eyes went flat and dark. I saw the fury rush into his face. My stomach somersaulted, but Memphis didn't even glance up.

Dad's voice sounded raspy. "What are you doing?"

"Building a cage," Memphis said, low and easy. He continued sanding the rough-edged wood as though it were part of his daily job to construct cages.

"And what do you expect to do with it?" Dad was speaking louder than usual.

Memphis ran his finger along the smooth line of the board. "Well now, Callie Anne here needs something better'n a box to put her turtle in." He straightened and looked my father directly in the eyes.

They stared at each other, momentarily locked in a standoff. I could barely find my breath.

Dad's jaw muscles twitched. "I was going to use that wood for something else."

Memphis picked up the sandpaper block he'd made and started working on another edge. "There's plenty more in the storeroom. If it ain't enough, I'll buy some next time we go into town."

Dad didn't answer. After what seemed like one of the longer minutes of my life, he turned to me, his legs spread to brace himself, his eyes hard as two black stones. "You clean up that litter yet?"

"Uh-huh."

He stood there another few seconds. Finally he hitched up his bad leg and limped off.

The trace of a smile flickered across Memphis's face.

The Starlite Drive-in

*   *   *

A few days later, Aunt Bliss came by, her hefty black purse slung over her arm, her red bandanna handkerchief pressed against her nose. Seeing her truck roll in, I took off running. I reached the picket fence just as her substantial brown shoes touched down on the gravel.

Dad was walking out the front door. Limping across the small patch of grass that made up our front yard, he stopped for a moment and nodded stiffly. "Bliss."

Her thick spectacles slid down her nose and caught the morning sunlight. She turned the two silvery patches of glass on him. "Claude Junior," she said sharply, "get your house in order."

His head jerked up.

For a moment, her words seemed to hang between them, like a hand-lettered sign dangling in the air. That was all she said, though. She was wearing a dress for a change and a straw hat that was decorated with fake flowers and fastened to her head by a monster pearl-tipped hatpin. As she marched by him, her sturdy nylon-covered thighs made a swishing sound.

Five minutes later, I was in her truck, rattling along the road to Jessup and gazing in dismay at my feet, which had somehow swelled in size over the summer from mere gunboats to full-attack battleships. Aunt Bliss was going to buy me a new pair of shoes. If it hadn't been for the embarrassment, I would have looked forward to the event. I liked wriggling my toes under the fluoroscope at Miller's Department Store. The hazy white bones inside my neon-green feet made me think of prehistoric creatures.

As much fun as the fluoroscope was, the shoe buying itself always turned out the same—a giant disappointment. The salesman

175

was a gaunt oily-faced fellow who smiled more than any other man I'd ever met. He greeted me as though I were his long-lost niece and asked Aunt Bliss how she was enjoying the hot weather. About as much as a sow enjoys a bath, she fired off tartly. While she surveyed the display of shoes, he winked at me twice and I wanted to throw up.

I couldn't look at the ladies' shoes. I had this idea that if I did, I'd jinx myself. Maybe just this once, if I didn't set my heart on the prettiest ones, I'd be able to cram my misshapen feet into something as dainty and elegant as my mother wore.

The salesman gestured at some brown Naugahyde-cushioned chairs as if he were the master of ceremonies at a circus. "Sit right here, please."

Aunt Bliss gave him one of her cold stares. "You go on ahead, Callie Anne. I believe I'll stand."

My aunt was funny that way. She didn't like sitting while some man was hovering over her.

The salesman brought out feminine flats with a rounded toe, lovely sandals, patent-leather Mary Janes with delicate straps across the instep. He struggled with each pair until the sweat broke out on his forehead and his smile faded. "Girls and ladies are supposed to have long thin feet. Yours are square with high insteps, like a boy's. I could put you in a pair of canvas sneakers."

Aunt Bliss snorted. "Those flimsy things'll ruin her feet."

He laughed. "Maybe she should forget the shoes and wear the boxes."

Aunt Bliss glared.

I sighed. Once again I'd have to settle for boy's oxfords, which were wide, bulky, well built and ugly. Tears stung the back of my eyelids.

"No, wait," the salesman said. "I almost forgot. There is a new style that just came in." He hurried toward the stockroom.

I didn't dare dream.

They were beautiful—a soft chocolate brown, not a sandal but low-cut with two delicate straps across the top. The salesman guided my right foot in, his jaw set, his mouth fixed once more in a broad grin. It slid on like butter left out in the sun. I nearly swooned. Suddenly, I was Cinderella, the golden slipper catching the light and winking like a thousand stars. If it fit, could my prince be far behind?

Aunt Bliss broke the spell. She was closely examining the fit, her berry-stained finger poking at the toe. "You got enough room in there, Callie Anne?"

"Oh, yes."

She frowned. "They don't look too substantial to me. How they going to hold up in winter?"

Oh, no, please. Couldn't she see how it made my foot look normal, even small?

"I'll wear my rubbers in the winter, Aunt Bliss. Honest I will."

The salesman's smile dazzled. He stood and rubbed his palms together. "They're good and solid. All leather." He picked up the left shoe and held it out. "See this stitching. . . ."

I tried them both on, walking back and forth across the carpet at least fifteen times to satisfy Aunt Bliss. "Why, they're the most comfortable pair I've ever worn." I intended to die before I'd admit the left one pinched my instep.

She eyed them skeptically. "How much they cost?"

Too much.

She bought them anyway, and we took them home.

The trouble began immediately after my aunt left. Once her

truck was out of sight, Dad slammed the empty shoebox down on the table. "Jesus Christ."

The hair rose on the back of my neck.

Mom was wiping up a spill on the counter. Her hand fluttered nervously, but I noticed she didn't cringe the way she might have a month or two ago. "She needed them, Claude Junior."

Dad set his lips together as tight as chimney bricks. "Your sister didn't have to buy the most expensive pair in the whole god-damned store, did she?"

Mom didn't answer.

He leaned his face toward her. "Well, did she?"

I stood there motionless, not sure whether I should stay or try to slip away. I knew better than to open my mouth.

Mom's eyes clouded. "She offered to pay for them."

He banged his fist on the table. "And how do you think that makes me feel?"

She was silent. My throat tightened.

Dad straightened to his full height. "Well, I'll tell you. It makes me feel like I can't even put my own kid in shoes."

It was a long moment before any of us moved. Finally Dad jerked the chair away from the table and sank into it, thrusting his bum leg out in front of him.

"She didn't mean to," Mom whispered. "She meant to be nice."

Not looking up, Dad absentmindedly kneaded the thigh on his twisted leg. "Maybe she did, but I don't want charity. What kind of man is it who can't take responsibility for his own family?"

"We gave her the money. We didn't take . . ."

"For Christ's sake, Teal, we can't be paying that much for shoes for Callie Anne, for any of us. I'm not making what I did last summer, and we still have the bill from her glasses."

"But . . . but last spring you said Mr. Sooter was going to increase your pay."

Dad raked his fingers through his hair in an almost violent gesture. "Well, he didn't."

Mom's voice became nearly inaudible. "But he said he would. . . ."

"Well, dammit, Teal, he didn't. He said he couldn't take on a fella to help me and raise my salary too. Of course, by that time, he'd already hired him."

A few moments passed while we all considered who it was Mr. Sooter had employed.

Finally, Dad said in a low, flat tone, "He cut it."

The blood drained from Mom's face. "He cut your salary."

"That's what I said. Jesus Christ, stop sounding like an idiotic parrot."

"But that's not fair. He can't do that, can he?"

Dad stood and shoved the chair in, nearly knocking it over. "And who's going to stop him?" he said, turning away from her with an air of defeat.

A moment later, he whirled on her. "What would you have me do, Teal? Quit? Get a job somewhere else? Should we leave this house and this goddamned sorry little town?"

Mom didn't move, but fear flickered in her eyes.

"Did it ever occur to you that you've trapped me here? And that I'm suffering as much as you. Did you ever once think of that?" Without waiting for an answer, he hitched his bad leg into position and stomped out.

Mom's face had gone so white I thought she might fall over.

I sat down on the floor, unfastened the straps of my new shoes, removed them and brushed off the soles with my fingers.

"I didn't wear them outside. We can take them back." I started

179

to wrap them in the tissue paper from the box. "I really don't like them that much anyway. The left one pinches my foot."

Mom stopped my hand.

I looked up at her. Two fiery pink splotches had risen on her cheeks.

"We're keeping them. It'll be all right."

"But Dad said . . ."

"I want you to have them. You don't have to worry. I've got a few dollars set aside."

I was never quite sure where the money in the cocoa tin came from, but I knew how my mother valued it.

"Okay," I said, but all the joy had gone out of the new shoes.

I laid them carefully in their box. "Think I'll go down to the creek," I said, tugging on my old brown oxfords.

I took John Wayne from his cage and carried him with me. As I trudged along, I considered the prospect of our family's poverty. It had never crossed my mind before. I knew we weren't rich, but I had never realized we were poor. I'd always believed we were somewhere in between. Now I thought of my mother scraping the last morsel from every container, turning the smallest leftover into soup. Maybe she did that because of me, because I demanded costly Cinderella slippers and sparkling eyeglasses.

I held John Wayne to my cheek and spilled tears onto his shell, repeating, "I hate those shoes and I hate my glasses."

Dad made it sound as though his pay cut was Memphis's fault. But how could Memphis have known Mr. Sooter would go back on his word? It was Mr. Sooter I hated now, that bloated, stingy man and his miserable unfairness.

When I reached the creek, I set John Wayne down near the water. After a few minutes he poked his head from his shell and ambled a few unsteady paces across the damp earth. He drooped noticeably on his injured side, but I could see improvement. I didn't move from where I was sitting. Eventually, he crawled over my worn brown oxford as if it were a rock and left a small wet footprint. For some reason it made me feel better.

Chapter Nineteen

By the time the water-well drillers out of Bloomfield arrived in early August, I was sure glad to see them, because we needed a distraction. It seemed like every time I looked up, Dad was tracking Memphis's movements with hunched shoulders and a hard, flat gaze, while Memphis, who was still seeing my mother nearly every evening, walked around like no one could touch him. I, on the other hand, wore a blank expression, not giving Dad anything he could grab on to.

The truck with the name FRICK AND SON DRILLING and the motto "WELL EXPERIENCED" lettered on the side pulled into the drive-in at about three in the afternoon. Harold Frick climbed out and shook hands with Dad and Memphis. It turned out he was the son in the company name, and he'd been digging wells in the tri-county area for more than twenty years.

Harold reminded me of a moving fireplug, short and solid. Chewing on the end of a toothpick, he peered down the shaft. "Nope, didn't put this one in. Pa says he don't remember doing it either."

I suppose he thought that excused them for the well running dry.

Memphis hooked his thumbs under his belt. "That's funny. Ben Sooter said your company drilled it when the theater was built."

Harold rubbed his hand across his neck, which had the color and texture of a brown-leather wallet. Ignoring Memphis's remark, he inspected the bright cloudless sky. "Sure as hell going to be a hot one, isn't it?"

Dad nodded but Memphis didn't answer.

Harold removed the toothpick from his mouth, turned and spat on the sand. "Don't look like we'll ever get a break in this weather." He stared toward the distance as though hoping for a raincloud to gallop over the horizon. When it didn't and nobody else said anything, he glanced around. "Well, guess we better get busy." He turned toward the truck. "Poke, get out here."

After a long moment, the door to the passenger side swung open, and a skinny guy in his early twenties climbed out and ambled toward us. His faded brown hair stuck straight up, bristly as a scrub brush. Grinning and showing a mouthful of bad teeth, Poke looked about two potatoes short of a blue plate special.

"Howdy," he said to no one in particular. No one answered.

Harold, Dad and Memphis conferred for a few minutes about the general location for the well while Poke hovered in their vicinity and eyed me with a grin that gave me the creeps. Harold broke up the discussion and meandered around, staring down at the ground.

I sidled up to Memphis. "Where's the water witch? Isn't there going to be a water witch?"

Harold had heard me. "Don't need one. I can sniff out water as good as any of them."

For the next fifteen minutes, he tramped around in deep concentration. We were in the northwest corner of the drive-in property, where the old well was located. I hung out close by, in the shadow of the screen. Occasionally, he stopped and stood motionless, as if waiting for the pull of underground currents. Then he bent down, put his nose to the earth and sniffed like a dog.

Memphis leaned against a tree, watching without comment. Dad returned to his office, telling Memphis to let him know when the performance was over.

Finally, Harold yelled over to Poke, who, from what I could tell, hadn't moved since the last time Harold had directed him to. Poke wasted about five minutes finding something—just a wrench, as it turned out—to mark the spot. The two men spent the next hour or so jockeying the truck into position, probably longer than necessary with Poke operating at half speed.

Memphis brought out the yellow barricades and set them up around the work site. Harold and Poke used blocks of wood to level out the rig.

As they unloaded the pipe they were going to drill into the soil, Memphis took a long look at it. "Kind of big, ain't it?"

Harold glanced up. "Not for these parts."

Memphis strode over and inspected it closer. "Can't see why you'd need one big enough to stuff a grown man into."

Harold squinted at him, unsmiling. "You want it as big as the old one, don't you?"

"Doesn't need to be. That one was oversized for the job it had to do. We're not irrigating the whole countryside."

Harold, who was squatting down, rose, pulled a fresh toothpick from his shirt pocket and stuck it between his lips. He rolled it from one side of his mouth to the other, assessing Memphis. "Let's see now, who's drilling this well?"

Memphis didn't answer, just studied him with a hint of amusement.

I was standing next to a truck tire as big as I was and watching the exchange.

Poke, who'd been pulling something from a toolbox, stopped to listen. His eyelids fluttered, leading me to believe he was processing the conversation through his dimly lit mind. When he didn't have that ridiculous grin on his face, I could see a family resemblance to Harold.

Harold finally gave up on staring Memphis down and turned away. He took one of the clamps off a long metal ladder anchored to the truck. "Poke, help me with this mast."

I got pretty excited as they raised the mast to the level of the trees and lowered the cable from it. Anything dropping from that high in the air was going to make a big hole. They hooked it into place, attached a drill bit to the cable, tightened some enormous bolts, positioned the length of pipe and cranked up the engine.

Talk about a letdown. The engine wouldn't start.

So Harold and Poke huddled over it and tinkered with it for the next hour. Occasionally, the motor coughed and spewed a puff of blue smoke, then died. Just about the time I thought I could easily find something more interesting to do, Memphis moved in to take a look.

Within three minutes, the engine jerked to life in a burst of smelly fumes. Unfortunately, they couldn't work very long because people would be arriving soon to watch the movie.

Later, I heard Memphis tell Dad they weren't the worst drillers he'd ever seen, but they sure as hell weren't the best either. Dad said they were good enough for what he wanted.

*　　*　　*

The *ker-plunkada-plunkada* of the drill sinking into earth jolted me from bed the next morning. Dad rose early to see how things were going. Memphis was already in the drive-in field checking to make sure there had been no damage to the speakers and poles the night before.

After a while, well drilling became a pretty boring process to watch. The big engine chugged, sputtered and belched oily smoke while Harold and Poke occasionally poured water in the hole or attached a new length of pipe. By Thursday, when they were a hundred and fifty feet into the earth and still hadn't hit water, Harold decided maybe they should drill a few test wells. He went off sniffing the ground again.

Dad watched him in disgust. "Keep an eye on him," he told Memphis. "Make sure he doesn't hit oil instead."

Memphis nodded. He gave no sign that it bothered him to stay behind while Dad and I made our usual trip to town.

In Jessup, I stopped at the public library, then headed toward the Empire Theater Organization to meet Dad. ETO occupied the second floor of a two-story limestone building on Main Street. The walls inside were a grimy beige and, as Dad said, possessed more coats of paint than a loose woman. There was no one in Mr. Sooter's outer office. Iris, the secretary, had left her desk so tidy that I wondered if she'd fallen ill or taken the day off. The frosted-glass door to Mr. Sooter's inner office was cracked open, probably to alert him to visitors. I could hear his voice and that of my father. They apparently hadn't heard me, but then I was still using my library manners.

I quietly slid onto a scratched metal folding chair. On the wall opposite me were photographs of the outdoor theaters ETO owned, fourteen in all, scattered around Indiana. There was our drive-in, the Starlite, third from the left, taken shortly after it was built. Another picture showed Mr. Sooter and several men in gray suits cutting a large ribbon with oversized, silver-painted cardboard scissors. I couldn't tell what the celebration was, but the photograph must have been taken several years before, because Mr. Sooter was missing one of his many chins.

Each week, someone thumbtacked a coming-attractions poster to a large corkboard in the office. This week's poster advertised *Kiss Me Deadly* and showed a man smooching a woman on her porcelain-white neck. I could see why he avoided her mouth. She was wearing lipstick the eerie crimson color of bats' eyes, not the sort of thing he'd want smeared all over his face. She held a gun loosely at her side as if he had simply overpowered her with one tender nibble. "Blood Red Kisses!" it said. "Mickey Spillane's Latest H-Bomb!" "Sizzling Hot Thrills!" I could see right away my father wouldn't like this picture.

I listened to Dad and Mr. Sooter drone on about box-office grosses and snack-bar inventories. A window fan ineffectively churned the muggy air, while a schoolhouse wall clock ticked off the minutes. I opened my book, but I hadn't read more than two pages when I heard Dad mention Memphis's name. There was a noticeable pause in the conversation.

Mr. Sooter's chair groaned, a noisy protest against his bulk. "You're sure the downstairs door wasn't open?"

"Yes. I'm careful when I handle money, even if no one else is around."

Mr. Sooter cleared his throat. He always had a lot of phlegm in it, even worse than Aunt Bliss. "Maybe you left the key in the lock."

Dad jingled his key ring. "I always carry it with me."

"What about Memphis?"

"I know he had his because he let himself in around midnight. I had already locked up by then."

There was a short silence, broken by Mr. Sooter's wheezy breath. "You could have miscounted."

I cocked my head to listen.

"No, sir," Dad insisted. "I counted the dollar bills twice, then went downstairs to get myself something to drink."

"I thought you kept a thermos up there."

"I do, but I'd run out. In this heat wave, a person goes through liquids pretty fast. Anyway, the money was all laying out there on the desk. I didn't think to put it away because I hadn't finished with the change yet. It was two o'clock in the morning. I always lock the downstairs door, but not the projection room door since any skeleton key could open it. Besides, only one other person could . . ."

"I know that," Mr. Sooter said abruptly. "You're saying he stole the money."

I sat straight up, feeling as though something round and hard had caught in my throat.

My father didn't answer, but his silence weighted the air. Dad was lying. He had to be. Did he do it the way I did? I wanted to rush into the room, to see if he was staring directly into Mr. Sooter's piggish eyes or at the mouth with the nicotine-stained teeth.

Mr. Sooter's chair made a loud complaining squeak. "Twenty dollars isn't much, not enough to call the sheriff about."

"No, but it's a nice little bonus to a man's pay."

"He's a good worker. Once that well drilling's done, the Starlite will be in fine shape. It looks better than it has in years."

"Yes, Mr. Sooter, I appreciate the help, but I don't need a thief."

"No, no, of course you don't. But Charlie Memphis saved us a lot more than twenty dollars when he caught those two men robbing the box office."

"There's something else, Mr. Sooter."

"Well, what is it?"

"Memphis killed a man."

"Where'd you hear that?"

I leaned forward, curious too.

My father's tone was cautious. "Well, sir, I can't say, but the rumor is he may have gone to prison for it."

I was starting to feel sick to my stomach.

Mr. Sooter was quiet for some time. Finally, he exhaled an audible breath. "I don't like this, Claude. I was thinking about asking him to manage the Sunset in Connersville. And now you want me to fire him, all based on rumor and conjecture."

"Well, sir . . ."

"I hate to be wrong about a man, Claude. Can't remember the last time I was. I have to think this over."

The phone on Iris's desk rang, and I jumped almost a foot.

I heard Mr. Sooter say, "The switchboard should be taking these calls." The ringing stopped. "Yes, I want to talk to you about that. Hold on." A chair scraped across the floor. "Claude, let me know if there are any more problems."

"I can't be responsible if . . ."

"For Christ's sake, you won't be." His tone switched to one of dismissal. "I said just let me know."

I was standing by the door as Dad came out.

He stopped abruptly, bracing his thigh with his hand to keep from losing his balance. He raked his eyes across me. "How long have you been there?"

I stared at his tight mouth, not his eyes. "Just came in. I didn't want to wait in the hot truck, so I thought I'd read my book in here until you were ready."

He glanced at *Love Stories of the Romans.* I could feel the track of sweat forming on my upper lip. He'd know I was fibbing. He glared at me for several seconds, then opened the office door and limped out. I trailed a few steps behind him.

After we returned to the drive-in, I helped Mom with dinner, cutting out the baking-powder biscuits with a flour-rimmed jelly glass and arranging them on a cookie sheet. Dad was unusually cheerful as we ate, and I don't think it was because Mom had fixed fried chicken with biscuits and gravy. I had cleanup chores to do so it wasn't until much later that I could get away. The first feature, *Lady and the Tramp,* had been playing half an hour by the time I ducked under the fence that separated our property from the Eggerts' farm. I had no need for a flashlight. The full moon was casting enough white rays to catch grasshoppers by. It must have set the cicadas off because they were fussing in some oak trees. The pasture gave off an earthy smell of clover and cows.

I walked down to the creek, not to my usual spot behind the Eggerts' farm but to one closer to the drive-in. I'd never passed much time there because of the weeping willow trees. Personally, I liked them, but I'd heard Aunt Bliss say they brought bad luck. She told Mom that Uncle Augie's sister's house burned down because there was one in her front yard. Up to now, there'd been no reason for me to hang around the willow grove. It didn't have a muddy bank with reeds and undergrowth like my other place did. Nowhere for frogs to hide. But then, I hadn't been interested in frogs much lately. I crawled under the trees' drooping branches. Tips touching the ground, they formed a natural shelter, a refuge for thinking. And these days I had plenty to think about.

I had been there about an hour, leaning my back against the

rough tree trunk and remembering the conversation in Mr. Soot-er's office, when I heard the voices. They weren't loud. In fact, they were soft, but Aunt Bliss was right in saying I had good ears. Because I wasn't used to having company near the creek, I tensed a bit. Then I parted the long thin branches of the willow just enough to see. I suppose I should have let them know I was there, but I couldn't just leap out from the foliage. For one thing, Mom thought I was in the projection booth with Dad, mainly because I'd told her that, and for another, Memphis had his arm tight around her waist and his head bent over her. The cicadas had stopped, and it was fairly quiet, just a few crickets chirping and a barn owl hooting occasionally.

Memphis must have said something that amused Mom because she laughed, the sound rippling with the night breeze. Her auburn hair glowed ember-like in the moonlight; her face was pale and content.

He kissed her, his lips brushing her temple. "You're not afraid to go out." It was a statement, rather than a question.

"Not as long as I'm with you."

He pulled her close. "I'll hold on to you. That's easy enough to do."

"Charlie Memphis?"

"Hmm?"

"Who did you love before, when you were working in those other places?"

He was quiet for a moment. "I could say nobody, but that'd be a lie. There were three or four I took a liking to, but for one reason or another nothing came of it."

"Didn't you ever think of marrying before?"

"Once."

"Why didn't you?"

He pondered that for a moment. "Guess you might say she had expectations. Her daddy owned a big company in the center of town. Hell, her father owned the town. She got this idea of me working in this fancy office he had, sorting through stacks of paper and making some sense of them. I tried to tell her I wasn't built like that, but she thought if I loved her . . . well, finally it began to occur to me a man don't love the way a woman does. He just loves."

This remark struck me as some morsel of wisdom I might not find in my books, and I stored it away for further thought.

He pulled back and looked down at her. "You're not like that though, are you, darling? You don't expect much at all. What is it you want?"

"Nothing, only this."

"We can't go along like this forever. You know that, don't you?"

She nodded, but the tilt of her head was so slight I almost didn't catch it.

"Would you be willing, you and Callie Anne, to leave with me?" He said it quickly, in a husky voice, the way someone does when he doesn't expect the other person to agree.

It took her less than a heartbeat to answer. "Yes."

I sucked in a sharp breath, wondering what Mom was committing us to.

He turned and looked out over the field for such a long time that I began to wonder if he was counting the trees on the horizon. "Are you sure you know me well enough? What if I don't turn out to be the man you think I am?"

"I know all I need to." She lifted her chin. "I'll take my chances."

There was a change in the sky now, a few dark, woolly clouds moving in and blotting out the stars. The breeze picked up.

"I won't have you living the way I do," he said, "moving from town to town, never staying more than a few months. That ain't no kind of life."

"Callie Anne and I don't need much."

He laughed, with a touch of bitterness. "I said something like that once to a judge when he was giving the divorce to my parents. Took me and my brother out on the back porch of the courthouse, gave us some hard candy and asked who we wanted to live with."

He didn't say anything for a minute or so. Mom waited, not pushing him.

"I told him we wanted to be with our pa, since Ma left us behind. The judge said she wanted to take us when she went away but couldn't, because of her financial situation, her money. I told him, 'Chet and me don't eat much.' The judge just smiled. So we went with our pa, not knowing he didn't really want us either. He was just getting back at her."

My mother gripped Memphis's wrists and pulled his arms tight against her, as though to remind him that was another time.

He kept his gaze on the short, bushy trees in the distance. "All of them are gone now—Ma and Pa, Chet too," he said, without any real expression in his voice. "I don't even know what happened to my brother Cal, who went with my ma."

I thought about my dream of meeting his mother and felt an unreasonable disappointment.

He looked down at Mom. "Did I ever mention I tried to enlist in the navy with Chet? They wouldn't take me on account of I couldn't make out the colored signal flags. Chet got shipped out of Pearl Harbor the day before it was bombed. I once told him that just went to show how lucky he was." He absentmindedly stroked her back. "Never did have any real family but him."

She burrowed deeper against his shoulder.

His mind was still somewhere else though. "It's been a long time since I had anybody to look after. I'm not used to it."

She gazed up at him. "Callie Anne and I don't need much, Charlie Memphis," she said again.

"We'll get married, Teal," he said. "After we leave, you can get a divorce and we'll marry. We'll have a real family with a house. I won't have you living hand to mouth. I'll figure out a way. . . ."

He kissed her hard then, slipping his hand around her waist and pulling her against him. She arched her back, allowing him to unbutton the top of her sundress and push the straps off her shoulders. He kissed her eyelids, the curve of her shoulders and the hollow at her throat. He moved his lips slowly across the pale skin that swelled gently above her breasts and leaned into the shadow between them. Her brassiere gleamed white in the moonlight.

She murmured his name, her head thrown back and her hair tumbling loose from its combs.

I turned away. I didn't want to see this. Even at that moment, I realized it would be an image I would always keep in my mind, Memphis kissing my mother this way. I crept from under the willow bush, on the opposite side of where they were standing, and so they wouldn't catch sight of me, I inched over the pasture on my belly, barely aware of the hard dry grass that pricked my skin. Halfway across the field, I stood and ran. When I reached the drive-in fence, I sat down hard and leaned against it, drawing in several deep breaths. I decided right then I was learning more about love and sex and everything else in life than I had ever wanted to know, and it was all much more complicated and scary than I had expected.

As for Memphis, I realized he'd already figured out a way to get the money he needed, and it was one that would put him in jail and break my mother's heart.

Mr. Sooter didn't fire Memphis the next day like I thought he might. He came out to the drive-in and inspected the well drilling. By that time, the northwest corner of the drive-in, the area behind the screen, looked pockmarked. That incessant *ker-plunkada-plunkada* was still going on, and I heard Harold tell him and Dad they'd be hitting water anytime, no question about it. They'd finally decided to stay in one spot, and they had drilled down three hundred and ten feet.

I saw Mr. Sooter corner Memphis alone, but from their expressions, it didn't appear as though they were discussing any missing twenty dollars. At one point, Mr. Sooter gave the top of Memphis's hard-muscled arm a quick light jab. They both laughed heartily, with Mr. Sooter's great bulk quivering like molded Jell-O. If Dad was watching from the concessions building, he probably didn't appreciate them being so chummy.

I followed Memphis around for a while, trying to figure out if he had really stolen that money. That twenty dollars represented more than his honesty. To me, it represented the kind of man he was, and I wanted to believe he was innocent. I could understand how, under certain circumstances, a good man might murder—after all, I'd seen it a lot of times on the big screen—but I couldn't understand how he could steal twenty dollars from people he knew. Memphis, who was standing at the snack bar, must have felt my gaze on him because he glanced over and winked at me. I quickly looked away.

At supper, I was so nervous I couldn't eat. Of course, that made Mom all upset and she wouldn't let me leave until she took my temperature, poking the familiar glass thermometer under my tongue. Finally, I slipped away to the willow grove, hoping a little quiet might straighten out my thinking. I laid my head against the cool bumpy root that jutted from the ground and gazed up at the arched branches and pointy leaves. Aunt Bliss had to be wrong. How could a tree hurt anyone, unless it toppled over and smashed a person's skull?

After pondering Memphis and the missing money for almost an hour, the answer came to me. I could easily find out if he had it. The weight of the day lifted, and through streaks of green willow, I watched the spent sun tumble into the Eggerts' dry pasture.

Chapter Twenty

Frick and Son Drilling hit water at three hundred and eighty-four feet, while Dad and Memphis watched from the shade of the concessions building. It was ten in the morning and the day was already a scorcher.

Memphis said the only good thing about this operation was they'd managed to avoid breaking the pipe at three hundred and eighty feet. "At least Sooter got a hell of a deal on the price. How'd he wangle that?"

Dad hesitated, and his gaze shifted uneasily toward Harold and Poke. "He promised them they could drill the wells for his next two outdoor theaters."

Memphis stuck his thumbs in his pockets. "When's that going to happen?"

My father threw his cigarette on the ground and squashed it into the dirt with his shoe. "It won't. What these morons don't know is that Sooter doesn't plan to build any more drive-ins. Says they're dying out. The next theater he builds will be a hard-top."

Memphis took off his cowboy hat and ran a hand through his damp hair. "I don't suppose Frick had enough sense to get Sooter to commit to the deal in writing."

197

Dad snorted.

They watched the drilling operation for several moments without speaking.

Memphis nodded toward Harold. "You gonna tell him?"

"Shit, no, and you better not say a word either."

Memphis didn't answer.

Dad squinted at him. "Makes no difference if you like it or not. If they don't know how business works, it's not Sooter's fault—or mine."

Memphis brushed the dust off his hat, pinched the fold in the crown and set it back on his head. "Well, Claude, it doesn't seem quite right engaging in a battle of wits when the enemy is unarmed."

Without the least bit of hurry, he adjusted his hat and strode off.

You'd think finding water would have been the end of it, but, no, it took them another several days to install a pump, get it working and hook everything up to the water main. I guess Memphis felt sorry for Harold and Poke because he helped them, and after that he wasn't so friendly toward Mr. Sooter. Maybe it was going to be easier on his conscience stealing money from the drive-in now. My heart dropped a few inches at the thought. By the time Frick and Son Drilling left, we were all glad to see them go. Memphis made a wood cover for the old well and nailed it on.

I had to wait until Dad and Memphis went into town together before I could try my plan. I was filling a glass with water and enjoying the strong spurt from the faucet when Dad walked into the kitchen. "Get ready. We're leaving in ten minutes."

"I thought I'd stay here and finish this book I've been reading." I raised the jelly glass to my lips and took a hearty sip, eyeing him over the rim.

He looked me up and down. Being stuck out here, I loved to go into town, and he knew it.

I set the glass upside down on the dish drainer. "It's a book about turtles. Tells what they like to eat, where they hide out, all kinds of information."

He rummaged around in a cabinet drawer, pushing aside pencils and old keys, coming up with the fountain pen he was looking for. He tucked it into his breast pocket.

Trying to keep my voice casual, I asked, "Memphis going with you, then?"

He eyed me suspiciously. "Yeah. And you don't want to ride along, huh?"

I set the jelly glass on the counter. "Not today."

He didn't say any more, but I suspected he didn't believe me. He knew I was up to something. He got the grocery list from Mom, who was in the bedroom folding laundry, and a minute later, he was limping out the door, the list stuffed in his pocket. I was standing at the kitchen window, waiting for him to drive off when Mom came in.

She glanced at me. "You're not going into town with your father?"

I shook my head. "Don't feel like it."

She smiled agreeably, took her writing materials from the shelf and sat at the table. That was the difference between my parents. I could have told her I was taking off for the moon and she would have believed me.

Dad and Memphis climbed into the pickup, and it pulled away, leaving behind a cloud of gray dust. Just as I started toward the door, Mom lifted her head from her papers. "Sweetheart, could you listen to something I've written and tell me what you think?"

I felt a small flash of panic. On Thursdays, Dad didn't stay in town very long. I wanted to get in and out of Memphis's room as quickly as possible, but Mom's face was so eager, so glowing, I couldn't refuse her. "Okay, sure."

She straightened her shoulders, cleared her throat and held up her notebook. "Give your breads and cakes a whirl," she said in a careful, exaggerated tone. "Reach into the cupboard for the Clabber Girl." She laid it down and, folding her hands together, looked at me expectantly.

"Well, gosh." I picked through my brain, trying to find something encouraging to say. "I like the part about giving breads and cakes a whirl."

"Uh-huh." She waited.

"But I think the rest of it sounds like the salt jingle."

She stared dejectedly at the scribbled lines. "I know. It's awful." Her gaze drifted off. "I just can't keep my mind on my writing lately," she murmured almost to herself. Then apparently remembering I was there, she lowered her eyes and turned a faint pink.

I shuffled my feet. "Uh . . ."

She gathered her papers together and tucked them back into her writing folder. "Thanks, sweetheart. You can run along now but I want you back in an hour or so to set the table."

I sprinted out the door, letting it bang twice behind me, and crossed the field to the concessions building. I knew the doors there would be locked, but I was prepared for that. In addition to his own key and Memphis's, Dad kept one in his top bureau drawer. I'd heard him tell Mom it was a spare, although Dad never lost anything.

The Starlite Drive-in

At the rear exit, I glanced around, mostly out of guilty nervousness. Hardly anyone ever came to the drive-in in the morning. The place was lazily peaceful, only the trill of a bird and the rattle of a truck on the nearby highway breaking the silence as I dug the key from my pocket and unlocked the door.

I climbed the steps to Memphis's room, my footsteps echoing through the eerily quiet stairwell. At the top of the landing, I hesitated before the closed door, suddenly realizing that what I was about to do was wrong, even worse than eavesdropping on other people's conversations. But I didn't plan to take anything. In fact, all I wanted was to make sure something wasn't there. That couldn't be so awful.

I turned the glass knob and the door swung open. Although the room still smelled musty, it didn't seem quite as grim as before. He had cleaned the windows, letting in more light, and swept the floor with a frayed broom that was still propped in the corner. With his possessions scattered around, the place at least looked lived in. The wooden table was pushed against the wall now and held a carton of Lucky Strikes, a half dozen cans of food and a small tin marked chili powder. There was a magazine opened to a picture of a sleek maroon Chevrolet. A square-jawed man with a proud grin patted the fender, while his smiling wife and their two freshly scrubbed children looked on. I wondered if Memphis was a Chevrolet man. That would be another reason for my father to dislike him.

Memphis had stacked his clean clothes in an apple crate and simply tossed the dirty ones on the floor. My mom would never have allowed that. His duffel bag lay in the corner, but I went to the mattress first because, in books and movies, that's where people always hide their money. I lifted the feather-filled, blue-striped ticking and ran my hand under it. No sign of the loot, but I did catch my finger on a sharp spring. I waited for it to stop bleeding, then patted the thin mattress and bedroll back into shape. Stepping over to the apple crate, I flipped through the jeans and shirts. I even checked all the pockets but came up empty.

The duffel bag leered at me now like a giant green toad. It was one thing poking into belongings that were right out there for anyone to see, but it was another, delving into something closed up.

I swallowed hard and crouched down. Unfolding the loose flap that covered the top, I reached my hand deep inside, latched onto something stiff and leathery and pulled it out. It was a small curved satchel with a strap that fastened on one side, a perfect container for hiding cash. But when I opened it, it held only a straight razor, a shaving brush, Lava soap, a can of tooth powder, a toothbrush and a comb. Sticking my hand into the duffel again, I dragged out a long-sleeved flannel shirt, wool socks, and a metal belt buckle embossed with a lariat before I ran into what felt like a heavy wool jacket. Crawling almost halfway into the bag, I rummaged around, finally hitting upon a square container. I withdrew my head, along with a cigar box that was tied with a black velvet ribbon.

If the money was going to be anywhere, it would be in here. I just had that feeling.

I untied the ribbon and lifted the lid. Inside were two photographs, one with a sharp-featured older man and a pair of scrawny boys holding fishing poles and grinning at the camera. The kids were shirtless and barefoot, wearing only bib overalls. In the next picture, which had been taken in a booth with one of those coin-operated photographic machines, the boys were older, arms thrown over each other's shoulders. Anyone could have seen the resemblance, although the younger brother had a longer nose and lighter hair.

Between the pictures was a yellowed newspaper clipping no bigger than the size of a matchbook.

SEATTLE—A twenty-eight-year-old man was beaten last night outside a tavern in Seattle's waterfront district. He died two hours later at Harborview Hospital without regaining consciousness. He has been identified as John Michael Huston.

Police said Huston had been at the same tavern the night before when an altercation resulted in the knifing death of a sailor, Chester Lee Mathias. No one was taken into custody at that time. Now authorities are seeking the sailor's brother, Charles Mathias, for questioning in Huston's death.

That was all there was to it. No date, no indication of which newspaper it came from. I returned the clipping to its place between the photos and picked up a military dog tag that was lying inscription side down. The name on it was Chester Lee Mathias. I dropped the tag back into the cigar box and lifted out an envelope that was addressed in a flowery script to "Charlie" and smelled faintly of lavender. I held it for a moment, debating.

As I began to slip out the pages, I heard the noise, the unmistakable clunk of the heavy exterior door, with the echo resounding through the stairwell. I sat straight up.

There was a brief, terrible silence. Then the steps began, without haste, the familiar thud of heel against wood. Cowboy boots. Frozen, I stared at the open door. He was supposed to be with Dad in Jessup. They were to be gone at least two hours.

If I hadn't panicked, I might have hidden under the bed or behind the door. But I stayed where I was, on the floor surrounded by his belongings. I wondered what he'd do when he saw me. I could already see the disappointment on his face, or, worse yet, the anger.

I could have sworn it took an hour for those boots to climb the stairs. In the meantime, I died at least twice.

He stopped at the landing and poked his head in the room. His freckles and the thin white scar on his chin disappeared into a golden tan, but his serene eyes stood out, bluer than ever. "Hi, Callie Anne."

I tried breathing again. "Hi, Virgil."

He gestured toward the stairwell. "The door was unlocked."

I nodded.

He glanced around, first at the signs of plunder, then at me. "This is Memphis's room, isn't it?"

"Uh-huh."

"What are you doing in here?"

My first instinct was to invent a story. But I couldn't. I simply couldn't fib to the slightly prominent Adam's apple or the turned-up nose that might cause him to drown if he lay down in the rain. And heaven forbid that I should try to gaze into those incredible lake-blue eyes and tell a lie.

"I'm trying to find out if Memphis took some money."

He curved his perfect mouth into a frown. "He wouldn't do that."

I had the sudden urge to cry and blubber it all out, but instead I drew an uneven breath and stood. Surprised at how wobbly my legs were, I sank onto Memphis's bed. "I heard Dad tell Mr. Sooter that some of the box-office money was missing and the only person who could have taken it was Memphis." I repeated word for word as much of the conversation as I could recall. My relief was tremendous. I felt as though I were shifting this burden, ever so briefly, to Virgil.

He listened carefully, seeming to turn it over in his mind but not registering the shock or concern I expected. "Your dad's real careful about the money, Callie Anne. I can't imagine him saying Memphis stole it if he didn't, but I can't imagine Memphis taking it either." There was a long pause. "I just don't think he's that kind of man."

"But I found something. Look at this." I still had the cigar box in my hand. I removed the newspaper clipping from between the two photos and held it out for Virgil to see.

He read it and shrugged. "So?"

"So-o, don't you wonder who Charles Mathias is or who killed John Michael Huston?"

"No."

"Don't you see? This could mean Memphis is Charles Mathias. You said he told you he murdered somebody."

"I did not. He said he was in a fight where someone was killed."

I picked up the dog tag and held it out, the chain draping across my fingers. "Well, look at this."

His gaze remained on me. "Callie Anne, you're poking into somebody else's private belongings. What you're doing is plain wrong."

I looked down at my feet, suddenly feeling pretty low.

He surveyed the scattered clothes, the toiletries case, the open cigar box. "You didn't find it, did you?"

"What?"

"The money."

I shook my head.

"I didn't think so. Where is Memphis?"

"He's in town with Dad. For a minute, I was afraid you might be him, that he might have returned for some reason." I tilted my head, a question of my own forming. "Virgil, why'd you come up here?"

His eyes seemed to fade a shade or two. He sat down next to me on the bed and rested his rawboned hands on his thighs. He was close enough to touch but not too close. "My dad sent me over. He said I have to quit working here right away."

I felt my insides sink. "Why?"

"To help with the haying. It starts tomorrow, and he's not going to let me get out of it."

"Can't you change his mind? Tell him it's just for a few more weeks, until the drive-in closes."

"I tried. Believe me, I tried real hard. We had a big fight about it last night. He said I'd better make up my mind the farm comes first."

"Well, doesn't he bring in men to do the work?"

"Yeah, but everybody in the family has to help too. Even my sisters and my mom have to cook food for the men."

I vaguely remembered Virgil's sisters, all tall, blond and stick-skinny like he was. It seemed to me the oldest one was already married and had a baby.

His shoulders slumped. "I hate farming, Callie Anne. I hate cows and hogs and manure and hay. Hay makes me sneeze. Most of all, I hate hogs though."

"I like horses."

"Well, yeah, I like horses too. I rode over here on Buck."

"You did?" I realized that's why I hadn't heard him outside. He hadn't driven the flatbed Ford that sounded like a metal pan rattling down the highway. The truck was probably half the reason why my father had hired him. Anyone who drove a Ford, no matter what its condition, had to be honest and hardworking. "Why did you ride Buck?"

"Dad says I can't drive again until I make up my mind about my responsibility."

There was that word again, the one adults used like a hammer. "Where's your sense of responsibility?" Aunt Bliss had asked Mom, stringing the word out, stressing each part of it. "What kind of man is it who can't even take responsibility for his own family," Dad had muttered, making it sound as though the word itself had weight.

We were both quiet for a moment, pondering the burden and the unfairness of it all. A bug, not an ant or a roach but something more like a beetle, crawled through a splash of sunlight on the wooden floor. We both watched it.

"I wish I had a brother my dad could turn into a farmer," Virgil said. "Then maybe he'd forget about me."

"What would you do if you could do anything you wanted?"

"That's easy. I'd build airplanes." His eyes brightened. "Pretty soon they'll have ones that can fly fifteen hundred miles an hour. Just imagine that. Fifteen hundred miles an hour."

"Gosh," I said. I had no understanding whatsoever of that speed. "Is there a place around here where you can build planes?"

"No, I'd have to go to California. That's where the biggest aircraft companies are. Of course, there's Boeing in Seattle, Washington, but Memphis says the weather's not so good there. He says in California it's summer all the time. They don't have snow, just palm trees and cactus and . . ."

His eyes blazed with passion. Watching him drift away from me, I burst into tears.

"Callie Anne, what's wrong?"

I didn't answer, just sobbed into the crook of my arm. Maybe it was the strain of worrying about Mom and Memphis and Dad or maybe it was my newfound loneliness, but for some reason I couldn't stop.

"Why're you crying?"

I could feel my whole body shaking like a wringer washing machine. Lifting my head, I hiccuped, "I don't . . . you . . . away."

He put his face close to mine, so close I could feel his breath on my cheek. "What?"

I swallowed hard. "I don't want you to go away."

He scooted closer and looped his arm around me, and I felt the warmth of his hand through my thin blouse. "I don't want to leave either, Callie Anne . . ."

"But you're going to California." I wiped my wrist across my nose. "You said so."

"That's not for a long time. I have two years of high school left and then I have to go to college. Memphis said you need a university degree if you want to work at those places. I could go to Purdue maybe and . . ."

I sat up straight. "Well, I'm not going to stay here, you know. I won't live in this drive-in forever—just cleaning and washing clothes and ironing, like Mom, or doing the same job day after day, like Dad. I don't want responsibilities. I'm going to do something exciting. I'll be a . . . a writer." I'd never thought before about what I wanted to do, but now it all seemed to fall exactly into place.

Of course, I could be a writer. I was good in English, a straight A student. I could spell and diagram sentences better than anyone else in my class. Visions of Louisa May Alcott and Mark Twain bobbed in my head. Why not? I took off my glasses and wiped the leftover tears with the edge of my blouse. "Yup, that's what

I'm going to do. A writer can travel anywhere. I could go to California if I want to."

Feeling his warm breath on my temple, I turned to gaze nearsightedly at him. His arm now loosely embraced my shoulder.

"You look pretty when your eyes are like that," he said.

I dropped my glasses on the bed. At least I think that's where they turned up later.

He reached down and softly, ever so softly, pressed his lips to mine. I noted with vague surprise that we didn't bump noses. In fact, I would never have guessed that it would work as well as it did. In time I felt only the touch of his mouth. The rest of my body, including a good part of my brain, floated away.

No boy had ever kissed me before, except in third grade when a dopey kid named Ellsworth Parsons had dropped a valentine on my desk, pecked me on the cheek and run away. I didn't think that counted.

I don't know how long the kiss lasted. Forever, I guess.

By the time he pulled back, I felt like cinnamon jelly, all tingly on the inside and quivering on the outside. I thought about Memphis kissing Mom, but now that it was happening to me, it felt different, not at all scary or wrong. Just as I realized I wanted Virgil to kiss me again, he rose to his feet. "We'd better clean this up before your dad and Memphis come back."

My dad? Memphis? I'd forgotten all about them.

He knelt down beside the duffel bag. "Do you think you can remember how all this went in?"

I nodded. I was confused. Is that what you were supposed to do? You kissed somebody and then pretended it hadn't happened? Maybe he didn't like it. Maybe I hadn't done it right. I felt bewildered and embarrassed.

I knelt down beside him. In the streak of light from the window, I could see the downy golden hair on his cheek. I desperately wanted to lean over and touch my lips to it, but I couldn't. A nice girl wouldn't do that, and above all I wanted him to think I was nice. We stuffed Memphis's possessions back into the green canvas bag and tidied up. Then he turned and smiled at me, and my disappointment vanished. I felt like a million bucks.

Dreamily, I glanced around the room. As far as I could recall, it looked the way it had when I came in. We walked down the narrow stairs, our hips bumping against each other every few steps.

I sighed. "I still don't know if Memphis took the money. He could have hidden it somewhere else."

At the bottom of the stairs, Virgil opened the door for me. "You don't have to know. As my mom would say, Memphis is a big fellow. He can take care of himself."

Maybe so, but who would take care of my mother?

After I locked the door, we headed across the drive-in field toward Buck, who was tethered to a speaker pole in a shady area. Virgil untied him, and we walked slowly toward the theater entrance. Almost without thinking, I brushed my hand lightly across Virgil's and he grabbed hold of it. We were standing halfway between the concessions building and the box office, staring wordlessly into each other's eyes, when Dad's Ford pulled in. We jumped apart.

Dad parked the truck, stepped out and considered us for a few moments without speaking. I couldn't tell what he was thinking.

Virgil stuffed his hands in his blue-jean pockets and walked over to him. "Mr. Benton, I was wondering if I could talk with you." He sounded stiff and nervous. He probably thought this was just about as bad as dealing with his father. He trailed Dad into the concessions building, his shoulders bent under the weight of what he had to tell him.

The Starlite Drive-in

Memphis was sliding a bucket out of the back of the pickup, but he'd been watching us, a smile working the corners of his mouth. I might have stared longer at him, trying to figure out what secrets he was hiding, but I had my own I didn't want to reveal. I don't know which secret I was more concerned about, raiding his room or kissing Virgil, but I was sure both were branded on my forehead.

I gestured toward the house. "Have to help Mom."

He nodded, but I noticed the expression of knowing amusement remained on his face.

I didn't go help Mom. I ducked around the back of the house and took off for the willow grove. I ran all the way to the creek. Lightheaded and out of breath, I parted the tree's long branches, dropped onto the dry matted leaves and leaned against the trunk.

I would never be the same. Virgil had kissed me.

I was a new person, not a kid anymore. No one had said it was like this, not even Betty Jo Babcock. The pure weightlessness I felt took me higher than any helium balloon could.

No shadows fell anywhere. The willow fronds created a hazy green kaleidoscope against the dazzling sun. I stared straight at the bright patterns, marveling at their beauty, at the beauty of everything. They floated, changed formation as I shifted slightly to the right.

I blinked twice. The foliage was blurry, fuzzier than it should have been. I shot straight up. My glasses! Oh, no, where were my glasses?

In my panic, I wondered whether I could have left them on the counter in the concessions building. Or whether they might have fallen in the grass as I ran across the pasture. But I knew with growing despair exactly where they were. I saw my glasses in the rumpled folds of Memphis's bedroll, just waiting for him to find them. My mind raced. Maybe I could get to them first. I saw myself creeping up the stairs, slipping into his room, hiding behind the door.

It was no use, of course. I couldn't sneak in there now without having him or my father catch me, and I couldn't ask him for them.

The memory of Virgil's kiss, delicate as mist, scattered in the gentle breeze. My stomach churned. My future spread out before me in all its bleakness. At dinner, Dad would want to know where they were. He'd say that's what he got for buying me expensive glasses, only for me to lose them. Memphis probably wouldn't return them until he came to our house in the evening. When he told Mom where he'd found them, she'd be disappointed. "What were you doing in his room?" she'd ask. They'd both stare at me with accusing eyes.

By then, having my glasses back, I'd be able to see them with perfect clarity.

My heart sank almost to my toes. Lacking the energy to run, I plodded through the dreary pasture, kicking dried-up cow pies, avoiding fresh ones, not bothering to lift my gaze.

Halfway across, I glanced up.

He was striding toward me at an even pace. Something in his hand caught the sunlight and reflected it. For a moment, he seemed to be carrying a tiny ball of light.

I stopped, unsure, as possibilities swirled around in my head. He would want to know what I'd been doing in his room, and I considered what I might say. Maybe I'd ask him questions of my own. Who was Charles Mathias and what did he have to do with

Charlie Memphis? Just maybe, I'd ask him that. But he reached me before I had time to make up my mind.

Giving me a long, searching look, he opened his mouth to speak. Then he seemed to think better of it. The tiny flecks of silver in the blue frames glittered and danced. He solemnly handed me the glasses and I put them on.

Before I could even say thank you, he turned and headed back toward the drive-in. After watching him disappear around the corner of the high board fence, I took off. I raced across the pasture until I ran out of fields and had to use the road. With my head down, I kept going until my face burned and my throat went dry.

It took me a full hour to walk back, and on the way I thought about how a short time before, still buoyed by Virgil's kiss, I had felt as weightless as a helium balloon. I came to an important realization: The higher a balloon rises, the farther it falls.

Chapter Twenty-one

$\mathcal{I}$ had the uneasy feeling I'd run into Mom and Memphis sometime, that I'd be out roaming and accidentally come face-to-face with them. And that's just what happened.

They were walking along White River Road, keeping to the shoulder although it wasn't well traveled. The sky was streaked pink and blue, setting itself up for a spectacular sunset, and I could smell clover drifting from somewhere. Although they weren't holding hands or kissing, my first instinct was to bolt into the nearby cornfield. But it was too late for that. They had already seen me.

Memphis waved, without a trace of embarrassment. "Hey there, pardner."

I reluctantly waved back.

Mom's gaze was lowered. I looked around, feeling the goose bumps rise on my arms. If I could come upon them like this, so could someone else. My father was at the drive-in, of course. The cars would be lining up on the gravel mounds now, row after row of switched-off headlights pointed at the screen. Once the movie started, he had to change the reel every twenty minutes. But what if . . . ? I hated what ifs.

Memphis gestured toward the barricaded cutoff that led to the

214

White River bridge. "We're going down that road a piece. Want to come with us?"

My jaw fell open in astonishment. I couldn't believe my mother would walk that way. There wasn't much danger of anyone seeing them. That section of road was no longer used, now that a new and better one linked the state route with Mechanicsburg. But her last visit to the old wooden bridge a quarter mile in that direction stuck in my mind like a splinter of glass.

I stared at her. "Mom?"

She brushed a strand of hair back from her face, which had taken on the damp sheen of perspiration, and looked at me. "It's all right. I want to."

"You do?"

She straightened her shoulders and nodded, but I saw the flash of uncertainty there. Memphis glanced from me to her as though he were trying to understand the foreign language we were speaking. Although I felt uncomfortable in their presence, I knew I had to accompany them. I stepped around the barricade of crossed white boards.

The road was narrow and rutted, with broken jags of asphalt poking up in places. Mom's gaze flitted nervously on the path ahead. When a tiny brown field mouse darted from the weeds and skittered back, she jumped. I'd never known her to be afraid of mice before. Once I'd even caught her feeding one that had found its way into our kitchen.

Memphis reached for her quavering hand but must have thought better of it because he pulled back. "You okay?" he asked.

She nodded.

"You don't have to do this. We don't have to come here tonight." His mouth was close to her ear, his tone more gentle than I'd imagined a man's could be.

She shook her head and kept going, hugging herself so tight even her shadow appeared to diminish.

Just beyond the curve, I heard the river's low steady rush and saw the plank bridge that arched over its banks. I'd been here hundreds of times before. The leaves of two big sprawling maples filtered the angled rays of sunlight. I glanced at Mom. Her eyes had the glazed look of a bird that's hit a window, but she didn't turn back.

I could see the concern in Memphis's face. He was protecting her now, just as I once had, ready to catch her if she toppled. I wondered if they even remembered I was there. Sunk in my resentment, I let them walk ahead.

She stopped at the very edge of the bridge. The planks were old and dry, thousands of splintered cracks running through the wood like dark threads. "Here," she whispered, her breathing deep and fast. "This is it."

He turned to her. "What happened here?" His voice was soft as cotton.

She locked her hands on to her wrists. "I couldn't walk across that bridge."

"You won't ever have to walk across it if you don't want to. There are other ways."

"Two boys from her school were fishing there, hanging their poles over the side. I made it to the edge of the bridge, but I couldn't go any farther. I couldn't move." She blinked the faraway stare from her eyes. Her voice grew low and husky, close to tears. "I scared and embarrassed her. I know I did."

"Callie Anne?" he asked.

"Uh-huh. She was such a little thing then."

But I hadn't been. I had been old enough to realize my mother

216

was breaking apart and there was no one but me to hold her together. I had tried to lead her away, but she had whimpered and
knotted her hands around my neck. When I had attempted to pry
them apart, they had been as stiff and unyielding as tree roots.
The Moen twins had gawked at my mother, as though she were
a curiosity at one of those sideshows that sometimes came to town,
and I had yelled at them to mind their own business.

Memphis waited for her to stop shaking.

"It's over," he said quietly, taking her hand. He put his other
hand on her shoulder, not exactly hugging her but holding her a
short distance from him, the way he might if they were dancing.

I turned away. It was obvious they didn't need me. I decided
I might as well go on home, where I could read a book or talk to
my turtle if I wanted some real company. As I stepped onto the
road, I heard a twig snap behind me, a sound as sharp as a bone
cracking.

I whirled around. In a nearby clearing stood a man. We formed
a triangle: My mother in Memphis's arms, the intruder, and I. A
single shaft of light caught me in the eyes so that I couldn't see his
face. I moved a few feet sideways and breathed again.

It was Billy. Only Billy.

Then I realized he was staring at Mom and Memphis in fish-
eyed astonishment. It was as if a curtain in his head had briefly
parted so that some form of understanding now mingled with his
craziness.

I wanted to run up to him and say, "They're just talking, Billy.
Not dancing. They couldn't be dancing. You don't hear any
music, do you?"

But how did I know what music played in Billy's head?

He opened his mouth. At first, only a hoarse rattle clawed its

217

way from his throat. His chest rose and fell with deep breaths. Then a howl of anguish split the air, a wail so deep and sorrowful it might have come from a dying animal.

Mom spun around, her eyes wide with alarm. "Oh, no. Billy?" She stepped toward him, her arms outstretched like a mother's. "No, don't, Billy, it's okay."

Then she seemed to realize she was leaving the safety of Memphis's arms, and she retreated. Billy watched her for one frozen moment, then twisted around and flung his arms across his head the way men do in the movies when bombs drop from the sky. He lurched toward the road, breathing hard.

I ran after him, my mother's worried voice fading behind me.

The sun had melted into the horizon, leaving a luminous pink glow. He hurried along the old, unused highway, his head bent, his pace twice as fast as usual. His shoulders shook either from sobs or rage. I couldn't see his face, so I didn't know which.

At the northern edge of the Morris farm, he cut in at a right angle and followed a rutted grass and dirt roadway that was used more by tractors and flatbed hay trucks than by automobiles. Occasionally, he made a sort of whimpering sound, but he never looked back. After a while, I gave up bothering to hide. I just stayed about fifty feet behind him.

A good mile later, we came to the railroad tracks. The moon was up now, not full, but bright enough to see Billy's bony hunched figure plodding between the rails. Every once in a while, heat lightning ripped the skyline, giving me an eerie feeling. I didn't really know why I was following Billy. I guess I thought someone should look after him. In his condition, I wasn't sure what he'd do.

What he did was walk, his unlaced shoes slapping against the wooden railroad ties. Fist-sized rocks that lay between the tracks made rough going for my short legs. I tried stepping from one tie to another, but after a while, my thighs began to ache and I wished he would turn back. I finally tried balancing on the rail the way a tightrope walker would.

We traveled some distance before I realized I didn't recognize the farms anymore. We heard just about every kind of nightlife there was, from coyotes howling to crickets sawing, but not a single train came by.

As we passed some open farmland, a dog charged from the shadows. Instead of targeting Billy the way you'd think he would have, he hurtled through the air like some blurry, snarling hulk and knocked me down flat. When I looked up, I was staring into a jawful of white teeth as big and pointy as a row of icicles. I blinked. When I opened my eyes again, that crazy dog was licking my face and pawing my chest.

"Go away," I hissed, swatting at the slobbering muzzle. "Stop it. Get off me."

Then he was lifted from my chest as easily as if he'd been a fallen leaf, and I was staring into Billy's sorrowful face.

I scrambled to my feet and brushed the grit off my hands. "That dog shouldn't be running loose. He's dangerous."

The mutt leaned against Billy's leg and licked his wrist. Billy didn't even bother pushing him away.

I rubbed my backside. "I suppose you're wondering what I happened to be doing . . ."

Billy turned around and continued walking down the tracks.

The dog, one of those yellow short-haired types, gazed up at me, his mouth slick with drool, his dark eyes gleaming in the moonlight.

"What are you staring at?" I said.

I took out after Billy again. I trailed him and the dog trailed me, so that in the moonlight we must have looked like some ghostly parade with a head spook who occasionally wept and sniffled.

We'd trekked another melancholy mile or so when Billy suddenly stopped. He peered into the darkness, seeing something I couldn't see. This area was much like the rest, a nearby grove of saplings, fields that smelled of alfalfa, a white farmhouse with darkened windows and a barn in the distance. I couldn't tell what made this particular spot special.

Billy drifted toward the trees. The dog looked at me as if he half expected me to know why we were stopping. I shrugged, jumped off the tracks and flopped down into a patch of grass. The dog crouched beside me, gazing up at me with his shiny black eyes and swishing his tail from side to side like a yellow whisk broom. Billy reappeared from the shadows with an armful of broken tree branches. He began to arrange them tepee-fashion between the rails.

I sat up. "Uh, Billy. . . ?"

He didn't even glance at me. He vanished into the shadows again and returned a few minutes later with some straw, which he added to the tepee. The three-quarter moon hovered over his shoulder like a shiny white egg.

I wiped the perspiration from my forehead and laughed uneasily. "A little warm for a fire, don't you think? Besides, everything around here's so dry . . ."

He produced a lighter from his pocket and flipped it open.

I stiffened. "Gosh, Billy, could we talk about this?"

He didn't answer.

I heard the scraping sound of metal on flint. A few yellow sparks shot out. The dog sank closer to the ground, flattened his ears and whined.

I felt my mouth go dry. "My mom didn't mean to hurt your feelings. Why, if you came to our back door tomorrow, I'll bet she'd . . ."

Again, I saw a streak of sparks. This time a thin blue flame flicked out and caught the straw and the withered leaves on the tree branches.

I sprang to my feet. "Oh, jeez, Billy. Oh, jeez."

The yellow dog leaped up, barked several times, ran back along the railroad tracks in the direction we'd just come from and barked some more. A few seconds later I heard what he had sensed, the low distant rumble of the train. I thought about jumping onto the tracks and scattering the kindling, but it was too late for that. The flames flared several feet in the air. I stood alongside the rails, looking for Billy. He had disappeared. The engine's enormous round light rolled along the tracks, glowing whiter than the moon. The wheels bore steadily down on me, clacking rhythmically. The whistle moaned, wild and mournful, urging me to do something, but I couldn't think what.

With the hot smells of the train and the smoke from the bonfire stinging my nose, I stood there for one nerve-racking second. When it came within a boxcar length, the train ground to a screaming, clattering halt, spitting up rocks and black gritty soot. I dove off the side of the tracks and tumbled into the weeds. I thought the dog was behind me, but I wasn't watching out for him.

I got up and ran, then fell again and pressed myself flat against the prickly grass. When I heard the voices, I lifted my head just enough to see what was happening. Two men dressed in gray-striped railroad overalls had hopped down from the engine. They stood in the bright glow of the single headlight, kicking out the fire with their heavy black boots.

"Goddamned kids," one of them growled.

He shaded his eyes with his hand and looked directly toward me. I buried my face in the dry weeds. They stomped around and cursed for several minutes, then climbed back on the long freight train. Eventually, it creaked, groaned and snaked back into the night.

Once it had gone, I stood up and looked around. There was no sign of Billy or the dog.

The next day I hiked back along the tracks looking for Billy. I couldn't find him, and the farmers along the way said they hadn't seen him either. I don't know why I bothered hunting him. In my heart I believed he had hopped that freight train and he was going to travel just as far as it would take him.

Chapter Twenty-two

Although Virgil was never far from my mind, I hadn't seen him in more than two weeks. Then, one Thursday evening, I wandered into the concessions building at a time when he had stopped by. The movie had been playing about twenty minutes, and Jerry and April, the teenagers working the snack bar, had temporarily run out of customers.

Jerry, who had teeth so large they reminded me of the slats in a picket fence, was refilling the straw holder and asking Virgil if he'd be coming to the softball game on Saturday afternoon. Virgil said he didn't think so.

April, one of the most popular girls in high school, tossed her long dark hair back, in what I thought was an overly dramatic gesture, and shimmied up to Virgil. She squeezed his biceps. "Goodness, is that your pitching arm?"

I couldn't help but roll my eyes.

Virgil blushed and inched away. April glided with him, her hand straying to his shirt, her red-painted fingernails toying with a button.

I coughed a little too loudly, then ended with a choking sound. They all turned.

I pointed to my throat. "Popcorn in it."

Virgil smiled in a way that made my heart trip over itself.

"Hi, Callie Anne," he said.

"Hi. I didn't hear . . . I mean, see your truck outside."

"I drove my brother-in-law's car."

Jerry laughed, showing his Bugs Bunny teeth, and slapped the lid back on the straw holder. "Hiding out so his dad can't find him."

Virgil frowned but didn't say anything.

"Did you come back to work?" I asked Virgil.

He shook his head. "Just visiting."

Jerry, whose slicked-back hair reeked of Brylcreem, rocked on his heels and eyed me as though I didn't belong here. "Looking for somebody, Callie Anne?"

I gave him a cold stare. "No."

Virgil took a step forward, closer to me. "I was hoping we could talk. . . ."

April shifted along with him as if stuck by chewing gum. She drew her rosebud mouth tighter. "Don't you have to run along, Callie Anne? It must be close to your bedtime."

For one brief moment, I saw red—her painted nails, her pouty lips, her blood flowing on the concrete floor. I may even have been lifting my fist when Virgil stepped between us.

"I want to talk to you for a minute," he said, guiding me toward the exit.

I glanced back over my shoulder and saw April's dark-chocolate eyes widen and blink several times. "But, Virgil," she said in a soft whine, "I thought you and me could go somewhere when the movie's over."

He hesitated. "Uh, well . . ."

I grabbed his arm and said in a low voice, "Come on. Let's get out of here."

He gave April an apologetic smile. "See you around maybe."

That was one of the things I disliked about him. He was unfailingly polite.

Just before we reached the exit, I heard Jerry bray, "Hey, Virg, ain't she a little young for you?"

Virgil held the door open and nudged me through it. "Don't mind them."

"Oh, they don't bother me." I tossed my head coolly, just the way Vivien Leigh would have, I thought.

I smacked right into a garbage can that fell over with a bang and a clatter, the lid dancing and reverberating for several seconds on the concrete pad next to the concessions building. As I collected popcorn bags, cups and paper that had scattered all over, I heard my dad's voice in my head. "Can't you take two steps without running into something?" I hoped Virgil couldn't see my burning face in the dim light.

Acting as though he hadn't noticed my clumsiness, he set the trash can upright and helped me pick up the litter. He talked the entire time about how Jerry was just one of those fellows who liked to tease.

We walked toward a Chevrolet that shone a gleaming two-tone white and celery-green under the canopy of light from the building's rear exit.

I gave a low whistle. "Somebody sure rubbed the dust off that car."

"My brother-in-law said I could drive it if I cleaned and waxed it."

I ran my hand over its glossy fender. "Is it true you're hiding out?"

He leaned his back against the passenger door and folded his arms across his chest. "Dad doesn't know I'm here."

"Would he mind if he knew?"

Virgil shrugged. "He believes farmers should go to bed when the sun goes down."

"And start working when it comes up?"

He nodded.

The excitement at the drive-in began when the sun set so it was difficult for me to think the way his dad did. It must have caused Virgil all kinds of problems when he was working at the theater until midnight or one in the morning.

I tilted my head up at him. "What did you want to talk about?"

He looked at me for a moment as though he wasn't sure what I meant, then seemed to remember. "I was wondering if your dad found the money."

I shook my head. "Mr. Sooter didn't fire Memphis, so I suppose he thinks someone else took it." I didn't say Dad might be lying in the first place because it didn't seem right to say that about my father.

In the semi-darkness I could see Virgil set his jaw. "Memphis wouldn't steal that money."

Aunt Bliss always said I had a stubborn streak so it was easy enough to recognize it in someone else. I leaned forward and said in a quiet voice that was intentionally sinister, "He killed a man, didn't he?"

Virgil shrugged. "I don't know."

"It was in that newspaper story. I don't see how you can deny it."

"The name in that story was someone else's."

"Yes, but the name on the dog tag in that cigar box matched the brother's."

"If Memphis did it," Virgil muttered, "I'll bet it was because he couldn't help it."

"Well, we don't know that, do we?" I wasn't going to allow him the last word.

For a few moments, we watched the insects swarm around the yellow light above the door, batting themselves into a frenzy. Virgil was right, of course. The more I thought about the possibility of its being self-defense, the better I felt about Memphis. I remembered Gary Cooper in *High Noon,* meeting the desperadoes one by one. But, in the movie in my head, Gary Cooper had Memphis's face, with Memphis's crooked smile. And he had plenty of reason to kill those outlaws. I didn't know what Virgil was thinking.

We could hear moms and dads and their little kids tromping toward the concessions building, their shoes crunching on the gravel, their flashlights seesawing through the darkness. It was part of the normal pattern of the drive-in evening. For the first half hour or so people stayed in their cars watching the movie, eating popcorn and drinking soda pop. But then the parade to the rest rooms started. As they passed the snack bar on the way back, they bought more soda pop and returned to their cars. About forty-five minutes later, the procession began all over again.

"How's your turtle?" Virgil asked.

"John Wayne? He's okay. I think he's getting better because he comes out of his shell more often and eats like an elephant. He's nuts about nightcrawlers. Yesterday he ate ten of them."

"Do you suppose turtles get stomachaches?"

I thought about it. "I don't know. It'd be hard to tell. I've never heard him groan, but he's hissed at me a few times."

"Hmm." Virgil tilted his head back and looked upward, inspecting the sky. The movie gave off too much light to see any but the brightest stars.

He was silent for a time, but I didn't mind. He wasn't one of those people who always had to be talking. After a while, I caught the reflection of the screen in his eyes and realized he was watching it over the corner of the concessions building. From where we stood, we could see most but not all of it.

I waved a hand toward it. "I've seen this picture six times. It's pretty good."

"I don't know anything about it. . . ." His voice trailed off with a strange wistfulness.

I knew how he felt. The kids who worked at the theater had the advantage of being the first in town to see a new movie. I suspect he missed the excitement that came along with it, and he no longer had the money to buy his way in.

"I can tell you about it," I said. "Ernest Borgnine plays a guy named Marty who . . ." I ran through the story to that point. "Right now, Marty's saying . . ." I recited the dialogue. Craning my neck, I tried to see the other actor's face, but he was just out of my view.

Virgil patted the car hood. "Hop up here."

"Will it hold both of us?"

"Sure, it's a good solid car."

He boosted me up and I scooted to the driver's side where I could see the screen. I leaned my back against the windshield and pressed my hands flat on the metal, feeling the lingering heat from the engine on my palms. Virgil climbed up and sprawled next to me, arranging his gangly legs so his knees were poking into the air. As we turned our heads toward each other, the pupils of his eyes absorbed the light and rippled like black water. He smiled and I grinned back.

He nodded toward the screen. "What's he saying now?"

I studied Ernest Borgnine's mouth for a few seconds, then told him.

An older woman came into the picture. "That's his mother. She never lets him do anything."

For the next half hour or so, I repeated the dialogue. I'm not sure if his hand brushed mine first or if the opposite happened, but when I felt our fingers touch I didn't move. We stayed that way for a few minutes, the warmth from that tiny patch of his skin seeping into my hand. Then I thought about how he always made me feel warm. He treated me nice, like someone special. The books I'd read said you were supposed to love only one person and I wondered if I was being unfaithful to Memphis. If I couldn't have him, maybe because he'd died young or married another— even if it was because he'd been sent to prison—I was supposed to remain true, going to my deathbed that way, if necessary.

Virgil folded his hand over mine, and my heart thumped like a drum. My voice fell lower and lower. I knew he could hear me though because our heads were just an inch or so apart. We might have been the only people for miles around, just the two of us on that car. And I didn't want to move for fear the tingling inside me would end.

I began to realize he wasn't watching the movie. He was star- ing at me. "You're pretty smart to be able to do that."

"Do what?"

"Read their lips." As if I might not understand what he was saying, he laid his finger on my mouth.

My lips moved under his touch. "You could learn how."

"Not as well as you do."

I felt a rush of pleasure. For some reason my gunboat feet and my eyeglasses no longer mattered. Virgil thought I was smart. He propped himself on his left elbow and bent toward me, blocking my view of the screen. I didn't care because I'd lost all interest in the movie.

As his face neared mine and my eyes slipped effortlessly shut, there was a bang and what sounded like the crash of a cymbal. We leaped apart as if we'd been shot.

"Virgil, are you out here?" a voice said.

It was April, and she'd tripped over the trash can. I noticed she made at least twice the clatter that I did.

"Virgil, where are you?" she called.

It was all I could do not to groan out loud. He slid off the car hood, and I hopped down after him.

April squinted in the darkness. "Oh, there you are."

"Yup, I'm here."

I heard disappointment in his voice, or maybe I was just hoping for it.

"I called my brother and told him he didn't have to pick me up. . . ." She spotted me and her voice rose several notches until it sounded like a carpenter's nail trailing across glass. "Are you still here? Shouldn't you be home by now?"

"I *am* home," I shot back.

That stopped her. For a moment, she just looked at me. Then she turned to Virgil. "I'm off work now. Let's go."

I glanced at the screen. The credits were rolling. Already I could hear car engines starting.

He shuffled his feet. "Well, I really have to get this car back to my brother-in-law."

She slipped into her whiny voice again. "But, Virgil, I don't have any way to get home. You were waiting for me, weren't you?"

I stared hard at him. Tell her you weren't. Tell her you were going to kiss me until she butted in. But he was looking toward the sky, for constellations maybe, or more likely for someone to save him.

"I suppose I could drop you off on the way," he said, with what sounded like a sigh.

"Good." She slid her arm through his and maneuvered him toward the shiny green and white Chevy. "I sure like this better'n your old truck."

Virgil gave me a backward glance. "See you, Callie Anne."

I didn't even say good-bye. I was crawling across the rooftop, my trusty Winchester rifle tucked under one arm, my white Stetson shading my eyes from the sun. I edged around a corner and caught sight of her long brown hair, her perky nose, her rosebud mouth. The money bags lay at her feet. She was leaning over a ledge, taking potshots at my deputies in the street below. One of them had already been wounded. She might be the most famous woman outlaw in the West, but she'd met her match now. She wouldn't get away with robbing the bank in my town.

I lifted my rifle and aimed. *Ka-boom.*

Chapter Twenty-three

*I*n the middle of the day, about two weeks after Billy and I took our midnight hike along the railroad tracks, a stranger came to the drive-in. I was emptying a bushel basket full of trash into the garbage can when he pulled his dusty black sedan into the shade of the concessions building.

For a minute or so, he sat in his car writing something in a notebook. Then he opened the driver's door, uncoiled himself from his seat and stepped out. What struck me immediately was that he wore a dark suit despite the ninety-degree heat. With his slick brown hair parted at the side and his gaunt, bony look, he put me in mind of a funeral director. His gaze fell on me, and I saw his eyes were a light hazel, almost eerily gold. He wiped the sweat from his upper lip with the back of his wrist and shook himself so that his slacks came unstuck from his long legs.

"Your dad around?" he asked.

I nodded. "Upstairs."

Without saying more, he walked to the front of the concessions building, and I set down the bushel basket and followed him. The sun beat down on the sand and gravel. Nothing moved, not a crow scavenging for food nor a fly buzzing in the air. His hard, pale eyes slowly surveyed the field, as though he thought someone might be hiding behind a speaker pole. Memphis had gone inside a few minutes before.

I felt the back of my neck prickle, as I wondered who or what this man was looking for.

I cleared my throat. "Uh, do you want me to get my dad?"

Not even glancing at me, he said, "Sure, honey, you do that."

I hurried around the corner to the back door of the concessions building and charged in, nearly colliding with Memphis, who was carrying a screwdriver in his hand.

He reached out to steady me. "Whoa there, where's the fire?"

"I was just going to fetch Dad." I glanced over my shoulder to make sure the man hadn't followed me. Turning back, I lowered my voice. "You weren't heading out, were you?"

He held up the screwdriver. "I've got the wrong size for that door hinge that's popped off in the storeroom. I think your dad's got one in his truck that'll work."

I backed toward the door. "I'll get it. You stay right here."

"It's okay, pardner, you don't have to . . ."

"No, really." My voice sounded a little shrill. "Don't go outside. There's a man I've never seen before. He's wearing a dark suit and . . . and . . ." I didn't know how to describe him.

Memphis gave me a long searching look. Finally, he said quietly, "All right. That door hinge will wait. You go on up and get your father."

I took the stairs two at a time and found Dad at his desk, entering figures in a ledger. The air in the projection room was so stifling and thick with cigarette smoke I could barely breathe. Dad glanced up.

I wet my lips nervously. "Someone's here to see you."

When he didn't move right away, I added, "He's out front. He didn't want to come in."

Dad grunted, not particularly happy about the interruption, and pulled himself to his feet. He clung to the rail as he descended the stairs, and following him, I could see how unsteady his leg was. Outside, the stranger, to my relief, had stayed where I'd left him. He shook hands with Dad and displayed some kind of badge or license in a leather wallet. I tried to get a look at it but he quickly tucked it away.

Dad leaned against the concessions building, taking the weight off his bad leg. "What can I do for you?"

"I'm looking for a man."

I sucked in a breath.

He studied Dad grimly, as though suspicious of everyone. "About six foot three. Lean. Thirty-five years old. No steady job, but you've probably seen him around."

I nearly fainted.

"His name's William Watson," the man said, his golden eyes flicking back toward the drive-in field, "and his uncle says he's been missing for two weeks."

In my relief, I must have sounded like a car tire deflating.

After giving the name a moment's thought, Dad shook his head. "Don't think I know him . . ."

"Yes, you do," I interrupted, "he means Billy."

Dad frowned. "Oh, him. Yeah, well, he hasn't been around for a while."

"His uncle said you ran him out of here on several occasions," the man said, his voice displaying the mistrustful tone I'd heard detectives use in the movies.

Dad folded his arms over his midsection. "Damned right I did. He was bad for business, always sticking his head in people's cars."

The man glanced at his open notebook. "Guess he had a little accident just outside the theater, is that right?"

"I didn't bump him off, if that's what you mean. He got clipped by a car on the highway," Dad said. "You new here? I haven't seen you around this area before."

"Moved to Jessup last month from Terre Haute."

Dad nodded as though that explained something.

"Look, Mr. Benton," the man said in a flat voice, "I'm just trying to get a lead on Watson. His uncle's worried he might be injured. Or still disoriented from the accident."

"The guy's sick," Dad said. "Came back from the war that way. Everyone knows that."

"The doctors at the hospital in Terre Haute said all he talked about after his accident was coming out here again."

"Well, like I told you, he hasn't been around." Dad turned to me. "How about you, Callie Anne? Have you seen him?"

The stranger's unblinking eyes settled on me. I shook my head, almost too quickly. How could I explain that ghostly moonlit procession that began with Billy's inhuman howl and ended with his disappearance? Dad's gaze dragged over me. I must have done something to give myself away because he gave a little sniff of skepticism.

The man scribbled in his notebook, tore off the piece of paper and handed it to Dad. "You can reach me at this number if you think of something."

"I'll do that," Dad said, with a trace of impatience. He was still eyeing me.

After the man left, I started toward the house.

"Hold on there," Dad said.

I turned, feeling the perspiration tickle my upper lip. "What?"

"When did you see him?"

"Who?"

"You know damned well who."

"I didn't," I said, my voice sounding high and thin.

"Yeah, right," Dad muttered dryly. He opened the door, then stopped and stared at me for a moment. "What's going on here?" he asked softly.

I looked down at my feet.

"What's going on here?" he asked again, and I knew he meant more than Billy.

I shook my head. "Nothing."

He leaned against the doorjamb for a moment and pushed his thumb and index finger against his forehead, kneading the spots above his eyebrows. "All right," he said wearily. He stepped inside, and the door shut behind him.

That evening, I came close to telling Dad he might be in mortal danger. At first, the prospect of Memphis as a murderer, a gunslinger in some faraway western town, had seemed thrilling, but the reality of it now in my own backyard gave me the shivers. Suppose he killed Dad so he could marry Mom, but nobody knew it was him. Then Mr. Sooter would hire him to run the theater and he'd live in our house with us. I could see all the frightening possibilities.

I walked up to the booth and stood in the doorway, watching the shadowy lights from the projector play over Dad's face.

He looked up. "What?"

236

"Oh, nothing."

"Why don't you come in?"

I sighed. "Maybe later." I couldn't seem to stay in that room for long anymore. If I sat there with him, watching the movies as we had so often done, I'd have to warn him about Memphis. But I couldn't warn him without telling him how I knew, and I couldn't betray my mother.

I left him shaking his head.

That evening I did something I'd never done before. I called a boy on the telephone. It took me more than an hour to work up the courage, and then I had to wait until Mom left the house with Memphis to carry through with it. We kept our telephone in the living room on a hip-high wooden cabinet with drawers for pencils and paper and shelves for books and magazines. I dragged out the barely used phone book that served Jessup, Mechanicsburg and a few of the other towns in our part of the county. It didn't quite stretch to Boagle Corner, where Aunt Bliss and Uncle Augie lived, but it did contain the number I wanted. I poked my finger into the cutouts on the black rotary dial and spun the numbers.

A man's voice, thick with a foreign accent, came on the line. I think I squeaked a little. "Is Virgil there?"

I almost hung up during the few minutes it took for him to come to the phone. When he did answer, his voice sounded too low to be the person I knew.

I gripped the receiver nearly hard enough to crack it. "Hi, it's Callie Anne."

He didn't say anything for a moment and I felt a click of panic, thinking maybe he'd be upset I was calling him.

"Oh, hello," he said.

We traded "how are you?" and cruised into another moment of silence. The receiver was slick in my damp hand, and I almost dropped it. "Virgil, there's something I want to talk with you about. Could we meet someplace tomorrow?"

The party line double-clicked, and I thought I heard another set of lungs puffing in the background.

"What?" Virgil said.

"Oh, nothing."

"Callie Anne?"

"Yeah."

"Where the highway meets the old quarry road. Three o'clock."

"Thanks, Virgil," I breathed.

I don't know what Virgil told his dad to get away from the farm. Standing alone at the turnoff to the quarry, we became shy and didn't say more than a quick hello. As we walked west along the rutted dirt road, I balanced on saw-toothed ridges that big truck tires had at some earlier time cut into the muddy ground. The summer sun had baked them hard as clay. We stopped once to examine the fresh carcass of a brown cottontail rabbit in the weeds. It looked plump enough to have been somebody's pet.

I studied the dark red trench from its throat to its abdomen. "What do you suppose got it?"

"Coyote, maybe."

On telephone wires across the way, two sleek black crows waited for us to pass so they could return to their meal.

I peered closer. "A coyote would have eaten it, wouldn't it?"

He shrugged and we moved on.

We'd walked no more than a few yards when we heard the sharp *clink-clink* of metal hitting rock. Past a grove of trees, we saw five bareheaded men standing like statues atop a grassy rise less than half a football field from the road. With their baggy black-and-white jailhouse pajamas, they looked as though they had just stepped out of *Unchained*, a movie about life on a prison farm. Another man, his brown pants cinched tight at the waist and his shirtsleeves rolled up his sunburnt arms, gripped a shiny-barreled rifle. A tan Stetson shadowed his face. It took me a moment to realize the five convicts were shackled at the legs, strung together like bass on a fish line. A tall muscular Negro was among them, his forehead a glistening chestnut color. There weren't many Negroes or chain gangs around Jessup, and I suppose I stared. The sky rose behind them like an intensely blue wall.

A white prisoner with shoulders the size of Sunday hams leaned on the shovel or hoe, or whatever tool it was he was holding, and let out a whistle that could have been heard to State Route 231. "Hey, girlie," he yelled. "Come on over."

One of the other men waved his arms. "Right here, honey. I've got something to show you."

I stood there longer than I should have, rooted in that spot, looking down at myself and wondering what I had done to make them talk to me that way. Even from a distance, I could see an eagerness in their stance, an invitation unlike any I had ever had from a man before. The thought I might have done something to deserve it filled me with a mixture of wonder and shame.

The convict with the burly shoulders pinned me in a thirty-yard stare. "Give her a couple of years and she'll be jailbait."

"Hell, I wouldn't turn her away now," someone else said, and they all hooted with laughter.

The guard waved his rifle toward them in a manner that was more wearied than threatening. "All right. That's enough."

I felt Virgil's hand on my wrist, tugging at me. "Come on, Callie Anne. Let's get out of here."

We ran the rest of the quarter mile to the quarry, the shackled men's catcalls still echoing in my ears.

The spring-fed pit was rimmed by limestone boulders, rocky outcroppings and a couple of hollows the stonecutters had fashioned when they scooped away the rock. Out of breath, we flopped onto an edge on one side of the quarry. I pressed my back and limbs against the hot dusty limestone. Here and there, gnarled trees split the rocks, but they hung so far over the water we got little benefit from their shade. The sun hovered above me like a bright yellow saucer, and when I closed my eyes I could still see it floating there. For several minutes, I lay drowsily motionless, letting the fuzzy warmth seep into me.

When I finally sat up, I saw that Virgil was watching dragonflies skitter across piercingly clear quarry water that was the color of new grass. He had his arms wrapped around his knees. A few feet from us, the rock shelf dropped off sharply.

I tossed a rock in the water. "Yesterday, a detective came to the drive-in."

His eyes widened. "Looking for Memphis?"

I shook my head. "Nope. Looking for Billy Watson."

He shrugged. "Yeah, I heard he was missing."

"You should have seen Memphis though when I told him there was a man outside hunting somebody." I squinted at him. "He acted awfully suspicious."

"What did he do?"

"Turned around and went the other direction. He didn't go out there and he didn't even ask me later what the guy wanted. I think he knows somebody's looking for him. Maybe not this guy but somebody else." I kicked off my shoes. "That chain gang back there made me think of something. Do you suppose Memphis was ever in prison?"

Virgil moved his head slightly, and I saw a glint of pale blond hair along his jaw line. "He worked in one, didn't he?"

"Yeah, that's what he said." I peeled off my white bobby socks and stuffed them into my shoes. "But I wonder if there's more to it than that." I leaned forward and lowered my voice. "First, there's the possibility that Memphis might have killed somebody. Then, there's the newspaper clipping about two men with the same first name as Memphis and his brother, and there's the dog tag with the name of the dead brother. Only it doesn't say Chester Memphis. It says Chester Mathias." I bent closer. "Come on, Virgil, you have to admit that Charlie Memphis has a dark, hidden past."

Virgil stared at me. "Why do you always assume he's so bad?"

I sat straighter. "I didn't say he was bad. In fact, I like him." It crossed my mind to say I loved him, but I had enough sense to edit that thought. I squinted at Virgil. "He did beat the piss out of that robber though, didn't he?"

His eyebrows rose a notch, whether in reaction to my argument or my language, I wasn't sure. I didn't' care. He didn't have to concern himself about Memphis the way I did. Memphis wasn't planning to run off with *his* mother.

I didn't like the way the conversation was going. When I had called Virgil on the phone, it had seemed so important to tell him about Memphis's reaction to the detective. Now that I had brought him here, my story seemed trivial.

241

He looked up at the blindingly bright sky. "You want to know what I think?"

"What?"

"I think you see too many movies."

I leaned sideways toward the water, cupped my hands under the surface and threw all that I could hold straight at him. Most of it drizzled onto the limestone before it hit his green-checked shirt, but it had the effect I wanted. With a lopsided grin, he lunged for me.

I jumped up and spun away, taunting him, "Guess that'll show you."

I don't know what I thought it showed him, because a few seconds later I was scrambling onto one of the limestone boulders and he was grabbing at my ankles. We were both laughing. When I skidded on the slippery rock, he caught me and gripped me by the back of my shorts and blouse.

I squealed, "Don't! My glasses . . ."

He held me with one strong fist and reached his long arm around me. "Give 'em here."

I laughed and shook my head.

He clutched tighter. "Better do it."

I could have fought harder, but I didn't mind the prospect of that cool velvety water. I handed my glasses over, and he slipped them into his shirt pocket. With the ease of a farmer handling a bag of feed, he tossed me over the edge. I curled forward and splashed headfirst, pinching my nose and clamping my mouth. I sank as if falling through silk.

I had been swimming in that quarry before and knew it was so deep I couldn't touch bottom. I rose slowly to the top, keeping my eyes open and watching a troop of minnows parade by. The rubber band on my ponytail had snapped when I hit the water, and now my hair floated loosely around my shoulders. Virgil was squatting on the rock, grinning. Although he had peeled off his shirt and folded it into a neat little bundle with my glasses on top, he didn't jump in.

It flashed through my head how strong he looked, in spite of his gangly limbs and rope-skinny torso. He had the broad shoulders a farm kid gets from pitching hay bales onto a truck all day. Dog-paddling around in that water, I felt a glow come over me and I had the sudden urge to perform for him. I had always been a good swimmer and could stay underwater until my lips turned blue. I dove deep so that my feet split the surface and pointed straight toward the sky. Coming up, I felt transformed from a scrawny tomboy into something quite graceful. I languidly curved my arms and scissor-kicked my way through the cool water, my legs rhythmically opening and closing.

Virgil was watching me with a glitter in his eyes. "You're beautiful," I thought I heard him say.

I smiled a proud little smile and glided and dipped as if I'd just been asked to swim with Esther Williams.

The sun was at a four o'clock angle when I scooted onto a silvery white rock, its heat warming my wet bottom. I twisted a stream of water from my hair. "Woulda brought my bathing suit if I'd known you were going to throw me in."

He didn't answer. I glanced up at him and realized he was staring at me. I squirmed under his gaze. "What?"

Looking down, I saw my white cotton blouse was plastered to my wet skin, my nipples showing through the flimsy fabric like pale pink scrapes. A year ago, I would have thought nothing about swimming in my clothes. But now I felt the heat rise in my face. I didn't wear a brassiere because no one had suggested I should. I silently blamed Aunt Bliss for this oversight because she lived out here in this world of men and should have realized I needed one.

My breasts had the shape of two soft buns rising, not as high as they should be but on their way. I worried he might think they were funny, but he didn't laugh or even smile. Except for the robbery, I had never seen him so serious. He knelt in front of me and leaned toward me, and for a moment his breath was warm and whispery on my cheek. He kissed my mouth, his lips tripping unsteadily sideways onto mine and remaining there for five seconds. I counted them this time, wondering how long the kiss would last and how I would know when it was supposed to end.

He pulled back, and with his head turned slightly away and his eyes lowered, touched his long knobby fingers to my bare arms. In spite of their warmth, I shivered.

"You're soft," he murmured.

He placed his palms flat on my breasts, directly on the pale pink nubs that hadn't yet begun to stick up like my mother's.

I didn't whack him. I didn't leap up and run the way I should have. I didn't even close my eyes. Neither did he. He pressed lightly. And then a little more until I felt a weakness inside.

The sun circled behind his head now, sparkles coming off it like slivers of glass. His shadowed eyes were so dark they didn't look blue at all. We rested on a boulder that a sea monster might have taken a bite out of. It formed a natural bench with a back that sloped into another mantel of rocks. He pulled me down onto the powdery stone, our knees and elbows bumping against each other as we stretched out on the rock. I lay so my back was flat against the slope and reached my arms around him, touching my fingertips to the bumpy ridge of his spine. Pushing my face into the hollow of his neck, I drew in the warm moistness of his skin. He smelled like hay and apples.

We lay locked together like that for several minutes, while I thought about what might occur next. I knew this was what Betty

Jo Babcock had talked about, but she had left out all the wonder of it, the feeling that something really important and exciting was happening to me. If it had been anyone but Virgil, I might have been scared. Maybe I wasn't afraid of him because his gentle hands were accustomed to tugging on cows' udders, or maybe because he possessed an easygoing, hardworking reliability. It might have been simply because he drove a Ford truck. Anyway, I trusted him.

A starling landed in a branch above our heads and scolded, knocking down thumb-sized seedpods that plopped onto the rocks. That noise seemed to bring Virgil back. He released me and sat up. His eyes turned blue again, matching the sky. In the center of his jeans, a wet spot about the size of a man's fist had formed. Somehow I knew immediately it wasn't quarry water or any kind of water at all.

He looked down at the stain, and his shoulders drooped. "I'm sorry," he mumbled.

I tugged at the edges of my shorts, straightening them. "It's okay," I said, knowing my words didn't begin to convey what I felt inside. I didn't exactly understand what had happened, but I had an idea, and I was amazed that I could have had, in some strange way, that kind of effect on him.

He offered his hand to pull me up, and this time I grasped it without goofing off or yanking him around. I retrieved my glasses and passed him his shirt. He tied it around his waist so the green-checked shirttails covered the blotch. There was a certain polite-ness in this gesture, but he turned away to let me know I shouldn't mention it. It occurred to me then that people in general don't often talk about what they've done, and men and boys talk even less.

Avoiding the chain gang, we chose another path back to the highway. Neither one of us said a word about what had happened.

Marjorie Reynolds

★　　★　　★

I phoned Aunt Bliss the next day and asked if she'd take me into town to buy a brassiere. She swung by that very afternoon in her mottled black and khaki Dodge truck. We drove into Jessup, her white-knuckled fists gripping the steering wheel as though it might spin right off.

I sat with my elbow jutting out the passenger window, something my dad never let me do because he said it was an invitation for some passing automobile to take off my arm. Aunt Bliss knew only one speed, so the trees and poles, not to mention other cars, whipped by. The blast of air from the open windows caused her reddish-brown hair to splay out.

She shouted over the din of the unmuffled engine, "Got the curse yet?"

I stared back at her. "'The curse?"

"Your period."

I nodded.

She gave me a basset hound look, as if to say this is the way life is. "Your mom talk to you about sex?"

I shook my head and studied my chewed fingernails.

"Thought so," she said, bunching up her cheeks the way a squirrel does when transporting nuts. "Well, then, this is how it is. The male of the species has got this puffy little thing between his legs called a pecker, and it don't make a bit of difference whether he's a dog or a mule or a snake or a man. I can tell you right now they're all in the same category, and when there's a female around, they've got just one thing in mind."

I wasn't sure she was right about the snake part because I'd

246

learned in sixth grade science a snake was a cold-blooded reptile. But I let it go.

She downshifted, and the truck squealed around a corner. "Their goal," she said, "is to shove that pecker directly inside you and pump away, spilling their seed every chance they can get. And believe you me, any man'll do that. They haven't got brains the size of walnuts, and the ones they have are below their belt. Your job, young lady, is to whomp the hell out of them when they try. After you get married, you can let them have their fun once in a while, but you gotta keep them under control. That's the important thing."

She pinned her eyes on the road with the same grim, determined expression I'd seen on her face when she'd wrung a chicken's neck. She didn't particularly like this job, but somebody had to do it.

"Now, after you marry," she continued, "the way not to have kids—and this is something my mama told me—the way not to have kids is to sleep back to back. 'Course she had six of them because she learned that too late. It's guaranteed to work though because it keeps a man in his place." She mashed on the brakes, fishtailed to a stop directly in front of Miller's Department Store and turned to look at me. "You got all that now?"

I gulped and gave what I suppose was a big-eyed stare. "Yeah, I think so."

"Good," she said, wrenching open her driver's door. It creaked like a vault that hadn't seen daylight in a hundred years. "That should do it."

While Aunt Bliss was bossing the saleslady into dragging out every bra Miller's Department Store carried, I considered her words. Her explanation of how it all worked sounded a lot like

Betty Jo Babcock's, which surprised me, because I never had put much trust in Betty Jo. However, none of the rest matched what I'd felt with Virgil. It didn't even match what I knew about mild-mannered Uncle Augie.

I was pondering these thoughts when Mrs. McGarry, the lingerie clerk, guided Aunt Bliss and me into the curtained dressing room and tugged my pink-striped shirt over my head. I immediately clapped my arms across my chest, but Mrs. McGarry gave me a comforting pat on the shoulder. "Now, don't you mind, honey. It's just us girls."

The three of us were wedged into that plywood cubicle that wasn't any bigger than a gas station bathroom stall, bumping into each other and sweating jelly beans. The place smelled like a combination of musty carpet and Mrs. McGarry's floral perfume working overtime.

She selected one of the white cotton bras from the foot-high stack she'd piled on a wooden chair and slipped it gently around me so the cups pooched out in front. "Now, bend over a little, dear, and shake your . . ."

"Lord amighty, she hasn't got enough to shake in there." Aunt Bliss elbowed in. "Here, give that to me."

"Well!" Mrs. McGarry said.

Aunt Bliss ignored her. "There's an easier way to cinch this contraption, child." She showed me how to fasten the hooks and eyes with the back of the bra slung across my tummy, then swing it around and yank the pointy white cones over my breasts. It was a slick operation, and after trying on about a dozen bras, I got pretty good at it.

Behind me, Mrs. McGarry was lecturing, "It's really important, dear, that you wear this every day to support those delicate tissues. And you mustn't ever run. You don't want breasts that sag to your waist."

We finally settled on a size 28A Playtex training bra. What I was training for, no one said. But it gave me far more bosom than I had ever dreamed possible. It was nothing like the sturdy cotton apparatus that hitched Aunt Bliss into place, but I strutted out of there like Marilyn Monroe. Aunt Bliss even bought me a spare, which Mrs. McGarry wrapped in tissue paper and placed inside a green Miller's Department Store bag.

Marching out Miller's newly installed revolving door, which sent people scuttling in circles, we nearly smacked right into Memphis. Aunt Bliss jumped back a little, her mouth forming a stony furrow.

He backed up a step, and I could see he'd recognized her too.

He nodded to me. "Hello, pardner."

I bounced forward, hoping he'd notice my new figure. "Hi, Memphis."

He tipped his hat to Aunt Bliss. "Ma'am."

"This here's Charlie Memphis, Aunt Bliss."

She reached out one of her hands, which had always made me think of small iron skillets, and grabbed his hand. I could have sworn I heard it crunch.

It was getting on toward late afternoon, and their bodies cast rigid shadows on the white sidewalk. Aunt Bliss was wearing a dress for a change, and the fabric looked as if rose-colored confetti had fluttered onto a pink background.

"Well, now," she said, and I could almost see the steam rising off her. Oh, Lordy, I thought, we're in for it now. I studied Memphis to see if he had any idea what was coming. He smiled comfortably, and I wondered how much Mom had told him about Aunt Bliss.

She jerked her thumb toward the truck. "Go on, child. I'll be there in a minute."

"Aw, Aunt Bliss," I have to admit I whined. I couldn't tolerate the thought of missing this conversation.

"No, you just get on over there," she said, not taking her eyes off him. "I need to talk to Mr. Memphis here for a minute."

The truck sat about ten yards away, its dented front bumper pressed against the high cement curb. I crawled onto the passenger seat, kicking aside a faded map and an empty paper cup on the floor, my bottom lip sticking out so far a fly could have landed on it. I poked my head out the open window and tried to catch what they were saying. I suppose I should specify, what Aunt Bliss was saying, because I didn't have to hear anything to know who was doing all the talking. I couldn't see her face, but the muscles in her back, which was turned toward me, rippled like those of a boxer going in for the punch. She practically shook her fist under his nose, and occasionally her voice sliced through the air like a buzzsaw. I heard "innocent Teal," "taking advantage of" and "what about that child?"

He listened to her without moving, a calm half-smile plastered on his face, his arms folded across the snap-buttoned front of his white denim shirt. There was a distance in his eyes, the way a man gets when his brain is sifting through important considerations. I don't know whether Aunt Bliss just stopped to draw a breath or whether she had finished speaking, but Memphis said, "I'm not going to apologize." And I realized I could read his lips, just as if he'd been an actor on the movie screen. He turned his head slightly to watch a young woman walk by and all I caught was "trapped inside that house."

He swiveled back to look Aunt Bliss square in the eye. "I done a lot of things wrong in my life, but Teal ain't one of them."

The Starlite Drive-in

"Why can't you stay away from her?" I heard my aunt ask, her strident voice carrying across to me.

"If you have to ask that, you don't know her very well." He tipped his hat. "Now, if you'll excuse me, ma'am."

He turned and walked away from her, the heels of his cowboy boots clicking on the concrete. He passed Miller's Department Store, Gibbons's Pharmacy and Woolworth's five-and-dime. I thought my aunt might run after him, maybe even thump him on the back of the head to let him know who was boss. But she stood there, her big hands dangling at her sides. When she returned to the truck, hoisted herself into the driver's seat and cranked the starter, she had the dejected look of a woman who's just lost her best dog. I was disappointed too. I had expected more of her.

Wearing my new bra, I returned to the quarry that evening an hour after sundown. I hadn't had the nerve to call Virgil again, but I hoped he would somehow know I was there. I wanted to see him, and as much as I worried it might be wrong, I wanted his hands on me again. Walking along the rutted road, I balanced on the saw-toothed tire tracks just as I had the day before.

The quarry was different at night, the water black and glittery, the bird songs replaced by the croak of tree frogs. The moon was so bright the surrounding boulders and foliage made deep shadows on the motionless pool. I didn't swim but sat on the edge of the still-warm rocks and dangled my feet in the water. I thought about how John Wayne would like it here and decided next time I'd bring him with me.

Crawling into one of the hollows the stonecutters had fashioned when they scooped out the rock, I lay with my head on my flattened palm and thought about what it might be like to marry Virgil. The floor of the small, man-made cave was cool on my back and smelled like damp leaves.

They came then, their feet padding softly on the limestone. I knew what their presence here meant. She had crossed the White River Road bridge. She had to, to get this far.

They moved slowly, quietly, as if under some spell. They stood close to the sandy boulder where Virgil and I had lain. Clenching my teeth hard, I willed them to go. I didn't want to spy on them anymore. The quarry was mine and Virgil's, and they were trespassing on my territory now.

I couldn't go, at least not easily. I had reached the scooped-out boulder by crawling onto the rock next to them. Leaving any other way meant a five-foot drop.

Memphis clasped Mom around the waist and pulled her against him. "Will she tell him?"

She shook her head, her pearl combs catching the moonlight. "I don't think so. Bliss doesn't mean any harm."

He cupped her face in his hands. "I told her I wouldn't give you up, that you're about the only thing I've ever done right in my life."

My mother said something that surprised me. "We have to leave soon."

"We will. I'll have the money in a few weeks."

He began to kiss her. She tipped her head back, closing her eyes and offering her face to him. He ran his lips over her, kissing her and urgently pressing words against her cheeks and mouth. "We'll go to New Orleans. Would you like that? I know people there and I can get a job."

"Yes," she said, allowing him into the curve of her neck. He lingered there a few moments, probably breathing in her fragrance. As a child, I had nuzzled that very place myself and knew its sweet softness.

He knelt on the sandy rock at her feet, and she leaned her back against the boulder, stroking his hair and face. He gathered the scalloped hem of her white dress in his hands and slowly lifted it to her waist. The triangle of her underpants flashed in the moonlight. He buried his face against that triangle, and she pulled him to her.

My face grew hot. I crawled out of my dark hiding place, scrambled over the rock away from their line of sight and jumped the five feet to the ground. I don't know if they heard me, and I no longer cared. I ran all the way back to the drive-in, knowing with a stomach-tightening certainty this couldn't continue.

An hour later, I was sitting cross-legged on the bench outside the concessions building trying to watch *Fire Maidens of Outer Space,* a silly movie but one that had attracted a fair number of people, when Dad came charging out of the concessions building, limping as fast as his legs would carry him.

He spotted me and jerked to a halt. "You seen Memphis?"

I shook my head too hard and too quickly.

Dad's hand came down on my shoulder like a vice. "Where is he?"

"I don't know."

His face looked pinched and dark in the yellow light from the concessions building fixture. He squeezed the muscle in my shoulder until it hurt, and I yelped.

"You're lying to me, missy. There are times I know you're lying to me."

He released me, and I stood up from the bench and moved a few steps away, rubbing the sore muscle with my fingers. "I haven't seen him. Why do you want him?"

"A pipe in the snack bar sprung a leak," Dad snapped. "I had to turn off the water, but I can't keep it off. People'll be wanting to use the rest rooms." He glanced at the screen, and images of light and dark played across his face. "I don't have time to fix it myself. That reel's going to run out in a minute." He turned back to me, but then his gaze caught something over my shoulder.

I looked behind me and saw Memphis walking from the direction of the house. Between the cars, I could see a single light in our kitchen, and for a moment I glimpsed my mother's silhouette on the drawn window shade.

Apparently unconcerned, Memphis moved with long, easy strides, his hands jammed in his pants pockets like a man who has just returned from an evening in town. My heart was thudding like a jackhammer.

Dad limped over to him. "Where have you been?"

A tense smile played across Memphis's lips. "I'm on my own time now."

I could see dad's shoulders straighten and tighten. Just then, the movie screen went black, quickly, like a curtain falling. Within seconds, the sounds of car horns split the night air.

"I got a pipe that's sprung a leak," Dad hissed. "Get in there and fix it." His glittery black eyes changed direction and focused on our dimly lit house. "I ever catch you over there, I'll break your fucking neck." Then he swung around and limped hurriedly into the concessions building.

The Starlite Drive-in

Memphis didn't rush to follow him. Passing me, he rested his hand briefly on my shoulder. "How you doing, pardner?"

I had barely enough breath in my lungs to answer him. "Okay."

Chapter Twenty-four

I kept thinking I should warn Mom about Memphis, that I should tell her about the newspaper clipping and the dog tag. But I knew she was even less likely than Virgil to believe me. In one of those books I had read, someone wrote that people in love tend to lose their good sense, and I could see that Mom's had fallen through a crack.

I was starting to have stomachaches about this time, the kind you get when your insides feel as tight as a fist, and no amount of Grape Nehi or chocolate bars seems to help. Sometimes the pain would wake me up in the middle of the night, and I'd have to hug my knees against my belly until it went away. I didn't complain about it to Mom though, because I didn't want to visit Doc Graham. He had a habit of giving me a shot every time I saw him, and the sight of that needle coming at me was more than I could bear.

Memphis had told Mom he would have all the money he needed in a few weeks, and the thought that he might steal it began to haunt me. If Mom really did plan for us to run off with him, we might be leaving with not only a murderer but a thief.

The Starlite Drive-in

In the short time left, I might not be able to find out if he had killed someone, but I figured I could at least determine if he was a thief. I came up with a plan, not a great one but a simple test of his honesty. To put it into effect, I needed a dollar bill, and that wasn't easy for me to come by. Money seemed to sift right through my fingers.

The most obvious sources of cash around the drive-in were the admission and snack bar grosses, but my father had set up such a tight system that more than once I'd heard Mr. Sooter refer to it as the model for his circuit. Besides, even if I could have filched a dollar, I wouldn't have risked it. If Dad had caught me, I probably would have wished I could be sent to Sing Sing for vacation. Almost more than anything else, my father believed in honesty. Every new employee at the theater got a fifteen-minute lecture on it, and, in general, I'm sure Dad practiced it himself. That's probably why it never occurred to Mr. Sooter to suspect him of lying about the twenty dollars.

I could have approached Aunt Bliss for the dollar bill, but I didn't know when I'd be seeing her again. And she would have grilled me backward and forward about what I was going to do with all that money until I wouldn't have been able to remember which lie I was using and which one she'd already figured out. The one person I thought I could go to for a loan was Memphis, but borrowing it from him made no sense at all.

That left Mom. After a good deal of soul-searching, I managed to convince myself that what I was doing was for her benefit anyway. I probably could have made up some fancy story, but I just couldn't bring myself to fib to her. I waited until I heard her in the bedroom snapping the clean bedsheets into place before I slipped a dollar from the cocoa tin in the kitchen cupboard. I felt pretty low in spite of my good intentions, but I told myself I'd return it before she ever missed it. And if Memphis swiped it? Well, then I'd just have to tell her why I couldn't give it back.

My plan wasn't complicated, but it had to be carried out when Dad was away. I knew Memphis started his day early and ate his dinner at noon. He prepared it in the snack bar, often using the hot plate and other equipment there. That's where the dollar bill would be, in plain view on the snack bar counter, with no one else around. All I had to do was hide nearby to see if he picked it up.

I knew my scheme wasn't as clever as one Tom Sawyer might have come up with, but I never expected it to cause the kind of grief it did. About the only thing that went as planned was the part where I laid the dollar bill on the counter. I hid near the entrance to the ladies' room scrunched against the wall to avoid detection. I cocked my head when I heard Memphis enter the concessions building. He opened a tin can and poured the contents into a saucepan, all the while humming "Red River Valley." After several minutes, I could smell his dinner cooking, something strong and spicy.

When I decided he'd had enough time, I pretended to emerge from the rest room. "Hi, Memphis."

"Hey there, pardner." He sprinkled some red powder over the pan. "How's that turtle of yours?"

"He's almost well. I'm going to let him go soon." It was a lie. Just stroking John Wayne's rubbery hide during the past few weeks had given me some measure of comfort, and I realized now I couldn't stand the thought of releasing the only pet I'd ever owned.

"Good," Memphis said, " 'cause you should turn him loose before winter comes."

"What are you making?" I asked, as my gaze swept the

counter. The dollar was missing, and I had the abrupt sensation of my heart nudging my belly button.

"Frijoles. Have you ever had frijoles?" He stirred the mixture, appearing as unconcerned as if he swiped money all the time.

"I don't think so," I murmured. "I don't guess Mom's ever made them." I glanced around, hoping that he had just pushed the dollar out of the way.

The powerful aroma of his dinner swept over me, and what had smelled so appealing while I hid in the shadows suddenly made my stomach lurch. My dollar, my mother's dollar, was gone, and I couldn't think what to do.

"Cowboy beans, we used to call them out west," he said, slurping a spoonful of the lumpy reddish-brown mush. " 'Course, I can't fix them the way we did then, simmering all day on the back of a woodstove. You want a taste?"

I peered woozily at him, tiny black spots dancing in front of my eyes. I was in a tunnel, and the dark walls were closing in on me. Reaching for something to grab on to, I swayed unsteadily.

"Callie Anne?"

His voice sounded distant, like someone slowly turning the radio down. The next thing I knew someone switched off the sound—and the light.

When I woke up, I was bouncing up and down and my head was tucked into warm, damp fabric that had a musky smell, one that was familiar but I couldn't quite identify. It took a few seconds to realize Memphis was carrying me, running with me, in fact, and my face was squashed against his tan shirt. He hitched me up and I found myself nuzzling his chest, the curly black hair there tickling my nose.

Mom must have seen him coming across the field because she met us at the door. "What happened?"

I could hear the hysteria in her voice.

I had always wanted to be in Memphis's arms but not like this. I pushed against him. "I'm all right. Put me down."

He had such a grip I could hardly move. "She fainted. Tumbled right onto the floor, but she ain't hurt."

I caught a glimpse of my mother's white, terrified face as she hovered over me. "This way," she said.

A minute later, he lowered me onto my pink chenille bedspread where I belatedly flailed my arms.

"What happened?" Mom repeated. She was smoothing my bangs back from my forehead and running her cool hand across my brow. I breathed in the rose fragrance of her skin lotion.

"I don't know," Memphis said. "One minute we was talking. The next minute she keeled right over. Came that close to hitting her head on the edge of the counter."

I suppose he measured the distance with his fingers, but I couldn't see it. Realizing everything was still a bright blur, I sat straight up. "My glasses. Where are my glasses?"

"Got 'em here in my pocket." He handed them to me. "They ain't broke."

Mom, who'd been sitting next to me on the bed, pushed me back down. "Watch her, please, Charlie Memphis, while I get a cold washcloth." She rose from the bed and dashed toward the bathroom.

He thrust a hand toward me, as though he didn't think he should touch me but he didn't want me bouncing up either. "You stay right there," he said.

Mom rushed back in with the damp cloth and pressed it against my forehead. "Tell me where it hurts, sweetheart. Do you feel sick to your stomach?"

"I'm okay. I just want to sit up."

"She's not really hurt. I caught her before she hit the floor."

"Mom, please."

"No, now don't try to get up. You need to rest a bit. Maybe I should call Dr. Graham."

I lifted my head, brushing away drips of water that had trickled from the washcloth onto my temple. "Aw, Mom, I'm all right. Honest."

"How can I tell if you keep moving around like that?"

I fell back against the pillow, exhausted by the conversation.

Mom untied my shoes and tugged them off, obviously glad to have something to do. She peeled off my white bobby socks so my feet stuck up, big and pink and bare, at the end of the bed. I hastily tried to cover them with the bedspread.

Memphis shifted nervously. "Well, I'll be running along."

Maybe he thought Mom was going to undress me right there or maybe he was worried my father might turn up. I personally was concerned about both.

Mom lifted her eyes to his and smiled. "Thank you, Charlie Memphis."

He put his hand lightly on her shoulder, and there passed between them a look so tender and affectionate no one could have misunderstood it.

"I'll check later to see how she is." He glanced out the window. "Claude should be coming back anytime, and I've got to take care of something with him before it brings me trouble." He looked down at me. "You get better now, pardner."

I was just about ready to smile when I remembered he had stolen my mom's money.

As soon as he was out the door, Mom pulled my pink-flowered cotton pajamas from under my pillow and shook them out. "Put these on while I get the thermometer. I think you have a fever."

I sighed, deciding I was probably destined to spend the rest of the day in bed. Just as I heard the door to the medicine chest creak, I remembered what Memphis had said about taking care of something that might get him into trouble with my dad.

I leaped from my bed and scrambled to the window. He was already halfway across the drive-in field. In the distance, my father had parked his truck in its usual place behind the concessions building and was walking toward the entrance that led to the projection booth.

I tore out of the house, running faster than I had ever run before. The hot sun pressed down on me and the gravel bit into my bare feet, but I kept on, thinking only of reaching Memphis before he got to my father.

Behind me, Mom was yelling from the door, "Callie Anne! What are you doing out there?"

I was sweating and puffing by the time I reached him. "Memphis, don't give the dollar to my dad. It's Mom's dollar, but don't give it to her either. She doesn't have anything to do with it. It was my plan, all mine, but it was a stupid idea. Please don't give the dollar to anybody. I'm sorry I ever suspected you. I'm really, really sorry."

He bent down, his tanned face so close to mine I could see the thin white lines that webbed the skin near his eyes. "I think you'd better tell me what's going on, pardner?"

I took a deep breath. I don't suppose he had any idea what he was in for. Nor did I. The words flooded out, cascaded over each other in one long, muddled confession. I told him everything, about thinking he had killed someone, about hearing Dad in Mr. Sooter's office and searching his room, about Virgil finding me there and taking off my glasses and kissing me, about borrowing the money from my mother and trying to entrap him in the snack bar. Midway through, tears clouded my eyes. A few sentences later, I was sobbing. I apologized again for mistrusting him. I may have even told him I loved him.

I can't imagine how he understood it all, but he didn't ask me a single question.

"Run along now," he said in a low voice, "and give the money back to your ma."

I gazed up at him through a wet film. His face had darkened, although at the time I had thought it was merely in shadow, the sun's bright light wavering behind him. My own relief was so tremendous, so deep and cleansing that I didn't immediately recognize the fierceness in his eyes.

"All right," I snuffled, turning back toward the house. I walked slowly, still feeling lightheaded and queasy. Mom was holding the door open for me, urging me inside. I made it all the way to our picket fence when I realized what was going to happen.

I whirled around and surveyed the parking field. A crow perched on the speaker pole near where Memphis had been standing, but he wasn't in sight. I started running.

"Callie Anne," Mom called from the house.

I didn't even turn back to look at her. I ran across the field, slowing down only when I approached the glass-windowed entrance of the concessions building. One of the doors was propped open with a cinder block to let in fresh air. I eased closer, listening for voices. It was too quiet.

I slipped into the snack bar lobby, wondering where Memphis had disappeared to. Standing there for a moment, I took in the lingering smell of his cowboy beans that sat cooling on the hot plate. The empty can and the tin of chili powder cluttered the counter.

When I heard the footsteps on the stairs, the uneven tread of a man with one leg he couldn't quite manage, I instinctively dropped to the floor, out of view behind the L-shaped bar, and waited.

Dad tromped over to the sink, emptied some liquid into it and ran the water for a short time. There was a clank and a splash, then an angry curse under his breath. I crouched against the sliding wooden doors of the glass-fronted candy case, holding my breath.

At that moment, I heard one of the exterior doors open and bang shut, followed by the slow *click-click* of cowboy boots crossing the tile floor. They stopped, and I didn't need to see either of them to know they were staring at each other.

"If you're going to cook here, I expect you to clean up after yourself," Dad said.

I eased the sliding door of the candy case open an inch and peeked through. Memphis was standing at the end of the snack bar, but Dad was out of my line of sight.

Holding the large wrench from Dad's truck, Memphis took a step forward. "That faucet's leaking again." His voice was tight, hard as a fist.

Dad grunted, and another silence followed. From what I could tell, he wasn't moving, stubbornly refusing to allow Memphis access to the sink.

Memphis laid the wrench on the counter, and I released a long breath. My relief was brief though because Memphis said, "I hear you've lost some money, Claude."

A chill ran through me, and I came close to passing out on that floor again. Miraculously, Dad didn't ask him how he had found out. As I watched through the crack, Dad came into view, a scowl on his face.

"Lost, huh?" He snorted. "Stolen is more like it. And I told

Sooter who took it. You think he's going to put up with your skimming money for very long?"

"He won't believe you."

"He will when I'm done." Dad's voice shook with triumph. "He's not going to believe a fuckin' drifter, I can tell you that."

Memphis's eyes turned so black, they looked like night water, but he didn't say anything.

"You think you can come in here and steal everything, don't you?" Dad still had that well-you're-finished-now tone. "Gonna just waltz right in and take it all. Guess you thought you'd move into my house, take my pretty little wife and my daughter too, huh? Is that what you thought, you two-bit son of a bitch?"

Dad's rage spilled out now and filled the room. It reached inside me and pressed down on my lungs so that I had to lean my head against the candy-case doors to catch my breath.

"And what did you think I was going to do?" Dad asked fiercely. "Just stand by and watch you? Watch you take my wife, my kid, my job too. Goddamn you, I'll never let you do that."

Memphis remained motionless, his arms folded across his chest, his mouth a thin dark trench. He said nothing.

"You think I'm dumb, don't you?" Dad's voice rose mockingly. "You think, dumb old Claude, sitting up there in that projection booth, showing those movies night after night, as trapped in this godforsaken place as she is. He'll never figure out I'm fucking his wife in his own home, right under his nose."

Dad strained toward him, his hands balled. "You've had your eye on her since the day you walked into this drive-in. I should have run your sorry ass out of here right then. You've probably got a woman in every town. You thought you'd just add her to your list of bitches and . . ."

Memphis swung his arm out, caught my father by the front of his shirt and with the snap of his wrist hurled him against the wall. Dad reeled, grabbed the edge of the counter and regained his balance. He charged Memphis, jamming his head into his midsection and locking his hands around Memphis's waist. They grappled and crashed so hard against the snack bar that an enormous jar of fruit-colored gumballs on the counter above me shook and tipped. I breathlessly reached a hand toward it, but it righted itself and settled back down.

I slid onto my knees and peered between the candy-case doors again. They were standing there, a few feet apart, their hands dangling by their sides.

Memphis's voice was a low rasp in his chest. "You shut up about her, you hear. I don't give a shit about your house and your job, but don't you ever talk about her like that. You don't deserve her, you measly little snake."

"You're a bum and a thief, and if she doesn't know that by now, she will soon."

Memphis went crazy. He caught hold of my father and jerked him forward, slashing his hand against Dad's face. Dad staggered back and struggled to keep his footing. He managed to recover and jam his fist into Memphis's belly but not with a great deal of force. Memphis grunted and swung his arm like a club, upward into Dad's chest, and Dad doubled over in pain, wheezing and coughing.

I gripped the edge of the candy case and murmured under my breath, "Oh, jeez. Oh, jeez."

With a deep roar, Dad straightened and grabbed Memphis around the neck, clinging to him like a pit bull. They crashed around the big open room, knocking over a small, round wrought-iron table and a chair. They hit the plate-glass window so many times I was sure it was going to break.

Finally, Dad managed to back Memphis against the counter where the wrench lay. Whether he intended to grab it first, I don't know. But within seconds, Memphis spun around and snared the hunk of metal. They were no more than six feet from me.

Memphis took a step forward and lifted the wrench with both hands. His black pupils shone like tiny pellets through the slits of his eyes, reminding me of how he had looked while beating the robber. My father hunched his shoulders, anticipating the blow. I opened my mouth to scream, but the sound lodged in my throat like a chunk of meat. I pulled back from my viewing place and slammed my shoulder as hard as I could against the candy case, hearing the sharp gasp of my own breath.

The gumball jar hit the floor with a cracking sound like a gunshot, and the air exploded with shards of glass. Tiny red, yellow, blue and green orbs clicked and bounced across the tile.

Dad stepped backward, stumbling and skidding on them, crunching them into multicolored pieces. Then I saw Memphis's eyes clear and he lowered the wrench to his side.

Sinking to the floor, I leaned my forehead against the cabinet in relief. When I no longer felt the pain of my breath pushing against my rib cage, I crept to the candy-case doors again and peered through.

Dad was slumped on the tile with his back against the wall and his bad leg twisted under him, coughing into a handkerchief. Memphis was breathing hard and his hands were bruised, but I saw no cuts or marks on his face.

He straightened and looked at Dad. "I'll leave this town when

I want to, not before." He glanced around the room at the mess but made no move to clean it up. He turned back to my father. "She ain't going to stay with you. You already know that though, don't you?"

Dad raised his head, revealing purple-red welts along his cheekbones. "You'll never pry her out of that house."

Memphis just shrugged. Then he turned and strode out the door.

If he had stayed a few seconds more, he might have seen what I saw, the absolute despair that had settled into my father's eyes.

As soon as I had the chance, I crept away from the snack bar and, almost doubled up with nausea, fled toward the willow grove. Upon reaching it, I knelt in the dry weeds and grass of the sharp-edged creek bank and vomited onto the mud and rocks until my throat ached and my insides felt hollowed out. I walked upstream a few yards, dipped my cupped hands into the clear water and rinsed out my mouth, then crawled into the sheltering arms of the willow tree.

What would happen now? I was afraid for both of them, for all of us.

Somehow, in the past weeks, I had come to think our departure would be easy and pleasant, a happy ending the way it was in the movies. I would discover that Memphis was an honest man, a good man, and all that business about murder and theft would have been simply rumors, as Mr. Sooter had said. Memphis would take Mom and me away, to exciting new places, to California and Idaho and Washington State. He would never yell at us. He would love us and look upon us with contentment, like the father in the

Norman Rockwell painting. We would be together day after fine sunny day.

And Dad? Well, I guess I had figured he would just fade away. Sure, I had expected to feel bad about him and even miss him occasionally, remembering the good times we'd had together watching movies and talking about them. The memories tugged at me even now. I had never thought it would be like this, the fighting, the hating. My stomach throbbed, and a sour taste rose in my throat again.

I slowly walked back to the house, across the fields and past the concessions building. Through the windows, I saw my father sweeping the glass fragments and gumballs into a dustpan with slow, stiff movements.

When I reached the house, Mom was about as angry as I had ever seen her. With her delicate features fixed in a frown, she held the door open for me. "Where on earth did you run off to? You get in here right now."

I drifted past her, feeling all shivery and damp with sweat. She must have seen right away how miserable I was, because her voice lost its edge. "Into bed, honey, before you fall over."

I didn't protest at all. I wobbled into the bedroom, tugged off my blouse, training bra, shorts and underpants, and slid into my worn, pink-flowered pajamas. Although Mom must have been standing close by, her voice came from a distance. "I phoned over to the concessions building, but your father said he hadn't seen you. He didn't sound right. Has something happened?"

I peeled back the bedspread and, without a word, crawled between the smoothly ironed sheets. Pressing my hot cheek to the pillowcase, I released a small cough. Mom rushed to my side, her thoughts only for me now.

I pitched feverishly in and out of sleep for the next several hours, glazing myself and my tangled bedsheets with a salty, burning sweat. Waking to the eye-stinging odor of Vicks on my chest, I sat up and groggily drank the 7UP Mom held for me, then plunged once more below the surface of sleep. I felt myself dragged into it, like an undercurrent pulling me down, like two hands tugging at me until I found myself on a long, slippery slide into a watery pit. Memphis was at the bottom of the slide, standing in a patch of clear blue light with the heavy wrench in his hand. His silver belt buckle gleamed like the eye of a fish, and two black crows, with bloody beaks and death in their eyes, perched on his shoulders. They reminded me of the birds that had pecked at the rabbit carcass on the old quarry road.

My father's twisted and battered body lay at Memphis's feet, the blood rising from his wounds like a red cloud.

I awoke with a start.

It was dark both in my room and outside, where the movie *Summertime* flickered on the screen. The overhead light was on in the hall. I heard the murmur of voices in the kitchen, Mom's and Memphis's, but I didn't have the energy to get up and eavesdrop on them. The talking stopped after a few minutes and I closed my eyes.

When I awoke again, Mom was sitting in a rocking chair next to my bed, her head propped against a pillow, her slender fingers draped across my wrist. My fever broke at one o'clock in the morning. I knew the time without looking at the clock because the cars were leaving the theater, their engines rumbling quietly, their headlights flashing wide, white bands across my bedroom walls. I pulled my damp sheet around me and sank back into sleep.

Chapter Twenty-five

*M*om was still in the rocking chair next to my bed when I awoke the next morning around nine o'clock. I stirred, and she blinked her green eyes open, looking a little blank for a moment while she probably tried to remember why she was there. She stretched out of her uncomfortable position and pressed her hand to my forehead. Although my fever was gone and I felt almost back to normal, she announced firmly that I would spend the rest of the day in bed. She even insisted on walking down the hall with me to the bathroom in case I should pass out again.

The bathroom door was open and Dad was at the sink, his face turned away from us. He was scrubbing his fingernails with an old toothbrush Mom kept for that purpose. The water gurgled in the drain.

"You're up early," Mom said to Dad. She stood behind me in the doorway, her hands on my shoulders. "I didn't hear you come in last night. Callie Anne ran a fever, and I stayed in her room. Did you wonder where I was?"

"You weren't in our bedroom," he said dryly. "Where else would you be?" He wiped his hands on the white towel, draped it over the edge of the sink and turned around. The welts on his cheeks were ugly—purple and puffy.

Mom gasped. "What happened, Claude Junior?"

"Fell down the stairs in the concessions building. Damned leg," he said, not looking at me.

Mom didn't offer to clean the cuts or put iodine on them. She went into the kitchen, fixed me unbuttered toast, which she permitted me to eat at the table, and prepared Dad his regular breakfast. Afterward, I went back to bed, and Dad limped off to the concessions building, looking tired and beaten. From my window, I watched for Memphis but saw no sign of him.

When Dad returned a few hours later, Mom was rolling out sugar cookies on a wooden board. She was dressed in her yellow seersucker dress and blue print apron, and she'd brushed her wispy hair from her face so many times she had streaks of white flour mixed in with the auburn. Since I wasn't running a fever, she gave me permission to sit at the table and drink a glass of 7UP.

Dad washed his hands at the kitchen sink, something I was never allowed to do. "Teal, I'm going into town right after dinner. Get your list ready."

Mom and I stared at him, and I knew she was wondering the same thing I was. Why was he going into town a day early? Something was wrong. I could feel it, like a chigger under my skin.

I approached the subject carefully. "Did you have in mind for Memphis . . ."

"He isn't here," Dad said, with an air of finality.

Mom blinked. With an unsteady hand, I set my glass carefully on the table. I hadn't seen Memphis leave this morning, but maybe he'd hitched an early ride into town.

"When's he coming back?" I asked.

"He's not. He left last night."

Dad wiped his hands harshly on the blue-striped dish towel, as though he couldn't quite get them dry.

I managed to squeeze out of my tight throat, "But where?"

"How the hell should I know? He's a drifter. What do you expect? Fellas like him never stay long in one place, just move on when they get the itch."

It was as though he were speaking to Mom, not me, but he didn't look at her, hadn't even glanced at her. My mother, holding a heart-shaped cookie cutter, lowered herself slowly and cautiously onto a chair, as if her legs wouldn't hold her. Her face went as white as the flour on her hands.

My own voice had the thinness of air. "He wouldn't."

Dad's laugh was cruel. "Sure he would. His type always finds something and someone else to take advantage of. Swiped some money too." He snorted harshly. "Wait till Sooter hears that. I warned him though. He can't say I didn't warn him."

"How much?" I asked softly.

"Three hundred dollars. Tidy little chunk. I'll tell Sooter about it today when I'm in town, but, hell, he's long gone. They won't catch him now." He threw the towel onto the counter. "Teal, have that list ready," he said, and strode out the door.

I put my head on my arms. My crying came in short, jerky sobs, like the fits and starts of a car engine.

I was only vaguely aware of her chair scraping the floor. Then she was kneeling beside me, her arms pulling me to her, and I was sobbing onto her neck, soaking her dress and skin.

"I love him."

"Yes, I know you do."

"He said he loved us. He said he'd take us with him."

Maybe she thought I'd just guessed at Memphis's promises, or maybe she realized I knew all along.

"He'll come back for us," she said. "He loves us too."

I raised my head and looked at her with streaming eyes. "Do you think so?"

"Yes, sweetheart, I do." She took her embroidered handkerchief from her apron pocket and wiped my face. "He said you're the prettiest little thing he's ever seen."

"Did he say that?"

"Yes, he did."

That sounded like him, and I wanted to believe her.

"Maybe he's just going to find a house for us all to live in and a job so we can stay in one town."

"I'll bet that's it." She handed me the handkerchief. "Here, now, don't you worry."

I blew into it. "What about the money though? Do you think he stole the money?"

"No, he wouldn't do that."

I wanted to believe she was right.

She brushed back my bangs. "He talks about your smile. He says we have the same smile, you and I."

"Really?"

"Uh-huh. The sweetest smile in Indiana, he says."

The corners of my mouth lifted.

"There, that's just what he'd want to see."

She wrapped her arms around me and hugged tightly. When finally she released me, I looked at her. Tears were streaking her cheeks.

At first, I couldn't believe Memphis had left without a word. While Dad was in town, I persuaded Mom to let me walk over to the concessions building, to visit Memphis's room, where I might find a note, a message, something. I was sure there'd be a letter that said he loved Mom and me and would return in a few days to take us away with him. It wasn't there. The sleeping bag was gone from the sagging mattress, and the battered wooden table was bare again. The only difference was, someone had shoved it back under the window. He'd left nothing, no sign he'd ever even lived there. I crept out, feeling as low as I possibly could.

The next day, Sheriff Jankowski and Mr. Sooter came to the drive-in. They checked around the concessions building and talked to Dad for more than an hour. The sheriff said he would put out word on Charlie Memphis, but drifters like him were hard to track down. Mr. Sooter growled something about shooting him on sight if they found him.

The hours, the days, then a week passed.

No letters came, and I could tell by Mom's face he hadn't telephoned.

My parents stepped around each other as if avoiding broken glass. Occasionally, their eyes caught, then darted away. Mom prepared the same delicious dinners she always had, but my insides were too twisted to eat them. More than once, I lay on the creek bank, the dry grass and weeds pressing against my cheek, my tears falling into the clear water.

Dad's temper, which made me nervous under normal circumstances, was shorter than a lighted fuse. When I poured iced tea for dinner, he said, "I told you not to give me any, goddammit. Now look at what you did. Jesus Christ, you're clumsy."

But he had never told me he didn't want any, and I'd spilled it because my hands were shaking.

At least twice a day now, he threatened to hit me. "I'll teach you not to do that, dammit. You want a good licking?"

When Mom was around to hear him, she glared at him with fury in her eyes. The tension built, like water rising steadily and relentlessly against a levee. A little more than a week after Memphis left, it crested. I heard my father return home that Tuesday night. He walked into the bathroom. The water ran, the toilet flushed, his heels clicked evenly down the hall. He shut the bedroom door, and a minute later the box springs squeaked. All was quiet for a few moments. Then I heard the murmur of two voices, one demanding and insistent, the other upset. It had been at least three weeks since I'd heard any noises come from their room on a Tuesday night.

I turned onto my stomach and pulled the pillow over my head. I had a bad feeling about what was going to happen.

"No!" Mom's voice cut sharply through the wall between the two bedrooms. "No, don't."

I jerked my head from under the pillow and listened.

"If you can give it to him," he said, sounding stone-cold and mean, "you can give it to me."

Their bed creaked furiously. The headboard banged several times against the wall that separated our rooms. In a muffled voice, she said, "No," over and over again. Finally, I heard his long, harsh groan, loud and unrestrained.

Then everything stopped. Several minutes later, their door opened and I heard my mother's slow shuffle toward the bathroom. I shivered, pulled the bedcovers over me and buried my head under the pillow again. I didn't sleep at all that night.

The next morning Mom's face was the shade of talcum powder. Her eyes were red-rimmed, and when Dad was around, she had a glint in them I'd never seen before. If I hadn't known her so well, I would have said she could have killed him.

My father, grim and haggard, limped into the kitchen and,

without looking at either of us, pulled a fresh pack of Chesterfields from the cupboard. He sat on the front steps and chain-smoked five of them, tossing the butts in a semicircle near his feet and grinding them deeply into the dirt. I trod carefully around him.

Mom didn't speak to him, not even during dinner. It was all "Callie Anne, would you like some more meat?" or "Callie Anne, would you please pass those rolls?"

Afterward, Dad produced his Chesterfields and his lighter. Tapping a cigarette a few times on the tabletop, he looked around. "I need an ashtray."

She didn't move.

"I said I need an ashtray."

She looked straight at him with eyes so hot and sullen they seemed to burn in her face. "You know where it is. Get it yourself."

If she had lighted a bomb, it could not have had any more force. He swung his arm around so that it swept across the table and sent his plate and glass and a bowl of biscuits all crashing to the floor. The cracked plate spun and reverberated before coming to a stop.

My mother didn't even flinch. She calmly and evenly folded her napkin and laid it next to her fork.

I sat there frozen.

Dad stood, his neck a fiery red, the entire upper half of his body shaking with rage. "Don't think I don't know what the hell went on here."

Mother turned to me. "Callie Anne, go to your bedroom, please."

After glancing first at one, then the other, I backed my chair up and scooted out. I had to step around the broken dishes and food on the floor. Once I got through the kitchen door, out of their sight, I slowed down, to about an inch per minute. I could have been halfway across the drive-in field, and I still would have heard my father explode.

"Well, he's gone, Teal. So you can just forget about him. He isn't coming back."

"What makes you so sure?" Her tone was measured, eerily calm.

"The law will get him if he does." Dad's voice lowered to a mean whisper. "Oh, I run him off, Teal. You better believe I did. But I guess he figured he'd take the money while he was going."

"He'll come back," she said, almost to herself.

"Jesus, what the fuck did you plan to do? Just keep carrying on right under my nose? You didn't really believe I'd stand for it, did you?"

A few moments passed before she said anything.

"Don't you want to know why, Claude Junior? Why I love him?"

I nearly gasped out loud, shocked that she had used those words.

"I love him for a lot of reasons, but one of them is that he doesn't treat me like a sorry speck of dirt. He cherishes me. Do you even understand what that means? To cherish someone?"

Dad's hand smacked something then. It made a cracking noise like an ax splitting wood, and I heard Mom's sharp intake of breath. At first I thought he'd hit the table or the wall with his hand, but the sound wasn't quite right. Then I realized in horror he'd struck my mother. I moved over a little to where I could see both of them. He was standing over her, in that peculiar stiltlike way he had when his leg was tired and he wanted to keep it from folding under him. She was still sitting, bent over slightly, her fingers touching a white splotch the size of a silver dollar on her left cheek.

She rose up, her body as rigid as I'd ever seen it, her face so pale all I could see were her two enormous dark eyes staring at him. "I swore to God I'd never let anyone hit me. When I was a kid, I saw my dad hit my mother more times than I can remember, and I promised myself I'd never put up with that from a man. Not ever." She was shaking but from anger, not fear.

He wiped his nose on the back of his hand. "And what are you going to do about it? Leave?"

"Yes."

He barked a little laugh. "Like hell. You can't walk two fuckin' steps out that door. That's just what I told him. I said, 'You'll never get her out of that house.' "

"Callie Anne," Mom called, not taking her hard, straight gaze off him.

It took me exactly two seconds to get there.

"Get a sweater, sweetheart."

"But it's hot outside."

"You might need it tonight."

"What about John Wayne?"

"Go get him."

When I returned carrying my pink sweater and John Wayne's cage, I found her taking coins and dollar bills from the Hershey's cocoa tin.

Dad was standing by the table, looking uncertain and somehow smaller, like a tire that's suddenly lost air. "Teal, what are you doing?" He walked over, took the dollars from her hand and stuffed them back into the tin.

She removed the money again and tucked it into a pocketbook

that I'd never seen her use before, probably because it had been five years since she had gone to town.

Dad turned to me. He didn't even seem to notice that I'd brought the turtle into the house. "Callie Anne, I didn't mean for . . . for . . ."

Seeing the hurt and confusion in his face, I squirmed and looked away, amazed that I could actually feel sorry for him. Somehow he'd managed to run Memphis off. He'd hit Mom, and he'd yelled at me and threatened to swat me more times than I could remember. Yet I still felt a stirring for him, and I couldn't understand why. Trapped in this grown-up crossfire, I wanted only to escape. I picked up John Wayne's cage and edged away.

Without a word, Mother took my free hand, and we walked out the back door. It was the third week in August, and the afternoon sun was already slanting in the sky. As we started across the field, I glanced over my shoulder at my father, who was standing in front of the house. He had the most stunned look I'd ever seen on a man.

Chapter Twenty-six

*M*om and I trudged along the dirt shoulder of the road toward the Eggert farm. It'd been hot and dry now for so long that crops were withering in the fields and there were reports of cows toppling over in their tracks. Preachers were praying for rain, and everyone was watching the sky for clouds. The sweater was making my arm itch, and John Wayne's cage smacked against my leg. My damp bangs prickled my skin at the hairline, but I didn't have a free hand to push them back. Until it cooled off, a sweater was the last thing I was going to need.

Mom was flushed and damp with perspiration. She stopped for a moment and stared across the Eggerts' pasture, which was dotted by a dozen or so motionless brown-and-white cows.

Her hand trembled in mine. "All that open space." She put her head down and walked on.

When we got to the Eggerts' house, Mom phoned Aunt Bliss. A half hour later, my aunt's decrepit truck barreled along their dirt road, spraying up a cloud of dust that probably reached the drive-in. Soon I was squished between Mom and Aunt Bliss, John Wayne and his cage on my lap, the pickup's round-knobbed gearshift poking into my leg. My aunt seemed bent on setting some kind of speed record. As the truck bucked and lurched along, my mother gripped my hand until it throbbed.

Since Aunt Bliss had last visited us, her windshield had suffered new damage, probably from a rock. It looked as though a giant colorless spider had settled directly in her line of vision, to the extent she had to stretch to see over it. At one point, Mom released my hand and reached over her own right shoulder to lock the passenger door. When she found nothing but a hole where the button had once been, she seized my hand and squished it tighter than ever. I yelped and she relaxed slightly.

Aunt Bliss was wearing a short-sleeved white T-shirt under her blue-denim bib overalls, and her bare, suntanned upper arm, which was pressed against me, swelled like a man's. Mashed between Mom and her, I felt like the filling in an Oreo cookie.

With the rattle of the truck and the road noise resounding through the open windows, she couldn't carry on a conversation with Mom, so she just grinned at her over my head. Once, she yelled, "It's great to see you out here, hon."

Mom smiled weakly.

Aunt Bliss and Uncle Augie lived on thirteen acres in Boagle Corner, in a white house with dormer windows and a sprawling front porch. Its paint was peeling off in large curls, showing patches of weathered wood and reminding me of a speckled Appaloosa pony the Eggerts had. My aunt drove her truck over the rutted driveway, stopping inches from an old garage that leaned dangerously to the left and didn't look as though it had ever been painted. Nearby, a panel truck, missing its tires, and a sloped-back Hudson sedan, its windows broken out, settled so naturally and permanently into the grass and weeds that they appeared to be two of nature's sculptures.

The Starlite Drive-in

My uncle's business, Boagle Corner Gas Station and Automobile Repair, was four miles down the highway from their house. It was actually closer to Daggett than it was to Boagle Corner, but since both towns were just bumps in the road, nobody remarked on it. The two communities together totaled no more than a hundred people.

As we walked from the truck to the house, Aunt Bliss wrapped her arm around Mom's shoulders and gave her a squeeze. "I can't tell you how good it is to have you out and around again. I was afraid I'd never see the day."

My aunt's brown dog, Boss, ran up, barked crazily and, with its tail fanning the air, circled everyone's legs several times. Aunt Bliss led us up the porch steps, still firmly gripping Mom. "Now, don't you worry about a thing, hon. You can stay here as long as you like."

Boss trotted off to my aunt's truck and whizzed against one of its tires. I set John Wayne's crate just outside the door and dropped my sweater on the porch swing.

In a voice that reminded me of my schoolteacher's, Mom said, "Well, we've just come for a visit."

Aunt Bliss acted as though she hadn't heard her. "You got every right to leave that bastard." She held the screen door open for us. "Many's the time I've come home and told Augie about the way that lowlife . . ."

Mom swung around. "Well, I certainly don't need this."

My aunt stared at her. "What? Don't need what?"

"Now look, Bliss, I don't need you carrying on about my husband. I've got enough anger inside of me for two of us. . . ."

"Well, sure you do," Aunt Bliss said soothingly. "And rightly so. He's a mean, selfish son of a . . ."

"Stop it!" Mom smacked the palm of her hand against the screen door. It broke free from my aunt's hold and slammed shut with a clatter.

We both froze. Aunt Bliss looked at her as though she didn't recognize her.

Mom grabbed my hand and started down the steps, walking in the direction of the road and half dragging me behind her. Aunt Bliss rushed past us, faster than I would have expected her sizable body to travel, and blocked our path. "Now don't go off, Teal. I'll shut my mouth."

Mom sighed. "I'm not asking you to do that, certainly not in your own home, but I simply can't deal with your carrying on about him. I don't need you telling me Claude Junior is mean and selfish sometimes. Don't you think I know that? I don't need you saying I made a mistake marrying him. Sometimes I've wondered that myself. But it hasn't been easy for him, Bliss. He's wanted to leave that drive-in for years. He had his dreams, things he was going to do, but he couldn't because of me."

Aunt Bliss's eyes flared. "You're just making excuses. No man has to be that hateful, whatever the reason."

Mom nodded slowly. "Maybe so, but he wasn't that way when I married him." She gazed directly at my aunt, and her eyes brightened. "Remember when we were young, Bliss, when we all had plans? Claude Junior and I were going to move out west and open a little movie theater, remember? All we had to do was save our money. But then Callie Anne came along, and Mr. Sooter didn't pay much, and I got so that I couldn't leave the house. And, well . . ." She lowered her eyes.

My aunt's shoulders slumped. "Aw, shoot, you don't plan on going back to him, do you?"

Mom stiffened. "What I do is my business."

"What about that . . ." She glanced at me. "What about you know who?"

"He's gone," Mom said in a low, steady voice, "for the meantime."

Aunt Bliss gave a knowing nod of her head.

Gripping my hand firmly, Mom sidestepped her. "Maybe it's best we find somewhere else to stay."

Aunt Bliss grabbed her wrist. "No please, I won't say anything more. Really, you're welcome here." In a tone of almost mournful resignation, she added, "I just want what's best for you, Teal."

Mom smiled and gave her a hug. Hand in hand, we all three walked back to the house. A breeze had come up, ruffling the leaves in the nearby oaks, and some dark clouds were swelling on the horizon.

"Callie Anne and I certainly will enjoy spending a few days with you," Mom said. "I'm going to have to ask you to take us home tomorrow to get our clothes, if you don't mind. We didn't plan ahead for our visit."

Aunt Bliss nodded and reached for the door handle. "Why, sure."

As my mother, her back arched and her head held high, stepped into the living room, I glanced at my aunt. She was giving Mom a long, assessing look. She started to say something, then bit it off.

In spite of what Mom had said about just visiting, it occurred to me she might get a divorce, and I wouldn't be living with Dad again, at least not the three of us together. None of the kids at school had divorced parents, except for the Pellman boys, and they were white trash. I felt like crying.

That night we slept in the upstairs bedroom with sloped walls and floor space only large enough to hold a double bed and an old pine dresser. I had stayed at their house overnight the previous summer, but my aunt had taken me into her brass bed and Uncle Augie had slept in the hot, stuffy room upstairs.

Mom opened the dormer window, and I could feel the cool air coming through it. She was wearing a muslin cotton nightgown that Aunt Bliss had loaned her. It hung off her shoulders and trailed along the floor. I wore one of Uncle Augie's white T-shirts and my underpants. At the bathroom sink downstairs, we had scrubbed our teeth, using a clean rag and baking soda.

Mom carefully folded the lavender chenille spread and laid it on the dresser. We crawled into bed, leaving the sheet and blanket draped over the footboard. Curled up, our heads on the pillows and both exhausted, we smiled at each other.

She took my hands in hers. "You okay?"

"Uh-huh." I wasn't, but I didn't want to worry her. I wondered where we would live now. Aunt Bliss's attic room was all right, but her pillowcases didn't smell like ours and her house didn't feel like home. Besides, school was starting in three weeks, and I didn't want to attend eighth grade in Boagle Corner.

Mom had a faraway look. Maybe she was thinking about home too.

"It's scary out here," she said.

I studied the faded rose-flowered wallpaper for a moment. "Yeah, I guess so."

During supper, Uncle Augie, who rarely spoke much, had mentioned that he smelled rain in the air. Now, thunder rumbled in the distance, and the wind picked up, ruffling the filmy nylon curtain on the window.

I snuggled in. "Mom?"

"Yes?"

"Do you miss Memphis?"

She smiled gently. "Yes."

It had been two weeks since he had left, and already the features of his face were starting to blur in my mind. "Do you still love him?"

"Yes." Tears fell from her eyes like sudden rain. Just as quickly, she wiped the back of her hand across them. I think she must have given in to them because she was all wound up and tired. She still didn't have much experience in going outside without Memphis, and I suppose it took a lot out of her.

She pushed my hair away from my forehead, the tips of her fingers as soft and cool as the air from the window. "I love your father too."

"You do?" I couldn't hide my surprise. "But how can you love both of them?"

"I just do, the same way I love you."

As I thought about this, a gust of wind blew the curtain inward so that it billowed like the puffed-out sail on a ship. Mom got up, pulled down the heavy sash, then crawled back into bed. A flash of lightning lit up the room. I counted one thousand and one, one thousand and two. Thunder boomed over our heads, and I scooted closer to her.

"Do you think Memphis will come back?"

"Yes."

"But how can you believe that, when we haven't even heard from him?"

"I have to, honey. Because he believed in me when I needed him to."

The rain came down then in wild, violent sheets. It hammered the shingle roof and slashed against our window. The sky cracked open with a blue-white lightning and throbbed with booms and crashes. The entire house seemed to shake. Mom pulled the sheet and blanket over us, and I burrowed my head under the feather pillow.

After several minutes, the storm eased into a steady downpour. I tried to think about what Mom had said about Memphis and Dad, but I couldn't keep my eyes open any longer.

Chapter Twenty-seven

Aunt Bliss drove us back to the drive-in the next day. When Mom asked us to wait in the truck, my aunt tried arguing with her.

Mom's tone was quiet but firm. "I appreciate what you're saying, but I can manage my own affairs."

Aunt Bliss clamped her mouth shut.

Reaching the front door to our house, Mom paused for a moment to smooth the skirt on her green print housedress, which she had ironed in Aunt Bliss's kitchen that morning. She patted her hair into place and straightened her back. The screen door closed softly behind her.

We waited inside that muggy, hot truck for what seemed like a long time. The rain hadn't cooled things off much. The back of my blouse kept sticking to the seat upholstery.

Finally, Mom came out, lugging a scarred brown-leather suitcase and a Miller's Department Store shopping bag. My father, his limp more noticeable than ever, trailed right behind her. He was wearing his short-sleeved white manager's shirt, and it was wrinkled, as if he might have slept in it the night before.

He hobbled along until he got close enough to grab her arm. "Teal, I want to talk to you."

With the car windows down, my aunt strained to listen. Their words hummed and rose and fell. We could hear my dad's deep voice, but not my mother's quieter tones. Then she turned to him and I read her lips.

"Don't, Claude Junior," she said. "Don't put your hands on me, until you can touch me like you should."

The way he jerked his fingers back, you'd have thought she was scalding hot.

Aunt Bliss elbowed me. "Can you hear her? What'd she say?" I just shrugged.

Dad jammed his hands in his pockets. "I only want to talk, Teal. That's all. Can't we do that? Just talk?"

"It's too soon to talk, Claude Junior. You need to consider how you've hurt me. . . ."

"I was only doing what was good for you, and for our marriage. Jesus, can't we just go back to the way it used to be, before all of this happened, before he came along?"

Her eyes burned dark. "I will never go back to that. You hurt me before Charlie Memphis ever set foot in this drive-in. All these years you've criticized and belittled me. You've treated me like I wasn't worth marrying or even caring about. That's not the way love is supposed to be."

"But I do love you, Teal. Can't you see that?" His voice cracked. "If we had a problem, it's because I've loved you too much. That's why I run him off. I couldn't tolerate seeing that man look at you the way he did."

Something was wrong with Dad. He was choking on his words. "He couldn't . . . couldn't ever love you like I do. He was just . . ." He searched for the word. "Just seducing you."

Mother shook her head slowly. "I don't know, Claude Junior.

Maybe you'll never understand." She hitched up the leather suit-case and started walking toward us.

Dad followed, a few paces behind her. "When you were stuck in the house, Teal, I didn't leave you. Another man might have picked up and moved out, but I didn't. I stayed by you."

She nodded. "Yes, you did, and I appreciate that."

He reached out his hand, but she kept on walking. His face reminded me of John Wayne's—my turtle, I mean, not the movie star. He looked old and wrinkled and sad, and I had to turn away so I wouldn't cry. I knew then what Mom meant about loving him and Memphis both. But Memphis had the whole world, and Dad's world was just my mother.

Chapter Twenty-eight

*A*unt Bliss eyed Dad's Ford as it pulled into her driveway. "When he gets to beggin', I hope you don't . . ."

Mom lifted her eyebrows, and my aunt shut her mouth.

"It's okay, Bliss." Mom laid a hand on her arm. "I can take care of this."

Shaking her head, Aunt Bliss headed for the kitchen. I was surprised she didn't want to hear what they were going to say.

Mom walked out on the front porch and across the grassy yard just as Dad, grim and determined, was climbing down from his blue pickup. Boss loped up and sniffed him, then made the rounds on the Ford tires. Dad's eyes had pouches under them, but he stood straight as a fence post beside the open truck door. He and Mom talked in low voices. She shook her head.

His face twisted into a grimace, and he gestured toward the front seat of the pickup. "Goddammit, Teal, get in there. You and Callie Anne are coming home where you belong."

Mom spun around and walked quickly toward the house, not once looking back.

I thought for a moment he might come after her. Instead, he

turned and slammed his fist down hard on the truck hood. When Mom reached the top porch step, he climbed in and drove away.

They repeated that scene, or something like it, for the next week and a half. He came regularly every other day, as if he kept track on a calendar.

With each visit, his white theater manager's shirt became more rumpled and dirty, until I began to wonder if he was ever going to change it at all. It struck me he might not be taking care of the drive-in either. If Mr. Sooter found out, he could lose his job. That gave me a whole new set of worries.

The next time Dad arrived, he and Mom stood beside his truck and talked in quiet tones. After a few minutes, she came back inside. I sat in Aunt Bliss's parlor, which was like a second living room with its upholstered love seat, its heavy dark-walnut side table and a tall bookcase with a curved glass door and a fold-down desk. I was reading *Huckleberry Finn* for the second time and pretending I hadn't recently had my nose pressed to the window screen.

She cleared her throat. "Your father would like to see you."

I stared at her in horror. I wanted to know everything that was happening, but I didn't want any part in this grown-up war. I was only a kid.

She smiled, wet the corner of her hankie and rubbed the tip of my nose with it. "It'll be okay. He's just going to say hello. He hasn't seen you for a while."

I nodded, swallowed hard and followed her outside.

He was leaning against the truck, still wearing the same dingy white shirt. His black slacks had gray dust on them, like he might have fallen in the gravel. "Hello, Callie Anne."

"Hi, Dad."

"How you doing?"

"I'm okay." I didn't ask how he was because I didn't want to make him fib.

"We're showing a new Casper cartoon this week."

"Oh." My excitement over the friendly ghost had faded a few years back.

"What have you been doing here?"

"Well, we've been helping Aunt Bliss put up bread-and-butter pickles, and sometimes I ride Ginger." I waved a hand toward the mare grazing in the pasture beyond the barn. Keeping my eyes on her, I searched for something to say. I knew better than to tell him Mom was learning to drive my aunt's truck. The silence hung between us.

He leaned over and brushed a strand of hair away from my eyes. Close up, he smelled old and sour, like cider that's turned vinegary.

I backed up a step. I wasn't used to his touching me anymore, except to grab my arm.

His eyes were moist. "You've gotten taller."

I nodded. I wondered if he'd noticed the bumps on my chest.

It wasn't until later, as I was sitting under Aunt Bliss's big maple and reading once again about Huck Finn's drunk pappy that it hit me. Dad's breath smelled like liquor. It wasn't the faint fresh smell of the beer he occasionally drank on hot summer afternoons, but a stale odor that swept over me when I passed the Buckshot Tavern in Jessup. I laid the book down and put my head in my hands. I was glad there was no one out there to see me cry.

A few days later, I was sitting on the front-porch swing with Mom, shucking the last of the summer corn into a galvanized pail when Dad drove up. He crawled out of the truck, his shoulders hunched as if he were leaning into a windstorm. He stumbled up the front steps, grabbed the porch column and fixed his bleary gaze on Mom. "You gotta come back to me, Teal. Otherwise, I'm not going to make it." His words were slurred, and he swallowed a fuzzy belch.

I stared at him. His skin had turned a yellowish gray and seemed to sag on his skull. His shirt gaped where it hadn't been buttoned up right, and the front of it was stained with brown streaks. This couldn't be my father. My chin started to quiver uncontrollably, and tears stung the inside of my eyelids. I looked over at Mom and saw her face contort as though she might cry too.

She gathered the ears of corn from her lap and handed them to me. "Take them into the kitchen, will you, honey?"

I stayed inside, watching and listening through a screened window.

Dad wound his arms around the porch column. "You're killing me, Teal."

Mom studied him for a moment. "No, Claude Junior, you're doing this to yourself." She rose from the swing and shook the corn silk from her apron. "I'm not going to listen to you while you're in this condition, and I should think you'd be ashamed to have your daughter see you like this. Did you really think I'd go home with you while you were drunk?"

He didn't answer.

She looked at him without expression. "I'm not punishing you. I'm waiting for you to stop thinking about yourself."

"I'm not thinking about myself, Teal, only you. I can't eat anymore. I can't sleep. You're in my mind every minute. I want you to know that everything I ever did was for you."

She shook her head slowly, in pity or maybe just in sadness. "You need to do something more then, Claude Junior. Consider what it means to respect someone. I won't ever again live with a man who treats me or Callie Anne poorly."

He was quiet.

She sighed. "I suppose the house is a mess too."

He wouldn't meet her eyes.

"I thought so." She took a step backward. "Go home. Clean yourself up and that house too. And don't even plan on coming back here until you're sober."

She eased through the door before I had a chance to back away from the window. Just inside the living room, there was a nubby old armchair, and she leaned against it, steadying herself. She closed her eyes, and for a moment, she looked like a doll that has lost all its stuffing. Blinking her eyes open, she caught sight of me and straightened. She put on a smile that was both sad and determined, walked over and held out her hand. "Come on, sweetheart, let's go see how Tabby's kittens are doing. I bet she'll let you hold them today."

I turned back to the window. Dad had crumpled onto the top porch step, his arms still reaching upward for the post. He began to cry, tearing the sobs deep from his chest. The tears ran down the lines of his face into the corners of his mouth. His shoulders convulsed, and he ground his head into the crook of his arm.

I wanted to run as fast as I could, to race across the pasture behind Aunt Bliss's house until I had no breath left in my lungs. But instead I took my mother's damp, trembling hand, and we walked slowly and steadily toward the kitchen.

The next time he came he was wearing a new white shirt that still had the creases from its cardboard wrapping. His eyes were watery and bloodshot, but at least he could walk across the yard without stumbling. He and Mom sat on the porch swing and talked in low voices.

"How did it come to this?" she asked. "It all started out with such hope. I still think about that night we met at the fairgrounds. You were so worldly and sure of yourself, nothing like the other boys I knew." She laughed softly. "I thought you were more interested in Sue Ellen."

"I didn't even see her. I couldn't take my eyes off you." Dad's arm rested across the slatted back of the porch swing. He lifted it slowly, just a little, but he didn't touch her.

"You tried to scare the daylights out of me in that funhouse."

"I just wanted to hold you."

She smiled sadly. "When did that all change? How did we get from there to here?"

He looked at her, not speaking.

"Well," she said, "I used to think if I could just be a better wife, you wouldn't have all that anger. But no matter how hard I tried, I couldn't do anything to make it right. I don't believe now it had much to do with me at all. It's got more to do with yourself and all that wanting you've buried so deep inside that it's festering like a sore. Don't ask me how it got in there. I couldn't tell you that, and I don't suppose you could either. Anyway, I'm not afraid of your anger anymore, so I guess I'll come back to you." She got up from the swing and walked to the screen door. "I don't know if or how long I'll stay. I don't even know if I can ever love you much again." She opened the door and leaned against it, studying him. "I'll never let you treat me the way you used to. And there'll be no second chances. Do you understand that, Claude Junior?"

He nodded slowly.

She sighed. "Well then, we'll have to see if we can make some new kind of life for ourselves. Come on back tomorrow if you want to."

She walked into the house, quietly shutting the screen door behind her.

All the rest of that day, I felt more confused than ever. I wanted to go home, and I didn't want to go home. I felt sorry for Dad, and I didn't feel sorry for him. I wanted Memphis to return and take us away, but I wondered what would happen to Dad if we left.

That evening, when Mom, Aunt Bliss and Uncle Augie were having their coffee after supper, I burst into tears and ran from the table. I threw myself on the bed in the upstairs room. I was sobbing into my pillow when Mom came in. She sat on the edge of the bed and stroked my hair.

I looked up at her. "We're going home, aren't we?"

"Probably. Don't you want to?"

I sniffled into a soggy tissue. "I guess so. I don't want to go to eighth grade in Boagle Corner."

She smiled and gave me a hug. "You won't have to. Is that all that's wrong, sweetheart?"

"Uh-huh."

But it wasn't. I didn't know how to express what was really bothering me. It was tied up with loving Charlie Memphis and losing a dream and thinking life was too complicated and hard on people. There was even something to do with responsibility, but I couldn't make sense of all that.

The next day, Dad came back, dressed in a new blue suit and carrying a florist's bouquet of yellow roses. He waited on the front porch and talked politely to Aunt Bliss while Mom and I packed the brown-leather suitcase. We rode home together in our truck.

I felt as though I'd been away for years. No one had picked up the litter at the drive-in while I was gone. There were popcorn bags and candy wrappers scattered across the parking field, and one of the speaker poles had toppled over. Even our house seemed dreary and smaller. Mom surveyed it without comment.

Dad wore a thin, apologetic smile. "It's not as clean as when you're here."

"Oh, it'll do." She pulled out a vase for flowers. "I won't have time to fix a regular meal for dinner, so we'll just have to have sandwiches."

"That's okay. I don't mind," he said.

When she told me I could keep John Wayne in my bedroom, as long as I cleaned his cage every day, Dad blinked but he didn't complain.

Mom put the roses in the center of the table. She couldn't find any bread for sandwiches so she made us eggs, sausages and baking-powder biscuits with butter and honey. Afterward, Dad leaned back in his chair and sighed contentedly. "That was great. Nothing I fixed ever tasted like yours did." He reached in his shirt pocket and brought out his Chesterfields. He shook out a cigarette and flipped open his lighter.

I held my breath.

I could see the realization of the moment flicker through his head. Springing from the chair, he limped across the room and grabbed the ashtray from the windowsill. He sat down and lit his cigarette. Mom hadn't moved at all.

Nothing was said, but, across the table, their eyes met.

Chapter Twenty-nine

$\mathcal{T}$he following Monday, school started, and not long after that, the drive-in closed for the winter.

When we had left Aunt Bliss's house, my aunt told Mom she was making a mistake, that leopards didn't change their spots. But after we'd been home a month I heard Mom tell her she was wrong about that. Dad had changed.

I guess Mom was right. He didn't say mean things to her much anymore, and whenever he forgot and started to boss her around, she could stop him with just a firmness in her expression. He'd get an odd distant look in his eyes as if remembering something and turn away. He didn't seem particularly happy, but at least he didn't take it out on Mom or me. At times he even tried to be nice. Once or twice he asked me how John Wayne was, and the week after school started he took me to the soda fountain at Bonnie Doon's and bought me a brown cow. Because Bonnie Doon's was a hangout for the high school kids, I kept looking around to see if Virgil might come in. But he didn't. Dad asked me what I thought about moving to a bigger city, Lafayette or South Bend maybe. I said I liked it here. If we moved, Memphis wouldn't be able to find us, although I didn't say that out loud, of course.

Without Memphis, Mom wasn't exactly contented, but she wasn't scared the way she had been before either. Every once in a while, I saw a sadness cross her face, and I'd know she was thinking of him.

And me? I wasn't the least bit happy about anything. Aunt Bliss said it was because of my age, but I'd like to know what made her think she knew so much about kids when she didn't have any. Besides, she was wrong. My problem was I didn't like junior high school. Although the school was bigger than my old one and I was making new friends now, the classes were boring.

I hadn't seen Virgil since our afternoon at the quarry, and with the high school being several miles from the junior high, it wasn't as if we'd run into each other. Betty Jo Babcock said she'd heard he was going steady with April, that pouty brunette who had worked in the snack bar. Maybe after he'd touched and kissed me, he'd decided I wasn't such a nice girl after all. Aunt Bliss said boys were like that, but I didn't want to believe Virgil was.

Apparently Sheriff Jankowski wasn't a very good lawman, because he didn't manage to track down Memphis or any of the stolen money. I missed Memphis, but at the same time I hated him for taking off and leaving us. As time went along, I began to believe he must have swiped the three hundred dollars, and that when it was staring him in the face, he forgot all about Mom and me. Maybe he decided he just didn't want the responsibility of us after all.

Then I started to wonder if anything he had told us had been true. Those stories about his friend Earl and the dog named Nickel and the water witch, even the one about the Indian whose people believed the world originated in the stars. Maybe all of them were just made up. After a while, I began to wonder if Memphis had ever loved us at all.

Mom must have guessed what I was thinking because more than once she whispered, "He'll come back. You wait and see." Or maybe she was whispering to herself. I wasn't quite sure.

We were both waiting, but nothing happened.

Chapter Thirty

*W*ith my books in tow, I trudged along the road from the bus stop to the drive-in. Cars whizzed by me.

Overhead, a flock of birds drove a black wedge into the gray autumn sky. We'd had a long Indian summer, all of September and part of October, but the days were starting to get downright cold now, and the trees that had flamed with brilliant color a few weeks before were nearly bare. Someone must have been burning leaves. I could smell the musty smoke.

I have never liked autumn. It has always made me think of things dying and cold weather coming. The only good part about it has been my birthday, which is October 20. In a week I would be thirteen. I had expected to feel more excited about it. It seemed as though I'd waited forever for my birthday, but now that it was here, I had just about lost interest.

When I reached the drive-in entrance, I flipped open the mailbox, a gesture that was mostly habit since we didn't get much mail. All the bills for the theater went to Mr. Sooter's office. I had to look twice to make sure the square white envelope that rested there now wasn't my imagination. The bold handwriting leaped out at me. It was a man's script, I was sure of that. I held the letter flat on my palm, staring at it.

Teal Benton, Starlite Drive-in, State Route 2, Jessup, Indiana. Not Mrs. Teal Benton. No, it wouldn't say that. My heart thudded so hard I could hear it in my ears.

Walking to the house, I carried the envelope in my outstretched hand because I had the crazy notion that if I took my eyes off it I might lose it. I wasn't worried about Dad seeing me. He was working at the county highway garage for the winter and wouldn't return home until six o'clock or later. In the kitchen, Mom was standing in her stocking feet on a chair, cleaning the window over the sink to a bright shine with the crumpled pages of a newspaper. Her cheeks glowed from her efforts. The days were shorter now, and with the light switched on, it already looked dark outside. The radio was tuned to *Lux Radio Theater*.

She glanced at me and smiled. "Hi, sweetheart. How was school?"

When I didn't answer, she didn't seem to notice. She went right on polishing. "I splashed some tomato sauce on the window pane, so I thought while I was at it, I'd wash the whole thing."

As I took a step forward, she turned around and looked at me. I held out the letter. "It was in our mailbox." Even as I said it, I thought it sounded silly, as though I usually found envelopes lying somewhere on the road. "It's addressed to you, to Teal Benton."

The color left her face. Slowly, she stepped down from the chair, walked over to the radio and turned it off. The room was suddenly too quiet. The only sound came from our cuckoo clock, the yellow bird sticking its neck out to chirp the quarter hour.

I handed her the envelope. She took it, sat down in the chair and studied the front of it. "It doesn't have a return address," she said.

"No, but it's postmarked Niles, Michigan."

"I don't know anyone there." She continued holding it unopened in the flat of her hand, much as I had done.

"Where is Niles?" I asked.

"Near the Indiana state line. Not far from South Bend."

My heart had not stopped hammering since I'd found the letter in the mailbox. "What if it's not from him?"

A moment passed before she answered with a smile. "We'll be all right."

I thought of my father, of how hard he had been trying to be nice, and I felt pulled apart. Mom turned the envelope over and slid her fingernail under the flap. She drew out the single folded sheet of ruled paper, opened it and read to herself. I thought I'd be able to guess what it said from her expression, but her face didn't change.

When she was done, she laid the page in her lap and looked up. "It's from a classmate of my brother's. He's planning a trip to California. He's lost track of Daniel's address in San Francisco and wants to know if I'll send it to him."

She didn't cry, and to my surprise I didn't either.

"He won't come back," I said.

"Yes, he will."

I carefully weighed what I was going to say next. It had been bothering me for some time. "It's not just the stolen money. He killed a man."

I didn't think it was possible for her to be any paler than she was, but her face turned the color of cotton. "How do you know that?"

"Well, first of all, he told Virgil he'd been in some kind of fight. And then I read a newspaper story about two murders in Seattle. I think one of the men who died was Memphis's brother and the other was the man who killed him." Deciding not to mention where I'd found the clipping, I hurried right along. "I think the police were looking for Memphis for murdering the second man. I'll bet that's why he didn't want to be in any newspaper photos after the box office was robbed. He was afraid someone would recognize him."

She laid her hand on her chest and released a long sigh of relief, as if to say she knew I was wrong and she could set me straight. "He didn't kill anybody, honey. He told me all about it."

I blinked several times. "He did?"

"That's right, and it wasn't the way you think it was. It's true his brother was killed in a fight. He'd just gotten out of the navy and they were in a bar celebrating when a fellow picked an argument. He stabbed Charlie Memphis's brother. By the time Charlie Memphis realized what had happened it was too late. The murderer ran off and the police never caught him."

I pulled a kitchen chair out and slowly lowered myself into it. "Memphis never killed anyone?"

"No."

I had been foolish enough to think I'd heard their most important conversations. What else had I missed?

Mom tucked the letter into its envelope. "He's never forgiven himself for his brother's death."

I thought of how Memphis had looked after the robbery, bone-weary and sad, how he'd refused to talk to the sheriff and how later he'd avoided the stranger who had come looking for Billy. Something still wasn't quite right.

"Mom?"

"What, sweetheart?" She propped the envelope against the radio.

"Wasn't the brother's name Chester?"

"That's right."

"What was his last name?"

"Why, it was Memphis. Chester Memphis. What else would it be?"

"Did Charlie Memphis ever mention someone named Mathias—or John Michael Huston?"

She thought for a moment. "I don't believe so."

"And the fight? Do you know where it happened? What city, I mean?"

She shook her head. "You'll have to ask Charlie Memphis that when he comes back." She pushed the chair closer to the sink, climbed onto it and went back to swabbing the window.

Chapter Thirty-one

$\mathcal{D}$ad tossed his cigarette down and ground it out with his shoe. "You been taking pretty good care of that turtle, Callie Anne, better'n I ever thought you would. You still feeding him worms?"

"Uh-huh."

We were standing outside the closed concessions building in the fading October light, watching John Wayne scoot across the gravel like a runaway stagecoach. I went after him, picked him up and brought him to where he'd started. After I set him down, he hesitated a moment, then hustled off.

Dad chuckled. "Travels faster than I do."

I went after him again and brought him back. "He's got that dent in his shell and he leans a bit to the side but he's mostly healed up."

I turned John Wayne upside down. He teetered for several moments and flailed his orange-speckled brown legs. Finally he caught hold of the ground with his beak, flipped over and hurried away. Anyone who says a turtle can't move quickly hasn't seen one that's got a good reason.

I blew on my hands to warm them and looked over at Dad. "I'm going to let him go soon."

He studied my face. "I didn't say you had to."

"I know."

I had a promise to keep, but I wasn't about to mention that.

"I've read up on turtles. If I wasn't keeping him in the house where it's warm, I think he'd be starting to hibernate about now. That's what the books say turtles do when winter comes."

"Like a bear, huh?"

"Yeah, I guess so."

I let John Wayne trek about twenty feet before I went after him and set him in his cage. He didn't hiss or squirt pee on me like he sometimes did, but he stared at me with such unblinking eyes that I felt like a prison warden. As I latched the cage, I sighed deeply, my breath making a steamy white cloud in the chilly air.

Dad picked up a smooth, round rock and bounced it in the palm of his hand. "Callie Anne?"

"Yeah?"

"How'd you like to move into Jessup?"

I swung around. "Jessup?"

Dad nodded with a self-satisfied air, as though he were passing out Christmas presents. "That's right. We'll be leaving in three weeks."

I glanced around us, at the small house across the deserted field and the blank white screen that seemed so sad and dreary against the cement-colored sky. Oddly enough, I didn't ask him where we'd live or how we'd survive. All I could think about was there'd be no movies each summer outside my window.

I looked at him. "What will we do without the movies?"

He frowned. "There's a theater there. You'd be sitting inside, that's all."

"It's not the same," I murmured. "It's just not the same."

But he didn't seem to hear me.

"I wasn't going to tell you this yet," he said, "but I might as well. I'm going to buy us a television set once we get settled."

"Oh," I said dully. I felt my insides shift, as if he were trying to take some part of me away from myself.

"I've got a new job lined up, a solid one with a big salary and benefits." His fist tightened on the rock he'd been tossing from hand to hand. "At that new Dodge plant they just built in town."

"You mean like the Dodge car? Like Aunt Bliss's truck?"

He nodded.

I couldn't believe it. "But you think Dodges are pieces of junk. You said so yourself."

"They make brakes at this plant. They don't assemble the automobiles there." He chucked the stone at a speaker pole about fifteen feet away. It hit with a ping and bounced off. "Besides, they pay good wages. It doesn't mean I have to drive one."

"Does Mom know we're moving?"

He nodded. "She's all in favor of it."

I wondered.

He stuck his thumbs in his pockets. "You'll be able to have all the new clothes you want this winter. Why, in a year or two, we can save enough money to buy a house. Then later, if we want to, we can move somewhere else, to some other state maybe."

I didn't think I'd ever seen my dad this excited about anything. But then I looked at the movie screen, and it seemed too much to give up. I shrugged and mumbled, "I don't know."

"You wait and see," he said. "Everything's going to be better."

He picked up John Wayne's cage by the bar of wood across the top and held it up so he could peer into it. "You can keep him if you want."

I shook my head. "I need to set him free before he forgets

how to find his own food. I figure if he hibernates this winter, he won't remember a thing about me when he wakes up in the spring." I turned away so he wouldn't see my tears.

We walked back to the house with the cage between us. It kept banging against the side of my leg, reminding me of my responsibilities and my losses.

I spent the next week digging a pit like the one described in *Reptiles and Amphibians of North America.* According to the book, a turtle needs to spend the winter in a hole in the ground below the frost line. John Wayne wouldn't eat, drink, move or leave his burrow until warm weather arrived. He'd have to live on his own fat. Thanks to his piggish ways with worms, grasshoppers and beetles, he had grown as chubby as an old sow.

I asked Dad how deep I'd have to dig to reach the frost line. He said eighteen inches, two feet to be safe. I hiked to the creek, farther upstream from where I used to play, and studied the thick underbrush for a place to fashion John Wayne's burrow. I hadn't been back to this area for a while. Could it have been only last spring I was sloshing around in the mud here, catching frogs and trying to make them stay in twig and grass houses I'd built? It seemed a lot longer. I didn't have the slightest interest in such child's play anymore.

I found a good spot between some tree roots that bulged out over the water like an old man's knobby knees. It was damp and chilly in the shadows and I shivered. I blew on my hands and, using a small shovel Dad had loaned me, began digging.

Every afternoon that week, I worked on the pit after school for a half hour or so. Already the ground was beginning to harden from the cold. When the hole looked deep enough, I measured it with a yardstick to make sure. Then, as the book suggested, I lined it with straw, grass and leaves. As an afterthought, I put in a dead beetle and a bottle cap filled with water just in case John Wayne woke up and wanted a late-night snack.

On Saturday morning, I rose at six o'clock, with a tightness around my heart. The house was silent in the early gray light. I pulled on a pair of navy-blue slacks that I hadn't worn since last winter. Either they'd shrunk or I'd grown taller. I slipped on an old blouse and a corduroy jacket and left by the back door, closing it softly behind me.

All the past week, I'd kept John Wayne in the garden shed to prepare him for the cold weather. That was Dad's idea. I found John Wayne in a corner of his cage, tucked tight inside his shell. As usual, he'd spilled his water and messed up the grass I'd piled into a bed for him. Lifting him up, I looked to see if any of the fat worms I'd left the night before were still there. Every one of them was gone.

He didn't stick out his head to see who was disturbing him so early, but when I held him up, I could see his beady red eyes peering at me. Wondering if he could somehow sense what was going to happen, I stroked the soft membrane-like web where his leg joined his body, then ran my finger over the leathery skin of his foot. It made me think of elephant hide, although I'd never touched an elephant in my life. I liked John Wayne's toughness. It didn't seem that anyone could care about a turtle, but I did.

I left the cage where it was and carried him in my hand. The eastern horizon was aglow with the rising sun, and the morning smelled of last night's rain. Skirting the puddles, I tramped across the drive-in field toward the Eggerts' farm. At the edge of it, the sun broke through the elm trees and glazed their branches. Steam

312

rose off some areas of the pasture, where a dozen Guernsey cows stood motionless, their bony legs rooted in a shallow layer of ground fog. I glanced over my shoulder. Clouds were moving in. Dull gray snow clouds.

I hiked toward the creek. Under the tree limb, I set John Wayne on a damp rock that was a little larger than he was. He was so sluggish now, he didn't even try to scramble off. It had crossed my mind to paint my initials on his shell with pink fingernail polish, but somehow it didn't seem right. Memphis could have explained to me why it wasn't, but I didn't have a reason other than I was sure I'd know John Wayne if I ever saw him again.

I set him in the pit and gazed at him for one last time. He didn't poke out his head or stretch toward me with a claw. I wasn't surprised. I no longer expected him to raise a foot in gratitude and farewell. With a final sigh that seemed to catch in my throat, I piled more straw and leaves on top of him, then filled the hole with dirt. I gave the loose earth a quick pat, then stood and walked away. I didn't look back.

For a while I had believed that if I released him, if I fulfilled my promise, my good deed would bring Memphis back. Now I knew that wasn't true. No matter what I did, he wouldn't return. But my anger over his leaving didn't well up in me as it had before. I remembered him telling me he wasn't any hero, and in some ways he might not have been, but I knew in other ways he was. When I thought about all the things that had happened during the summer, I began to feel more than a year older. There are some things we gain at a terrible cost, and Memphis was one of them. As I crossed the pasture, I wept.

When I came to the road, I started to run. I didn't know where I was going but I couldn't seem to stop. It was spitting snow. The falling moisture, mixed with my salty tears, chafed my face. I ran along Logan Highway and turned left where it crossed Bear Creek Road and eventually the river. Three cars and a hay truck drove by, but otherwise the country blacktop was deserted. My chest heaved and my legs ached. The land around our area may appear flat, but it isn't. There are plenty of dips and rises in the road, and I covered all of them. I ran miles and miles, passing a few dozen homes and farms before I ended up where I must have been headed all the time.

Off the road, down a long graveled driveway, a plain two-story white house rose proud and tidy on a lot that was marked on the front and sides by carefully arranged whitewashed rocks. Behind it was a collection of barns, coops and silos, as well maintained as the fields that stretched into the landscape. The buildings looked so new and clean they might have been painted yesterday.

Halfway down the driveway, I stopped, put my hands on my knees and gulped lungfuls of air while the blood pounded in my head. I expected a dog to run out and bark, but none did. It was so quiet that I wondered if anyone was home. I felt the overwhelming need for him to be there.

I heard a faraway tractor start up, but I couldn't see it. As I studied the horizon, a tall gangly figure carrying two pails came around the corner of the barn. Something released in my chest, as if a spring had popped free. If it hadn't been Virgil, I'm not sure what I would have done. I would never have had the courage to walk up to his front door. When he saw me, he set the buckets down and rubbed his hands on his blue jeans. Then he headed toward me, his strides long and easy.

Snowflakes big as quarters were falling now. I felt one land on the end of my nose and I brushed it away.

He stopped a few feet from me and stuck his thumbs in his pockets. "Hi. I thought that was you. Where'd you come from?"

"The drive-in," I said.

We both stared toward the neighboring pasture as though the drive-in were visible from where we were standing, instead of a good seven or eight miles down the road.

I turned back to him. "So, how have you been?"

"Okay." He studied my face, which must have been red and tear-stained. "How about you?" he asked.

"All right." Feeling the chill now, I began to shiver. I hugged myself and looked down at my feet. "I heard you were going steady with April."

"Well, I'm not. She's dating the Italian foreign-exchange student."

"Hmm. Doesn't surprise me," I murmured under my breath. I dug my toe in the gravel. "You haven't stopped by the theater lately." I heard the accusation in my voice. I didn't like it but I couldn't seem to help myself.

"My dad's buried my nose in the work here."

The snowflakes were piling on his head, resting on his crewcut like a white cap.

My teeth started to chatter. "G . . . Guess I'd better be going." I turned and took a few steps.

"Callie Anne?"

I looked back. He had unzipped his green wool jacket and was holding it open. I dove into it like I was sliding into home. He wrapped his arms and jacket around me and held me so close I could hear his heart beating.

"I let John Wayne go."

"Your turtle?"

"Uh-huh."

"It was the right thing."

I swallowed hard. "Then why did it hurt so much?"

He pulled me in tighter.

There was a great deal I wanted to tell him. I wanted to say something about my mother, who was no longer afraid to leave the house. And about Billy, who I was sure had hopped that train and would never come back. I wanted to talk about Memphis, about my certainty he would never return, about my sense of betrayal and the terrible aloneness I sometimes felt. But I couldn't think how to put all that into words.

So I said instead, "We're moving to Jessup in a couple of weeks."

"I'll come visit you there."

"We won't have the movies."

He didn't say anything, but he nuzzled the top of my head with his chin.

I burrowed against his warm chest. "I thought you liked April," I said in a muffled voice.

"Nope."

"She's beautiful."

He didn't hesitate. "Not like you."

I pulled back and stared at him. I knew I was smart but never for one minute had I ever thought I was beautiful. April was gorgeous. My mother was pretty. Men paid attention to them, but the boys at school hardly noticed me. Through fogged-up glasses, I gazed at the intelligent blue eyes that, like Memphis's, saw things others couldn't. And I wondered how I ever could have thought of him merely as Memphis's sidekick.

Chapter Thirty-two

$\mathcal{I}$ ran my fingers over the engraved letters on the lighter. C.M. I had always thought it stood for Charlie Memphis, but it could have been Charles Mathias.

And the other things in the grave? The belt buckle with the grizzly bear embossed on it, the metal box, the big heavy wrench, even the partially decomposed leather cowboy boots with their wooden heels told me he was Charlie Memphis. In a few days the coroner would probably rule that he'd died from a blow to the skull.

But I didn't need his verdict. I was already constructing the scenes in my head. They played there as clearly as if they had flashed across some large white screen: Dad watching the cars exit the drive-in that night after he and Memphis had fought, counting the evening's receipts in his tiny projection-room office, locking the money away, lingering in that building until nothing and no one but the crickets and the night animals were stirring. He must have wakened Memphis with some story he had concocted. A faucet wouldn't shut off or a pipe had burst in some dark recess of the building.

I can imagine Dad luring Memphis to that spot, waiting for

him to bend over to assess the damage, then smashing him across the back of his head with the wrench. He had dragged him to the hole he'd excavated and buried him, along with the metal box and the murder weapon. Between the septic tank and the new water well, there were holes dug all over the drive-in that summer. Any freshly turned dirt wouldn't have attracted attention. As for the box, I knew exactly what the sheriff would find in it. Three hundred and twenty dollars—the original missing twenty and the three hundred Dad later accused him of stealing. My father could never have spent that money. That was his strange brand of honesty.

With Dad's bum leg, the ordeal of burying him must have taken all night. I can see him limping across the grounds to our house afterward, the sun raising its head on the eastern horizon, the birds chirping furiously in the fresh, still air. He must have been exhausted, probably even horrified and full of guilt about what he'd done. I know Dad wasn't an evil man, and I'd like to think he felt some shock and repugnance.

I had always wondered how Mom's threats alone could have changed him so dramatically. Now, another reason for his transformation shone clear as a window to his heart and his mind. He carried a tremendous amount of guilt. He took Memphis's life, and he owed him something in return, even if it was no more than to treat my mother the way she deserved.

And Mother? What about her? Did my father rob her of the happiness she might have had with Memphis, that radiant, almost transcendent love he brought her those sweet, steamy nights?

I don't know. After he was gone, I had wondered if her heart would break, but it might have been more the cracking of my own heart I was hearing. Who can say how the affair would have ended? She has always been a decent woman, a loving woman committed to her husband and family. What happened to her in those few summer months may have changed her, but it didn't alter her basic nature or values. For all his wonderful, seductive, romantic qualities, Charlie Memphis—or whatever his name was—was a drifter. He had no home he was coming from or going to. He'd had a rough life, one that I still believe included murder.

I suspect we saw only the best of him. What transpired between my mother and Memphis was suffused with a rosy glow. It was a fairy tale, an encapsulated fantasy that flickered to life when the sun went down. And in some ways it was an incredibly beautiful love story that could have played out only on a movie screen. It didn't take place in a little white house at an ordinary drive-in theater in the middle of rural Indiana. It occurred in an exotic café in Casablanca or the South Pacific island of Bali Hai.

Okay, so maybe those were just the romantic notions of a twelve-year-old girl. After all, that was the summer I believed I could rise from my body and glide around like a ghost. It was also the summer I was looking for heroes. But romantic notions or not, Memphis gave Mother back her self, and I'll always thank him for that.

Strangely enough, or perhaps not so strangely if you consider who she is, Mother has never stopped believing in Memphis. More than once she's whispered to me, "He'll come back. Just wait and see. One of these days, he'll come walking through that door. . . ."

And I smile and hug her. Well, in a way she's right. I did see him again.

I can't help but think about such ironies of life, that one and others. In 1973, Mother entered a jingle contest conducted by an Indianapolis radio station and won a trip to Paris. Dad grumbled and said he had too much work to do, and besides there was no way his unhinged leg was strong enough to traipse all over some country, and a damned foreign country at that. So she took me.

That woman who'd never even been to Chicago and who'd once trapped herself in her house for five long years had more fun than most women ever have. And I did too.

I'm glad she had that time, that we had it together, because the following year Dad fell ill with cancer. He'd turned withdrawn and moody with age, and if I were to speak in parables, I'd say the guilt ate away at him. But I've known many an innocent person to suffer a long hard death. It took him eight months to die, my mother nursing him with devotion.

Mother still lives in the two-bedroom house she and Dad bought twenty-eight years ago on Union Street in Jessup. My home's about three miles away in one of those developments with curlicue streets and the nonsensical name of Oak Palisades.

I didn't marry Virgil. I wasn't allowed to date until I turned sixteen, and by that time Virgil had gone off to Purdue University to study aeronautical engineering. Armed with his master's degree, he moved to Los Angeles to build airplanes. After graduation from Indiana University with a degree in business, I married a high school classmate named Alan Dicksen. Occasionally, I'd hear Virgil had returned to town for a brief visit, but I didn't see him again until he was home for his twentieth high school reunion. I ran into him at a restaurant in Jessup—literally ran smack into him and got lipstick all over his blue tie. We talked for several minutes and met twice for coffee after that. He was coming off a divorce, and my relationship with my husband wasn't so great at the time.

We flirted with possibilities, until one of us—and I can't remember who—said, "Before, when we were kids, it was too soon. Now it's too late."

I drop by Mother's every few days now that she's alone. I can't imagine what I'd do without her. I once told her she was the nicest person I've ever known.

She just looked at me with a smile from my childhood. "A person can never be too kind."

I won't be going back to the drive-in again, and I won't tell the younger Sheriff Jankowski that the man in the grave is Memphis and the man who killed him was my father. There's no point in it now. In a few weeks, the drive-in will be leveled. Nothing from the years I spent there will be left, none of the funny little humps for cars to drive up to, no massive screen that glowed with fantasies on a warm night, no tiny frame house that held love and hate and all the complexities and mysteries of life for a young girl. It'll all be gone, along with Memphis and the mystery of what happened to him.

As I returned the cigarette lighter to its plastic bag, bits of dirt and grit sloughed off and fell to the bottom of the pouch. I laid the stolen evidence on the passenger seat and backed the car from the driveway. I wouldn't tell the sheriff who was in that grave, but I would tell my mother. Finally, she would know what had happened to him. She'll pray his spirit escaped that small closed space before he felt its terrors. She'll grieve, as I will, for a long time to come, but at least she'll know he never meant to leave us.

I parked the old station wagon close to the curb, tucked the plastic-shrouded lighter into my purse and stepped out. The sky was cobalt blue, the deep shade of midafternoon, and for a moment I wondered if Memphis could have recognized that color, whether he could have identified it from a spectrum when there was no sky overhead for comparison. He couldn't distinguish red and green, he'd said, but what about the other colors? There was so much about him I'd never learned, and so much I'd been too young to ask.

I passed the flowering shrubs in my mother's front yard, the orange begonias huddling in the shade of the porch, the honeysuckle dripping from a trellis near the entry and sending out its warm, heavy scent. The screen door was unlatched and I stepped into the living room. I should tell her to lock that door, I thought. Anyone could wander right in. But I knew she would smile and say, "Well, that's the idea, isn't it, dear?"

I found her in the backyard, weeding the cabbage patch. She stood, leaving small, shallow depressions in the black earth from her knees. "Hello, sweetheart. When did you get back from Chicago?"

"Last night."

She took off her garden gloves and draped them over the edge of a bushel basket filled with crabgrass, leaves and tomato vines. "How did it go?"

"Looks like we're going to get the contract."

"Good for you."

I kissed her cheek. "How are you, Mom?"

"I'll be better when that cabbage-eating bunny and I come to an agreement on how much he's allowed to nibble," she said, brushing the dirt from her housedress, a faded print I seemed to remember from my childhood.

I hadn't been successful in persuading her to abandon dresses for blue jeans or even slacks. She made me think of a little white-haired Englishwoman puttering among her plants. She gave off a fresh light fragrance, perhaps from touching the lavender that populated her garden. I wondered if she went inside the house much at all these summer days when her flowers were blooming.

She looked around. "Is my favorite granddaughter with you?"

"She's still at work. Alan's going to pick her up on his way home."

She pushed back a tendril of runaway hair. "Oh, good, you

can stay a minute then. It seems like we hardly ever have a chance to talk anymore."

Her face was so bright, so full of imperturbable good cheer that I wondered if I could tell her about Memphis.

"I dropped by Aunt Bliss's house earlier today," I said.

"Oh?"

"Irma Schmidt called while I was there."

"She called here too." Her gaze drifted back toward the garden.

I sucked in a breath. "She told you then, about the bones at the drive-in."

Mother nodded. "I said I didn't know whose they could possibly be." She looked at me then, her eyes as clear and guileless as they had been when I was a child. "Can you imagine someone being buried there?"

This was going to be much more difficult than I had expected. I took the hands that were folded together like petals and rubbed my thumbs over her finely wrinkled skin. "Mother, I know whose bones they are."

I felt a tremor run through her. "They're Billy's, aren't they?" she whispered. "I didn't want to think it."

I gripped tighter. "They belong to Memphis, Mother. I'm sure."

She hunched her small shoulders and shook her head.

I clasped her face between my hands. "It's okay now. Don't you see? He didn't run off. He didn't leave us behind like we thought he did."

She stood unmoving, tears slipping from beneath her long, lowered lashes, which were still nut-brown. "Of course he didn't," she murmured. "Because it's not Charlie Memphis buried

323

there. You're mistaken. It's Billy, poor sad Billy, all alone in that grave."

"It can't be. Billy hopped a train. I saw him. Besides, there were things with the bones that could only belong to . . ." I rummaged inside my shoulder bag and pulled out the lighter. "Remember this?" I held it in my outstretched hand. "See, it has his initials on it."

She glanced at it and drew away, her body stiffening. When she looked at me again, I found the strong light in her eyes jarring.

"I don't know who that belongs to," she said, her chin tilted up. "I've never seen it before in my life."

In the long silence that followed, a wind chime suspended from the branch of a nearby tree jingled its endless tune. I stared at her and realized I was doing a terrible thing. I didn't need to prove anything to her. She had not been the one with unanswered questions, with troubling doubts.

I stuffed the lighter back in my purse, out of sight, and murmured, "For a moment there, I thought it belonged to Memphis, but I was wrong." I gestured toward the small, round table under the plum tree and the painted metal lawn chairs. "Shall I make us a pot of coffee and set out some cookies?"

She had already turned away. "That would be nice, sweetheart. The percolator's on the drainboard." She reached for a nearby tomato plant and snapped off a withered vine, releasing what I thought was the most wonderful heady fragrance in the garden.